NIGHT JOURNEY

NIGHT JOURNEY

by Goldie Browning

A Publisher of Quality Fiction

ISBN-13: 978-0984725403

Book Website
www.GoldieBrowning.com

Give feedback to:
goldie_browning@hotmail.com

NIGHT JOURNEY is a work of fantasy and historical fiction. Apart from the well-known actual people, events and locales that figure in the narative, all names, characters, places and incidents are the product of the author's imagination or are used fictitiously. Any resemblance to current events or locales, or to living persons, is entirely coincidental.

Storyteller Publishing
www.storytellerpublishing.com
Email: info@storytellerpublishing.com

Printed in U.S.A

ACKNOWLEDGEMENTS

Giving thanks to everyone that helped in the writing of a book is a difficult task, but here goes:

First and foremost, I want to thank my wonderful husband Alan, for putting up with all the general craziness involved in the writing and rewriting and rewriting again of Night Journey. It was a long and difficult process and I truly appreciate your cheerfulness every time I needed you to drive me across three states to do research, for taking care of me when I was sick, as well as being nice about late or missed meals while I was in writing mode. You are the love of my life.

I also want to thank my daughter Kari, for her keen eye in detecting typos and her other valuable input. Thanks also to my mother Juanita, my stepfather Ralph McHan, my sweet mother-in-law Joyce Browning, my sister-in-law Glenda Margerum, my aunt Norma Farmer, my aunts-in-law Naomi Burris and Elizabeth Edwards and my cousin-in-law Colleen Gunter, for reading an early manuscript and telling me it was wonderful, even if it wasn't. Thanks for the same reason to my BFF's Kellie Hurst, Liz Woodruff, Bob Barnes, Debbie Brown, Mozelle Palmer, Tiara Roberts, and Jean Wood. And thanks so very much to my brother, Stephen Ray Roberts, who has been my biggest fan.

Thanks soooooo much for all the wonderful people who helped with critiques: Mary Gruhlke (aka Mary Tyler), Caroline Smith (aka Caroline Clemmons), Ashley Kath-Bilsky, Fran Fletcher, Clyde Powell, and Stephen Sullivan. You all taught me a lot about the writing process.

A special thanks to Jonny Haydn, my friend and editor. While working as a tour guide for the Crescent Hotel ghost tours, you took the time to read my chapters and helped make them sparkle. As the son of Hiram Haydn, who was once Editor-in-Chief of Random House and other major publishers, you seem to have inherited his editorial abilities. Thank you.

I'd also like to thank the management of the Crescent Hotel for their help in the publication and marketing of Night Journey. Thanks to Elise Roenigk, owner of the Crescent Hotel, for allowing me to base my story on her wonderful old hotel. Thanks also to Jack Moyer, General Manager, and Bill Ott, Director of Marketing, for so graciously working with me. Thanks so much to Linda Clark, Concierge at the Crescent Hotel, for her support. Thanks also to all the Crescent Hotel ghosts, named and unnamed, for your fascinating stories.

DEDICATION

THIS BOOK IS DEDICATED TO ORGAN DONATION
WORLDWIDE

Please sign up with your drivers' license office to be an organ donor. It's easy and it's free. If everybody does it, we won't have any more long lists or shortages.

Do it for the ones you love. Do it for the human race.

PART ONE

THE JOURNEY BEGINS

CHAPTER ONE

If anyone had asked Emma Fuller to choose between spending the weekend at a luxurious haunted hotel or a low-budget motel, she probably would have opted for the latter.

It wasn't that she was afraid of ghosts, exactly—she didn't even believe they existed. Yet for as long as she could remember, she had always felt uncomfortable in old buildings. Creaky floors, shadowy hallways, and musty smells would invariably trigger something in her imagination and she would end up scaring herself silly, sometimes to the point of panic. She didn't know why she reacted the way she did, she just knew she couldn't help herself.

Now here she was, four hundred miles from home, learning via text message that the Ozark Mountain resort her brother-in-law had booked for his wedding party was supposedly infested with spirits—and she might even have to sleep with one. She didn't know whether to laugh or to cry.

ChAng of plans. Rehearsal dinr muvD 2 6. Ghost 2R @ 8. Haunted r%m reserved az U requestD. Mega kewl hotel. Full 2 overflowing w spooks.

"What the heck is your moron of a brother talking about?" Emma frowned and thrust the BlackBerry toward her husband. "Did you ask for a haunted room?"

Zan hesitated as he negotiated the Lexus up a steep mountain switchback before he glanced at Emma's phone. "Nope. It was Allen's idea." He downshifted when the road began to descend. "Ghost hunting is his and Phoebe's newest passion. I think it'll be fun. Don't you?"

"Not really." Emma cracked her neck back and forth and then stared out the window. She had an uneasy feeling, but what could she do about it now? She should have researched the hotel before they left. "I suppose it'll be okay. Just wish you'd told me about it earlier."

Emma wasn't sure how long she'd been sleeping, but it must have been quite a while because they were almost to their destination. A sign reading *Eureka Springs City Limits* whizzed by.

"Sorry, Miss Cranky Pants. You've been snoozing since we passed Little Rock and that's about the time I first learned about my brother's kooky plans. Didn't want to wake you for something like that."

"In five hundred feet, turn left," said a nasally feminine voice.

"I wish you had woken me. I had another scary dream."

"The one where you're being chased by a slasher down a long dark hallway?"

"I don't know who's chasing me. It was the same as always, except this time I think I saw a number on a door. Then Allen's text alert woke me."

"In three hundred feet, turn left."

"What was the number?"

"Can't remember. Too scary." She shivered and rubbed her arms.

Zan reached across to squeeze her hand and then he zapped her with one of his irresistible, puppy dog smiles. "We don't have to stay at the hotel. We can get a room somewhere else, if you want."

"In one hundred feet, turn left."

"No, no. Its okay, honey. Sorry I've been so grumpy. I promise I'll behave. The reservations are already made and we need to stay with the group." She remembered passing a Best Western earlier and made a mental note—for future reference, in case their hotel was too, too scary.

Ding...Ding...Ding... "Off route. Recalculating."

"Shut up." Zan punched the GPS off. They drove a little farther through winding residential streets before he pulled into a parking lot. "Ready to get out and stretch your legs?"

"More than ready." She shivered as she emerged from the warm cocoon of the car. Hunching her shoulders against the wind, she zipped her nylon jacket and followed Zan to a roadside gazebo. "How much farther to the hotel?"

"We're almost there, but Allen specifically said we should stop here first and take a look." He leaned against the railing and gazed at the mist-enshrouded scenery. "Man, oh man. Would ya just look at that view."

"I don't see anything but fog." Emma shifted from one foot to the other and gazed across the tree-covered valley. Jeez, but this trip was gonna be rushed. One night before and one night after the wedding, then they'd have to hurry back home in time for her to check into the hospital bright and early Monday morning for day surgery. Seemed to her it would have made a lot more sense for them to hold the wedding in Dallas than for them to drag everybody all the way to Podunk, Arkansas. "What are we supposed to be looking at?"

Zan inhaled deeply and pointed toward the vista. "You'll see. That's West Mountain over there. Mmm...don't the woods smell great?"

"Um hm, it's nice...but cold." She shivered as a brisk wind danced in from the north, puffed up her dark brown curls, and snatched playfully at the swirling mist that hovered over the emerald Ozarks. As the veil parted, bright blotches of orange and gold set the woods ablaze and the dwindling light of the late-afternoon sun crept closer to the horizon, casting shadows across the wilderness.

When Zan's arm slid around her shoulders, Emma closed her eyes and leaned against him. Too much tension from the long ride in the cramped car and the unsettling dream had her nerves on edge. She took a deep breath and willed herself to relax. The scent of the pines filled her lungs and the music of the songbirds generated a feeling of peace within her. Maybe this weekend get-away was what they needed after all.

"Honey." Zan gently shook her. "Look over there."

Emma opened her eyes and stared in the direction he pointed. A fairytale castle floated in the clouds. "Oh, my gosh. What is that?"

The stately turrets of the building rose high and proud above the tree line, and then disappeared as the mist enveloped it once more. It looked eerie with the fog drifting in and out, like a brooding old mansion in a Penny Dreadful. The beautiful vision seemed like a dream and her heart beat faster. It captured her imagination and reminded her of something—but she couldn't quite grasp it. Had she been there before? No, she knew she hadn't.

"It's the Crescent Hotel. The Grand Old Lady of the Ozarks."

"*That's* where we're going?" Emma gazed at the hotel with wonder. "It looks so familiar. Like I've been there before."

"Maybe in a former life. There's some kind of family connection, I understand. Something about my grandparents being here when they were young. Will it bother you?"

"Will what bother me?"

"The ghosts."

Emma shrugged and stared at the exquisite vision on the mountainside as it drifted in and out from behind the clouds. She didn't believe in ghosts, but if they did exist, this is certainly where they would be. Deciding not to let her silly fears get the better of her, she smiled and replied, "I don't care. As long as the spirits don't keep me awake, they can spook you all they want."

Tires crunching on gravel interrupted their laughter. She glanced to her left and saw a young woman step from the passenger door of a white mini-van. A man walked around from the driver's side, pulled open the sliding door, and unfastened a child's car seat. He lifted a rosy-cheeked toddler dressed in a bright red hooded jacket from the backseat and set him on the ground. Emma melted at the sight of the happy family. Tears pooled in her eyes. She fished in her pocket for a tissue.

"Are you okay?"

"Uh-huh." She dabbed at her eyes and gazed lovingly at Zan. "I'm so glad we're being proactive. If the doctor is right, we could be like those people in another year or so."

"I'm glad too. I just wish you didn't have to go through such a hassle. I think it's the fertility drugs that're giving you those headaches and nightmares."

Emma patted him on the arm. "I know I've been a basket case with raging hormones lately, but if it works it'll all be worth it. Then the real fun will start. Morning sickness, stretch marks, swollen ankles, labor pains…" she ticked off a list of ailments. "Then it'll be your turn, with the two a.m. feedings and diaper changing. I can't wait!"

"We'll suffer together." He kissed her on the top of her head and asked, "Ready to go?"

Emma nodded and followed him to the car. They'd been trying to have a baby for such a long time. Five years of marriage and she still hadn't conceived. Now they had renewed hope and she was looking forward to the outpatient procedure her doctor had scheduled for early Monday morning. Following right on the heels of her brother-in-law's wedding they'd be in a rush, but she'd been lucky to get the procedure scheduled so quickly. Thank goodness she'd already taken care of the paperwork. There'd been so many forms to sign—consent for this and that. Authorizations. Releases. Whatever. Just sign on the hi-lighted blank lines. All she had to do now was show up and get it over with.

Emma stared at the passing countryside while her husband zigzagged the car through the narrow, winding streets of Eureka Springs. She marveled at the shops and the lovely Victorian homes built into the side of the mountain, which seemed to defy the laws of gravity. Two slender does ambled down from the steep hillside, crossed the road, and nonchalantly flicked their white tails. Despite the annoying GPS's instructions she was certain they must be lost, but to her surprise, they rounded a bend and the massive structure suddenly loomed into view.

She caught her breath when she saw the building up close. It was a beautiful, erratic jumble of architectural styles. The exquisite gothic arches and purple brick chimney spires seemed out of place with the concrete verandas that dominated the first three floors. Her impression of familiarity grew stronger. A sense of foreboding washed over her as she stared at its towering limestone walls; the hotel seemed as if it were alive and waiting to swallow her up.

"What do you think?"

"Very impressive," Emma replied, dismissing her initial feeling of dread. She stepped out of the car and followed him up the entrance steps, mesmerized as she entered the elegant lobby. A prickly sensation of déjà vu enveloped her when she saw the Victorian-era front desk and antique furnishings. "What time is it?"

"Four-thirty. We've got just enough time to check into our room and relax a little before the rehearsal dinner."

While Zan turned his attention to checking into their room, Emma wandered around the lobby. In one corner near a small sitting area a battered old sign propped up on an easel read *Cancer Curable Baker Hospital – Eureka Springs, Arkansas.* An odd feeling of recognition washed over her.

Something didn't seem right; the colors were all wrong. The walls should have been purple and the window blinds lavender. She looked at the huge columns and beamed ceilings. The beautiful varnished wood seemed oddly out of place. In her mind she saw them painted bright orange, red, black, and yellow.

A uniformed bellman appeared and Zan showed him to the car parked in the circular driveway. He placed their bags on a rolling cart and waited with Emma in the lobby while Zan moved the car. The bellman led the way to the ancient elevator. The door creaked and groaned as it slid open.

"Welcome to the Crescent. My name is Jimmy," said the bellman. "What's your room number?"

"419," Zan replied, glancing at the key tag.

"Ah. Theodora's room." Jimmy punched the button marked four.

Emma's body prickled and her heart raced. She stared at her husband, who was happily chatting with the bellman. *That was the number—the one in her dream.*

"Who's Theodora?" asked Zan.

"She's the resident ghost in room 419."

The elevator gave a little jerk and they began to rise. Emma grabbed for the wooden railing to steady herself. *Breathe. Don't think about the dream. Just breathe.*

"So, is she the only ghost you've got here?" asked Zan.

"Oh, no. The Crescent has many ghosts. Well, here we are. Fourth floor." The door creaked open and Jimmy pushed the cart out of the elevator.

They stepped into a long, pink plastered hallway. Emma squinted to see in the dim light as they made their way through the eerily quiet passage. They walked toward the far end of the huge building, passing a sign halfway down the hall that read *Dr. Baker's Lounge.* Another small twinge of recognition jolted.

When they reached the end of the hall, they made a right turn to a shorter hallway. There it was, just like in her dream. *Room 419.*

Jimmy opened the door and they stepped into the parlor. At first glance, it was like walking into the nineteenth century. The suite of rooms had a Victorian style ambience, yet all the modern amenities. An antique turquoise swooning couch in the parlor faced a flat screen TV. Set into an alcove near the bathroom was a small refrigerator, microwave, and coffee maker. The sloping attic walls were painted bluish-green, decorated with gold stenciled stars. A locked, child-sized door built into the parlor wall appeared to lead nowhere. The next room was almost filled by the massive king-size bed, which faced yet another television atop an antique sideboard.

Emma raised the mini-blinds to reveal a spectacular panorama of mountains and trees. In the distance, she saw an odd-looking structure, standing like a huge white cross above the trees. "What is that?"

"That's the Christ of the Ozarks statue. It's where they have the Great Passion Play every summer. Thank you, sir. I hope you both enjoy your stay at the Crescent." Jimmy pocketed Zan's tip and left.

Emma remained standing at the window. That statue hadn't been there before. *Before what?* She frowned and watched a pigeon land on the windowsill. It paced back and forth, and then preened its feathers. She stared at the bird, trying to occupy her mind with anything but the irrational thoughts creeping into her head. Quit being such an idiot. It was only a dream.

The warmth of her husband's breath on her neck brought her to awareness. She leaned against him as his hands gently massaged her shoulders. She closed her eyes and relaxed.

"This place is pretty romantic," he whispered, nuzzling her neck. "What do you say we christen the bed right now?"

"Do we have time? We still have to shower and change."

"That's okay," he replied, holding her tighter. He reached up and pulled the blinds closed, then drew her toward the bed. "We'll make time."

Her heart pounded as she kicked off her sneakers. She lay with him and returned his kisses. To heck with thermometers and cycle charts—they were on vacation. She'd worry about all that next week.

A flowery scent filled her nostrils and she wondered if Zan had changed brands of cologne. He always wore Ralph Lauren Polo, but now something smelled more like Chanel Number Five. Her eyes opened into lazy slits when he let her go to pull his tee shirt over his head—and that's when she saw the blinds move, rippling out in a cascading wave from one end of the room to the other. She sat up and screamed. "Zan! Somebody's in our room!"

Zan lost his balance when Emma shifted on the bed. He tumbled off the side, with his shirt still up over his face. For a few seconds he grappled with it, then jerked it back down as he sprawled on the carpeted floor. But he was back on his feet in an instant. He grabbed the nearest weapon—the television remote control—and stalked the room, searching for the intruder.

"Where?"

"By the windows. The blinds moved. Like this." She tried to demonstrate by waving her arms like a hula dancer.

Zan jabbed at them with his remote control sword, then pulled each one forward and shook them. Two dead crickets and some dust bunnies fell out. He looked annoyed. "There's nothing here."

"Well, I can see that. *Now.*" Emma bristled at his tone. She knew what she'd seen. "It's gone."

"What's gone?"

"I don't know. Whatever moved the mini-blinds." She pursed her lips and then shivered. "It's cold in here."

Zan joined her on the bed and started nuzzling her neck. "Come on, honey. I'll warm you up." He tickled her and started chanting, "I do believe in ghosts... I do believe in ghosts... I do believe in ghosts…"

"Now you're making fun of me." She laughed and buried her head in his chest. She snuggled in his arms, then pulled away and sat up as a thought popped into her head. "If the procedure next week doesn't work, do you think we ought to try adoption?"

"I think we need to just stop thinking about it for now. Wait and see what the doctor says." He gently stroked her arm and bussed her neck with his lips. "Pay attention to *me*."

"Stop it. That tickles." She squirmed and batted at his hand. "You know, my parents adopted me and a year later they had Tommy. The same thing might happen to us."

"Uh huh. Could be." He slid his hand underneath her top and started pushing her backward on the bed again with the other.

"We are gonna be soooo late for dinner."

"I don't care." He ran his hands up and down her torso. "I thought you wanted to make a baby?" His voice lowered to a whisper, "Let's make one right now."

Emma flinched when she saw a shadow move on the ceiling and she turned her head toward the windows. The mini-blinds quivered. She went rigid with fear. Zan released her and sat up, holding up his hands in defeat.

"*Okay.* I get the point. I'll leave you alone." He stomped into the bathroom and began unpacking the champagne gift basket left by Allen and Phoebe.

Emma saw by his clenched jaw and red face he was angry. Well, so was she! She stared at him in disbelief. "I saw what I saw and you don't believe me." She jumped from the bed and stood glowering, her legs planted far apart, hands on her hips. "You are the most thoughtless, self-absorbed jerk!"

"*What* did you say?" Zan came into the bedroom and glared at her.

"You heard me."

Two loud thumps from the closet startled them both. Their

attention diverted, surprise replaced anger. They stared at each other before hurrying to open the door. An ironing board lay cattycornered on the closet floor and an iron dangled by its cord, which was looped around its wall bracket.

"How in the world did that happen?" asked Emma.

Zan thought for a moment before answering. "I remember seeing what looked like a penthouse right above this room. I think the stairs are up there." He pointed to the corner of the room nearest the bed. "Somebody must have gone upstairs and caused the ironing board and iron to vibrate off. Yeah. That's got to be it."

Emma stared at the mess in the closet, rolled her eyes, and shook her head no. "I didn't hear anybody in the penthouse a minute ago, did you? Somebody would have had to be stomping like crazy to have done this."

"Well, what's your explanation then? Ghosts?"

"You know I don't believe in that stuff. Maybe it *was* somebody in the penthouse, but I seriously doubt it."

Goose bumps rose on Emma's arms when a sudden blast of frigid air permeated the room. Hairs at the back of her neck stood on end when she again heard a crashing sound followed by a pop, this time from the bathroom. They ran toward the sound and stopped, staring in awe at the destruction. Moet & Chandon puddled on the white tile, while the remains of two long-stemmed crystal flutes created a mine-field of broken glass across the bathroom and parlor floors.

Within seconds the temperature returned to normal. Zan was the first to recover. He grinned at Emma, scooped her up, and carried her back to the bedroom. "Have we been into the bubbly already?"

She giggled as he dumped her on the bed. Ha! He'd seen it too. She wasn't the only one who was crazy. "If we have, we must have had a lot—'cause I don't remember having any."

"Did you see what I saw?" he asked.

"I don't know. What did *you* see?"

Zan craned his neck and peeked into the parlor. The shards of glass were still scattered all over the floor. "I think I saw you throw the champagne basket."

"You did not," Emma cried and punched him in the arm. "You know very well it just fell all by itself and smashed into a million pieces."

"So you didn't see me throw it?"

"No."

"Well, if *I* didn't throw it. And *you* didn't throw it..."

Emma shrugged. "Maybe we've had a *visitation*."

Zan smirked and picked up the telephone. "Hello, front desk? This is Zan Fuller in Room 419. We need a broom and dustpan up here ASAP...No, something just got broken ...Yes, ma'am. A bottle of champagne and two wine glasses...No, I don't know how they got broken...Uh, yes. We were...Okay... Thank you very much."

'Well, what did the desk clerk say?"

Zan shook his head and hesitated. "She sounded like it was the most natural thing in the world and then she asked me if we'd been quarreling."

"What a strange question."

Zan nodded and looked pensive. "I figured she would think we broke the stuff while we were fighting, but I couldn't imagine why she would care. But when I told her yes, she said *'Theodora doesn't like it when couples argue.'*"

CHAPTER TWO

The vacuum cleaner's roar sliced through the silence. Emma's mind swirled with wonder as she watched the hungry machine suck up the last bits of the wine glasses. She smiled when Zan squeezed her hand, feeling more excited by their experience than she could ever remember. Her fear of the paranormal had vanished, replaced instead by a sense of exhilaration.

"Thank you very much." He stood up when the maid finished her work, reached into his pocket to hand her a folded bill, and helped her with the door. She nodded and lumbered away, dragging her cleaning supplies.

"Well, that's that," Zan said and closed the door. "So what do you want to do? Do you want to move to another room?"

"No. I love this one."

"You're not afraid of things going *bump in the night?*"

"Zan, it's the weirdest thing. You know I've always been a skeptic, but I feel so comfortable now. I get the impression we're being watched over. Like we have a guardian angel or something."

"Do guardian angels throw breakable objects?"

"Oh, she was just trying to get our attention." Emma giggled.

"So you're calling our ghost a *she* now?"

"Yes." Emma leaned forward and playfully kissed the tip of his nose. "*Our* ghost is named Theodora."

"You're a nutcase." He slapped her on the rear.

"Hey, watch it. We've gotta get changed. It's almost time to meet everyone for dinner. No time for a shower now." Emma peeled off her sweater, unzipped her jeans, and shimmied out of them. As she reached around to unhook her bra she noticed her husband lounging on the bed, staring. Their eyes met and she smiled seductively, then pursed her lips and wagged her index finger. "Stop looking at me like that, you horny old goat—later—I promise."

The chandeliers glistened in the Crystal Dining Room, bathing the linen-covered tables in a rainbow of iridescent colors. Soft piano music wafted lightly through the room, evoking an impression of peace and relaxation. The delicious aroma of gourmet food caused Emma's stomach to growl in anticipation.

"We're here for the Fuller party," said Zan.

"Very good, sir. Right this way."

The hostess led them to an elegant table occupied by the small wedding entourage. Allen saw them approach and jumped from his seat. He looked like a redheaded, slightly younger version of his sandy-haired brother. His dancing green eyes and impish smile gave away his mischievous nature. He caught them both in a bear hug. "Hey big brother, it's about time you dragged your skinny ass downstairs. We're all about to starve."

"Always thinking about your stomach, aren't you Allen? I think he cracked one of my ribs." Zan rubbed his side and pulled out a chair for Emma. "Phoebe, I hope you know how to cook."

"I know my way around a kitchen," retorted Phoebe. "I was once a sous-chef at Spago Beverly Hills."

"Yeah, her cooking's great if you like sushi and bean sprouts." Allen made a face and grinned at Phoebe. She stuck out her tongue and then smiled brilliantly.

Emma watched the banter with amusement. Would the two brothers never grow up? They always acted like roughneck little boys when they got together. Allen and Phoebe came from such different backgrounds. She hoped he would be happy with his beautiful, Malibu Barbie bride. It still amazed her at times to think that Zan's crazy little brother was a top trial attorney in Fort Worth.

Phoebe was a free spirit with a healthy California glow and flower child innocence. She looked gorgeous in a yellow empire-waist tunic with flowing sleeves and designer jeans. Emma felt plain and mousy compared to her sister-in-law-to-be with her silky blond mane, long slender legs, and perfect figure. She instantly regretted her choice of a sensible navy blue business suit.

"Okay, now that we're all here…" Jonathan clinked a silver knife on his water glass. "I'll make the introductions for those of you who haven't already met. My name is Jonathan Fuller. I think everyone already knows Allen and Phoebe here on my left. I'm the groom's father and to my right is my lovely wife Barbara."

Barbara smiled and nodded. Emma noticed the rope of pearls on her neck and wondered if it bothered Zan that another woman was wearing his deceased mother's jewelry. She regarded the diamond and sapphire ring on her own hand with pride, knowing that it too had once belonged to Zan's mother.

"Next to Barbara is my beautiful daughter-in-law Emily and my eldest son, Alexander," Jonathan continued. "I believe you all know them as Emma and Zan. He will be the best man at the wedding."

"Of course I will be," Zan quipped. Allen made a face and shrugged.

"All right boys, try to act your age," Jonathan scolded, his eyes twinkling. "Continuing on—across the table is—Miss Moonbeam. Is that right?"

"Just Moonbeam." Her voice was low and sultry, with an odd intonation. Emma noticed the stud in her tongue when she spoke, which explained the lisp. She had closely cropped spiky black hair that contrasted harshly with her pale complexion and kohl-rimmed gray eyes. Dressed in a black satin pantsuit, her blood-red lips and gold gypsy hoop earrings provided the only color to her Goth look. She waved a claw-like hand with long, black painted fingernails and pointed to herself. "Maid of honor."

"All right then. On the opposite side are Phoebe's parents, Professor and Mrs. Lowenstein. Sydney, I understand you teach philosophy at Stanford University?"

"Not any more. Maurine and I have retired to Sedona, Arizona now. We're both leading seminar retreats in Yoga and metaphysics." Professor Lowenstein appeared relaxed and comfortable. A long, gray ponytail and full beard compensated for his receding hairline. Maurine Lowenstein wore a floor length, multi-colored silk caftan. Her pale hair was piled on top of her head, held tight by a clasp covered with brightly colored beads.

"Seated next to the Lowensteins is Pastor Barnes, who will be officiating the wedding," said Jonathan. "And next to him is Chief Whitefeather of the Yavapai Apache Nation. He is a Native American shaman who will bless the marriage."

Emma fought to suppress a smile at the contrast between the two men. Pastor Barnes was a husky little man in a conservative blue suit, with friendly eyes peering out from above rounded cheeks. Chief Whitefeather, although dressed in slacks and a sports coat, looked the part of an Apache holy man, with his black braid, high cheekbones, and intelligent eyes. The assortment of character types at the table amazed her.

"What are you going to have, Zan?" Emma studied the menu.

"I don't know…Ooh. The Chicken Boursin looks good. I think I'll have that. Do you want an appetizer?"

"I'll have the same, but no appetizer. I want to save room for dessert." Emma's mouth watered at the prospect of Crème Brûlée.

"We'll have your biggest rib-eye, mashed potatoes and pinto beans—with cornbread." Allen drawled with exaggeration, pointing to himself and Phoebe.

"*I* will have the Vegetable Wellington." Phoebe shot a disgusted look at Allen and closed the menu. "*Thank* you very much."

"Hey, Zan. Are you and Emma going on the ghost tour with us later?" asked Allen. "Phoebe and I can't wait to see something spooky."

Zan almost choked on his wine. Reminded of the earlier events, Emma blushed, torn between the excitement of her experience and the need for prudence. Should they tell everyone what happened?

"What?" Allen looked from Zan to Emma. "Don't tell me you've already seen something?"

"Shall we tell 'em?" asked Zan.

"I guess so," said Emma. "He'll never let us rest if we don't."

Zan relayed the story to the astounded group, omitting only the personal parts as to why Theodora resorted to minor violence. Emma considered telling everybody about the coincidence between their room number and her dream, but instead decided to keep it to herself.

The only person who seemed to be alarmed was Pastor Barnes. "This is very, very extraordinary," he muttered. "I think we should all bow our heads in prayer."

Emma lowered her head and closed her eyes. She listened respectfully as the minister droned on and on, asking the Lord to bless everyone at the table and protect them from evil spirits. Wasn't that Chief What's-his-name's jurisdiction? She covered her mouth with her hand in a make-believe cough to hide her smirk. When she sensed someone staring at her she sneaked a peek. Moonbeam smiled mysteriously when they made eye contact.

"…In the name of the Lord, amen."

"Amen," Jonathan echoed. "Well, that was a very interesting story, Zan. What did you call the apparition?"

"Theodora. That's what the people at the hotel call her—it—whatever. But I wouldn't exactly call it an apparition. Don't they have to materialize somehow to qualify for that? We didn't see anything except the stuff that fell." Emma shot him a dirty look. "Oh yes. And the moving mini-blinds," he added.

"The term is *discarnate*. She is a lost soul," interjected Phoebe, and then exhaled rapturously. "This place is a hotbed of activity."

"Perhaps she's trapped in a vortex and needs help finding her way to the next level," offered Phoebe's mother.

"No, no," Professor Lowenstein replied. "It's more likely that Zan and Emma encountered some sort of anomaly on another astral plane…"

Emma listened in silence as almost the entire party argued about the source of her and Zan's purported supernatural experience. Everyone seemed to have an opinion except Emma. What she felt was simply a sense of peace and homecoming. The debate finally died down when the entrees arrived.

"Allen, were you and Zan aware that my parents—your grandparents—met each other in Eureka Springs? Your great grandmother Turner was staying here at this very hotel," said Jonathan. "That's the main reason I suggested this place for the wedding. I've always wanted to visit."

"They met here? At the Crescent?" asked Allen.

"Yes, in 1938. But it wasn't a hotel then. It was a hospital."

"Jonathan, remember that sign we saw in the lobby? Did one of your parents have cancer?" asked Barbara.

"No, but family legend has it that Grandma Ivy's mother was being treated for cancer here when she met Grandpa Harry. Then later on *she* became a patient here too, although she said there was nothing really wrong with either of them."

"I read somewhere that the guy who ran this place in the late thirties was some kind of quack who injected his patients with strange concoctions and claimed to cure everything from cancer to hemorrhoids." Allen winked at Zan. "Too bad you weren't living here then. He probably would have given a lot of business to my brother, the drug dealer."

"Very funny—pharmacist," Zan corrected. "So what was Grandpa Harry doing here?"

"I don't know a lot of the details. They didn't talk about it much," Jonathan mused. "My understanding is he had been working with the CCC building a dam. His family lost everything after the market crash of '29 and ended up as sharecroppers in Oklahoma. Then when the Dust Bowl hit, they gave that up and headed west. I don't know what became of them after that, but I believe Grandpa Harry just drifted around a lot looking for work."

"What's CCC?" asked Phoebe.

"Civilian Conservation Corp," Allen volunteered. "It was an agency President Roosevelt created to help get people back to work during the Great Depression. They built lakes and dams and parks and things. It was part of the New Deal."

"Oh," Phoebe said. "I never was any good at history."

"So, Dad. Why did you ask about Theodora's name?" asked Zan "Is there some significance?"

Jonathan frowned and hesitated. "A couple of times my mother mentioned two lady friends she met here when she was hospitalized. I had forgotten all about them until now. I can't remember one of them. Something common. Like Ann or Alice...But the other one I remember vividly—you're not going to believe this—her name was Theodora. Such a startling coincidence." He shook his head and added, "Remember the bobtailed cat in all the family photos? It used to belong to one of them."

"Oh, my goodness! Do you think Zan and Emma's ghost

could be the same Theodora your mother knew?" Phoebe grinned widely and her eyes danced with excitement. "We need to have a séance."

"Honey—Phoebe…"

"What is it, Allen?"

He lowered his voice and handed her his napkin. "You've got a piece of spinach stuck in your teeth."

"Good grief." She rubbed furiously at her mouth, then opened wide and tilted her head toward her intended. "Is it gone now?"

"Yes, dear." They kissed blissfully and Emma couldn't control her laughter.

"Yuck," said Zan. "I think I'm gonna be sick."

A strolling photographer approached the table. "Would you guys like a group picture?"

"Yeah, that'd be nice," said Allen. "Everybody smile."

The photographer walked around the table, snapping several photos from different angles. "I'll have the prints available at the front desk tomorrow afternoon. If you're interested in any of them, you can purchase them there. Thanks."

The party continued their dinner after the brief interruption. When Emma reached for the saltshaker she glanced to her left and noticed Jonathan gazing intently at her hand. The antique ring sparkled brilliantly, its facets bouncing light off the refracted crystal prisms overhead. "What's the matter, Dad?"

"May I see your ring for a moment, please?"

She extended her hand. "Beautiful, isn't it? Didn't it belong to Zan's mother?"

"Yes, and to Grandma Ivy—my mother—before that. It was her engagement ring."

"So, Dad. If Grandpa Harry was so poor, how could he afford such a valuable rock?" asked Allen. "Was it an heirloom?"

"This is the part that's so strange," Jonathan replied. "It originally belonged to one of Grandma Ivy's friends. I don't know how Grandpa Harry ended up with it. It's all kind of a mystery. But supposedly, the friend gave it to him and stipulated that it was to be worn by the eldest son's wife and then handed down to their son for his wife. And so on and so on."

"No way," cried Zan. "This is just too, too weird."

A sharp stab of guilt brought Emma's euphoria crashing to earth when a voice whispered in her head. *You have no right to wear the ring. You can't have Zan's child. You know the medical tests scheduled for next week will crush your last shred of hope.* Fear and nausea suddenly overwhelmed her and she rose, almost knocking over her chair. She held her napkin to her mouth and prayed she could make it to the restroom in time.

"Emma, are you all right?" Zan asked. Ten sets of eyes watched her as she stumbled away.

"I don't feel well..." She fled, searching for the nearest ladies' room. Her sickness passed as soon as she opened the door, but fatigue and sadness overwhelmed her. She collapsed into a chair in the lounge area and began to weep. How could she have been so happy one minute and devastated the next? She'd never heard voices before and she was terrified. Was she losing her mind?

A moment later the door opened and Moonbeam walked in. She moved gracefully, like a sleek black cat stalking its prey. But her eyes seemed kind as she knelt on the floor next to Emma and reached for her hand. "Don't cry, Emma. Everything's going to be all right."

"You don't even know me," Emma protested and jerked her hand away.

"I know a lot about you, Emma. Just from holding your hand." Moonbeam passed her a tissue.

"I suppose you're one of Phoebe's psychic friends." Emma took the tissue and wiped her face. "Can you read my mind?"

Moonbeam smiled and sat on the floor, crossing her legs in a lotus position. She reached for Emma's hand again, turning it over and studying her palm. "I can't read your mind, but I can sense impressions. You're suffering from a lot of fear and anxiety right now."

Emma bit back a sharp retort. Anybody with observational skills could make the same diagnosis. Why was she so angry with this woman? She didn't like the hostile feelings that roiled within her, especially since Moonbeam had been so patient and nice to her. Hormone overload or not, this was not good.

"Wouldn't you be more comfortable in a chair?"

"Shh..." Moonbeam held a black tipped, talon-like finger to her lips. "I feel another presence in the room with us. Its energy is the source of your discomfort."

"You can't mean Theodo..."

"No," Moonbeam interrupted. "This entity is full of rage. For some reason it has directed its anger at you and is bombarding you with negative thoughts. I first noticed its aura hovering above you at the table."

"You mean it followed me to the bathroom?" Emma furtively scanned the room.

"It's gone now." Moonbeam inhaled deeply. "The atmosphere has already cleared. It didn't like being discovered."

Emma closed her eyes. The faint aroma of lavender hung in the air. A sensation of well-being wrapped itself around her like a blanket. Now where had she noticed that smell before? "We really ought to be getting back. They'll be starting the rehearsal soon."

"In a minute. May I?" Moonbeam reached for her hand again. "I want to show you something."

"Are you a palm reader?" Emma's eyes widened with fascination.

"Yes," replied Moonbeam, tracing her finger across the lines in Emma's palm. "My grandmother taught me, and my great-grandmother Cordelia taught her."

"Can you really tell the future?"

"I can only make predictions based on the signs. Your palm is like a roadmap. There are so many junctures in life that are affected by your choices. If you choose to take the wrong path, your fate may be permanently altered. My purpose is to provide you with guidance."

"This is all so unbelievable." Emma shook her head. "I'm a systems analyst and I design web pages. My whole life is based on logic."

"Don't you think the Internet is a little bit like magic?" asked Moonbeam, then returned her attention to Emma's palm. "You've suffered great loss. Some sort of accident. Was it an airplane?"

"Y-yes. My parents and little brother were killed in a plane crash six years ago." Emma was stunned until she realized Phoebe must have told her. Her heartbeat slowed and her skepticism returned.

"I'm so sorry for your loss," said Moonbeam before continuing with the reading. "Okay, this is your Life Line. See how long and deep it is? This represents a long life full of health and vitality."

"Well, that's good," Emma said, disbelief edging out her earlier enthusiasm. She thought about her scheduled hospital visit and had her doubts. The negative thoughts that had invaded her mind still lingered.

Moonbeam pointed to another crease above the Life Line. "This is your Head Line. It's deep and long, which indicates logical thinking. This next one is your Heart Line. It curves upward sharply, which says you have a romantic nature. You also tend to give yourself completely to love, no matter what the cost."

"Is everything okay in here? Zan's getting worried," interrupted Phoebe, walking into the ladies' lounge and staring at the two women.

"I'm giving Emma a reading. Sit down." Moonbeam

motioned toward a chair in the corner. "Okay. Now *this* is your Fate Line. See how it starts clearly at the wrist and then joins the Life Line? This indicates a point where you have to surrender your own interests to those of other people."

"What? I don't think I like that."

"But wait. Now see how it separates again from your Life Line? This means that you will again gain control of your life."

"Oh, this is all so confusing." Emma glanced at Phoebe sitting quietly, seemingly absorbed.

Moonbeam smiled and continued. "See this line down here? This is the Travel Line. See how it crosses the Fate Line? This indicates that you will take a trip that will present a life-changing experience."

"What about children?"

"See this tiny line just below the base of the little finger? This is the Marriage Line. You only have one, which means you'll have one spouse." Moonbeam pointed to a tiny crease. "This line that connects with the Marriage Line tells me there will be children born to this marriage."

"Okay, thanks." Emma tensed and tried to pull her hand away. She had heard enough. She was beginning to believe what Moonbeam was telling her until she came up with the part about children. She knew that wasn't going to happen. "Don't you think we'd better get back to the party? They'll be wanting to start the rehearsal."

"Please. I have one more thing I must tell you." Moonbeam refused to relinquish her hand. "This is very important."

"Listen to her, Emma," said Phoebe. "She knows what she's doing."

Emma stared at the two women with indecision. She didn't want to be rude. "I'm sorry. This is just all so new and strange to me. Please continue."

"Thank you," Moonbeam replied. Phoebe scooted her chair closer. "I didn't tell you this at first because I didn't want to frighten you. Look at your Life Line. I told you earlier that it was long and deep. And it is. But look right there, where it completely disappears for a fraction of an inch. See?"

"Uh huh. What does that mean?"

Moonbeam hesitated and glanced toward Phoebe before continuing. "It means that your life will have a slight interruption."

Emma shook her head in confusion. She shivered as a cold chill of dread spread through her veins. "I still don't get what you're saying."

"It means that you will die—and then come back."

CHAPTER THREE

Reality struck like a slap in the face. Emma recoiled, jerking her hand away. She rose abruptly and stared at Moonbeam in shock and disbelief. Why was this freaky woman saying such absurd things to her? She had gone way too far; she was nothing more than a sideshow fortuneteller. How could she have allowed herself to be sucked into accepting such nonsense?

"I've heard enough." Emma bolted for the door. Determination replaced anger by the time she returned to her place at the table.

"Are you all right?" asked Zan. "I've been worried sick about you."

"Sorry, honey. I think I'm just tired from the long trip." Emma patted his hand and smiled. She deliberately ignored Phoebe and Moonbeam when she saw them approach the table. "I feel much better now."

"Will you be okay while we have the rehearsal?" Zan's obvious concern softened Emma's mood.

"Of course I will, darling. I'll just sit right here and watch. You go on."

Grateful for the opportunity to be alone with her thoughts, Emma quietly observed the wedding party rehearse in a corner of the dining room. Intermittent streaks of lightning illuminated the darkened windows, but Emma didn't care about the impending thunderstorm. It was a relief not to have to make small talk and be sociable for a little while.

She had to get a grip, for Zan's sake. For better or for worse,

Phoebe was going to be a part of the family. But after the wedding tomorrow they would all go back to their own lives. Then Emma could forget about ghosts and mysterious falling objects and broken lifelines.

"All finished?" Emma flashed a smile at her husband when he approached after the small group had dispersed. She stood and followed him out of the dining room and down a corridor to the lobby.

"Yeah. I think it'll go a lot better tomorrow night. There should be a lot more room to spread out at Thorncrown Chapel."

"So are we still going on the ghost tour? It's almost eight." She knew Zan was looking forward to the tour. She didn't want to be the one to put a damper on the pre-wedding festivities.

"Do you feel up to it? We don't have to go if you're too tired."

"Oh, I wouldn't miss it for the world. I want to find out what's behind all the weird stuff that goes on around here. I have a theory."

"Oh yeah? What is it?"

"I think it's all a big hoax. I suspect the hotel manipulates stuff to scare people out of their wits and make them believe the place is haunted. They've probably got wires or something to make the blinds move around and the ironing board fall. Why else would they sponsor ghost tours if it wasn't a money-making scheme?"

"I don't know." Zan folded his arms and squinted. "They probably do capitalize on the ghost stories—but how did they make the champagne basket fall off the sink?"

"I already told you. They've got everything rigged."

"Hm. If that's true, maybe they've got the rooms bugged—hey, what's that thing on the ceiling? Is that a hidden camera?" Zan craned his neck and pointed at a small red blinking light. "I remember seeing one of those in our room."

"Okay. Cut it out. I know a smoke detector when I see

one." Emma rolled her eyes and leaned on the concierge desk. A flicker of recognition shattered her train of thought and she stared at the unusual piece of furniture. Colorful brochures advertising gift shops and tourist attractions were scattered across its surface, belying its sinister past. Now what made her think that? She shuddered as she ran her hand across the rich patina of the black walnut hexagon-shaped desk.

"What's the matter?"

She shook her head, bewildered by the elusive awareness that seemed just out of her grasp. "I don't know. I just had this weird feeling. Like I've seen this desk before—and something bad happened here. I think I'm losing it."

"Now you're creeping me out." Zan cocked his head to one side and searched Emma's face. "You're messing with me. Right?"

Emma returned her husband's gaze, struck by the childlike innocence of his question. The purity of his love for her showed clearly in his eyes, reminding her why she had fallen in love with him in the first place. Resolving to put his mind at ease, she donned her best fake smile and cried, "Gotcha!"

Zan returned her grin and reached for her elbow to guide her toward the stairs. "Come on, crazy lady. Let's get up there before we miss out on the tour."

Emma held onto Zan's arm as they climbed the crooked old staircase to the fourth floor. The boards creaked and popped with each step. Although solid, the ancient stairs leaned under the weight of more than a century. A small crowd of potential ghost hunters milled about the hallway across from Dr. Baker's Lounge. Allen and Phoebe caught sight of them and waved.

"Hey, we've got your passes," said Allen. He handed two long paper tickets to Emma and Zan. "Come on. They're about to start."

Emma glanced behind her and saw her father-in-law leaning against the wall, chatting with a middle-aged couple wearing

Hard Rock Café – St. Louis tee shirts. Barbara stood next to a boy, who appeared to be eleven or twelve. She dangled a camera cord while a calico kitten lunged and pounced playfully. Moonbeam loitered in the back, laughing and whispering with Chief Whitefeather; her voluptuous body pressed seductively close to the tall, handsome man. Emma supposed Phoebe's parents and the preacher had decided to skip the evening's entertainment.

"Do *not*—under any circumstances—blurt out to this tour guide what happened to me and Zan this afternoon," Emma warned Allen. "If you do, I'll have to hurt you."

"You're such a party pooper." Allen stuck out his lower lip, then turned to Phoebe and gave her a hug. "I'm glad I'm marrying *you*."

A pretty redhead wearing a green turtleneck sweater and stonewashed jeans came out of the Faculty Lounge. She motioned for the people to enter, while a distinguished looking gentleman with silver hair and laughing eyes collected their tickets. When everyone was seated she waved for attention. "Thanks, Johnny. Not too many tonight. Are ya'll ready?"

A murmur of agreement wafted up through the small crowd. Zan put his arm around Emma. She smiled and put her head on his shoulder, ready to listen to the guide's opening monologue.

"Hi, everybody. My name's Cheryl. I'll be your tour guide tonight." She was cute and bubbly, putting everyone at ease with her homey, easy speech. "So. How is everybody? ...good...are you scared?...no?...you will be."

Twitters of laughter drifted through the group. Someone snapped a picture.

"Okay, I'm gonna take you on the ghost tour of the Crescent Hotel. I think some of you are staying here tonight and if I mention your room and it scares you, I'm sorry. But if I don't mention your room, don't think that makes you immune. Walls don't hold ghosts. They go wherever they want to. If they want to go in your room, they're gonna do it—so you never know."

Allen, sitting one row back, leaned close to Emma. He blew on the back of her neck and said, "Boo!"

Emma flinched and then gave him a withering glance over her shoulder. Zan shot a good-natured warning look at his brother, cuddled her protectively and said, "Hush, dimwit."

Cheryl smiled at Allen and continued, "This is not a Halloween party tour. We don't have anybody hiding in a corner that's gonna jump out and scare you. That would be cheating and this is very, very real. It's not just the hotel that's haunted; it's the whole area. Three-fourths of the people who live in this town will tell you they have somebody extra staying in their house."

"Do you have a ghost living in your house?" asked the young boy, his eyes wide with wonder.

"As a matter of fact, I do," replied Cheryl. "The place I live in now used to be an orphanage, so there are some children who are still there. My kids play with them. You see, my whole family is clairvoyant, so I grew up with it. When I was a little girl I thought everybody had ghosts in their houses."

"I'm clairvoyant too," volunteered Phoebe. "But I've heard that everybody is, to a certain extent. It's just a matter of sensitivity to the forces of nature. Some people have more highly developed ESP than others. That's why some people see ghosts and others don't."

"That's right," said Cheryl. "We get reports from people in the hotel all the time about things that happen. But it's not like Hollywood. It's not like the *Poltergeist* movie where people get sucked through a TV. Ghosts were people just like we are who have died and for whatever reasons are emotionally bonded to an area. You have to understand that whatever happened to them when they failed to cross over has to do with why they're still here."

"Do you ever see any ghosts on the tour?" asked the boy.

41

"Oh, yes," replied Cheryl. "We've had ghosts materialize on the tour, but I can't guarantee you'll see something tonight. It takes a lot of energy for them to do that. You see, this isn't a material world for them anymore. You have to understand that time is different for them. What may be a century for us could be like five minutes to them."

"Do you conduct scientific experiments like on the ghost hunting shows?" asked Jonathan.

"Some. We've used equipment to measure electro-magnetics, spirit boxes, night vision cameras, etc. But the only way to get real proof is to die. I haven't done that yet and I hope nobody here plans to do it any time soon. So just take what anybody tells you—including me—with a grain of salt. All I'm gonna do here tonight is present you with different things we've experienced and what we've researched about the history and legends of the area and the building."

"Fakes. What'd I tell you?" Emma whispered to Zan. She tried to ignore the nagging memory of Moonbeam's prediction. He grinned and squeezed her ribs.

"If you have questions, please feel free to ask," Cheryl continued. "This is a really, really laidback tour. If something happens to you that's outside the norm, say something. Raise your hand and say *'this happened to me.'* Nobody will say you're crazy. After all, you've just paid eighteen dollars to go on a ghost tour. So scream your lungs out if something happens—well, don't scream. You'll scare everybody else to death."

Someone's cell phone played Taps. A buzz of laughter drifted through the crowd.

"Be sure and take lots of photos," said Cheryl. "We've had tons of people capture pictures of ghosts on this tour."

"What do they look like?" asked the wide-eyed boy.

"Well, if you're very lucky, you'll get a picture of ectoplasm, which looks kind of like smoke. But mostly they show up as balls of energy, called orbs. If you're using a regular camera, be sure to tell the developer you want every picture back. A lot of times what happens is there'll be funny spots on the film and the developer will throw them away, thinking it's a flaw in the film. You don't want them to throw away your ghost."

Barbara gasped when she scrolled through the images on her digital camera. A bright, glowing ball of light hovered in a far corner of the hallway on one of the pictures. "I think I got one. Look at this."

"Yeah, that's an orb all right." Cheryl smiled and nodded. "That's the kind of thing to look for."

Emma craned her neck and stared at the camera display. She whispered to Zan, "Dust particle caught in the flash." She smiled and continued to listen politely.

"Sometimes on this tour you may hear somebody talking and it's not me and it's not anybody on the tour. You may smell something you know shouldn't be there. Sometimes you'll get touched." Cheryl rolled her eyes when Allen made a face. "No, this isn't a groping ghost, so you're not gonna get lucky. You may see somebody walking down the hall and then just disappear into the wall. It happens. Sometimes you just see the outside shape or you'll see shadows in your peripheral vision.

"Okay! Any questions so far?" asked Cheryl. "No? All right, a little bit of history. The Osage Indians lived here for hundreds of years. They believed the water that came from springs in the Ozarks was magical and could cure whatever was wrong with you. They basically worshipped the water that was in this area. Legend has it that when Ponce de Leon was searching for the Fountain of Youth he was actually headed just south of Eureka Springs. But he never made it this far and wound up in Florida."

The man with the Hard Rock tee shirt raised his hand. "I read somewhere that Eureka Springs is supposed to be so haunted because the springs that flow underneath the mountain create a lot of energy that attracts spirits."

"Yes, I've heard that theory before," Cheryl admitted.

"Anyway, lots of people believed the waters were curative, so they settled here and in the 1870's Eureka Springs was turned into a resort town. The Crescent Hotel was built in 1886 and became a five-star hotel that attracted wealthy people from all over the world. It was operated as a hotel until 1907, when it became an exclusive finishing school for wealthy young ladies. The school operated until the Depression and then everything fell apart. Eureka was just about boarded up. It was during that period that it became a cancer hospital…yep. The Crescent has gone through some tough times over the years."

The man interrupted again. "The first time I came to the Crescent was in the late 1980's and it was literally falling apart. It had nasty 70's carpeting; the plaster was falling off the walls; it looked like something out of *The Shining*."

"I remember that period," said Cheryl. "We're very grateful to the present owner who's been refurbishing it for the past few years. It's been a huge project. So. Are you guys ready to take a walk?" asked Cheryl, glancing around the room. "Uh huh, you are? Well, come on then!"

Cheryl turned left after exiting the Faculty Lounge and led the way down the hall. The group followed, huddling closely when she stopped and gestured toward a short hallway that split off to the right.

"Okay, over there are a couple of our most haunted rooms. The North Penthouse and Room 419. But I'm not going to talk about 'em just yet. Okay? Time to go down," said Cheryl and then headed down the stairs.

"She's talking about our room," whispered Emma.

"I know," Zan replied. "Pretty cool, huh?

Emma nodded and continued trudging with the group down the winding staircase. A black cat lay on a bench in the stairwell; its orange eyes gazed disdainfully at the intrusion.

Their first stop was the third floor. Cheryl resumed her spiel. "Now over here at the end of this hall is a square building called the annex. It connects to the main building on both the second and third floors. This is where the servants would stay during Victorian times—and later it became an asylum for cancer patients who had gone insane."

Allen and Phoebe's eyes widened as they stared at each other. Zan grinned and poked his brother in the ribs. "Guess you feel right at home, huh?"

Cheryl laughed and continued her story. "It's been renovated into luxury Jacuzzi suites now. But right about in this area on the second floor, usually around 9:00 or 9:30 at night, you might see a nurse pushing an older gentleman in a wheelchair down the hall. Then they fade out and disappear—all right—let's continue on."

Emma rolled her eyes. Zan noticed her look and placed his finger over her lips. She suppressed a giggle as they continued walking.

Cheryl stopped near the elevator and resumed her speech. "Okay, on this floor is another nurse—not the same one—pushing a gurney. On the gurney is a body covered with a sheet. We've never been able to see who it is. She's very noisy and the gurney wheels squeak. They're coming up the hall toward the elevator, where they just disappear. It's always around 2:00 or 3:00 in the morning. Now technically, these nurses are not really ghosts. It's called *old energy*. It's an imprint on time because the same thing replays over and over again, kind of like watching a movie on a VCR. Every time you rewind it, it never changes.

"Another ghost seen frequently is a girl about eighteen or nineteen in a long white dress, like a school uniform. Dozens of people have seen her climb over the third floor balcony and jump. The legend is that from 1907 until the Depression, when this was the Crescent College for Young Ladies, this girl got killed. People often see her out in the garden darting between the trees like she's hunting for someone.

"One of two local legends is she had an affair and got pregnant, and to save her family honor she jumped from the third floor balcony and killed herself. The other story that floats around town is that she was having an affair with a male professor in the building, and to save his job and his tushy, he pitched her over."

"Which one do you believe?" asked Phoebe.

"We don't know which one is true, but most likely the first one, since nobody ever sees anyone but her. What we do know is that people will consistently see this girl fall from the third floor balcony. Now you don't see her land. If you really do see someone fall and go splat, please call 9-1-1."

"This is getting sillier by the minute," Emma mumbled. She glanced around and noticed expressions of polite amusement on other people in the group.

They followed Cheryl on down the stairs, where she stopped halfway down the hall of the second floor. Moonbeam and Chief Whitefeather stayed in the back, oblivious to anything but each other.

"Okay, the first thing we're gonna talk about is this room right here." Cheryl pointed to Room 218. A man and woman carrying suitcases passed the tour crowd. "Are you guys needing to get by? Everybody, let them pass, please."

"Thanks," said the man. "Which one's the haunted room?"

"They *all* are," replied Cheryl. "But Room 218 is the most famous one. It's probably rented. It's the most asked-for room because of Michael. People think it's their best shot at seeing a ghost."

"Who's Michael?" asked the talkative boy.

"Michael was an Irish stonemason who was brought here back in the olden days with a big crew to build the Crescent. They had finished the outside structure, but the inside was still just scaffolding. Michael supposedly fell to his death right there where Room 218 is now. Whether this story is true or not, we don't know. But what we do know is there is someone who likes the attention and has taken up permanent residence in that room."

"Whoa!" The little boy grinned at his grandmother.

"Michael is a poltergeist," said Cheryl, smiling warmly at the buzz of excitement that swept through the group. "If you check your dictionary you'll see that it literally means a noisy ghost. A poltergeist can move things. He turns off and on lights or the water in the bathroom. He has a habit of moving all your stuff around and putting his hands through the mirror while you're applying your makeup or fixing your hair."

"Oh, my goodness," said the middle-aged woman. "That would scare me to death."

"He's just playing," replied Cheryl. "Okay, now we're not gonna go back up to the fourth floor again, but I want to talk to you about a particular room up there. Room 419. That's Theodora's room."

Allen's eyes lit up. Emma stared at him with a warning look. He sighed loudly and appeared resigned. She had to smother a laugh.

"Is Theodora a ghost?" asked the boy.

"Oh, yes. She's our sweet little grandmother," replied Cheryl. "We found her literally by accident. One of our guys was up on a ladder one day doing some stenciling work in the room. He heard this little old lady's voice say *'I really like what you're doing to my room'*. He turned around to say thanks and nobody was there. So he went back to work. Then she said it again and this time he saw her.

"She's an elderly lady about five feet tall. He asked her who she was and she said *'I'm Theodora. I'm one of Dr. Baker's patients'*. Which means she had cancer. The next day we asked the hotel staff about her and they said they talked to her all the time, but they never told anybody because they didn't want to scare her off. They tell everybody about Michael, on the other hand, 'cause he's ornery and he loves the attention."

"Have you seen her yourself?" asked Allen in a serious voice, locking eyes with Emma.

"Oh, yeah. Many times. She's a little bitty thing wearing a long black dress with a white crocheted collar. She looks frail, but she's not quite as helpless as she seems. She's notorious for standing right outside her door rummaging through her purse like she can't find her keys. People from surrounding rooms will ask her if she needs help and she'll say *'No thanks. I do this all the time'* and then disappears. Freaks 'em out when she does that."

"I've noticed a door right next to 419 that seems to have its own staircase," said Zan. "Is that some sort of penthouse?"

"Um hm," said Cheryl. "That's the North Penthouse— directly above 419. It was Dr. Baker's private residence—I'll tell you all about him when we get to the basement. He used to keep machine guns hanging on the walls. That room is very, very active."

Goose bumps rose on Emma's arms. She thought about the little door in the wall in the parlor and shivered. Zan squeezed her shoulder and she felt better.

"What were the machine guns for?" asked the boy.

"We'll get to that in a little while," said Cheryl. "All right. Is everybody ready to go to the basement? Before we do, I just want to tell you a couple of rules. One of them is no running. The other one is no poking anybody on the back. By the time you get to the basement, this tour gets pretty intense, so I don't want anybody getting hurt if they panic. Okay? Let's go."

The noise of a dozen people descending the ancient stairs echoed throughout the building. Hotel guests waited patiently for the group to pass. Emma laughed to herself when she compared their polite reverence to a funeral procession.

"Isn't this exciting?" Phoebe held tight to Allen's hand, practically dragging him down the stairs. "I can just feel the vibrations of all the spirits who still walk these halls."

Emma laughed at Phoebe's exuberance. Her earlier anger had dissipated, caught up by the adventurous spirit generated by the tour. Intellectually she knew the stories were hogwash, but she was still having fun. She felt like a twelve year old at a pajama party listening to ghost stories.

"Emma—psst! Over there." Zan poked Emma on the arm. She glanced up just in time to see Moonbeam and the Chief break away from the group and head back upstairs.

"Well," exclaimed Emma. "I guess some people just can't wait for the tour to get over."

"I know how they feel." Zan nuzzled her ear. "Don't forget. I'm gonna hold you to your promise, you know."

"Zan, there are other people trying to get down the steps too," Emma scolded and pulled him forward. "Don't worry, I haven't forgotten. Just don't *you* get all worn out from running up and down these stairs."

When they reached the basement, Cheryl motioned for them to sit on the steps while she stood and talked. Emma smiled when she felt her husband pull her into his lap as he settled himself on the stairs. The whole group—minus the two who had sneaked off—made themselves as comfortable as possible.

"Okay, is everybody here?" Cheryl scanned the group. "Did we lose some people?"

"I don't think they'll be back," said Allen, raising and lowering his eyebrows.

"All right, whatever." Cheryl smiled with understanding. "On this level everything changes. Once we go through that door we'll go back through the laundry room and to the maintenance department. You'll be going into an area you would never get to see unless you were on this tour. It's gonna look different. It's gonna feel different. The walls are a little bit closer. The ceilings are a little bit lower. You're going to see the stone structure that was put in place in 1886 that actually holds the hotel up as a grid work. It kind of looks like the dungeon of a castle. It makes great special effects for us, but it tends to make your imagination run away with you. So don't run and trip over your own feet or I guarantee everybody is gonna laugh at you."

The calico suddenly appeared and began rubbing against Allen's pant leg. He jumped in fright. Laughter rippled throughout the basement.

"He'd better not get himself locked up down here or we'll have another ghost kitty, like Morris."

"Who's Morris?" asked the boy.

"Morris was the Crescent's marmalade tabby for over twenty years. Everybody referred to him as *The Manager*. He's buried in the back of the hotel near the patio. There's also a picture of him in the lobby."

Emma turned toward Zan and buried her face in his chest to hide her mirth. Ghost cats. What would they come up with next? She straightened her face and continued to listen.

"Now there are only three years of history we deal with on this level which makes up a big percentage of the entities at the Crescent—1937 through 1940. In 1937 Eureka was flat broke. The only industry they had here was tourism and during the Depression not many people could afford to go vacationing.

"There was a man who drove into town one day in a purple Cord convertible. He was only five foot five. He had on his trademark outfit, which was a white suit and a lavender shirt with an art deco tie. Everything about him was very colorful and flamboyant. He was throwing cash around like it was water. Now when a town is broke, the mayor and everybody rolls out the red carpet for somebody like him. They're thinking *'Oh thank God. He's going to save the town.'*"

"Was this Dr. Baker?" asked Phoebe.

Cheryl nodded. "He came from Muscatine, Iowa where he owned a radio station. He was the youngest of ten kids and he had three goals. He wanted to be rich—he wanted to be famous—

and he wanted to be a doctor. Well, he got rich by inventing something called a *Tangley Calliaphone*. It's an instrument sort of like a calliope, but it was smaller and it operated off air pressure instead of steam. Anyway, he made a lot of money from it and he became famous by talking on his radio station for hours and hours about how he had discovered the cure for cancer. Prior to that, he'd been a mentalist in a Vaudeville act."

"How did he find the time to do medical research with all his other enterprises?" asked Jonathan.

"That's just it," replied Cheryl. "He never went to med school, so he just skipped that part of his formal education. He only made it through sixth grade. Anyway, he opened up a clinic where he took in over a hundred cancer patients. And he called himself Dr. Baker, with absolutely no training and no degree. His name was Norman Baker."

"Are you sure it wasn't Norman Bates?" Allen interjected.

"No, not Norman Bates," Cheryl laughed. "Same personality type, maybe."

Cheryl regained control of the laughing group and continued. "Now the Feds were after him because he'd published a book and some pamphlets that actually stated he could cure cancer no matter how bad you had it. He gave people a written guarantee. He said if it wasn't too far advanced he could cure them in two weeks. If it was a little worse, maybe four weeks. Worst case scenario, he'd say *'Give me three months and I'll have you cured and going home.'*"

"Quack, quack." Allen held his nose and made a face.

Cheryl grinned and continued. "Well, of course thousands of desperate people were flocking to his hospital. We're talking about the thirties. They didn't have many options. They'd try anything. The American Medical Association was trying to shut him down, but he did have licensed physicians on staff, so that made his hospital legal. He told them he was just the administrator. So they waited for him to make a mistake—and he did."

"How horrible." Barbara shivered and snuggled up to Jonathan.

"He held a public demonstration one day in a Muscatine city park. Thirty-two thousand people showed up to watch him perform surgery on a gentleman who had brain cancer. They put this guy up on a platform and had Dr. Baker's surgeon open up his skull. Then Baker waltzed up there with all his fanfare and poured his miracle cure directly on this guy's brain— watermelon seed, carbolic acid, and mineral water—real brain washing. Sewed him up, called him cured, and sent him home."

"Did that *really* happen?" Emma could no longer hide her skepticism. Something about this story nagged at her, but she refused to acknowledge its truth. She was fighting not to believe.

"Oh, yes. After the tour I can show you the pictures and newspaper article," Cheryl replied. "Baker was a master at deception, but he messed up. He craved publicity, so he invited the newspaper there and they published the article. So after this stunt, the authorities filed charges against him, shut down his radio station, and issued a warrant for his arrest. He high-tailed it and ran, with his clinic still operating. He went to Laredo, Texas and crossed the border into Mexico where he opened up another radio station and started it all over again."

"Couldn't the authorities get him there?" asked Zan

"No, that's why he went there. But pretty soon they managed to shut his hospital down in Iowa, so his staff called him in Mexico and asked him what to do with his patients. So he crossed back across the border and started looking for a place. That's when he came across Eureka Springs and heard about all the healing water they were supposed to have. He found the Crescent, which was all boarded up, and bought it for $40,000." Cheryl pursed her lips and glanced around the room. "Doesn't that make you sick? It cost almost $300,000 to build in 1886 and he got it for practically nothing. He spent another $50,000 tearing out the balconies and putting in those ugly concrete porches. And he painted the whole place bright colors, mainly purple."

Emma frowned, remembering her earlier reaction to the lobby. How had she known about the purple paint? And when Cheryl mentioned the machine guns in the penthouse, a distinct picture of where they'd hung had formed in her mind. Her certainty that she'd figured everything out began to crack.

"When the Baker Hospital opened here in Eureka, he made sure he was the only one who checked in the patients," Cheryl continued. "He wanted total control. He would ask *'Where are you from? Who's your family? Is anybody visiting you while you're here? How far advanced is your disease?'* All of those questions were logical and things he would need to know. But somewhere in the interview he would slip in *'You know, during your treatment you may need some cash. So where's your bank account? How much do you have in it?'*"

"Surely no one gave him that sort of information?" remarked the middle-aged man.

"This was the thirties. He was their doctor who was gonna save their lives. Nobody had ever heard of identity theft back then," replied Cheryl. "He only did this to people who fell into a certain group. He had a lot of wealthy widows who came here for treatment, and some of them didn't have any close living relatives near Eureka Springs.

"Get the picture? Let's pretend I have a Great Aunt Joan who's a patient at the Baker Cancer Hospital. I don't really know her, but she has a fortune and I'm her closest living relative. So her lawyers send me a letter and tell me she's in the hospital and while she's there she puts me in control of her money. When Baker finds this out during the interview, he gets her to sign three letters to the effect *feeling better, love it here, send more money.* And he'd stuff them into a file in case she died, for future use."

"Now the nurses we've seen on the second and third floors are simply repeating things that happened over and over. If someone died in his or her room, Baker's nurse would lock the remains in during the day and then move it out at night. His staff couldn't move them during the day because Baker had given the patient a written cure guarantee."

"Surely somebody saw what was going on and would tell?" asked Emma. How could something like this have gone on without detection? She felt her blood pressure rise just thinking about it. Such a terrible, terrible thing. Somebody needed to do something.

"We used to wonder how they got the bodies out, since the elevator doesn't go to the basement...excuse me, management prefers we call it *garden level*. But we discovered that originally it did go down there—and they always did this *body shuffling* late at night, when patients were sleeping and the rest of the staff was gone.

"Now there have always been rumors of secret tunnels and passageways, but we never could find them—until they started renovating the building and knocking down walls—supposedly, they found human skeletons hidden inside some of the walls. That's when they discovered the secret trap door and escape hatch leading from Baker's office on the first floor. It had a ladder that went right up to what is now room 203. They found another hidden passageway in the North Penthouse going down to the fourth floor, but I understand it's never been explored because of structural instability due to fire damage. Who knows what might be in there now?"

Emma stiffened and her eyes widened as she realized the penthouse was directly above her and Zan's room. Terror suddenly gripped her and she clutched at her palpitating chest. Zan sensed her fear and tightened his embrace.

"You okay?" he whispered in Emma's ear. She nodded and patted his encircling arms, grateful for their comforting strength. She fought to regain her composure.

"I heard a rumor that there was an underground tunnel," the middle-aged man interrupted. "They said he had little safe paths hidden everywhere, so he could escape when the Feds came to arrest him."

"That's right. And that's why he had the machine guns. But nobody knew where the passages were until a few years ago when they put in a new telephone system. They found a tunnel adjacent to the elevator that runs to the west and on out into the woods. Okay. Is everybody ready? Time to go." Cheryl unlocked a door and led the small group through a dimly lit hallway.

A frisson of apprehension coursed up Emma's spine and she clutched Zan's arm. She wasn't sure she really wanted to go in there. He pulled her close as they trudged through the narrow channel. They passed the hotel's huge laundry room before stopping in front of a plain looking door at the farthest end of the building.

Cheryl entered first, yanking on an overhead light chain and motioning for the group to gather around. The room was a hodgepodge of paint cans, tools, and various objects. A cluttered metal table with a built-in sink lined one wall. An old battered freezer case was built into the wall; its door was tightly padlocked.

Emma felt as if her breath was cut off when she saw the room. Icy fear twisted around her heart and a cold knot formed in her stomach. She clenched her hands until she felt her nails digging into her palms. She held her breath and waited. She knew what was coming.

Cheryl's eyes gleamed brightly as she surveyed the group. She leaned nonchalantly against a cabinet and said, "Welcome to the morgue."

CHAPTER FOUR

Emma scanned the room with apprehension as an eerie hush settled like a shroud over the small group of explorers. Shadowy forms quivered on the bare stone walls, waxing and waning in the harsh glow of a naked swinging light bulb. The room smelled of dust, mildew, and stale varnish.

The muffled sound of thunder, followed by pelting rain on the window casements reverberated throughout the hotel's underbelly. A tomblike chill penetrated the fabric of Emma's jacket; she shuddered and moved closer to Zan. She breathed in the dank air, trying not to dwell on the sensory overload.

"Where're all the dead bodies?" The young boy's innocent question shattered the tension; the adults laughed, transforming the tour's somber mood.

"Oh, honey. It's not a morgue anymore," said Cheryl. "It's the hotel's maintenance room now." She flipped a switch and the room was flooded in bright fluorescent light.

"Oh," he replied. He lowered his eyes and smiled shyly. "I thought there'd be a bunch of tables and freezers and stuff like on *CSI*."

Cheryl laughed and pointed to the farthest corner. An ancient wooden door built into the wall rose from floor to ceiling. "Well, there are a couple of artifacts here that prove it was the hospital morgue. That's a refrigeration unit and I understand it's original to the Crescent.

"They had freezers in the 1800's? I would have thought they'd only have ice boxes," remarked Phoebe.

"I'm sure the technology was different back then. But remember, the hotel was built with electricity and in 1886 that was a miraculous thing. There's a dumbwaiter out there in the laundry that goes up to the kitchen, so we think the hotel used this freezer down here."

"Why's it padlocked?" asked Allen.

"Because it's not used anymore and we don't want silly people crawling into it and getting locked up," said Cheryl. "But Baker used it."

The young boy gasped and pointed, "Did he put the bodies in there?"

"You got it," answered Cheryl. "Remember my Aunt Joan? Well, of course she didn't make it. So they brought her down here and stuck her in the fridge. Baker pulled her file and found those letters. *Feeling better; send more money.* He remembered me and hoped I wouldn't come here to check on her. So he sent the first letter and I sent the money."

"What a scam artist." Zan shook his head in disgust.

"Um hm. He mails those letters out for a couple more months. But now he has a two-month-old body he's got to do something with. So he sends out a regret letter saying *'We've done everything we can. Would you like us to make the arrangements for you?'* Sure, I say. What a relief not to have to deal with that. Here's a bunch of her money for the burial and I get to keep what's left over. Very convenient. So to keep the body count down and to make sure all this stays hidden, he would take her corpse out and put it in the incinerator."

"Ohmigod," exclaimed Phoebe. "Is that what that huge smoke stack is at the end of the building?"

"No," replied Cheryl. "Everybody thinks it is. It's just the boiler room for the hotel. The incinerator doesn't even exist anymore. After they caught Baker, the people in the city were so horrified they came here and tore the incinerator apart. They actually talked about tearing the hotel down, too."

"The angry villagers—armed with torches intent on burning the monster—march on Castle Frankenstein." Allen lowered his voice dramatically, then executed an evil laugh. "Bwa-ha-ha-ha-ha-ha."

"Hush." Phoebe snickered and slapped the back of Allen's head.

Cheryl smiled and continued, "After they destroyed the incinerator, people actually found human bones in the ashes. I know a woman who saved a skeletal hand she found in there. Now *that's* weird."

"Euwww!" several people remarked in unison. The group laughed, but Emma couldn't join them. Her sadness was too deep and personal, but she didn't understand why. As if sensing something wrong, Zan held her close and gave her little reassuring pats.

"Okay. Now the room in the back is where they took the bodies before they transferred them to the funeral homes—the ones they didn't cremate. Undertakers did a thriving business during that time. We only have one mortician now, but when Baker was here there were eight." Cheryl pointed to a small room filled with broken furniture and assorted junk.

The group wandered around for several moments, speaking in hushed tones as they tried to imagine the macabre activities that had taken place in the basement. Emma managed to calm herself, but a sudden impulse compelled her when she noticed Allen and Phoebe leaning against a steel table. She pointed to it and asked, "What is that?"

"That's the last of Dr. Baker's autopsy tables," replied Cheryl.

"Ack!" Allen shrieked and jumped away just as a violent bolt of lightning flashed outside, followed by a clap of thunder.

Jonathan joined the laughter at his son's antics and asked, "So what happened to Baker?"

"The Feds finally gathered enough evidence to indict him

on mail fraud for sending fake guarantees. He was tried and convicted in January of 1940, and the hospital was shut down. He served four years in the penitentiary at Leavenworth, and was fined four thousand dollars."

"Is he still alive?" asked the boy.

"Oh, no," said Cheryl. "After he was released from prison he bought a yacht and lived off the coast of Florida until 1958. He died of liver cancer."

"That's ironic," said Zan. "He couldn't even cure himself."

Cheryl shook her head. "Nope. They say he was a quack who never cured anybody."

"Are a lot of his patients buried here in town?" asked Jonathan. "For instance, is Theodora's grave in Eureka Springs?"

"There are a lot of people from the hospital buried in the city cemetery," said Cheryl. "But we've never found any record of Theodora. We don't really know anything about her. She may have been one of the ones who ended up in the incinerator."

A tear escaped and traveled down Emma's cheek. Zan reached over and wiped it gently with the back of his hand. She closed her eyes and nestled back against his chest. Weariness overwhelmed her. What in the world was wrong with her? It was ridiculous to be affected like this by a bunch of silly stories.

Cheryl reached inside the door of a small pantry-like room and flipped a switch. Above the door a sign read *Parts Room*. Dim light bathed the shelf-lined interior. Buckets, paint cans, and shop supplies cluttered the floor and shelves. "Now *this* is called the Parts Room—for more reasons than one. It was kept sealed and locked until 1985. I'm told that when they opened it they found dozens of jars full of human organs preserved in formaldehyde."

Gasps of disbelief echoed through the crowd.

"Where are they now?" asked the man in the Hard Rock tee-shirt.

"Nobody knows," answered Cheryl. "They sat on those

shelves for forty-five years because people were afraid to touch them—afraid they'd get cancer. But when the building was for sale in '85, someone decided those jars wouldn't look too pretty to prospective buyers and moved them. We've been trying to find out what happened to them for years."

"How did they keep something like that secret for so long?" asked the man.

"We have a theory. We think there must have been a guard posted down here and they kept this room heavily secured. There's somebody in this room we think must have been a watchman. When we first started doing these tours he would get very perturbed and start materializing."

"Is he here now?" asked the boy, his voice quivering.

"I'm not sure," said Cheryl. "He doesn't show himself much anymore. But when *TAPS Ghost Hunters* filmed here they actually caught his image on thermal photography—a tall man wearing a billed cap, right there in front of that locker with the stenciled numbers."

"His name was Andy." Emma opened her eyes when she noticed the silence. Everyone stared at her. A chill worked its way down the length of her body.

"What did you mean?" asked Zan. "Who's Andy?"

Emma blinked and tried to clear her mind. Now why did she say that? "I don't know. It just came out."

The fluorescent lights suddenly dimmed, the incandescent bulb flickered and popped, and then the room was plunged into darkness. Chaos ensued as the entire group screamed. Cheryl found a flashlight and the frightened people scurried toward the light and huddled together. As if on cue, a loud clap of thunder roared outside, contributing to the confusion. Emma clung to Zan in shock as Cheryl worked to regain control of the frightened group.

"It's okay. It's okay." Cheryl fanned her face with her hand. "I think Andy's just feeling kinda mischievous tonight. But don't worry, he won't hurt anybody. It *is* nice to know his name now."

Emma's head swam. She looked around the darkened room in confusion. What had just happened? Had the storm caused the lights to blow? Or had it been the result of some force beyond her understanding? How could she have known the name of some alleged guard who was now a ghost?

Zan appeared to be in shock. The young boy began to whimper and he clung to his likewise-frightened grandparents. Jonathan attempted to console a visibly shaken Barbara. Allen and Phoebe hugged each other and giggled. Even Cheryl seemed stunned.

Seconds later, the frightened people streamed out the door. Cheryl aimed the light down the hall and waited until the last tour guest had passed before she followed. Nobody lingered to thank her or add to the tip jar. "Well, I guess it's about time to end the tour anyway. Hope ya'll had a good time. Thanks for coming."

Emma held tight to Zan's hand as they trailed behind the mass exodus. Her heart raced from the adrenaline rush, but slowly calmed at the sight of lights blazing in the laundry room. The clatter of rushing footsteps in the narrow hallway gradually abated as the group distanced themselves from the morgue; within moments they began to laugh and talk about their experience.

"Goodness, gracious. I've never been so glad to get away from a place in my life. I'm never coming down to this basement again," Barbara exclaimed when the carpeted staircase came in sight.

"But all you gals have appointments at the beauty parlor tomorrow." Allen pointed to The New Moon Spa sign across from the stairs.

"If you don't want to come back down here again we can find another salon in town somewhere." Jonathan patted his wife's arm.

"I'll have to see how I feel in the morning." Barbara shuddered and began climbing.

When they reached the first floor, the couple and their sobbing grandson headed for the lobby door. The Fuller party gathered around the elevator. Emma flinched when a loud clap of thunder fractured the silence. The elevator door squeaked open and they climbed inside.

"Sounds like it's raining cats and dogs out there," said Zan. "That family's gonna get wet."

"Yeah, glad we don't have to go out in it," remarked Allen.

"Well, that was fun. So do you guys want to go up to Dr. Baker's Lounge for a little while? I think they've got some guy singing and playing guitar tonight. I could use a good, stiff drink after that ghost tour."

"Honey, you know I can't drink right now," said Phoebe.

"Not me, I'm exhausted," said Barbara.

Jonathan nodded in agreement, holding the elevator door open for his wife when they reached their floor. "We'll see you all in the morning. Good night."

"G'night Dad, Mom," Allen embraced Jonathan and Barbara.

"What do you want to do?" Zan turned to Emma.

"I think I'm ready to call it a night," she replied.

"Sounds good to me. Phoeb—whadda ya say we test out that big whirlpool tub?" Allen grabbed Phoebe and nuzzled her neck. She purred happily. The two lovebirds exited the elevator hand-in-hand.

"Alone at last." Zan bent down and kissed Emma lightly on the lips. She raised up on her tiptoes to meet him. Even with heels he towered over her. The elevator door squeaked open and they headed down the hall. A sense of exhilaration filled her now that she was out of that awful basement. She couldn't wait to get back to their room.

A light floral aroma pervaded the suite, welcoming them home. The mini-blinds remained still and she sensed they were now alone. Her earlier fright from their experience in the morgue had dissipated. She felt happy and contented and excited, all at the same time. Emma sat on the edge of the bed, kicked off her shoes, and dangled her legs. Zan followed her into the bedroom, pulling his tie loose as he walked. She stopped him before he could unbutton his shirt.

"Honey, I'm thirsty. Could you go downstairs and get us some ice and sodas please?"

"Oh, okay. Where's the machine?"

"I think I saw it down on either the second or third floor. I'm not sure which. By the elevator."

"Be back in a jiffy."

When she was certain he was gone, Emma raced to her suitcase. She pulled out a Victoria's Secret bag and emptied its contents on the bed. She was glad now she'd put it in her luggage at the last moment. She'd bought it to wear for their anniversary, but decided instead that tonight would be the perfect night. She quickly undressed, tossed her clothing on a chair, and put on the lingerie.

The red satin merry widow tucked her in and pushed her up in all the right places. A matching thong flattered and showcased her derriere. Black silk stockings caressed her legs as she pulled them in place and attached the garters. A pair of red stilettos completed the sexy effect. She felt excited, as if she was dressing for a very naughty costume party.

When she finished changing, she stood in front of the floor-length bathroom mirror, turning back and forth to assess her appearance. She bent over and tousled her shoulder-length hair to give it a poufy, sensuous look. She applied blood red lipstick, doused herself in perfume, and then scampered to the bed.

Allen was at the vending machine trying to feed a dollar bill into the slot when Zan approached with the ice bucket. He cursed when it spat the money back out. Zan laughed and reached for the bill. He turned George Washington's picture in the proper direction, the dollar disappeared, and the buttons lit up.

"Thanks, Bro." Allen grinned and pushed the button for Diet Coke. "Don't think I'd have ever learned to tie my shoe laces if you hadn't been around."

"I'm glad I ran into you alone."

Allen fed another dollar in, correctly this time. "What's on your mind?"

"Please correct me if I'm wrong, but I thought I picked up on something when we were back at the elevator."

"Oh, yeah? Like what?"

Zan hesitated. "Is Phoebe pregnant?"

Allen's face lit up. "Yeah. Isn't it great?"

"Yes it is, little brother. I'm astounded. Congratulations." Zan smiled and patted him on the shoulder. "You never were one to waste time."

"Well, you and Emma had better get busy too. Don't tell anybody about us yet. Okay?" Allen glanced over his shoulder and stuffed the soda cans into the pockets of his jacket. "We just found out last week and we didn't want to announce it until after the wedding."

"I understand. Nobody's gonna hear it from me." Zan made his purchase and filled up the ice bucket. "Just make sure you show up at the chapel on time. We wouldn't want the old hippie coming after you with a shotgun."

Zan felt empty inside as he walked slowly back to the room. So he was going to be an uncle. He should have been elated, but he knew Emma would be crushed when she found out. Not that she would be unhappy for Allen and Phoebe, but the irony of the situation was incredible. He and Emma had been unsuccessful for the past few years to get pregnant and his brother had hit the jackpot without even trying. Just his luck. He put the key in the lock, opened the door, and went inside.

His mouth fell open when he saw Emma posing on the bed in what appeared to be her best imitation of a *Playboy* centerfold. His gloom vanished instantly. He dropped the ice bucket and a soda can went rolling across the floor, hissing and spewing. She looked like a goddess. He had never seen anything so beautiful in his life.

"What's the matter? Cat got your tongue?" She gazed at him through lowered lashes.

"God, Emma. I've never seen you so, so…" He bent to pick up the cans.

"Leave it."

She sprang to her knees in the middle of the bed and leaned forward provocatively, revealing her cleavage. He couldn't take his eyes off her, enthralled by the power of her sexuality. He'd never seen her more alluring. She had to know she was tantalizing.

"Come here. I want you. Right now." Her voice was low and seductive. Her outstretched hands were an invitation to heaven.

She drew him to her like a magnet. A delightful, white-hot streak of wanting ran through him as he stumbled to the bed. He stood there and drank in her beauty. He was her slave, enchanted by this glorious role reversal. She'd rarely been the instigator in their lovemaking and it thrilled him beyond words.

Zan's skin tingled where Emma touched him as she gently urged him to sit beside her on the bed. Her hands caressed his face, and she bent to give him soft little kisses on his forehead and cheeks and ears. He groaned and reached for her, but she caught his hand and shook her head, indicating she was in control. Okay, he would let her lead the dance.

Her slim fingers undid the buttons of his shirt. Languidly she caressed and kissed the dark curls on his chest little by little as the gap between cloth and skin widened until the shirt fell in a heap on the floor. With a gentle push to the bed she urged him to lie prone while she unzipped his trousers and then pulled them away and dropped them on the floor. His boxers went next. She gently raked her fingernails upward from his knees to his hips, teasing him until he thought he would go mad with desire. "Oh God, Emma. I can't stand much more of this."

"Hush, I'm seducing you now," she crooned.

He closed his eyes and let her have her way. She hovered and kissed him deeply, while her hands roamed his body. Her tongue seared a burning path along his neck and ears, sending shivers of desire throughout his body. He was on fire. He couldn't take it anymore. He wrested control and she acquiesced, responding with more passion than either had dreamed possible. Primal instinct completed its circle. Man and woman. Flesh became as one. Ultimate joy realized.

The faint sound of creaking floorboards barely roused Emma from her deep slumber. Her mind still groggy from sleep, she reached across and patted the other side of the bed. Her fingers found her husband's warm body lying beside her and she sighed with contentment. Her touch disturbed him slightly and he shifted from his back to his side, but did not awaken.

She heard the noise again and opened her eyes. She blinked and raised herself slightly. The clock on the bedside table told her it was after midnight. She peered around the darkened suite. A light from the hallway shone faintly under the door; the tiny red eye of the smoke detector blinked monotonously. An occasional lightning bolt flashed across the ridge of the mountain, momentarily illuminating the inky blackness.

The pleasant scent of flowers filled her nostrils. She relaxed against her pillow and breathed deeply. When she looked toward the window near the bathroom, she saw it. A blue, neon-like cloud floated in the corner. She watched in fascination as it hovered, moving very slowly toward her.

An impression of contentment worked its way through Emma's thoughts. She wanted to keep watching the beautiful vision, but her eyelids felt so heavy, she had to struggle to keep from drifting back to sleep. She sighed serenely as the blue mist took on a hazy human form.

"Good night, Theodora," Emma whispered, then fell into a peaceful sleep as the wrinkled hand lovingly pulled the blanket up around her shoulders.

Two-fifteen.

The red numbers on the digital clock seemed to waver as Emma blinked to focus her eyes in the darkness. A blustering wind wailed mournfully outside and rain pelted the windowpanes. She sat up in bed and scanned the dark and misty chamber. Instantly alert, her heart shifted gears. Something was in the room—something evil. She wrinkled her nose at the smell; the cloying odor of camphor and alcohol permeated the air.

She gasped when she saw the shadowy wraith hovering just inside the bathroom door. Intermittent flashes of lightning illuminated the sky like a strobe light and sifted through the shuttered window just enough to reveal the outline of the apparition. Emma clutched the blanket to her chin and stared, too horrified to move or speak. She felt icy cold, yet sweat beaded on her forehead. She turned toward Zan lying beside her. He snored peacefully, oblivious to the terror lurking so near.

Emma heard the creak of footsteps moving across the floor. Whoever—or whatever—was in the room passed from the bathroom and headed toward the door, leaving a bitter chill in its wake. She watched in horror at the murky ectoplasm's metamorphosis. Even in the darkness Emma could make out the shadowy form of a woman wearing a mid-calf length dress and a handkerchief-shaped cap.

The rasp as the deadbolt disengaged and the groan of ancient hinges fractured the silence; the door began to open.

Light flowed in from the hallway, casting uneven shadows on the parlor walls. The apparition became more distinct. Emma trembled at the intense hatred that emanated from the mad, cold stare of the spectral woman.

Emma summoned all her strength just to move her hand enough to touch her sleeping husband. The warmth of his skin reassured her and she shook him harder, but he didn't wake up. She tried to call his name, but her vocal cords refused to respond. Terror gripped her heart like a vise and squeezed until she thought she might faint.

She closed her eyes and prayed to wake up from this hideous nightmare. It had to be a dream—a terrible, horrible hallucination. She opened her eyes and looked toward the door. The phantom was still there. It watched Emma for several more seconds, and then passed through the open door and into the hallway. The door hung halfway open as if to remind her she wasn't imagining things.

An overpowering compulsion swept over her. She climbed out of bed, slipped a nightgown over her head and crept toward the door. The coldness of the doorknob surprised her. She glanced back toward the bed. The back of Zan's head was all she could see with his body beneath the mound of covers. She pulled the door all the way open and stepped into the hallway.

The ghost was clearly visible now. Emma stared in horrified fascination at the figure standing near the stairwell. Could it be one of the phantom nurses Cheryl had talked about on the tour? Or was it the pursuer in her reoccurring nightmare? Perhaps they were one and the same?

The woman was dressed in an old-fashioned nurse's uniform, with starched cap and apron. Her dishwater blond hair was pulled back in a severe knot at the nape of her neck. She looked young, no more than thirty. But the expression of madness in her eyes, combined with the grotesquely scarred cheek, lips, and forehead made Emma flinch with revulsion.

As if she were hypnotized, Emma followed the woman down the stairs. The black cat on the bench arched its back and hissed as the specter passed it on the stairwell landing. Emma stumbled, almost tripping on the hem of her long nightgown. When she looked up, the ghost had vanished.

Emma scanned the third-floor hallway, searching for the nurse. She didn't know why she followed her. She only knew that some irresistible urge pushed her. When she saw a movement at the farthest end she gathered her nightgown in her left hand and hurried toward it.

Whatever she had seen turned left. She came to a glass door leading onto one of the observation decks. The wind formed a vacuum and she had to tug with all her strength to open it. She gasped when she felt the full force of the storm. The battering rain pelted down on her, immediately soaking the thin material of her gown.

Emma flinched when she saw a girl standing there. From her profile she looked young and beautiful. She wore an ankle-length white dress; her long, pale hair was plastered to her head from the driving rain. She turned her back to Emma and slung one foot over the balcony railing. A scream rose in Emma's throat. "No!"

The girl turned and looked at Emma, her face a mask of utter despair. She gazed sadly, then pulled her other leg over the balustrade and jumped. Emma ran frantically to the edge of the veranda and searched the ground. The storm lashed violently around her, making it difficult for her to see. A bright lightning flash momentarily lit up the night sky. She could see no body on the ground below.

Emma turned and stumbled back inside the hotel. Her teeth chattered; her hair and nightgown were completely soaked. She stood shivering in the hallway, trying to calm her spinning nerves. The clattering screech of unstable wheels approaching from the end of the hallway arrested her attention.

The ghostly nurse advanced, pushing a long cart on wheels. A white sheet covered the object on the gurney. Emma stood paralyzed as it drew closer; the shrill noise grew louder.

She couldn't move—she couldn't think—she couldn't breathe.

The nurse stopped and smiled at Emma. Her scarred lips twisted into a leer as she pulled the sheet forward. A woman's corpse lay on the gurney, its face contorted in the final throes of agony.

She hadn't been told who the dead woman was, but somehow Emma intuitively knew. She'd seen that face before— somewhere—sometime.

Overcome with grief, Emma collapsed in the hallway. She pounded on the door of the room where she sat, crumpled and sobbing. She heard voices from inside the chamber; someone fumbled with the deadbolt. The door opened and Emma cried with relief when she saw Moonbeam and Chief Whitefeather.

"Emma, what's wrong?" Moonbeam clutched her wrap with one hand and helped Emma with the other. "You're soaking wet."

"She's dead," Emma babbled, shivering and sniffling. "Anna's dead…."

"Who's Anna?"

Eyes wild, confusion painted on her face, Emma scanned the hallway. "I don't know…I know Anna's dead…but I don't know who she is."

CHAPTER FIVE

Zan's heart raced as he pounded barefoot down the stairs. He pulled the tee shirt over his head while he ran, and then cursed when he felt the tag at his throat. Damn. He'd put it on backward. With shaking fingers he yanked it back up and twisted it around, then pulled his arms correctly through the sleeves. He didn't stop moving until he reached the half-open door. Chief Whitefeather motioned him inside.

His breath caught when he saw Emma huddled on the couch, dressed in a terry-cloth robe, a white towel draped around her head. Her legs were tucked beneath the robe and her head rested on Moonbeam's shoulder. She looked so small and sad and bedraggled. His heart ached at the sight. Moonbeam stood and discretely moved out of the way when she saw Zan approach.

"Emma. Baby. Are you all right?" He sank down beside her and cradled her in his arms. "What happened?"

"I...don't...know," she replied, between sniffs. She buried her face in his chest and sobbed harder. "My head hurts..."

"It's okay. I'm here now." He held her tight and tried to soothe her by patting and caressing her back. He glanced toward the others, uncertain what to do.

"Very evil spirits here," Chief Whitefeather muttered. He shook his head and paced.

"I think Emma must have had a nightmare," said Moonbeam.

"No." Emma pulled away from Zan and shook her head. "It was real...it wasn't a dream...so horrible..."

73

"Honey, how did you wind up down here in Moonbeam's room? I've never known you to sleepwalk before."

"I told you. I wasn't asleep," babbled Emma. "I saw a woman—a nurse—in our room and I followed her into the hallway. Then I thought I saw her go outside on the porch, so I went there, too. But it was raining and I got soaking wet." She stopped and sniffed before she continued. "And then I saw a girl jump off the balcony. I tried to stop her, but I couldn't…"

Zan interrupted. "You saw somebody jump off the balcony? Did they get hurt?"

Emma lowered her voice and her eyes darted about the room, scanning every corner. "I don't know. She disappeared—and then I came back inside—and I saw the nurse pushing a gurney in the hall. She showed me a corpse and I recognized its face, but I don't know how I could have known who it was."

"Where are the nurse and the body now?" Zan turned to Moonbeam and the Chief. "Did you see them?"

"We didn't see anything but Emma crying at the door," replied Moonbeam. "I'm sorry."

Zan took Emma's hands into his and pulled her gently around to face him. "Sweetheart, I know this all seemed very real to you. But you've been under a lot of stress lately and I really believe you just had another very vivid nightmare."

"No…"

"Wait." Zan held his finger to her lips. "Think about it. Everything you've told me has gone along almost exactly with what we heard on the ghost tour. It's probably all mixed up with the nightmares you've been having. Why, I'm surprised I didn't have the same dreams myself."

Emma hung her head, a frown of confusion on her face. "I suppose you could be right."

"Come on, honey. Let's go back to bed." He pulled her gently to her feet. "I'll give you something for your headache and we'll leave first thing in the morning."

"But what about the wedding? We can't let my foolishness ruin Allen and Phoebe's big day." She looked at him with pleading eyes.

"I'm not going to risk your health. They'll understand."

Emma drew a deep breath and composed herself. "I'm okay. I see that I was just overreacting. Please don't tell Allen and Phoebe about this. I'll be all right now," she said, and then turned to Moonbeam and the Chief. "I'm sorry for all the trouble I've caused."

"No problem at all," replied Moonbeam. The Chief grunted.

"Thanks for calling me. We'll return the robe in the morning."

Zan carried Emma's wet garments with one hand, put his arm around her with the other, and gently guided her back to their room. He helped her change into fresh nightclothes and climb into bed, then went to the bathroom and brought her headache medication. She melted into the mattress with a whimper.

He lay down beside her and held her until her rhythmic breathing told him she slept. Savoring the warmth of her skin and the fragrance of her hair, he thought about how much he loved her and how worried he had been. The thought of losing her was almost unbearable. What would he do without her?

When he knew he wouldn't disturb her, he carefully removed his arms from underneath her body and settled onto the pillow. She moaned and shifted onto her side. He punched his own pillow into a ball and tried to relax, but his thoughts ran rampant. His mind refused to shut down.

If he'd had any idea how this place would affect her he would have never brought her here—brother's wedding or not. She'd been so excited at the prospect of a weekend at a big hotel in the mountains; he'd thought it would be a great getaway for them both. But then after her doctor's appointment last week, the nightmares had begun and her chronic headaches had resumed. He supposed he should have mentioned the ghost business before they left, but it had slipped his mind.

She could be so hyperactive sometimes; it was hard to get her to unwind. When things didn't go on schedule, he could always tell it stressed her by the little crease that formed in her brow and the way she tightened her mouth. She tried so hard to be perfect and that was probably why this setback of her hopes to get pregnant had been so hard on her. She internalized too much and the cracks were beginning to show.

Zan remembered the first time he'd seen Emma. She'd looked beautiful yet pale when she walked into the little neighborhood pharmacy where he worked with his father. He didn't get to see a woman like her every day, with long brown hair, an hourglass figure and a face like an angel's—unless he looked at the movie magazines against the back wall. He couldn't resist snatching glances at her from behind the counter as he filled her prescription. The headaches, he'd discovered, came after the loss of her family in a jetliner crash.

He didn't normally flirt with the customers; in fact, she was the only one. But the sight of her bare left hand had excited him and given him hope. Surprised at himself, he had managed to be witty and charming as he rang up the sale. Usually such a klutz around women, there was something special about her that inspired him. Her sweet laughter sounded like music to him and he knew he was hooked.

The afternoon rush hit the drugstore soon after she left and Zan was too busy for a while to think much more about her—until he saw two pills lying on the measuring tray. Her prescription had been for thirty tablets and he'd accidentally shortchanged her. He decided to take advantage of the situation. He had her phone number, her address, and a perfect excuse to contact her.

Zan gazed wearily at the clock on the bedside table—four a.m. God, he was so tired. But he couldn't relax. He closed his eyes and tried to lull himself with deep breathing. After what seemed like an eternity, exhaustion finally overtook him and he slept until the morning sun peeked over the mountain, bathing the bedchamber with golden light and the promise of a new day.

Emma awakened refreshed the next morning, brimming with renewed determination. She inhaled deeply and glanced around the bedchamber. The stormy weather from the night before had passed. Sunlight filtered through the gaps in the blinds and dust motes danced playfully on the air currents. She felt Zan's strong arms encircle her and she sighed with contentment. Memories of the night before came flooding back, but she no longer felt the horror of the experience. Everything seemed different now.

Zan's grip tightened when she stirred and she turned to face him. Her mouth moved across his in a whisper-light contact and he responded with increased passion. She curled into the curve of his body and they made slow, sweet, exquisite love. They slept and woke and loved again.

By the time Zan and Emma rose and dressed, it was almost time for lunch. They left the hotel, drove down the mountain, and parked the car in a downtown lot. The crisp air exhilarated her and the narrow twisting streets appeared renewed, washed clean from the previous night's rain. Birds rejoicing overhead lifted Emma's spirits. She smiled and turned toward the sun to let the warmth caress her face.

They strolled hand-in-hand along the sidewalk, glancing into shops filled with brightly colored merchandise. A horse and buggy clattered down a steep incline. A green bus shaped like a trolley stopped on the opposite side of the street and discharged a horde of tourists. Emma and Zan ducked into a restaurant to escape the crowds.

After lunch they continued their exploration of downtown Eureka Springs. Emma loved the olde-time atmosphere and the beautiful artwork on display. They stopped to pet a cocker spaniel tied to a light post. Zan bought a hideous hillbilly wood carving of a razorback hog as a gift for the newlywed's fireplace mantle. He bought fudge at the *Two Dumb Dames Fudge Factory*. They sat on a bench near a public spring, fed each other chocolate, and laughed at the mess they made.

Emma glanced at her wristwatch. "Oh, shoot. We've gotta get back."

"Yeah, I guess it's time for you girls to start primping for the wedding."

"Are you sorry you missed out on playing golf with the guys?"

"Are you kidding?" Zan reached over and flicked a tiny dab of chocolate from the corner of her mouth. "I can't think of a better way to spend the day—or anyone I'd rather spend it with."

"Are old married people like us supposed to be this happy after all these years?" She felt like her heart would burst with the love that filled her. "How did I get so lucky?"

"You know it's all your fault, don't you?"

"What?"

"That I'm never gonna win the lottery."

"And why is that?" She tilted her head. "'Cause you never buy a ticket?"

"No." He reached across and kissed her on the forehead, then stared deep into her eyes. "'Cause I used up all my good luck when I met you."

Seven thirty-five.

Dusk settled quietly across the western edge of the Ozarks, casting a faint purple glow in the distance. The car's headlights lit up the rocky hillside as they climbed and twisted up the steep switchbacks.

Emma gasped at the sight of Thorncrown Chapel, shining like a brilliant jewel in the twilight. Lights twinkled through the floor-to-ceiling windows and illuminated the towering trees that surrounded the magnificent structure. Nearby sat the Thorncrown Worship Center, its towering bulk resting on giant girders that climbed high into a peak and then jutted out across the mountain, like a huge glass and steel fortress.

Zan walked with Emma from the car and led her inside the chapel. He looked dashing in his dove gray tuxedo. He kissed her before relinquishing her to an usher, who then escorted her to a seat next to Jonathan and Barbara. The scent of roses and the relaxing sound of organ music filled the hall.

She peered around the chapel, amazed at the glass walls that soared more than four stories through the forest. Attendance was small and intimate.

"Emma, you look lovely, as usual." Jonathan rose while she found a place on the pew. Barbara smiled and nodded.

"Thanks," replied Emma. "This is such a beautiful place for a wedding."

"Prettier than that casino wedding chapel where you and Zan tied the knot?" asked Jonathan.

"Much prettier." Emma laughed at the irony. Zan and Emma were the practical ones, yet they had eloped and married in Las Vegas. Wild child Allen and hippie chick Phoebe, on the other hand, had planned a traditional ceremony.

The processional began with a flourish of trumpets as a recording of *Rondeau's Fanfare* filled the chapel. Zan escorted Moonbeam down the aisle. She wore a long, slinky, cowl-collared dress that dipped daringly in the back and changed colors from black to a shimmering, deep purple as she moved. A glistening, cut glass beaded Mata Hari headdress hugged her head and she carried one Sterling rosebud. Phoebe and Professor Lowenstein followed behind.

The bride was a vision dressed in an elegant vintage gown of silk satin charmeuse. The halter wrap neck of the ivory wedding dress dipped low in front as well as in the back. It showcased her perfect form and revealed a tiny rose tattoo at the small of her back, near her slender waistline. The long bias cut skirt hugged her hips before flaring outward into a full flowing train. A pearl-encrusted snood held her long golden hair in a plump roll that brushed her shoulders and accented the seed-pearl choker at her throat. She smiled at the guests as she glided down the aisle on her father's arm, clutching a silvery lavender rose bouquet.

"She looks absolutely incredible," said Emma. "Where did she ever find such a gorgeous dress?"

Barbara leaned across Jonathan to reply to Emma's remark. "Maureen told me she bought the dress from a vintage auction and that it was once worn by Jean Harlow."

Emma's eyes misted as she watched the simple yet elegant ceremony. With love in her eyes, she gazed at Zan standing next to his brother. She had never before seen Allen look so emotional. For the first time since she'd known him, he appeared quiet and awestruck.

Pastor Barnes conducted the service and the couple made their vows. Chief Whitefeather looked regal in his buckskin and beads and feathers. His poignant blessing, spoken in the *Pai* language, seemed dreamy and lyrical. Emma relaxed, watched his graceful symbolic gestures, and listened to the slow, musical chanting. *"... Apa—Pakri—Asitam."*

She bent toward her father-in-law and whispered. "What does that mean?"

"It means *man—woman—one.*"

A short time later the wedding party gathered for the reception at the Basin Park Hotel in downtown Eureka Springs. It wasn't quite as old as the Crescent, but it also exuded an atmosphere of elegant by-gone times. Emma thought it was the perfect setting for a raucous celebration, with its fascinating history as a hangout for famous gangsters such as Bonnie and Clyde, Al Capone, and Pretty Boy Floyd, as well as its listing in Ripley's Believe-it-or-Not for being the only building in the world with all eight floors on ground level.

"Woo hoo! Way to go, Moonbeam," yelled Allen. He put his fingers in his mouth and whistled.

The wedding party clapped and cheered as the smiling bridesmaid triumphantly held the bouquet high above her head. Phoebe squealed with delight when she saw who had caught it. Chief Whitefeather's eyes glittered, but his expression remained unchanged.

Emma laughed and took a bite of her cake. She glanced up through the glass ceiling of the Atrium. A silvery crescent moon peeked through the scudding clouds. The night sky filled her with a momentary, irrational feeling of sadness. The darkness pressed down on her, but she steeled herself and mentally pushed it back. She smiled at Zan and sipped her champagne. "Neat place for a reception."

"Yeah. After that fancy wedding, it's nice to go somewhere just to have fun," replied Zan. "I'm itching for a game of pool in the Billiards Room. You want to play a game or two?"

"I don't think so." Emma lifted her feet and wriggled the red-soled *Christian Louboutin* pumps that peeked from beneath her floor-length skirt. "You guys can take off your jackets and roll up your sleeves, but we women still have these dresses and uncomfortable-yet-gorgeous shoes to get in the way—and I forgot to bring something to change into."

"What's everybody looking at over there?" Zan pointed to a group huddled around a table on the other side of the room.

"I don't know. Let's go see."

Jonathan appeared worried and then smiled when he saw the couple approach. Emma sensed tension as she met the curious stares of the others. Something was wrong.

"What's going on, Dad?" asked Zan.

Emma's heart lurched when she saw the photographs spread out on the table. "Where did these come from?" She froze when she picked up the one on which everybody focused. Her heart pounded and blood slid through her veins like cold needles. She stared in bewilderment at the image of her and Zan seated at a table. A dark, cloudy mass hovered behind her head.

"I bought them at the front desk of the hotel this afternoon," Jonathan replied, his face etched with concern. "They're from the rehearsal dinner last night."

"What in the world is that?" Zan indicated the dark spot on the picture.

"Looks like *Pigpen* and *Charlie Brown* to me," Allen remarked with his usual droll wit.

"Allen—that's not nice," exclaimed Phoebe.

"Very funny, little brother. Like you've got room to talk," replied Zan, pointing at the butter cream icing all over Allen's shirt and vest from the wedding cake Phoebe had crammed into his mouth.

"I meant the little black cloud that always follows Pigpen around…you know, the *Peanuts* cartoon?" Allen saw that nobody was laughing. "Oh, never mind."

"It's just a flaw in the film." Moonbeam waved her hand in dismissal. She met Phoebe's eyes and shook her head.

"Oh, man," Allen exclaimed and pointed at the picture. His eyes danced with mischief. "Remember what that lady on the ghost tour said last night? She said not to throw away the film if it had a flaw in it or you'd be throwing away a ghost. Remember? I think Emma's got a ghost following her!"

Emma's eyes widened. She remembered Moonbeam's statement about the evil spirit's aura hovering above her at the rehearsal dinner. Could it be an actual photograph of a ghost? Surely not the horrible nurse who haunted her dreams.

An awkward silence fell among the party. Emma noticed the embarrassment spread across Allen's face when he realized he was the last one there to catch on. Everyone waited in silence to see how she would react.

Emma took a deep breath and composed herself. This was a

party and she was determined not to cause a scene. She would not let this shake her. No more worrying about ghosts and nightmares. She pushed the memory of last night's terrifying events out of her mind, turned to her father-in-law, and asked, "May I keep this one?"

"Of course you may, Emma," replied Jonathan. "If anyone else wants one, please help yourselves."

Zan seemed relieved she showed no more concern about the odd-looking photo. She straightened her posture and willed herself to be calm. She picked up a champagne glass and sipped. The tension in the room dissipated. The reception wound down and guests began trickling out of the hotel.

"Who wants to go upstairs to play some pool?" asked Allen.

"Wait a minute," interrupted Phoebe, grabbing Allen's hand and lowering her voice. "Don't we need to make our big announcement before everybody leaves?"

"Oh, yeah." Allen agreed and turned to Phoebe. "Ready? Drum roll please."

Phoebe giggled and nodded, then together they stood before the waiting group of people. They held hands and smiled at each other before announcing in unison. "We're pregnant!"

Emma's breath caught and her body stiffened. She felt torn by conflicting emotions. *Why does Phoebe get a baby and I get haunted by an evil spirit?* A bitter jealousy stirred within her, followed by an agonizing stab of guilt. A burning sense of shame filled her heart when she saw everyone else laughing and congratulating the newlyweds for their joyous news.

What kind of horrible person was she? She glanced toward her husband and noticed him searching her face with a worried expression. She couldn't let him know how deeply she had been wounded. She drew a deep breath, pasted a smile on her face, and joined in the celebration. Her heart ached and the beginnings of a headache germinated. Zan reached over and squeezed her hand.

"Our time will come, you know," he whispered.

Emma nodded and clenched her jaw to stifle her emotions. She ached with an inner pain, but was determined not to let it show. The pain in her head grew stronger. A line formed to congratulate the newlyweds and she joined it, intent on proving her good will.

"Oh, honey. When's the blessed event?" Barbara embraced Phoebe first and then Allen. Jonathan wiped away a tear and did the same.

"She's just barely pregnant," Allen said with obvious pride. "Not much more than a month. We only found out a few days ago."

"Sydney, can you believe it? We're going to be grandparents! This is such wonderful news." Maureen Lowenstein grinned and hugged the newlyweds. "But Phoebe, how can you be sure this early?"

"Those test kits are extremely accurate, Mama," Phoebe answered. "But we also had it confirmed with a blood test."

The reception having ended, the rest of the guests made their goodbyes and began to leave. Those remaining started to migrate upstairs to the more casual atmosphere of the Billiards Room. Phoebe and Moonbeam disappeared to the ladies room to change out of their formal attire. Emma closed her eyes, rubbed her temples, and tried to mentally banish the streaks of light beginning to flash rapidly across her vision.

"What's the matter, babe?" asked Zan, putting his arm around Emma and searching her face. "Are you getting one of your headaches?"

"I'm afraid so," she replied. She winced when she felt the tension build, as if a tight band pressed relentlessly against her skull. The floaters increased their pace.

"Come on, sweetheart. I'll take you back to the hotel."

"No, you stay here with the others," Emma protested. "Your Dad and Barbara are leaving now. I'll ride back with them."

"Are you sure?"

"Yes, Zan. I'm just going to take a pill and go to sleep. There's no reason why my migraine should ruin your fun."

"Well, if you think you'll be all right..."

Excruciating pain stabbed like a knife. She winced and put her hand to her head, wishing with all her heart he would go back with her. She really didn't want to be alone...especially in that haunted place.

"I don't see how I can leave you like this." He put his hand under her chin and tilted her head toward him.

Her guilt overwhelmed her when she looked into his worried eyes. She had been nothing but a problem since they'd started on this trip. How did he manage to put up with her? She couldn't stand the thought of ruining his time with his little brother on such an important occasion. Struggling to compose herself, she ignored the throbbing ache and her growing fear. She smiled and pretended.

"Please, honey. I'll be okay. Your dad and Barbara will be at the hotel if I need anything." Her mouth hurt with the strain of smiling. "Go have a good time with your brother."

He wavered. "Okay. I won't stay long...keep your cell phone turned on."

"I will."

"I love you."

"Love you too."

Nauseated by the pain in her head, Emma endured the short, winding ride up the side of the mountain in silence. She politely, but firmly, refused her step-mother-in-law's offer to accompany her to her room and help her into bed. All she wanted to do was take her headache medicine and be alone.

Her hand trembled when she worked the lock on the door. Almost total darkness filled the room until she found the light switch in the parlor. The floor creaked and shadows danced in the corners. Her right foot throbbed from the pressure of her high heels. She limped to the bed and kicked off her shoes. Emma's head seemed to pound even harder and her hands shook as she strained to reach the zipper on her dress. Finally done, she tossed her clothing on a chair, too ill to hang them up. She reached into the suitcase, grabbed one of Zan's tee shirts, and pulled it over her head.

She found the case containing her medication and carried it into the bathroom. Forgetting about the raised threshold between the two rooms, she tripped and almost fell, dropping the bag. Her right hand grabbed the pedestal sink and she stopped herself from falling.

When she was sure of her balance, she stooped to pick up the pouch and placed it on the edge of the sink. She fumbled with the cellophane that wrapped the glass. When it finally broke free, she turned on the faucet and filled the glass with water. She unzipped the bag and pulled out an orange plastic prescription bottle. Her fingers trembled as she tried to pull the cap off. Stupid child-proof lids. She squeezed the sides of the lid, struggling with it until she found the correct combination. After what seemed an eternity, the cap came free and she poured the contents into her right palm.

Pain stabbed Emma from all sides as she prepared to down the pills. Only two of them remained, but that was okay. It would be enough to get her through the night. When she raised her hand to swallow them she glanced in the mirror—and saw the hideous, leering face of the nurse standing behind her.

She flinched and spun around, dropping the pills into the sink. Her heart pounded as she scanned the room.

The apparition was gone.

She held her breath and strained to listen for any signs of an intruder. A chill, black silence surrounded her.

The pain in her head shrieked at her as if to remind her of its presence. Her suffering overshadowed her fear and she turned her attention back to the sink. She could still see the tiny tablets, trapped in the drain.

Emma cursed when her ring caught as she tried to fish out the pills. She pulled her left hand back out, slipped the ring off her finger and placed it on the edge of the bathtub. Turning back to the sink, she tried again to retrieve the pain pills, but they slipped farther down into the drain and disappeared.

Emma slumped in despair, bracing her hands on the sink. Her knees felt as if they would give way. She sank down onto the white-tiled floor and began to sob. Tears flowed freely down her cheeks and she held her throbbing head between her hands. She closed her eyes, feeling utterly miserable and alone. Her pills were gone forever, but the agony remained to torment her.

The creaking of a door in the next room fractured the silence. Emma lifted her head and stared with bleary eyes, wondering if—no, praying that Zan had come back early to their room. She hoisted herself up off the floor and crept out of the bathroom. The door to the hallway was still closed and locked.

Disappointed, she scanned the parlor and saw that the tiny door in the wall hung partially open. A sense of desolation swept over her when a voice inside her head began to berate her. *You are worthless—defective—barren. You promised him you would give him children. But you can't do it, can you? The ring should go to Phoebe, not you. It must be passed on. He's too good for you. You're nothing but a little throw-away who got lucky. You don't deserve to be loved by a man like Zan. The world would be better off without you.*

Like a zombie she turned and walked back to the bathroom. She stared at the ring, glittering brightly beneath the incandescent light. She felt cold and numb and dead as she picked it up and carried it into the parlor. The voice echoed in her head.

Just throw it away—throw it away—throw it away!

Shuffling toward the little door she reached out and pulled it open wider. The voice screeched louder and her headache

intensified. If only if would stop screaming at her!
She couldn't stand it any more.

She stared sadly into the dark hole in the wall, but she couldn't bring herself to do it. The ring fell from her fingers onto the floor.

The discordant sound of crazed laughter reverberated through Emma's head, raging against the rhythm of her heartbeat. The stench of disinfectant swirled in the air and burned her nostrils. The temperature plummeted.

She trembled when a shadow in the corner advanced toward her, growing with each step, taking the form of the nurse she had grown to dread. She cowered, rooted to the spot, unable to move.

The terrifying specter stopped and stared. Emma shriveled inwardly at the scrutiny, but was powerless to move or even to blink. The room was as still and as quiet as a tomb. No sound emanated from the ghost, but Emma could hear the awful voice in her mind.

Climb inside the door. Nobody will ever find you in there. You can just curl up and hide—and die. That's what you really want to do, isn't it? Just go to sleep and never wake up. Go ahead—do it—do it!

The wraith's eyes glittered and her lips twisted into a grimace. She pointed to the door in the wall and it slowly opened wider. Emma watched in horror as the ghastly nurse snatched up her ring and then hurled it through the door. Emma's anguish peaked and shattered the last shreds of her control.

"No! Not Zan's ring!" Emma screamed. She fell to her knees and began searching frantically for the ring, with her head and shoulders just inside the door. The evil nurse cackled and then a massive force lifted her up and slammed her whole body face first into the hole.

As soon as she was inside, the door slammed shut.

The darkness was absolute; a horrifying oubliette.

Dust choked her and she couldn't stop coughing. Crawling on hands and knees, she searched desperately for a way out of the prison. She screamed and banged on the door, but she couldn't get it to budge. Nobody could hear her. She felt as if she was buried alive.

She gasped, panting in terror. She felt dizzy. Then, realizing she was hyperventilating, she tried to calm herself and think of a way out of her predicament. Her head throbbed again, but she pushed the pain from her mind. She had more important things to worry about now.

She stood up straight and her bare foot touched something small, soft, and furry. She cringed when she heard the tiny squeak and felt whatever she had stepped on scurry away. She shuddered, afraid to move, lest she encounter something worse.

Emma's nose twitched from the dank, musty smell of rotting wood. Summoning up her courage, she inched her body along the wall, carefully testing the environment. Cobwebs brushed across her face and a spider skittered across her arm. Her skin crawled and she frantically brushed at herself.

She had to do something. She blinked and tried to focus her eyes. A faint pinprick of light was barely visible high above her. Searching with her hands she found something cold and metallic. She ran her fingers across it and determined it was a ladder. Tugging on it to test its strength, she decided to try it. Anything would be better than being trapped in this place.

Emma closed her eyes and prayed she was doing the right thing. Her head throbbed again, reminding her of the pain that had been replaced by terror. Moving with great care, she placed her hand on an upper rung and then her foot on a lower. When it held her weight, she climbed higher. She repeated this action several times until she could feel the change of temperature in the narrow space. She shivered and she felt her hair rise upward from the extreme vertical current that blustered through the shaft.

A scraping noise from above alerted her to trouble. Her heart pounded when she felt the ladder shift under her weight. She heard the brittle snap of rusted metal just before she fell. Something sharp scraped against her shoulder and she felt searing pain.

Then something crashed down on her head. Her fear went away. All of her thoughts left her.

CHAPTER SIX

Zan gripped his cue stick and carefully studied the balls on the table. Choosing his target, he leaned into position, drew back the stick and aimed, then followed through with the shot. He banked the six-ball off the side cushion and it rolled into the pocket.

"Yes!" He thrust his fist into the air and strutted around the pool table.

"Way to go, Zan!" Phoebe and Moonbeam yelled in unison. Phoebe jumped up and down, waving her arms like a cheerleader. The Chief smiled and rubbed the tip of his stick with chalk. Allen pretended to sulk.

Zan walked around the table and prepared his strategy. Feeling cocky, he decided to really show off and try for a *cut*. But just as he was about to make his shot, the eerie sight of an old woman standing in the corner distracted him. Startled, he missed, and the cue ball went flying across the table without hitting any of the balls.

"Scratch!" Allen yelled in triumph.

Zan lowered his cue stick and stared at the elderly woman. The others noticed his odd behavior and turned to see what had arrested his attention.

"Who is *that*?" Allen broke the silence.

She looked tiny and ancient, standing forlornly in the shadows. Her thin gray hair was pulled back in a bun and her face was lined with age. She wore an old fashioned, long black dress with a white lace collar and carried an old, worn reticule.

A prominent dowager's hump contributed to her shrunken stature; the expression in her deep-set eyes seemed to cry out in unspoken pain and sadness.

A heaviness centered in Zan's heart as an ominous premonition engulfed his mind. Something was wrong with Emma. His voice broke. "What's wrong with my wife?"

"She needs you now," the old woman answered in a shaky, solemn voice. "You must go to her. Quickly." She paused to search his face, and then disappeared.

Zan stood frozen. The Chief and Moonbeam exchanged worried looks. Phoebe's eyes widened and her hand flew to her throat.

"Jeez, that was freaky," said Allen.

Zan threw down his stick, headed out of the game room and rushed down the stairs. The others chased after him. When he got to the parking lot two blocks away he fumbled in his pockets and stormed, "Where're the friggin' keys?"

"You probably left them in your jacket upstairs," Phoebe volunteered, panting from their mad dash down seven flights of stairs and across the street.

"Let's take mine." The Chief motioned for the group to follow. He led them to the far end of the parking lot and stopped in front of a big 4X4 pickup with oversized wheels.

"Are we all gonna fit in there?" Allen asked, staring at the truck's single cab.

"I don't give a damn where I ride, as long as I can get to Emma," Zan replied, fighting to hold back his panic. He boosted the women up into the cab, climbed into the bed of the truck, and motioned to Allen. "Get in."

The pick-up's engine came alive; its row of bright off-road lights lit up the darkness as they sped away. Zan and Allen clung to the roll bars as the Chief zigzagged his way up the side of the mountain. He dodged parked cars on the narrow streets and swerved into a rock wall to avoid a head-on collision. Zan could see the lights of the big hotel grow closer as they bounced along, but the ride seemed interminable.

"Come on, Emma...answer..." he barked into his cell phone, almost dropping it when the Chief made a sharp turn. Her voice mail came on and he hit *cancel*. He dialed again, this time trying to reach Jonathan. Same thing. They'd probably already gone to sleep.

Moments later they pulled into the hotel's driveway. Zan jumped from the bed of the truck while it still rolled and loped up the front steps. He dashed through the lobby and took the stairs two at a time, winding round and round until he reached the fourth floor. He didn't stop to catch his breath until he saw the room marked 419.

"Emma—Emma are you in there?" he pounded on the door, realizing he'd left the room key in his jacket along with his car keys. Frustrated, a primitive urge to kick in the flimsy barrier overcame him. He stepped back from the door and picked up one leg, preparing to batter it down.

"Zan...wait!"

He hesitated when he heard Moonbeam's voice and the clatter of running feet on the ancient stairs. He peeked around the corner and saw the group coming toward him. Jimmy the bellman huffed and panted from the exertion of running upstairs. A big ring of keys dangled from his right hand. Zan stepped back and let Jimmy open the door.

Zan rushed into the parlor, searching for his wife. Lights blazed in every room of the suite, but Emma wasn't there. Her clothes were sprawled across a chair beside the bed and her shoes were on the floor. The bed was still made up. The suitcase was open, as if someone had been rummaging through it. The others streamed in behind him, glancing around with worried expressions.

"Emma? Emma, where are you?" Zan called. He went into the bathroom, saw the empty medication bottle on the floor, and panicked. "She's not in here, either."

"Check the closet," Phoebe suggested. Empty. Allen lifted up the bedspread, and searched under the bed. Nothing.

"Is anything of hers missing?" asked Moonbeam.

Zan shook his head, "Not that I can tell. It looks like all her clothes are still here. Her shoes too."

Allen picked up the phone and dialed his father's room. "Dad, this is Allen...sorry to wake you, but we've got a problem...we can't find Emma...no, she's not in the room... yeah, looks like she's been here, but she's not here now...okay, we'll see you in a few minutes."

"Do they know where she could be?" Zan pleaded.

"No. Dad and Barbara said they got off the elevator on their floor and just assumed Emma came up to her room and went to bed. They had no idea anything was wrong."

"Have there been any reports of anything strange tonight?" Zan turned to Jimmy.

"No, sir. Not until just a little while ago with this—uh—situation."

"Is everything okay in here?" a bald man dressed in green pajamas stepped into the open door from the hallway. "I'm staying up in the penthouse and my wife and I heard the commotion."

"I'm sorry if you were disturbed," Jimmy said. "Have you heard anything unusual tonight? Within the last couple of hours, I mean."

"Well, we did hear some banging sounds from inside the wall," he said. "We just assumed it was pipes or something."

"What kind of banging?" Zan asked.

"I don't know...kind of a tapping sound, I guess. Then there was a crash and everything got quiet."

"She's in the wall." Moonbeam's eyes grew wide and she pointed toward the little door in the parlor. "She's in there."

Zan rushed to the door and tried to open it, but it wouldn't budge. He stared at Moonbeam in confusion. "That's impossible. It's nailed shut."

"Yeah, look." Allen pointed to the door. "It's even been painted over."

"I'm telling you, that's where she is," Moonbeam stated and then glared at the men.

"I think they're right, Ma'am," Jimmy interjected. "I'm not sure why, but I don't think that door's been opened in years."

In his silent, business-like manner, the Chief reached into a hidden pocket in his buckskin shirt and unsheathed a Bowie knife with a ten-inch blade. He walked purposefully toward the door in the wall and used the knife like a pry-bar. The green painted wood splintered and cracked, along with a bead of caulk that had completed the seal. The door creaked open. Silence momentarily filled the room as everyone strained to peer into the dark interior of the wall.

Zan poked his head into the hole, but he couldn't see anything. "Does anybody have a flashlight?"

"Here, try this." Jimmy produced another key ring with a tiny pin light attached.

Zan took the key ring and swept the light back and forth. He gasped when he saw her, crumpled into a ball several feet inside the wall. "Oh, my God. There she is…she looks like she's hurt….Emma!"

He tried to climb inside, but his shoulders wouldn't fit through the opening of the debris that surrounded her. Panic greater than he'd ever known before welled in his throat. He wanted to rip the place apart—anything to hold her in his arms and know that she was safe. He tugged on a board that lay across the opening, but stopped when he felt the dust and dirt raining down from above. The cracking sound of splintering wood caused him to freeze. He didn't want to make things worse for her. His face ashen, he turned around and shouted, "Somebody call an ambulance. Hurry!"

Jonathan and Barbara hurried into the room and saw the group huddled around the door in the wall. Sydney and Maureen Lowenstein trailed behind. "Did you find her?" Jonathan asked.

Phoebe held the telephone in one hand, nodded, and pointed toward the bedroom. "Hello...yes, we have an emergency at the Crescent Hotel....uh, it's a woman trapped inside the wall...they can't get her out because they're afraid it'll collapse on her...we don't know her condition...I think she's unconscious...okay... room 419...thanks."

Turning to Zan, Phoebe said, "They're on the way."

Soon the room bustled with activity as other hotel guests, most of them wearing nightclothes, crowded the hallway to find out what was going on. Larry, the night maintenance man, bustled into the suite wearing a pair of overalls and carrying a toolbox. He set it down and pulled out a big torch lantern.

"Shine that light in here," Jimmy commanded. "We need to see what's fallen on her before we can start digging her out."

Zan felt helpless. He wanted to rush into that hole and carry her out and never let her go, but he knew it would be too risky. He was terrified he might cause an avalanche that would do more harm. Thank God somebody had finally come with a bigger light. At least now maybe they could see what they were up against.

"Oh, man," Larry sucked in his breath. "She's bleedin' pretty bad."

"Let me see," Zan cried. The maintenance man handed him the light and moved out of the way. "Emma, Emma—it's Zan— can you hear me?"

Blood trickled down her arm and pooled on the floor. She was slumped to one side, her eyes were closed and her head was resting against a rotted post. Her brown hair looked wet and matted from the wound that still bled on the top of her head. The tee shirt she wore was soaked and red. He noted a big gash on her shoulder and her legs seemed to be covered with debris.

She didn't move or respond in any way.

"Oh, my God. We've got to get her out of there," Zan cried.

"Mr. Fuller—please," Jimmy touched Zan's shoulder. He motioned for Larry to take over. "Why don't you let us see what we can do?"

Zan stepped away from the door and gave back the flashlight. His powerlessness crushed like a heavy weight against his chest. He closed his eyes and prayed silently *Dear God, please don't take her from me. I love her more than life itself. If I could only trade places with her, I would. Please give us another chance.*

"The paramedics are here," someone yelled.

Two fire fighters and two EMT's entered, carrying a portable gurney, as well as other emergency gear. Dissonance and confusion filled the room. People were everywhere, shouting and standing and pointing.

Zan endured a feeling of helplessness as he watched the emergency crew prepare to rescue her. Emma would hate this. She couldn't stand being the center of attention. He wished she would just wake up and give them a sign she was still alive. Stricken with concern for his wife, he barely noticed the worried hugs and reassurances from friends and family. All he could think about was getting her out alive and well.

The buzz of the saw seemed surreal and distant. Zan tuned out the din around him and watched the firemen work. He hated this feeling of impotence, of not being able to help. He was a hands-on type of guy and this was like torture to him.

A young man wearing a dress shirt and slacks joined the growing throng and went straight toward Jimmy and Larry. Something about the hotel employees' expressions worried Zan further and he strained to listen to their conversation.

"How the hell did she get in there? I thought you told me that door was nailed shut."

"It was, Mr. Hutchison" Larry replied. "And painted over

and caulked, too. Nobody's opened it in a long, long time. Don't got a clue how she did it."

"She must have found one of Baker's escape hatches." Jimmy shook his head. "I thought that was all just legend."

"I thought this whole floor, along with the penthouse, burned back in the late sixties," said Hutchison. "Baker hasn't been here since 1939."

"That was the *south* penthouse that got destroyed." Larry frowned and shook his head. "This room and the penthouse above us are just about all that's left up here that didn't have to be rebuilt."

"Jimmy, you come in here all the time. Have you ever seen that door opened before?" asked Hutchison.

"No, sir."

"I'm tellin' you, Mr. Hutchison. There ain't no way she did it on her own. She must've found some other way to get in. Sealed that place up myself twenty-four, maybe twenty-five years ago," said Larry.

"With all the renovations that've been going on around here, how come nobody's done anything about this? We can't have guests getting hurt like this." Hutchison appeared both worried and angry.

"I swear there warn't no way she got in there from this room. Course, it's sealed up from the topside too. Cain't imagine how she did it. Like I said, closed it up tight years ago."

Zan stopped his eavesdropping and interrupted the conversation. He stared at Larry and asked, "Couldn't somebody else have found another opening somewhere and put her in there?"

"Oh no, sir. There ain't no more openings. I've been here comin' up twenty-six years. I know every inch of this ol' hotel—explored just about every crawl space there is 'cept that one," Larry pointed to the door where the firefighters were laboring to rescue Emma.

"And why haven't you been in that one?" asked Zan, a tingling sensation of dread coursing through his body.

"Well, I ain't never told nobody 'bout this before." Larry hung his head before he continued. "I got a real bad feelin' when I tried to go in there one time—and I seen somethin' real scary." His eyes were wide with fright. "I 'member it had shiny blue eyes…just starin' at me…" He shivered and shook his head. "If it hadn't been for your missus in there I wouldn't a stuck my head in there tonight—not fer a million bucks."

"Good grief, Larry." Hutchison pulled at his tie and wiped sweat from his brow. "What are you talking about? Don't tell me you're buying into this ghost crap?"

"It ain't crap, Mr. Hutchison." Larry straightened his posture and stared at the manager. "There's all kinds a spirits hauntin' this place. I ain't afraid a none of 'em, 'cept whatever's inside there. That's why I boarded it up. It's evil."

Zan thought about the old woman in the billiards room. She must have been Theodora, come to warn him that Emma was in danger. There had been nothing sinister about her and he had reacted instinctively. He hadn't really believed in ghosts, even after the champagne and ironing board incidents. But now apprehension consumed him.

"They got her loose!" someone yelled.

Zan turned his attention back to the rescue scene. His heart pounded as he watched the men pull Emma out of the wall. Her legs emerged first, then the blood stained tee shirt, and then her head. The paramedics cradled her neck carefully as they carried her out and placed her on a gurney.

"Emma!" Zan choked back a sob when he saw her. She looked so pale and lifeless and she was covered in blood. He rushed toward her, but a paramedic held up his hand.

"Please stand back, sir. We need room to work."

Zan retreated, but craned his neck to see. Tears blinded him and he felt sick to his stomach. His emotions were a crazy mixture of hope and fear. He felt dazed as he stood by helplessly waiting to hear the diagnosis of her condition, yet terrified at what the answer might be. He strained to understand the jargon of the paramedics as they ran through their protocol.

"Is she breathing?"

"Yeah, but her BP's low. We've gotta stop the bleeding."

"She needs oxygen—intubate, but stabilize her neck."

"Okay, her spine's immobilized. Is she conscious?"

"No. Unresponsive... pupils are dilated...she's going into shock..."

"Start a lactated Ringer's I.V. ...I'm gonna call for a chopper...we need to transport her stat."

Zan listened to the exchange with growing trepidation. At least she was still alive. When they'd first pulled her out of the wall he hadn't been so sure. There was still hope. Thank God Theodora had come to him when she did.

"Mr. Fuller, I need to talk to you." One of the paramedics tapped him on the shoulder. "I believe your wife is stable now, but she's still very critical. We're going to transport her by CareFlight to Northwest General in Rogers. It's too far to go by ambulance. They have an excellent trauma center there."

"All right," Zan replied. He felt numb. "Can I ride with her?"

"I'm afraid not. There's not enough room and regulations prohibit it. I'm sorry."

"How far is it?"

"About thirty-five miles. But the roads here are twisting and steep, so you need to be very careful."

"We'll drive you, son," said Jonathan. He placed his hand gently on Zan's shoulder. "She'll be all right."

"God, I hope so." Zan's shoulders slumped. He was so tired, yet he knew he'd never be able to rest until he knew Emma was going to be okay.

The crowd parted to allow the firefighters and paramedics

to wheel Emma out of the room. Zan followed closely behind, heartsick by the sight of the IV and the oxygen tank and the blood stained shirt. They had a hard time getting her into the tiny elevator with all the paraphernalia attached. Zan made it down the stairs and into the lobby just as they were maneuvering her out.

Moments later he heard the *whoosh whoosh whoosh* of the helicopter. Dust and dirt flew in every direction as it hovered momentarily and then set down in the parking lot that had been cleared of all the cars. The paramedics wheeled Emma out on the gurney and lifted her into the aircraft. The door slammed shut; it lifted off, and disappeared into the black night.

"Here, you drive." Jonathan tossed his keys to Allen. The family hurried toward the Lincoln Town Car and piled inside. Zan sat in the front seat beside his brother. Jonathan, Barbara, and Phoebe rode in the back. Moonbeam and the Chief followed in his truck.

The forty-five minute drive was the longest, most tense experience Zan could ever remember. A hollow emptiness washed over him when they passed the chapel in the woods where only a few hours ago they had all been so happy. He clenched his teeth and held onto the grab bar to steady himself as Allen weaved back and forth through the hairpin curves.

"You don't need to kill us all, Allen," Jonathan scolded. "Slow down a little."

"Sorry, Dad." Allen eased up on the accelerator and the car slowed.

Zan tensed. He knew his father was right. If they all ended up at the bottom of a ravine it wouldn't help Emma. But all he wanted to do was hurry and get there. He set his jaw and stared out the window at the passing gloom.

CHAPTER SEVEN

The first thing Emma noticed was the smell. Her nostrils twitched at the odor of disinfectant mixed with blood and sweat. Then she heard people yelling and machines buzzing and doors banging. She opened her eyes and tried to focus. She blinked, wondering where she could be.

She appeared to be in a hospital, looking down from some high vantage point. She could see doctors and nurses frantically working to save some poor soul on a bed. She frowned at the sight of the blood and the tubes and the machines. Who could it be down there and why was she here watching?

A radio played her favorite Eagles song and she hummed along with the music while she watched the activity below. Her body seemed light, detached from the earth. Her feet didn't touch the ground and she could move simply by thinking herself there. Emma glanced around the room, trying to remember—something. She couldn't remember what she was trying to remember. She put her hand to her mouth and giggled at the ludicrous thought. On impulse she reached up and touched the light fixture. Now what was she doing on the ceiling?

"She's coding!" someone shouted. Squiggly lines jumped erratically on the monitor and it beeped loudly.

"Crash cart. Stat!"

"Stand back!"

Emma watched in fascination as the nurse applied the paddles. The body on the table jerked in response to the electrical jolt.

"Again!"

She watched for a while, then lost interest and floated through the double doors when they opened. Two people wearing scrubs ran inside as she exited. Now she was in a long, sterile hallway. A janitor ambled by, pushing a mop bucket.

Emma felt like Peter Pan when she realized she could control her movements. Delighted by her new ability, she lightly touched down and began walking down the hall. Her feet and legs were bare and she felt the thin cotton of a hospital garment against her skin. But she wasn't cold. Something dangled down her back and brushed against her legs. It must be a loose tie from the gown. She tried to reach around to grab it from behind, but it was just out of her grasp.

A heavy-set woman sat slouched behind a reception desk reading a magazine. The sign above her read *Emergency Room*. Emma walked toward her, but the woman didn't even look up. An old man wearing a plaid shirt and dirty overalls snored loudly from his seat in the waiting room. A younger man sat beside him, staring bleary-eyed at a late-night infomercial on the television.

Emma heard footsteps clattering down the hallway and she turned around. A tingle of recognition coursed through her and she waited with anticipation. Somehow she knew it was Zan— and suddenly he was there. She watched him run toward the woman behind the desk, followed closely by his family and their friends.

"We're here about Emma Fuller," said Zan, his voice coming in short breaths, eyes wild with fear.

"Um—is she the one they brought in by CareFlight?"

"Yes." Zan nodded. "Is she okay?"

"I'm not sure. I'll call the nurse's station."

"Zan, I'm right here. Look at me." Emma walked toward him and stared into his face, but he looked right through her. They were all ignoring her. What was the matter with him?

What was the matter with everybody?

"Okay...I'll tell them." The clerk frowned when she turned back to Zan. "They're still working on her. She went into v-tach and they're trying to resuscitate her now. I'm sorry I can't tell you more."

"Oh, my God!" Zan's face paled and he sank into the nearest chair. Jonathan and Allen hugged him and he began to cry.

"Zan, I'm okay. Just look over here. Please..." Emma tried, but she couldn't move forward.

Powerless now, she felt herself moving backward and up, like being sucked into a vacuum cleaner. Her arms reached for Zan, but she continued on, swept into a dark, swirling vortex. And at that moment she realized the truth.

So this is what happens when you die. Emma didn't understand why, but she wasn't scared, only curious. At first she'd been startled when she began to rise so swiftly. But after a moment, the force became gentler and she relaxed, enjoying the new and wondrous sensations. Her head no longer hurt. She felt light, free, and marvelous.

Whatever propelled her didn't seem dark or frightening. It was like riding on a giant Ferris wheel that never quite reached the top. She saw the hospital roof below and the twinkling lights of the city. The dark outline of the mountains against the horizon appeared smaller and smaller.

Emma watched in wonder, as the earth grew more distant. The lights from a jet pierced the night and she realized she must be very high in the sky. No need for oxygen or pressurized cabins anymore. Gazing up into the grandeur of the universe, she savored its peace and beauty.

Emma knew when she crossed into another layer of the atmosphere because she could see the lightness fade into darkness at the very edge of the planet. A derelict satellite, painted with a red hammer and sickle, wobbled in its orbit. She stared in amazement at the earth, so big and round and blue, swirling with oceans and clouds and continents.

Just ahead, another dazzling sight appeared. It began as a faint glow before transforming into green and red flames that swept majestically across the sky. A glowing curtain of light waved and swirled into a shimmering oval that seemed to cling to the earth below. Emma had seen the Aurora Borealis once from the ground, but nothing could compare with this awesome vision.

A strange looking object, like a huge robotic dragonfly under construction whizzed by. She wondered what it could be and then she remembered seeing magazine photos of the International Space Station—back when she was still alive. Journeying on, everything seemed to change and she realized she had entered outer space. No rocket—no space ship— nothing but her spirit hurtling through infinity.

Emma wondered how long it would take to reach her destination. At least she was going up, which was a good sign. She thought about Heaven and what it would be like. Would there be angels to guide her? Would she herself become an angel? The thought of what lay ahead filled her with exhilaration.

Emma floated past the moon and saw herself back in the hospital, lying on the emergency room table. A crowd of doctors and nurses worked frantically to save her battered body. She remembered seeing Zan in the waiting room, sobbing in despair. Never before had she seen him break down like that. An acute sense of loss washed over her.

Poor Zan. Guilt overcame her when she thought about how happy she felt to be on her way to Heaven, while she left her husband behind to deal with his sorrow alone. At least he was young and oh, so good-looking. He'd marry again and have the children he deserved. Emma sighed wistfully at the thought. She was grateful that their last words to each other had been *I love you.*

Her view changed and now she was at her gynecologist's office. Her hands trembled and she shredded a tissue as she tried to make sense of the shadowy image on the sonogram. Zan sat beside her, nodding politely as the doctor discussed possible diagnoses and options. The doctor wrote up an order for tests and told her to see his secretary for an appointment—he had an opening first thing Monday morning. His nurse would help Emma pre-register for the hospital outpatient services. He instructed her to fill out all the forms today to avoid any delay.

Emma realized she had lived this before. Was this what was meant when they said you relived your whole life after you died? Visions of memories proceeded in reverse. Emma saw herself at home staring at the computer screen. A tingle of excitement pulsed through her soul when she saw Zan creep up from behind and nuzzle the back of her neck. She laughed and reached for his hand. Moments later they were making love on the futon.

Her life story continued to rewind, pausing now and then at significant milestones. Jonathan Fuller retired and Zan became the owner of the pharmacy. Emma quit her job and started her own computer consulting business. She and Zan bought a house and they had their first spat—over a wallpaper pattern. With her brother-in-law Allen's help as her attorney, she settled with the airline over her family's death.

Emma grew excited when her memories displayed the giant shining pyramid of the Luxor Hotel in Las Vegas, where she'd gone with Zan on a mad, crazy, spur-of-the-moment impulse. She'd heard somewhere that astronauts could see the beam of light from its obelisk all the way into space, but she guessed she had already traveled too far now. Earth was no longer visible.

She giggled when she saw Zan catch her as she lost her balance on the hotel's *inclinator*. They were more than a little drunk by then. The flight attendant on the red eye from Dallas had been very generous with the alcohol when Zan told her they were on their way to Vegas to get married—which was news to Emma.

Tears formed in Emma's eyes when she saw the view of The Strip from their pyramid room. The memory of Zan's hands on her arms and his breath on the back of her neck as she stood at the sloping window was almost tactile. She turned to face him, ready to give him her body as well as her heart. But instead, he took her hand and pulled her toward the door.

Thirty minutes later, at four in the morning, they stood in line at the county clerk's office applying for a marriage license. By then her buzz had worn off, but neither of them had come to their senses, or even wanted to. Marriage license in hand, they set off for the nearest wedding chapel.

Giddy with excitement and overflowing with love, they stood hand-in-hand at a cheesy little wedding chapel. They made their vows beneath a ceiling of draped gold lame' fabric, in a room decorated with red velvet wingback chairs, gilt cherubs, and silk ferns, as Elvis serenaded from a scratchy-sounding speaker. Emma held a bouquet of plastic daisies and repeated the words *till death us do part*. She never thought it would come so soon.

The vision of her wedding faded away and she saw herself at Del Frisco's in Dallas on her first date with Zan. Emma could almost taste the delicious Double Eagle strip steak, the sautéed mushrooms, and the Cabernet Sauvignon. Afterward, they'd gone to a club in Deep Ellum. They danced, and drank, and fell in love. She never dreamed they would be husband and wife less than six months later.

Now she was in the drugstore. She remembered how badly her head had ached that day; it took all her strength to drive from the doctor's office with the prescription. Emma was under so much stress, still overcome with grief from the loss of her family.

At first Emma had gone to a big chain pharmacy, but the line was so long she decided to try a smaller place. Maybe she could get the prescription filled a little quicker there, she'd reasoned. She remembered it had taken her a few minutes to catch on to the good-looking pharmacist's flirtation. She didn't feel like laughing, but he was so cute and funny, she couldn't help herself.

The happy memories faded into the darkest period of her life. She wished she could skip over this part, but whatever controlled these revelations refused her any leniency. She saw herself at the graveyard, alone in the world, staring sadly at three caskets draped with red roses. Next she was at home in her tiny apartment, numb with shock as the policeman explained about the plane crash.

Emma's life continued its regression. She saw herself receiving her diploma at her college graduation. Now she was a freshman at UT Austin, standing nervously at a frat party, holding a warm bottle of beer and trying to shoo away a drunken jock determined to make out with her.

She smiled when she saw herself all dressed up for the high school prom, her hair permed into a huge mass of spiral curls. Emma cringed when she saw herself climb into the stretch limo with a group of friends. Her best friend's date lit up a joint and passed it around.

Now she was sixteen. She'd just gotten her drivers license and her first car—an old Chevy Nova a year older than Emma. She felt grown up as she cruised the streets and drove to the Dairy Queen to show off to her friends. That's where she saw Dylan, the boy she'd had a crush on all year. Emma sighed as she watched her young counterpart slide over to the passenger side. Her parents had specifically told her not to let anyone else drive—the insurance wouldn't cover other kids—blah, blah, blah.

He drove too fast, they ended up in a ditch, and he left her by the side of the road. She lied and told her parents she'd been driving. They never questioned her further.

Time continued to retrogress. She saw herself in the ninth grade, marching in a parade, and playing a flute. She and her family drove to Florida and spent a week at Disney World. She played miniature golf with her little brother. At a church retreat she received her first kiss from the minister's son. The visions seemed so real, she felt like she was there all over again.

Emma winced when she saw herself at thirteen, wearing a Rude-Dog T-Shirt, a hot pink Ra-Ra skirt, and matching leg warmers. Her bangs stood at attention, ratted and moussed into submission. She flitted through the Galleria with her best friend, Heather, and they both got busted shoplifting.

Her memories continued to wind downward, going deeper into the past. She fell off her bicycle and broke her arm. She received her first Cabbage Patch Doll. Her little gray kitten ran away and she cried for three days. She lost a tooth and received twenty-five cents from the Tooth Fairy.

When the visions reached back into her very early childhood, Emma looked on in amazement at life events that happened when she was much too young to consciously remember. The tiny little girl she recognized only from photographs sang along with The Muppets, learned to use the potty, took her first steps, and splashed happily in the bathtub while her mother gently soaped her back.

But the most disturbing scene of all was that of a tiny newborn, wrapped in a dingy yellow blanket, lying in a battered-looking infant carrier. On a chair beside the baby was a vinyl diaper bag, with two bulging pouches in front. A milk bottle poked out from one of the pockets and the other contained the antique musical powder box she hadn't seen since she'd been in college.

A young woman with long brown hair and sad-looking eyes bent down, kissed the baby's cheek, and then stared wistfully before she handed it over to a stern-looking man behind a desk. He gave the woman a long piece of paper and an ink pen.

Emma strained to see as she watched the woman sign the document—T-e-r-e-s-a—something. Her birth mother's name was Teresa, but she couldn't make out the last name. She caught a quick glimpse of an old woman in a nurse's uniform standing in the corner. Then she noticed the nameplate on the man's desk. *J. R. Covington, Attorney at Law.* A lot of good this information did her now—she was dead. Things like this didn't matter any more.

The journey ended abruptly and the transcendent visions ceased. Emma now stood at the mouth of a long, dark tunnel. In the distance she saw a light. A warm glow of anticipation flowed through her. The dangling tie on her gown tickled her legs and she swatted at it. Then she stepped inside the tunnel and began to walk.

The light became brighter as Emma drew closer. Finally, she came to the end of the tunnel and stepped into a beautiful garden. The light she'd been following was still in the distance, but she stopped to stare at her surroundings. She'd never seen anything so exquisite.

Flowering trees and bushes were everywhere. Lush, green meadows stretched out endlessly. Brightly colored birds flew overhead and butterflies danced from flower to flower. The fragrance of the blossoms gently drifted on a zephyr wind, bathing the garden in a heady perfume.

Emma reveled in the beauty of this paradise. The sound of trickling water arrested her attention and she saw a clear, blue stream cascading down the side of a bluff. At the base of the waterfall a small group of people waded and swam in a tranquil, natural pool. Her breath caught when she recognized her family, standing at the edge of the water, watching the swimmers.

Joy bubbled up and overflowed within her. She ran to meet them, arms outstretched, tears flowing down her cheeks. "Mama—oh, Mama!"

Her mother embraced her, and then she felt herself enfolded

by the arms of her father and brother. They laughed and cried and hugged. Emma had never experienced a more joyous reunion.

"Daddy—Tommy—I didn't think I'd ever see any of you again," said Emma. She pulled back a little so she could look at them. They were just as she remembered. Tommy wore a raggedy pair of blue jeans and a Dallas Stars jersey. Her father was wearing the outfit he always wore around the house—a loose pair of khaki pants and a plaid shirt. Her mother was dressed in the blue silk frock she'd worn to so many important functions.

"What are you doing here, Emma?" asked Tommy.

"Don't you know?" Emma was puzzled by his question. "I died—just like the rest of you."

"Honey, it's not your time," said her mother.

"What do you mean?" Emma paused, searched their faces, and spread her arms. "I'm here. Just look at me."

"Emma, we know you're here," her father answered. "But look at the way we're dressed and then look at yourself."

Emma glanced down. She still wore the thin cotton hospital gown, barefooted and bare legged. She didn't understand. They were all wearing their favorite outfits from life, yet she was still dressed in this old thing.

She glanced around and now she could see other people standing in clusters. It looked like a costume party. Some were dressed casually in shorts, or sweatshirts, or jeans. But others were decked out in formal wear, or uniforms, or clothes from bygone eras. There were ballerinas and figure skaters and football players. Where were all the white robes and harps?

"I'm confused." Emma shook her head.

"When it's your time to be here, you get to wear whatever you liked best when you were alive," said her father.

"Yeah, and you get to do your favorite things, too." Tommy grinned and showed her a handheld video game.

"Good grief, Tommy. You're twenty-two. Haven't you outgrown those silly things yet?"

"Remember my favorite saying?" Tommy winked at his sister. "He who dies with the most toys, wins."

Emma laughed. "Well, it all sounds great. Where do I go to sign up?"

"No, Emma," her father shook his head. "You have to go back. Zan needs you back on earth."

"How did you know about Zan?"

"That's one of the benefits of being in Heaven," said her father. "We get to see what's going on down there whenever we want. Come here, I'll give you a preview."

Her father waved his arm and Emma's perspective suddenly changed. It was like looking down through a window in the floor. Below them she could see her body again in the emergency room. Nothing much had changed since she'd last been there. The activity was still frantic as the medical personnel fought to revive her. How long had she been gone?

Tommy put a hand on her shoulder. "See, Emma? You've got to hurry back down there before it's too late. If your brain's deprived of oxygen too long you'll be damaged."

"But it's already been hours," Emma argued.

"No," her father said. "It only seems like it to you. There's still time."

Emma peered down through the window again. Her body looked so frail and vulnerable, overwhelmed with all the tubes and machines. It felt so good being at the threshold of Heaven. Why would she want to go back?

Emma turned back to her family. "Why do you think it's not my time? Just because I'm not dressed in my favorite clothes? That seems silly to me, if that's the only reason."

"Sweetheart, just look at this." Her mother reached behind Emma's back and held a slender, glowing cable. "This is your silver cord. It's like an umbilical cord that connects your soul between life and death. Once it breaks, you can never go back."

"Ours broke instantly when the plane crashed," her father added. "That's how we know it's not your time. When you get back, you won't remember this experience. And if you do recall any of it, you'll think it was all a dream."

Emma stared at the cord. It wasn't much thicker than a piece of thread, but she now realized it must have been what caused the tickling sensation on her legs. Its light pulsed and wavered, and she could see now that it was attached to her mortal body down below. She felt sad when she thought about all the pain she'd have to face if she went back. Was she strong enough to do it?

"Emma, you've got to be brave and think about Zan and my grandchildren now," her mother urged.

"What grandchildren?" Emma's eyes flew to her mother's face.

Her mother's eyes sparkled. "The ones that will never exist if you don't get down there right now."

Emma's eyes widened and she took a deep breath when she realized what her mother meant. "What do I have to do?"

"Okay, Emma. See this faint little glow here?" her father pointed to a hazy, shimmering mist in the window. "This is the portal. You've got to go down very quickly, like sliding down a very high toboggan run. But you need to be careful not to break the cord."

"All right." Emma nodded. "How do I do it?"

"Climb up here, pull your knees up underneath your chin, keep your head down, and your arms close. But whatever you do, keep your eyes straight ahead and make sure you don't waver off the path," her father instructed. "Don't even look around."

"Why? What's in there?" Emma's heart skipped a beat when she saw the look that passed between her parents.

"All I'm going to tell you is that sometimes there are bubbles in the portal, and if you don't stick to the path you could be pulled off somewhere you don't want to go, or your cord could break—go on, Emma. Just do it while there's still time."

Emma nodded, embraced them all one last time, then looked again through the window. She swallowed the lump in her throat, climbed into position, and propelled herself forward.

Her hair billowed upward as she made the deep, sliding descent. Mysterious sounds resonated and fabulous colors quivered all around. The portal was a glowing, liquid tube, with intermittent bulges that writhed and squirmed like quicksilver. Were these the bubbles her father had warned her about?

Going down seemed much quicker than going up, but she was still anxious to get back to Zan. She had so many things to do and so much to tell him. Was she almost there? She lifted her head to see. The hospital emergency room appeared very close; it would only be a matter of seconds now.

Her will to live intensified as she zipped toward earth, thankful she'd been granted a second chance. She vowed to live life to the fullest and waste no more precious time on insecurities and anxieties. She would be the best wife and mother ever. Just the thought of seeing Zan and sharing her secret with him made her tingle with anticipation.

Then something moved on the periphery. Emma turned her head to look. She gasped when she saw it. The evil nurse of her nightmares emerged from one of the bulges in the portal and advanced on her, wielding a knife. Startled, Emma jerked slightly and her course veered from the heavenly track that guided her.

She panicked when she realized she now careened toward the bubble, with no way to stop or turn. Emma wasn't sliding anymore. She was falling.

Her thoughts centered on the silver cord—her lifeline. She must protect it, but she didn't know what to do. The blade looked sharp and she knew it would easily slice through the slender thread.

She plummeted on and on, hurtling out of control. Panic-stricken, Emma raised her arms, hoping to fend off the attack. Then a scream of pure rage, like the wail of a banshee, pierced the air. She looked up in time to see a second figure climb out of the bubble—an old woman wearing a black dress. Emma felt a hard jerk on her arm when the woman suddenly grabbed her and pushed her off in another direction.

The malevolent nurse grew more distant as Emma tumbled farther and farther away. Then her spirit entered the body with a thud, her silver cord still intact.

And then she slept.

CHAPTER EIGHT

"Your wife is back, Mr. Fuller." Dr. Richard Wilson wiped his forehead with a towel, smiled wearily, and extended his right hand.

"Oh, thank God," Zan said and then exhaled in relief as he clasped the other man's hand. "Is she going to be all right?"

"We don't know yet," the doctor replied. "She's still extremely critical. Hopefully, I'll be able to give you a better prognosis within the next twenty-four to forty-eight hours."

"Why so long?" Jonathan asked.

"The lady's been through a terrible trauma," explained the doctor. "She's lost a lot of blood and she's in a coma. I don't know how long before she comes out of it—if she does."

Zan gasped. "Are you saying she may never wake up?"

"Sir, I just don't know. Her heart actually stopped for two or three minutes. Until we've had time to run some tests, I can't give you a definitive prognosis."

"May I see her?" asked Zan. He felt like a condemned man who'd just been reprieved, and then told they might hang him after all.

"Okay, but only one person at a time for now," answered the doctor. "As soon as her blood pressure's stabilized we're going to take her down for a CT scan—oh, by the way. Were you aware that your wife's blood is AB negative?"

"Uh, no. I don't think she ever told me her blood type. Is that a problem?"

"No, not from the standpoint of a recipient. It's just an

unusual blood type. Very rare. But we did have to give her quite a bit of blood before we got the bleeding under control. I don't suppose any of you might care to donate, just to help renew our supply?

Moonbeam spoke up. "That's not my blood type, but I'll be glad to give whatever you need."

"Me too," said Barbara. The entire group nodded their agreement.

Dr. Wilson turned to a nurse standing beside him. "Bridget, would you please direct these people to the lab? Mr. Fuller, why don't you come with me."

Phoebe and Allen hugged Zan before he turned and followed the doctor down the hallway. He'd never felt so forlorn in his life. He swallowed a lump in his throat when he entered the emergency area.

He barely recognized her. Tubes and IV's surrounded her and an oxygen ventilator mask covered her face. A machine beside the bed beeped monotonously, but the steady zigzag of the heart monitor gave him hope. The top of her head was bald on one side where they'd shaved her to stitch up the cut. She wasn't going to be happy about that.

"They're ready for her in radiology, doctor," said a nurse.

"Okay. Sorry to rush you out, Mr. Fuller." Dr. Wilson patted Zan on the shoulder. "We'll call you when we have more information."

"I understand."

Zan hung his head as he walked slowly back to the waiting area. Everyone else had gone to the lab. He sat on an uncomfortable plastic chair and stared at the television. A perky blonde wearing bright yellow leotards demonstrated aerobics to a quick-paced disco beat, but Zan didn't even notice. All he could think about was Emma.

An eternity later Dr. Wilson reappeared in the waiting room and motioned for Zan to follow him into a small office. The rest of the group, who had joined him in his vigil, watched hopefully as he rose. His cheeks and chin felt like coarse sandpaper when he tried to rub the grit from his eyes. His mouth tasted sour from too many cups of coffee and his whole body felt stiff and sore. The doctor pointed to a set of x-rays illuminated by a viewer on the wall. "Your wife has an epidural hematoma—a blood clot at this section of the covering of the brain."

Zan gasped. "Can you operate?"

Dr. Wilson nodded. "Yes, but we've got to relieve the swelling first. We'll have to put in a catheter to drain the fluid and an intracranial pressure monitor."

"Doctor—is she going to make it?" Zan's voice came out in a rasp.

"It's just too soon to say, Mr. Fuller." The doctor patted him on the shoulder. "We'll do our best. Your wife isn't pregnant, is she?"

"No, why do you ask?"

"It's just a routine question when a woman is in her child-bearing years."

"We've been trying to have a baby, but haven't been successful. She was supposed to have outpatient tests next week to try to figure out the problem. She pre-registered and everything."

"Be sure and give all that information to the nurse. We'll get your doctor to fax her records to us."

"Can't we take her back to Dallas for treatment?"

"Not at this time, sir. She'll be in ICU here for a while." Doctor Wilson shook his head at Zan's disheveled appearance. "You look like you could use some rest. Where are you staying?"

"In Eureka Springs."

"You'd better move to a motel here in town."

Rachel Hughes sipped her coffee and frowned. God, how she hated Mondays. Heaven forbid she take a Friday off. It was barely nine o'clock and already her phone was lighting up, her in-box was overflowing, and her messages numbered in the triple digits.

And where the hell was her assistant? Did she have to do the job of Hospital Administrator and receptionist both? No, she wouldn't. Those calls could just go to voice mail and Dorinda could deal with them when she got back from wherever she was. If it was the last thing she did, she was going to chain that girl to her desk, pregnant or not. How many friggin' bathroom breaks did a person need?

She sighed and opened her e-mail, then sighed again. She'd need a snow plow to get through all this. Well, better get to it. She wrinkled her nose when she saw the request from the homeless shelter asking for an increase in free medical services—delete. Another message was an invitation to speak at a medical symposium in Las Vegas—now that looked interesting. Memos—budget meetings—the usual stuff.

Oh, no. Not him again. Another urgent message from the office of United States Senator Grayson Talmedge. The poor guy was getting desperate. He'd been bombarding hospitals all over the region for weeks, reminding them about his twenty-one year old daughter. She'd been on the list for quite a while now waiting for a heart transplant. Rachel shook her head. She wished her luck, but she knew how tough it would be to find a proper match. Even though she was at the top of the list, she kept getting bumped because donors with her particular blood and tissue type just didn't come available very often.

"Good morning, Ms. Hughes"

"G'morning, Dorinda," said Rachel, glancing at her assistant over the rim of her reading glasses. She looked like she was about to pop. Oh, well. Rachel had already warned her that her expectations would remain the same after she gave birth. Sick babies and doctor's appointments would not be an excuse for absence or tardiness. So, the ungrateful little wench had decided to turn her maternity leave into permanent retirement. Fine. Maybe then she'd get to replace her with somebody competent.

"I've typed up all the stats you requested and I've updated the hospital calendar," said Dorinda. She slowly lowered her bloated body into a chair across from Rachel's desk.

"Thank you. Now, will you please fill me in on what's happened over the weekend?"

"Yes, ma'am." Dorinda scanned through her notes. "Let's see...CareFlight brought in a woman in the wee hours Sunday morning—a severe head injury case. She's in ICU in a coma right now and she can't breathe without life support."

"Really?" Rachel's interest was aroused. "Is she brain dead?"

"Mmm...I don't know. It says they're still trying to control the swelling and keep her vitals going. Won't know her prognosis for a few days."

"Who's the attending?"

"Dr. Richard Wilson."

Rachel couldn't control a sneer. "I should have known. How old is she?"

"Twenty-eight. She had an accident over in Eureka Springs. A cave-in at a hotel? That's weird."

"We don't need your opinions, Dorinda. What else does the report say?" Rachel leaned back in her chair and laced her fingers together. She smiled with satisfaction, knowing how annoyed Dorinda was growing by having to sit and read to her.

Rachel relaxed while Dorinda read until she heard something that arrested her attention. She put up her perfectly manicured hand and said, "Stop."

"Ma'am?"

"Go back. To the part about the Living Will."

"Oh, okay. Living Will with executed organ donor affidavit included with other documents faxed from Dallas."

"What does it say about life support?" questioned Rachel.

"It's just the standard form," said Dorinda. "I can pull up her file for you if you want to see for yourself."

"Yes, Dorinda. Please do." Rachel wheeled her chair away from her desk and waited while Dorinda bent over to work on Rachel's computer.

"Is there something else wrong with her?" asked Rachel. "What's she doing with a Living Will?"

"The report said she's been trying to get pregnant and she was set to go in for outpatient tests next week in Dallas. From what I've heard, her family is frantic with worry and they'll do anything to keep her alive. They probably don't even know she signed a Living Will. It was one of those routine forms they get you to fill out whenever you go into the hospital for anything. Everybody's pushing 'em like crazy ever since that woman in Florida with the feeding tube case."

"Still, it's a binding legal document. Right?"

"I suppose so," replied Dorinda. "Do you want me to continue reading the report?"

"No, I'll read through it myself. You really should get back to your desk and take care of those messages. The phone's been ringing off the hook while you've been dawdling," said Rachel. She pretended not to notice the glare of hatred on Dorinda's face before waddling back to her desk.

Rachel stared at the advance directive on the computer screen and wondered. What if? No way. It would be too much of a coincidence. On impulse, Rachel logged into the transplant data base and read the information for Monica Talmedge. Then she pulled up the file on the new patient. Emily Jean Fuller. She compared the data. Close—extraordinarily close. She picked up the telephone.

"Frank? This is Rachel...I need you to take over a patient from Dr. Wilson...head trauma...she's in a coma...no, I'll explain when you get here...okay, bye." Rachel placed the telephone receiver in the cradle and smiled.

Dr. Richard Wilson. The son-of-a-bitch. She couldn't wait to show him who's boss. They'd clashed on many subjects, but their opinions were polar opposite on the right-to-die/right-to-live issue. She thought about her own mother-in-law, wasting away like some vegetable in a high priced nursing home. The old woman wasn't ever going to get any better. She was eighty friggin' years old, for God's sake, and she'd had Alzheimer's for the past three years. The dementia had grown progressively worse, yet Rachel's husband still refused to accept the fact that his mother's life was as good as over. She couldn't even eat or drink anymore without a feeding tube, so what was the point?

She thought about the thousands of dollars being wasted every single month on the old bat—her husband's inheritance was slipping right down that tube. Rachel could certainly think of better ways to put the money to use. They desperately needed to re-plaster the swimming pool—and he'd been promising her a trip to Italy for ages.

The news had been out less than forty-five minutes when Dr. Wilson banged on Rachel's office door. She looked up and smiled demurely. "Yes, doctor. May I help you?"

"Rachel, I want to talk to you." He stormed into the room and slouched onto a chair that faced her desk. He ignored Dr. Ballew, who was sitting in the next chair.

"I'm listening." She leaned back and gave him her attention. Her right foot tapped impatiently beneath her desk. That stubbly chin and the graying hair curling down his neck set her teeth on edge, but she pretended not to notice.

"Just give me one good reason why you're transferring my patient to Dr. Ballew," demanded Dr. Wilson.

"Which patient are you referring to?" she asked, with sugar dripping from her mouth.

"You know very well which patient I'm talking about—Emma Fuller."

"All right. I'll give you two reasons," Rachel replied. "Number one—Frank's a neurosurgeon and you're not. Number two—your shift is over. You've already pulled two doubles and you need a break."

"That's bullshit and you know it," Dr. Wilson raged. "Since when did either of those reasons justify removing a doctor from his patient?"

"Don't you have someone else to go bother?" Rachel stared up through the half-rimmed glasses resting on the tip of her nose.

"You're such a bitch." Dr. Wilson's eyes blazed with anger.

"Richard, don't take this personally." Dr. Ballew tried to intervene. His bushy black eyebrows rose higher on his forehead and he seemed unsure of how to react to the looming battle.

"You're just as bad as she is." Dr. Wilson whirled and pointed at the other man. "You've both had it in for me ever since your organ procurement buddy called me by accident and started trying to ring me in on his deals."

"I *thought* we'd already addressed that issue. The Board of Directors established that Frank and I did nothing wrong. Thanks to you, the OPO was able to catch on to the agent's scheme in time and fire him." She drummed her fingernails on the desk. "That's all water under the bridge. Can we please give it a rest?"

"Humph," Dr. Wilson folded his arms. "The whole thing leaves me with a bad taste in my mouth. He should've gone to jail. The government needs to have stricter regulations for these organ procurement organizations. There's way too much potential to make money the wrong way. And I think you're both trying to punish me now for foiling your plans. "

"Don't be so paranoid, Richard." Dr. Ballew glanced toward Rachel before he continued. "Ms. Hughes and I just think this new case should be handled by a specialist."

Dr. Wilson folded his arms and grimaced. "Okay, so why

the nasty little comment about my bothering you?"

"Richard, I'm sorry," Rachel said. She hoped she could keep the insincerity out of her tone. "I shouldn't have said that. You've just pulled a double shift and it's time for you to get some rest. We think this patient would be better served if Frank were officially the treating physician. That's all."

"No. I don't trust you." Dr. Wilson leaned down, put his hands on Rachel's desk and stared at her. "I think you've got some evil agenda."

"You will *not* speak to me like that." Rachel's eyes narrowed and she straightened her posture, moving closer to meet his stare. "The decision is made."

Dr. Wilson stood poised for battle. Rachel could see how angry he was by the redness of his face and the tightness of his jaw. But she wasn't about to give in. She'd fought her way through life and she knew that continuing to fight was the only way to stay on top. A show of weakness now and he would win. He'd almost brought her down once before. She couldn't let it happen now.

"I'm going to check on my patient now." Dr. Wilson maintained eye contact with Rachel, trying to stare her down.

Rachel laced her fingers together and smiled. Her eyes were cold and her words were clipped and precise. "You will go clock out of your shift right now and leave this hospital, doctor—do I have to call security to have you removed?"

"Richard, please..." Dr. Ballew mopped at his brow with a handkerchief. "I'll take good care of the patient."

"I'm sure you will." Dr. Wilson's lip curled in an expression of loathing, then he turned and shrugged before he stalked out of the office, leaving the door hanging open.

"God, that was intense," said Dr. Ballew.

"I wish he'd get a haircut." Rachel wrinkled her nose. "He looks disgusting."

"You don't think he'll cause any trouble, do you?"

"Am I the only one with any balls around here?" Rachel rolled her eyes and stared at Dr. Ballew with distaste. "Shut the door."

Rachel got up from her desk, walked to the window, and stared down at the street below. She could still see the fat, sniveling excuse for a man out of the corner of her eye. Dr. Wilson's insubordination had infuriated her, but Dr. Ballew's meek compliance was worse. He'd quietly done as he was told, which irritated her further. She counted to ten before she returned to her desk and composed herself.

"Okay, now that the unpleasantness is over we can get down to business." Rachel crooked her finger at Dr. Ballew. He jumped to attention, his eyes wide with fright. "How long until we can contact the Senator?"

"Oh, I don't know," Dr. Ballew replied. Sweat beaded on his forehead and his hands shook. "We're being a little premature, don't you think?"

"Frank, I thought I explained everything to you. Time is running out for Monica Talmedge."

"Yes, but it's too soon to tell about Mrs. Fuller's recovery yet."

Rachel sighed and picked up a piece of paper. "I'll repeat what I told you earlier. She signed an Advance Health Care Directive of her own free will. Let me read what it says. *END-OF-LIFE-DECISION: I direct that my health care providers and others involved in my care provide, withhold, or withdraw treatment in accordance with the choice I have marked below; Initials EJF—check mark on (a) Choice NOT to Prolong Life. I do not want my life to be prolonged if (1) I have an incurable and irreversible condition that will result in my death within a relatively short time, (2) I become unconscious and, to a reasonable degree of medical certainty, I will not regain consciousness, or (3) the likely risks and burdens of treatment would outweigh the expected benefits. Then it goes on and she's*

126

marked the box that says 'Upon my death I give any needed organs, tissues, or parts for the purposes of transplant.' How much more clear could it be?"

"But it hasn't even been forty-eight hours yet. We don't know if she's going to die or not," Dr. Ballew argued.

"There's a young woman who is *definitely* going to die if she doesn't get this heart. Her father is an extremely important man. Who knows? He may be the President someday. Do you want to be the one responsible for letting his little girl die?"

"Of course not, but..."

"But nothing!" Rachel felt her anger rise at his ignorance. "All you have to do is go through the motions. Just fill out the paperwork and certify her as PVS. You and I both know that even if she comes out of this coma she'll probably be severely disabled."

"That's not necessarily true. People come out of comas all the time and make full recoveries. It could happen."

"Yes, and you could win the lottery, too. But what are the odds?"

"She's my patient now. Don't I have an obligation to her?" his voice took on a shrill quality.

"Yes, and we both have an obligation to the Board of Directors." Rachel waved her arms and paced. "Can't you imagine all the accolades and rewards if *we* were instrumental in saving Senator Talmedge's daughter? Why, it's no telling what he would do for the hospital in gratitude."

"Does Richard know about all this?"

Rachel laughed. "Of course not. Why do you think I pulled Sir Galahad from the case? You know he'd mess everything up. That's why we've got to hurry up and push this thing through before any of the do-gooders have time to start screaming."

Dr. Ballew hung his head, clasped his hands together and stared at the floor. Rachel watched him intently. He was weak and a coward. She knew she had him where she wanted him.

"Do what you have to do. I'll be notifying Senator Talmedge we have a heart donor at precisely three o'clock tomorrow afternoon. Let's keep a low profile until then." Rachel's eyes glistened. "I want her dead before anybody has a chance to react. Do *not* let me down."

Zan pulled his tired body from the chair beside Emma's bed in the Intensive Care Unit, cracked his neck back and forth and then stretched. He glanced at his watch—just after four in the afternoon. He tried to remember the day of the week. Oh yeah, Tuesday. Three days since the accident. For three days he's been talking to her, telling her how much he loved her and how happy he'd be to have a whole houseful of kids with her, if only she'd wake up. He glanced up in surprise at a man in a white coat standing in the doorway, holding a clipboard and looking nervous.

"Hello, Mr. Fuller. I'm Dr. Ballew." The doctor smiled and extended his right hand.

"Where's Dr. Wilson?" Zan returned the shake, but did not smile.

"He had to leave for a while. I'll be your wife's attending physician from now on." Dr. Ballew motioned toward the hallway. "Do you think we could go into my office and talk?"

"Sure." Zan lovingly caressed the only patch of skin on Emma's arm that wasn't covered with IV tubes or pressure cuffs and then followed the doctor down a short corridor.

"Have a seat," Dr. Ballew pointed to a chair and then sat behind a desk. He rummaged through some files, avoiding eye contact with Zan. "Let's see, I believe Dr. Wilson already showed you the results of the CT scan."

"Yeah, she has a blood clot that needs to be removed. Are you going to do that now?"

"Well, Dr. Wilson installed the ICP Monitor and he's got a shunt drawing off the excess fluid from the brain. But her EEG's not showing much activity...I'm not sure surgery will do any good at this point. She can't breathe without a respirator. I'm worried about damage to her brain stem." Dr. Ballew knitted his brows, shook his head and rambled on. "Let's see...she's classified a three on the Glasgow Coma Scale...rostral-caudal deterioration...cerebral anoxia...probable persistent vegetative state..."

Zan's mind reeled as he listened. As a medical professional, he understood enough to realize Emma was in serious trouble. But he sensed a reticence in this man's demeanor. Something didn't seem right. What was he trying to hide?

"When will Dr. Wilson be back? I think I'd feel more comfortable with him."

"What?" Dr. Ballew looked flustered. "Oh, he won't be caring for your wife any more. The hospital's reassigned her to me."

"With all due respect, Doctor...I believe I have the right to decide who I want to treat my wife." Zan stood up and headed for the door. He shook with anger and suspicion. "I'd like to speak to whoever's in charge."

"Mr. Fuller, please. Wait. I understand you're upset."

Zan stopped, turned around and stared at Dr. Ballew. "You're damn right I'm upset. You're acting like my wife is dead already. Like there's no hope."

"Please, Mr. Fuller. I know this is hard for you. I'm just trying to explain the futility of continuing treatment."

"Look." Zan's eyes widened. He clenched his fists to suppress an impulse to punch the doctor in the nose. "I've got insurance. I've got money. You do whatever it takes to get her through this. I don't care how much it costs or how long it takes."

Dr. Ballew sighed. "If only it were that easy—by law we can't continue treatment."

Zan felt as if his breath was cut off. A cold numbness

invaded his body. "What are you talking about?"

The doctor appeared almost as anxious as Zan before he replied. "Apparently your wife executed a valid Advance Health Care Directive. She's requested not to have her life prolonged by extraordinary means if she finds herself in the—ahem—position she's now in."

Zan felt like he'd been pole axed. "When the *hell* did she have time to do something like that? She's been unconscious for three days!"

"Yes, yes. But apparently she signed it last week when she pre-registered with the hospital in Dallas." Dr. Ballew fished in his pocket for a handkerchief to wipe the sweat from his forehead. He handed Emma's chart to Zan and pointed to her signature on the form. "They faxed it along with her other paperwork."

Zan paced the room and read the form. "Okay, let me get this straight. You're saying that just because my wife signed this *bogus* form—which by the way, was thrust on her very quickly—we're just supposed to undo all the machines and let her die?"

"Basically—yes. According to the law, that's what we have to do."

Zan closed his eyes and composed himself before he spoke. "Look, I was there at the doctor's office with her that day. They were in a hurry to get everything buttoned up, so they just shoved forms at her to sign. She had no idea of the implications when she signed this."

"I understand your concerns, Mr. Fuller." Dr. Ballew spread his hands in a helpless gesture and wrinkled his brow. "But there's nothing we can do. The law clearly states we must follow her wishes."

"Isn't there some sort of waiting period?" Zan pleaded. The reality of the situation began to set in and he grew frightened. "Dr. Wilson said we had to wait and see…"

Dr. Ballew interrupted. "Dr. Wilson is not a neurosurgeon. He doesn't understand the complexities of the human brain the way I do."

"I'm her next of kin. I want a second opinion."

"Sir, I'm very sorry, but that's not an option. She was a rational, consenting adult when she made her wishes known. Her records don't indicate a Power of Attorney assigning you or anyone else as her advocate. We have no other alternative."

"I *demand* she be evaluated by somebody else right now!" Zan approached the doctor and pounded his fist on the desk.

Dr. Ballew flinched and shrank back before he took a deep breath and continued. "Mr. Fuller, I assure you I did not make this diagnosis lightly. We've followed all the rules. I've consulted extensively with two other specialists and they concur with my opinion—you've got to accept reality and let her go."

Numb with rage, Zan felt an overpowering urge to start breaking things. He began backing out of the office, frightened of losing control. Something evil was happening, but he didn't know what. He pointed his index finger at the doctor. "You'd better not unplug one single machine or so help me God, I'll kill you!" He turned toward the hallway and yelled. "Allen—Dad—where are you?"

"Please lower your voice." Dr. Ballew followed him into the hall, glancing nervously at the staring onlookers. He returned to his office and slammed the door when Zan entered the waiting room.

"Zan, what's wrong?" asked Jonathan.

"They're trying to kill Emma," said Zan. His shoulders slumped in despair. "We've got to do something."

Gasps of disbelief echoed throughout the group.

"Mr. Fuller." Bridget, one of Emma's ICU nurses walked toward Zan and motioned for him to follow her to the TV in the waiting room. She glanced nervously around the room, put her finger to her lips, and turned up the volume.

Zan stared in confusion at the reporter on the television. What was she talking about? And then realization set in. When he understood the implications of the news report he was stunned. His mouth felt like old paper, dry and dusty. He sensed his father's hand on his shoulder, but he was too numb to actually feel it. He heard someone in the room sobbing uncontrollably, but didn't even realize the person crying was himself.

"Good evening. This is Lora Lapinski, reporting live from Northwest General Hospital in Rogers, Arkansas with breaking news. An anonymous source has revealed that a suitable donor for Monica Talmedge's long-awaited heart transplant has at last been located right here in Rogers. Monica is the daughter of US Senator Grayson Talmedge, who is regarded as one of the front-runners in a bid for the White House next term... we have Senator Talmedge on the line right now...Senator, congratulations on your good news...so tell me, how does it feel now that the wait is almost over?"

PART TWO

INTERLUDE IN TIME

CHAPTER NINE

June 19, 1938
St. Louis, Missouri

BABE RUTH NAMED FIRST BASE COACH FOR BROOKLYN DODGERS. Caleb Turner pondered the headline sprawled across the front page. He shook his head and sighed. What a low blow for such a great career. A little farther down, in smaller type, another caption read *JAPAN DECLARES WAR ON CHINA.* He shrugged with disinterest and thumbed through to the financial section.

The telephone rang. Once. Twice. Three times.

He glanced up from his newspaper and frowned, annoyed by the incessant ringing. He squirmed in his chair, rattled the paper and scanned the parlor. Would nobody answer the damned thing?

Exasperated, Caleb stood up and stubbed out his cigar. He threw down the newspaper and stalked toward the yammering contraption. He picked up the instrument by its long, thin base, jerked the earpiece from its cradle, and bellowed into the mouthpiece.

"Hullo?"

"May I speak to Ivy?" asked a feminine voice.

Without bothering to acknowledge the young lady on the telephone, he grunted and yelled toward the stairs. "Iv-ee!" Caleb tapped his foot impatiently. He dropped the earpiece and let it dangle while he craned his neck and watched for his daughter to come downstairs to take the call.

Where was the blasted maid? He was already in a bad mood from all his employees at the sawmill loafing around, all puffed up about Eleanor Roosevelt's pet project. What did they call it? The Fair Labor Standards Act. Humph. Overtime *and* a minimum wage. It certainly wasn't fair to the business owners. Thank God it didn't include domestic help, or he'd never get any service anymore. But where was that woman? He paid her good money to clean the house and answer the telephone, yet here he was doing it himself. Couldn't a man enjoy a Sunday afternoon of peace in his own home?

"Who is it Papa?" Ivy walked halfway down the stairs and peeked through the banister. She clutched a thin cotton robe with one hand and a towel on her shoulders with the other.

Caleb eyed her wet head and pin curls suspiciously. "I don't know. One of your friends." Three o'clock in the afternoon and she was still in her chemise! "What are you doing up there?"

Ivy came down the rest of the way and reached for the telephone. "Margot's curling my hair." She put the earpiece against her ear and spoke into the mouthpiece. "Hello? Oh, hi toots….you're kidding…*Betty* from school went to Atlanta and auditioned for the part of Scarlett O'Hara? But she's never even acted before. I thought they were gonna cast Talullah Bankhead?"

Caleb returned to his chair and tried to read the stock market report, but he couldn't concentrate. Too much hen cackling. And the smell was overpowering. Whatever hair tonic she'd put on her head made his eyes tear up and his nose twitch.

"Whatcha been doin'?…Margot's trying out a new hairdo on me…um hm. We used Jo-Cur Waveset…yeah, the one you told me about from the radio…really? He's a good egg…" Ivy glanced toward her father. "I don't know. It's kind of iffy… he's been trying a lot of sweet-talk, but between you and me, my patience is about gone. I think he's gonna get the ol' eighty-

six....oh, that's just Mrs. Hooper listening in on the party line...
she's such a Nice-Nelly, I've gotta be careful what I say."

What kind of language was she speaking? He just did
not understand young people nowadays—that infernal slang.
His patience was almost to the breaking point. Even though
Ivy thought of herself as grown up, he knew she needed her
mother's influence. He wished Winifred would hurry up and get
over whatever it was she thought was wrong with her this time
and come home from that expensive hospital.

Between his wife's constant, elusive illnesses and his
daughter's bull-headedness, he would be bankrupt before the
year was out if something didn't change. Now he had to pay
some ding-blasted Social Security tax on top of everything
else—he gave the government a year to come to its senses and
put a halt to such foolishness. And just when he thought this
damned Depression was about to turn around and he'd ventured
out with some investments, the stock market had crashed again.

"Okey-doke. Bye, now." Ivy returned the handset to its
cradle and set the telephone back on the hallstand. She turned
to Caleb and asked. "When are we gonna get rid of this relic and
get a modern desk phone?"

"Humph. Might I remind you there's a depression going on,
young lady? Most people nowadays don't have telephones at
all."

"You're right, Papa. I'm sorry for being so selfish. We
should all count our blessings."

Caleb grunted his acknowledgement, but his dander was
still up about the lack of loyalty from the hired help. He was
tired of having to do everything around here. "Where's—uh—
what's-her-name—the housekeeper?"

"Yolanda? It's her day off. Remember, you told her you had
to cut back on her hours." She hesitated at the foot of the stairs.

"Humph. I thought you were going out with Jared tonight?"

Ivy stopped. Her expression grew pensive and her tone was

guarded. "I canceled."

"To do your hair?" Caleb felt his anger rise. He narrowed his eyes and stared at his daughter. "Did you bob your hair?"

"No, I did *not*. It's just curled."

He exhaled a sigh of relief. "Good. You know how Jared feels about bobbed hair."

Ivy rolled her eyes. "I don't care what he thinks about my hair."

"Don't be a flibbertigibbet. Are you toying with his affections?" Caleb felt his blood pressure rise. "You know he wants to marry you."

Ivy set her chin in a stubborn line and replied, "I'm not going to marry Jared."

He clenched his jaw to control his fury. He was sick and tired of her impertinence. Why, in *his* day a girl married whomever her father told her to—and that was that. "And why, pray tell, do you not want to marry Jared? He's been courting you for months now."

"Because I don't love him—and he's old—he's almost thirty!"

Caleb glared at Ivy. He'd just spent a small fortune to make sure she was properly presented to St. Louis society at the Veiled Prophet Debutante Ball and he thought his plan had hit pay dirt. Jared Covington was one of the richest bachelors in Missouri. He was counting on Jared's investments in his business to keep him afloat until the economy turned around. Their whole future hinged on this match.

He sighed as he looked at his little girl—so petite and graceful. She looked more and more like her mother every day. Even with her chestnut hair in pin curls, Ivy was like a delicate, porcelain doll. It was no wonder Jared had been smitten with her charm and beauty. Smart too. Graduated high school with straight A's. But she had a mind of her own—which could be a dangerous thing in a woman.

Caleb's attention was diverted when he heard someone coming down the stairs. His bushy eyebrows raised in surprise when he saw the girl—he supposed it was a girl. She was wearing trousers!

"Hello, Mr. Turner. I'm Margot Hollander." The girl smiled, extended her right hand, and proceeded to pump his with a strong, firm grip.

"Afternoon," he responded warily, returning her handshake. He looked her up and down. She was tall and thin, with coal black bobbed hair that hugged her head in finger waves. She would have been almost pretty if not for her slightly enlarged nose and her loosey-goosey stance. But those slacks and that masculine-looking blouse set his teeth on edge. He hoped she wasn't one of those lesbians he'd been hearing about.

"Papa, Margot's going to be an aviatrix," said Ivy. "Her boyfriend knows Adela Riek, who's been taking flying lessons from one of Lindbergh's friends, and he's teaching her too."

"Flying lessons!" Caleb was horrified. "Do you want to wind up like that Amelia Earhart person? Women don't have any business flying planes."

"With all due respect, Mr. Turner. Miss Earhart's navigator was a man," said Margot. "He's the one who got them hopelessly lost."

Before Caleb could reply, the doorbell rang. Ivy opened the door and stared. Three young men dressed in Western Union garb stood on the porch. One of them held a crystal vase filled with a dozen red roses and read from a card. "Are you Miss Ivy Turner?"

Ivy appeared confused as she accepted the flowers. "Yes, that's me."

"This is from Jared Covington—with love. Okay fellas, hit it." The leader turned to the others. They immediately began harmonizing a popular Bing Crosby tune.

Caleb chewed on his cigar and watched Ivy's expression.

He wondered what was going through her mind as she stood politely and listened to the Sing-o-Gram. He chuckled to himself. That Jared was such a scamp. He certainly knew how to charm the ladies.

When the song ended, they began another, more fast-paced song. Ivy glanced helplessly toward her friend, but said nothing. When the songs were finished, Caleb gave each boy a quarter, which lit up their young faces. Ivy's shoulders drooped as she carried the roses into the dining room and set the vase in the middle of the table. She stood and stared at the arrangement, seemingly deep in thought.

"That was really swell," said Margot. "Kid, I've got to run now. When your hair's dry and you comb it out, let me know how it looks. Okay? Nice to meet you, Pops." She bounced down the sidewalk, climbed into a silver Horch Cabriolet, and roared away.

Caleb closed the door and beamed at his daughter. "Now don't you feel badly for the way you treated poor Jared?"

Ivy's face suddenly contorted and she put her hand to her forehead. She sank into a chair and stared at the floor. "Papa, you just don't understand about him."

Now what was the matter? "Understand what?"

Ivy looked up at her father with a pleading expression. "Haven't you ever wondered where he got his money?"

"He's a businessman. He's very smart and he's made a lot of wise investments. What are you getting at?"

"Doesn't it bother you that he and his brother took advantage of a lot of poor farmers who lost everything they had to foreclosure during the bad times? That's how they amassed their fortunes in the first place, you know."

"That's just business. Buy low, sell high. That's the name of the game." he reached over and patted her hand. "I think he was very shrewd. If he hadn't done it, somebody else would have."

"But that doesn't make it right!"

"Look," Caleb spluttered, amazed that his little girl even thought about such things. "Those people were losing their farms because they couldn't pay the mortgage. Those are the breaks when you can't pay your debts."

"It wasn't their fault." Ivy's face grew red with anger. "The banks closed down and they lost their life savings. And then the prices for their crops tumbled so low they couldn't make a living. It wasn't fair. He took advantage of those poor people."

"Well, the farmers had their own methods of cheating too, you know. Didn't you ever hear about the penny auctions?" Caleb bristled. "They all got together like a band of thugs and scared off the honest bidders. Then they intimidated the auctioneer so bad he sold the farmers back their land for a penny. It was either that or get his head bashed in."

"Good. That's what they should have done."

"God's teeth, girl! Who's putting these notions in your head?" His eyes narrowed. "Is it that Margot? Is she a Socialist or something?"

"No, Papa. She's Jewish."

"Um." Caleb leaned back in his chair, lit his cigar, and took a puff.

"What's the matter? Do you have something against the Jews?"

"No. No, of course not," said Caleb, puffing his cigar thoughtfully. "But you've got to admit they're certainly stirring up a ruckus over in Europe."

"What are you talking about? The Jews haven't done anything wrong. It's that Hitler person who's causing all the trouble. He's the one who annexed Austria and now all the Jews are scared to death over there."

"Humph. Since when did you take such an interest in politics?"

"Margot says Jared is selling lead out of his mines to the

141

Nazis. She says Hitler is planning to exterminate the Jews and then take over the world. He's using it to make weapons to use against all of us. She says there's going to be another big war. Bigger than the last one."

"What a bunch of folderol! There aren't going to be any more wars, especially not like the Great War," Caleb stormed. His bad leg throbbed at the reminder of his time in the trenches. "I was *over there*, remember? Armageddon will come before we see anything like that again."

Ivy continued, despite her father's reaction. "Margot has relatives who were run out of Germany because of the Nazis. They moved to Amsterdam, but she doesn't think they'll be safe there much longer. She has two little cousins she's very worried about—the youngest wants to become a writer. Margot sent her a journal for her birthday, but she doesn't know if it got there or not."

"I'm not so sure this Margot is such a good influence on you." Caleb tapped his ashes into the ashtray. "I don't want you seeing her any more."

Ivy bristled. "I am eighteen years old, Papa. You can't control who my friends are any longer."

"Well, young lady," he replied, his fury building. "You may be all grown up according to the law, but as long as you're under *my* roof, you will do what I say."

"Very well." She lifted her chin defiantly. "If you will excuse me, I'll go pack my things and be on my way."

"Where do you intend to go?" He clenched his fists and forced himself to be calm. "You can't go out on the street with those thingamajigs in your hair."

"They're called bobby pins—and I'll wear one of Mama's turbans." She glared defiantly and began to climb the stairs. "I'll go stay with Margot. She's going to college in the fall. I'll go too."

"College? How're you going to pay for that?"

"I'll get a job." Ivy appeared determined. "I can be a secretary, or a telephone operator, or a sales girl." She continued to climb the stairs, her head held high.

Caleb flinched when he heard the door slam upstairs. He sank into a chair, defeated. Now what was he going to do? He knew Ivy possessed enough stubbornness to follow through with her threats. She wasn't like her mother, who wilted at every crisis. In the past he'd been proud of the fact she was so much like her old man, but now he was worried.

Several moments passed before he decided on a plan of action. He would just have to beat her at her own game. He crept up the stairs and knocked on Ivy's bedroom door. "Ivy, are you still in there?"

The door opened slightly and she stared questioningly at her father. A stretchy turban covered her head and he could see her opened suitcase on the bed. "Yes, Papa?"

"Ivy, I'm sorry I spoke so harshly with you earlier. It's just hard for me right now, with your mother away. Please don't leave."

"Oh, Papa." Ivy ran toward Caleb and hugged him. "I'm sorry, too. I miss Mama so much—but I just don't like being pressured about Jared."

"Well, don't you worry your pretty little head about that any more." He patted her on the back. "I just had an idea. I really need to go down to Joplin to take care of some business, so I thought maybe you and I could take the train to Eureka Springs and visit your mother. How would that be?"

"That would be just grand!" Ivy's eyes danced and she clapped her hands. "How long will we stay?"

"Well, I can only stay for about a week. But I thought you might spend the rest of the summer there at my sister Tyme's house. She's probably lonely since Chauncey died and she could use the company." He smiled benevolently and added, "Then, if you still don't want to marry Jared, you can come back home and go to business college in September."

Ivy squealed with delight. "Oh, that sounds perfect! I'll go and pack."

June 24, 1938
Baker Cancer Hospital
Eureka Springs, Arkansas

Ivy fidgeted in the rocking chair and sipped her bottled spring water, feeling ill at ease by her surroundings. On either side of where she sat with her parents were row after row of hospital beds full of cancer patients sunning themselves on the third-floor veranda. But despite the cool mountain breeze and her short-sleeved cotton frock she felt her temperature rise uncomfortably, because every time she stole a glance toward her mother that horrible Dr. Baker would be staring at her.

She'd never seen a man dress so strangely—a white suit, with a lavender shirt, purple suspenders, and a purple tie. Dr. Baker wasn't much taller than Ivy, but she got the impression he thought of himself as a big man. He seemed to be constantly bristling for a fight; he made her think of a banty rooster. He gave her the willies, but her parents seemed to be enchanted by him. She patted her wide-brimmed straw hat and attempted to position it to better hide her face so she wouldn't have to look at him.

"Well, well." Caleb leaned back in his chair, puffed his cigar, and gazed at the vista. "Now I see why my wife wanted to come here. This is quite a place you've got, Baker."

"It certainly is, isn't it?" Norman Baker sighed, inhaled his own cigar, then blew three dark smoke rings in succession. "My own little castle in the air—high atop the Ozarks. We consider it to be more like a health resort than a hospital—where relaxation is a big part of the treatment. We like to think of ourselves as one big, happy family living in a newly 'furbished mansion—

but we're all just plain folks."

Ivy scrunched lower in her seat, trying to hide her discomfort at Baker's proselytizing. She didn't understand why her parents thought the hospital was so beautiful. Certainly the mountain scenery was spectacular, and she supposed this former hotel had once been very grand. But now she could only think of one word to describe its furnishings—tacky.

She'd been shocked when she'd walked into the lobby and seen the paint scheme. Every wall was painted purple and the Venetian blinds were lavender. The beams and pillars were a hodge-podge of bright colors. Dr. Baker was apparently enamored of the Art Deco style of furnishing, but Ivy was not impressed with the garish-looking posters adorning the walls and the *moderne* style furniture.

Winifred Turner exhaled rapturously. "This place is so comfortable and everyone here is absolutely wonderful. It's so nice to have both those rooms to myself and not have to share a bathroom with a stranger. I feel better now than I've felt in years." She reached for Dr. Baker's hand and squeezed. "I don't think I would have been alive by Christmas if it weren't for you."

"There, there my dear." Baker patted her hand and smiled imperiously. "That's exactly what we're here for."

"So, Baker. How much longer until I can have my lovely wife back home?" asked Caleb.

"Oh, at the rate she's progressing, I'd say she should be completely cured by the end of July."

"Do you really think it will be that soon?" Winifred's penciled-on eyebrows moved up even higher than usual. She seemed alarmed at the prospect of going back home. She placed her hand on her abdomen as if to nurse a pain.

"Don't you worry, Mrs. Turner," said Baker. "We'll make absolutely sure all that nasty cancer is completely eradicated before we send you back out into the world."

"So, what kind of treatments are you giving to my wife?" asked Caleb.

"We use only the latest, most scientifically formulated treatment available." Dr. Baker's eyes gleamed as he began to describe his procedure. "Everything is completely natural. We use only the finest ingredients, which I have personally formulated and tested on hundreds of cancer patients. We do *not* use any radium, x-ray, or surgery of any kind."

Two giant Saint Bernards trotted over to Dr. Baker, nuzzled his hand, and lay down at his feet. Ivy loved dogs, but she'd never in her life seen such gigantic ones. She turned in her chair and reached down to pat one of them on its massive head. It gazed at her with sad-looking brown eyes and slobbered on the concrete porch.

Dr. Baker continued his lecture. "Ya know, it's a cryin' shame, but it's a fact—modernization has increased our susceptibility to illness. Too many of us have deviated from nature's gardens. We live our lives out of tin cans and fancy labeled boxes."

"Humph. That's for sure," agreed Caleb.

"Yes—a poor diet, vaccinations, and the use of aluminum cooking utensils are the major cause of cancer nowadays." Dr. Baker tapped his cigar in the ashtray, gazed out across the mountain and continued. "Now *my* treatments include all natural ingredients such as roots, barks, and herbs, which help to purify the blood and tone up the system. When the blood is pure, disease cannot exist."

"That a Cuban cigar you got there?" Caleb leaned forward and sniffed the air.

"Direct from Havana," replied Baker. He reached in his pocket and handed one to Caleb. "Wouldn't smoke anything else. Sure is great to be an American where you can always get the very best of everything from anywhere in the world. The day I can't get the real thing is the day I quit smoking."

The wind shifted suddenly and the acrid smoke drifted

toward Ivy. She covered her mouth to keep from choking and tried to wave it away. She wondered how they could possibly think what they were doing was healthy.

"Say, Baker, did you see in the paper what happened to Red Pollard yesterday?" asked Caleb.

"Who?"

"Pollard. That jockey who races Seabiscuit. Got his leg crushed in an accident on another horse. Guess he won't be riding for a while."

"Aah, that nag's days are over anyhow." Baker waved his hand in dismissal. "If Seabiscuit ever does get the match they keep promising, my money'll be on War Admiral."

Winifred gathered her silk kimono and straightened her fashionable turban before she leaned toward Dr. Baker. "I am so grateful for your wonderful radio broadcasts. Because of them, you've managed to get your message out to thousands of people who would have otherwise died."

"Oh, yes. Many's the evening we've sat around the wireless listening to your shows," Caleb reminisced. "But we always had to keep a close eye on the daughter, or she'd be cranking the dial over to hear *Fibber McGee and Molly* or *Charlie McCarthy.*"

Ivy turned bright red from embarrassment as the older people laughed. She hated the way she felt when Dr. Baker turned his attention toward her. When he stared at her with those cold, calculating eyes through wire-framed spectacles, she felt as if she were being examined like a bug under a microscope. She nervously increased her motion in the rocking chair and tried to ignore him.

"Little girl doesn't talk much," remarked Baker.

"I'm not a little girl. I am of age." Ivy retorted. She turned and gave Dr. Baker a cold stare. If it weren't for her mother, she would get up and leave right now.

Dr. Baker smiled and resumed his conversation with the elder Turners. "Y'know that's another thing that's wrong with

147

this country. The *radio trust* got together and formed the Federal Radio Commission so they could poison American's minds with all that frippery—yet refused to renew my license for KTNT because the *medical trust* didn't want the world to *Know the Naked Truth* about how the American Medical Association is gouging the public and not providing any cures for what ails them." Dr. Baker paused while the Turners laughed. "The medical establishment profits too much from treatments. If they actually *cured* somebody, their purses would be considerably flattened."

"Amen to that," replied Caleb.

"Yes, we got one of your advertisements in the mail," commented Winifred. "That's what made me decide I just *had* to come here. I've been to so many doctors, but you're the only one who's ever promised me a cure."

"D'you still own that station down in Mexico?" asked Caleb.

"Yessiree. X-E-N-T—100,000 watts of pure power." Baker's eyes gleamed as he related his story of persecution. "They closed me down in Iowa, but I came back bigger and better south of the border. Ran for governor while I was exiled down there, but the *medical octopus*—the AMA—made sure my name didn't even appear on the ballot."

"Humph. Sure is hard to make any headway when you've got all the powerful cards stacked against you," said Caleb.

"Yep. They got a kangaroo court up against me and put out a warrant for my arrest. Said I was practicin' medicine without a license." Baker grinned and puffed his cigar. "So I showed 'em. Come back to Iowa, turned myself in and served one day in jail. Then I ran for the US Senate on the Republican ticket. Did purty good, but then somebody put out a *March of Time* newsreel about me at the picture shows and called me a quack. So that's when I decided to give up on the thugs in my home state of Iowa and I found this lovely place here in Arkansas."

"Well, it's probably a blessing in the long run," said Winifred. "I'm sure you can help a lot more people with your healing than if you were up there in Washington butting heads." Baker nodded and smiled. "You just might be right, Mrs. Turner." He suddenly rose and extended his hand to Caleb. "Well, I really must be about my duties. It was so nice to meet you, and I hope you enjoy your stay with us—is the little missy going to stay? We can always bring in an extra bed."

Ivy's skin crawled at the thought. She spoke up in what she hoped was an appropriately icy tone. "I will be staying at my aunt's house in town."

Norman Baker grinned, gave her a wink, and whistled. Both dogs jumped to attention and trotted after their master. Ivy shuddered, took another sip of water and tried not to think about him any more.

Ivy stood next to her Aunt Tyme and waved at the train as it chugged out of the Eureka Springs depot. She hadn't been surprised Mama'd felt too weak to see Papa off—she was used to it by now. A black cloud of soot billowed up from the coal-powered steam locomotive and the whistle's shrill blast drowned out the chirping of the pond frogs. When the caboose was out of sight, she reached for the red rose pinned to her dress, jerked it loose, and tossed it into a nearby garbage can.

"Ouch." She winced and examined the drop of blood oozing from her fingertip.

"I see you got pricked by your corsage." Tyme smiled knowingly and handed Ivy a linen handkerchief. "Men can be like thorns at times."

"Thanks, Aunt Tyme." Ivy wrapped the cloth around her finger. "I'm sorry Jared's been such a pest all week. He's about to drive me to distraction."

"Don't feel bad, kiddo. I've been through the same thing." Tyme reached into her bag and pulled out a package of Camels and a Zippo lighter. She placed the cigarette into a holder and lit it. Taking a long, sensuous drag, she closed her eyes and exhaled. "Please don't call me *aunt*. It makes me feel so old." She held the cigarette toward Ivy. "Here, you wanna try it?"

"Oh, Papa would have my hide if he knew!" Her eyes grew wide and then she grinned. "Well, Papa's not here. Maybe I'll try it just once." She reached for the cigarette and tried to mimic her aunt. She sucked in too much smoke and bent over in a fit of coughing.

Tyme took back the cigarette and pounded Ivy on the back. "Now you've tried it and it's done. Smoking's a nasty habit you should never start. I wish I hadn't." She put it back in her own mouth and inhaled, then blew out a cloud of smoke. "Come on, let's go."

Ivy's throat still felt raspy from that one brief puff. How in the world did anybody ever get hooked on those things? She grinned at her aunt, whom she'd grown to love and admire in the past week. Her father's baby sister was so young and pretty, it seemed a shame for her to have to dress in black widow's weeds all the time. She followed Tyme to a brown 1930 Model A Ford Fordor and climbed into the front passenger seat.

"Ahooga!" Tyme honked the horn and a flock of chickens scattered.

Ivy held onto her hat and grabbed for the dashboard as Tyme's old car chugged through the winding streets. She giggled at the sight of a middle-aged lady standing on the sidewalk, gazing suspiciously at the two attractive young women driving unaccompanied. Tyme waved and puffed on her cigarette. The woman's disapproving stare made Ivy feel very grown up and scandalous.

She saw the telegraph office and tugged on her aunt's arm. "Tyme, can we stop there for a minute? I want to send a telegram."

Tyme nodded, flicked out her smoke, and parked the car

near the curb. The women climbed out and they strode into the building. Ivy adjusted her eyes to the dim room and walked up to the skinny, bald-headed man behind the counter.

"Yes'm. May I he'p you?" His Adam's apple bobbed up and down in a comical way as he spoke. He grinned broadly when he saw Tyme. "Afternoon, Miz Renfro."

"Afternoon to you, too, Darlin'," purred Tyme. "Please call me by my first name. It's pronounced Tie-mee. Okay?"

"Yes'm, M-Miz Ren—I mean T-T-T..."

Ivy interrupted the clerk's stammering and unfolded a piece of paper. "I'd like to send a message to this address."

"M-hm," he composed himself and held the paper at arm's length, scanning the address through his thick, bi-focal lenses. He plucked a pencil from behind his ear and asked, "Whatcha' want it to say?"

"I'd like it to say 'No more flowers please—stop—developed allergies—stop—sick in bed—stop.'" Ivy giggled and Tyme roared with laughter.

The thin man quirked his brow and shook his head at the laughing women. "That it?"

"Yes, that's all. Thank you." Ivy fanned herself and tried to catch her breath from all the laughing. She reached into her bag and handed the man some money.

He gave Ivy her change and said, "Here you go, Miss. Nice to see you T-T-T..." but he couldn't manage to get it out.

"You really mean business, don't you?" Tyme laughed as she started up the car and yelled. "Hey, Jared—twenty-three skidoo!"

Ivy felt liberated. She smiled as she imagined Jared's face when he got the telegram. He would be furious. She hoped he would get the message to back off.

Tyme drove the car into an alley behind a red brick storefront building and parked inside a rickety old garage. She unlocked the back door of the Renfro Dry Goods Store and they went upstairs. Ivy walked around the parlor gathering up the various containers of roses that had been delivered in the week since she'd arrived. She dumped them all into a garbage can and then dusted her hands together.

"Beaulah the florist is sure gonna be disappointed," remarked Tyme. She sat on the high-backed sofa and crossed her legs.

"Oh, well. She'll get over it. There are a lot of nice vases here. Maybe you can use them in the store."

"You're gonna break that poor fella's heart, you mean thing."

"I don't care." Ivy flopped down in a wingback chair and closed her eyes. "Papa's the one who's so crazy about him. Too bad *he* can't marry him."

Tyme giggled. "So what's the problem with Jared? Is he cross-eyed and hare-lipped?"

"No." Ivy laughed. "He's actually very handsome. Some people say he looks like Errol Flynn."

"Oooh."

"Yes, and he's filthy rich. That's what Papa loves about him."

Tyme lit another cigarette. "So what's the problem?"

Ivy thought for a moment before she answered. "Lots of things. He's unscrupulous in his business dealings and I'm not happy with the way he made his money." She sat forward and searched her aunt's face. "But the main thing is the way he makes me feel—as if I'm just one of his trophies."

"Trophies?" Tyme exhaled a cloud of smoke that wafted slowly around the apartment.

"He's a big-game hunter. He's got these animal heads hanging all over the walls of his den." Ivy shuddered. "He keeps telling me he loves me, but I don't really believe it. Sometimes I feel like if he ever really catches me, I'll just be another one of those heads on the wall."

"That's pretty severe," Tyme reached over and squeezed

Ivy's hand. "Whatever you do, don't let your guard down. Follow your instincts. If you don't love him, then for God's sake, don't marry him."

"What about you, Tyme? Are you lonely since Chauncey's been gone? Do you miss him a lot?"

Tyme snorted. "I just wish he would go the hell away."

Ivy tilted her head, confused. "What're you talking about?"

"Oh, it's nothing." Tyme shrugged dismissively and re-crossed her legs. "Forget I said anything."

"No, Tyme. I will *not* forget it." Ivy leaned forward and searched her aunt's face. "What do you mean about him not going away? He's dead, isn't he?"

"Hm." Tyme frowned and looked down, her right foot swinging nervously.

"Now you're being just like Papa." Ivy scowled at her aunt. "Don't treat me like a child. He always tries to brush me off just like that whenever he thinks I'm too delicate to know something."

Tyme raised her head, stared sadly at Ivy, and sighed. "Sometimes the dead don't leave."

Ivy felt a sudden chill and shivered. The air in the parlor felt heavy, as if it were electrically charged. The hairs stood up on the back of her neck. An odd sensation of depression washed over her. She had to fight an overpowering compulsion to jump up and run.

"Tyme, you're scaring me." Ivy looked furtively around the room. "Are you trying to tell me Chauncey is a ghost?"

"Do you believe in ghosts?"

"Well, Mama believes in ghosts, but Papa says all her stories are a bunch of claptrap." Ivy smiled sheepishly. "I've never seen one, but I'm getting really scared right now just thinking about it."

"Oh, sweetie, don't be scared. I know you're gonna think I'm crazy, but yes. That is what I meant—and he won't leave me alone. He's a lot like that Jared beau of yours." Tyme grimaced and pointed across the room. "He's standing over in that corner right now, as we speak."

Startled, Ivy stared in the direction Tyme pointed. She didn't see anything, but her heart thumped so hard she thought she would faint. She squealed and covered her face with her hands.

"Humph. He's gone now. I guess he didn't like me talking about him, so he left."

"He's gone? Are you sure?" Ivy was afraid to look up.

Tyme relaxed and puffed happily on her cigarette. "Um hm. Just feel the difference in the air. It's so much nicer around here now. He never would allow me to smoke before. I had to sneak around to do it. But now I just do whatever I want to and I don't care if he sees me or not—you can't hurt me anymore, Chauncey. To the Devil with you! Ha!"

"Are we safe here?" Ivy's heart still palpitated and she glanced warily around the room.

"Oh yeah, don't worry about it," Tyme waved her hand. "It's just Chauncey and he can't do anything to us now. Of course, I didn't know that at first. Right after he passed on it scared me pretty badly, I can tell you. I'd wake up from a deep sleep and see him standing over me in the bed, just staring. Gave me the heebie-jeebies the first few times he did that."

"Oh, my God," Ivy clutched at her throat. "Now I'm really afraid to stay here. What if he comes into my room?"

"Just ignore him, Ivy. That's all he ever does, just stands around looking sad. I finally talked to some people who know about this sort of thing and they assured me he just hasn't figured out what he's supposed to do yet. When he does, he'll move on and leave me in peace."

Ivy shivered and warily scanned the room. "You're still scaring me. Was he cruel to you?"

"Kid, you don't know the half of it." Ivy frowned and took another drag on her cigarette. "He acted all proper and *holier-*

than-thou in public, but he didn't think twice about knocking me across the room if the notion hit him. The church doors were never opened without him and I passing through 'em, but you know what's funny? I haven't been back to church since the funeral!"

"That's terrible," said Ivy. "Papa always talked about what a good and righteous man Chauncey was. Wasn't he all upset when they repealed Prohibition?"

"Oh, yes," Tyme smiled and nodded. "The ol' Volstead Act was his bread 'n' butter. I didn't know it until long after we got married, but he ran a couple of speakos here in town. He was the bootleggers' best friend. Repeal cut way down on his business."

"Aunt Tyme, I'm really frightened," Ivy felt like crying, but she certainly didn't want to go up to that hospital and stay with her mother. What was she going to do?

"Oh, it's okay, sweetie. I promise, if he bothers you I'll kick his ass right out of here—pardon my French—I used to be a Flapper and it's all comin' back to me." Tyme flicked her ashes into a Mason jar lid. "But he's not the only spirit here, you know. There's a woman and two little children downstairs in the store."

"Really?"

"Um hm. They're real sweet and don't cause any trouble. The kids'll throw stuff around a little, but the mother always picks up after 'em. You'll find it's no big deal in this town." Tyme stubbed out her cigarette and stood up. "There's something about Eureka Springs that attracts ghosts. I'm not sure why, but just about everybody in this town has *extra guests* in their homes—say, I just had an idea. Come on."

Tyme reached for Ivy's hand and pulled her down the stairs. Ivy scanned the darkened store for ghosts. Shadows in the corners played with her imagination and a dressmaker's dummy in a window display startled her. Tyme rummaged around underneath a display case and pulled out a box.

155

"Here we go. What do you think of this?" Tyme pulled an evening gown from a bed of tissue paper and shook it out to its full length.

The dress took Ivy's breath away. It was long, slinky, and sleeveless. Cut low in the front as well as in the back, it was constructed of copper-colored silk, with scalloped, shimmering fringe from bosom to toe. She'd never seen anything so beautiful.

"It's lovely." Ivy knew this humble description didn't do the dress justice.

"The color's called *parisand*—although everybody around here just calls it copper. It's the latest rage." Tyme held the dress toward Ivy. "Here—it's yours."

"Oh no, I could never accept anything like this."

"Sure you can, kiddo." Tyme smiled and her eyes lit up. "You're gonna need it, 'cause you and I are going dancing!"

CHAPTER TEN

"Hold still now— almost got it."

Ivy squinched her eyes, held her breath and tried not to move as she endured the painful process. Her fingernails dug into her palms in anticipation of the next assault. She had no idea it would hurt so badly. How did anybody ever get used to plucking one's eyebrows?

"Please don't make them look like my mother's," Ivy begged. She opened one eye and peeked at her aunt.

"Silly girl. I'm not gonna pluck 'em all." Tyme jerked one more time with the tweezers.

"Ouch!" Ivy furiously rubbed her stinging forehead and turned toward the mirror, surprised no blood ran down her face.

"See, just a nice slender arch. All I did was get rid of those wild-growing hairs. You don't look so much like a terrier anymore."

"Thanks for the compliment—I guess."

"You're welcome." Tyme smiled and placed a Princess Pat cosmetics kit on the dresser. "Okay, you're going to need lipstick, powder, rouge, mascara...."

"Oh, I've never worn mascara before—or rouge. Papa always said it makes a woman look fast."

"Well, we're gonna be doin' some fast dancing tonight, so you need it." Tyme handed the mascara to Ivy. "I'll show you how to do the eye shadow and liner, too."

When Ivy looked in the mirror, she was amazed at the transformation in herself as well as in her aunt. For the first time in her life she felt all grown up and beautiful. And Tyme was a complete knockout, with the carefully applied makeup and her newly bleached platinum blond Marcel waves.

"Nobody's gonna recognize the Widder Renfro," said Ivy. "They'll just think a movie star has come to town."

"Um hm, and with her young protégé starlet by her side. All right, we're gonna try you with an up-do, since you've got that beautiful shoulder-length hair." Tyme worked skillfully and soon Ivy's red-brown hair was swept up in an exotic twist, crowned with a little mass of ringlets.

The dress fit perfectly after only a few minor alterations. Ivy laughed as she twisted from side to side before the mirror. The gleaming fringe shook and shimmied with every move. Her eyes lit up when Tyme showed her the strappy high-heeled shoes and the long, satin gloves that would complete the elegant ensemble.

"One more thing." Tyme pinned in place a tiny feathered doll's hat with a short net veil that brushed Ivy's forehead, yet showcased her curls. "Now I'm going to get dressed."

Ivy squealed with delight when Tyme emerged from behind the dressing screen. The bias-cut satin gown clung to her curves, rippling in shiny black waves with every move she made. She pulled on her evening gloves, stuck one slender, silk-clad leg through the daring slit in the skirt and struck a pose.

"Whadda ya think?"

"May I have your autograph, Miss Harlow?"

Tyme's face crumpled slightly. "Poor thing. I can't believe it's already been a year since she died. She was my favorite."

"Mine too. So sad."

"Well, are you ready to go have some fun?" asked Tyme.

"I think so." Ivy's heart fluttered nervously. "Where did you say we were going?"

"The Independence Day Ball. They always hold it on the Saturday night before July fourth," replied Tyme. She adjusted her bosoms in the halter-top of the daringly backless evening gown and turned sideways to look in the mirror. "I've wanted to go for years, but Chauncey never would take me. He was more of a Blue Grass and jug band type of guy."

"Is he still hanging around?" Ivy glanced around the room. There hadn't been any more signs of Chauncey's ghost since last evening. She'd decided not to be scared of him unless he gave her a reason.

"Oh, I'm sure he's around here someplace watching from the wings. But I intend to ignore him until he just gives up completely and goes wherever it is he's supposed to go—and I seriously doubt that it'll be up."

Ivy giggled and searched through her jewelry box. She pulled out a pearl choker, and held it up to her neck. "How's this?"

"Perfect. Turn around. I'll help you fasten it."

"Why on earth did you marry him?"

Tyme appeared sad before she answered. "Oh, Ivy. It was a different world back then." She sighed, sat down at the dressing table and picked up a powder puff. "You just can't imagine what it was like."

"Please tell me."

Tyme smiled. "I hope Chauncey doesn't start throwing things."

"Me too." Ivy shuddered and glanced around the room. "I thought you said all he did was stand around?"

"Well, one time soon after I first started seeing him, I was sitting here smoking. I think he got mad at me 'cause I was using his favorite shaving mug for an ashtray. It just went sliding off the table all by itself. Boy, was I startled!"

"Oh, my goodness. I would just die if he did something like that now."

Tyme waved her hand in dismissal. "Nah. He has to use up a lot of energy to move things. Stuff like that wears 'em out. I didn't hear a peep out of him for a couple of weeks after that. It was a really nice respite."

"Okay," said Ivy. She tried to ignore her quickened pulse. "Now tell me your story."

Tyme relaxed and appeared thoughtful before she began. "I came of age in the twenties, and people were pretty free-wheeling in those days. Ya know what I mean?"

Ivy nodded. "I was small, but I remember. Papa always called it the *decade of debauchery.*"

"Well, he wasn't too far off." Tyme powdered her nose and then pulled out a cigarette. "You know, I'm not that much older than you—only nine years. But compared to our experiences, it might as well be a hundred."

"I know. Papa has been very protective."

"Yes, and he's right to be—up to a point." Tyme lit her cigarette and took a long drag. "I'm just afraid he's repeating the same mistakes with you that he did with me."

"What's Papa got to do with you? He's your brother, not your father."

"Let me tell you the whole story. Then you'll understand." Tyme looked pensive before she continued. "As I said before, everything was very different when I was your age. We thought we had the world by the tail. Daddy was rich then, and getting richer every day."

"I thought Grandfather stayed solvent after the market crashed?"

"Oh, he did. Daddy was very conservative and he didn't have everything tied up in the stock market. He didn't go in for the get-rich-quick schemes and lose his shirt like Caleb."

"*My* father?"

"Um hm," Tyme nodded and took another puff. "Daddy had to bail him out of debt more than once. And me—I just went completely wild before the bottom dropped out of everything. I think that's what killed your grandfather so young—his children

160

broke his heart." Her voice cracked.

"Tyme, you don't have to tell me if you don't want to."

"No." Tyme held up her hand. "I need to tell someone. It's been eating at me for years."

"Okay." Ivy settled into a chair.

"Like I said before, I went totally wild. I was a real *Jazz Baby*. Dropped out of school, started drinking and smoking, and spent my time at parties just about every night. I lived to party. Nobody could tell me what to do."

"What did Papa and Grandfather do?"

"Oh, they tried their best to get me to behave. Your father was so much older than me; he thought he could control me. But he couldn't." Tyme's eyes teared and she tapped out her ashes. "Nobody could—until Walter."

"Walter?" Ivy felt a slight chill in the air and shivered.

"Um hm. Walter Montgomery. I fell hard for him." Tyme wiped away a stray tear. "He was from old money back East. Your grandfather and Caleb thought he was the answer to their prayers."

"He wasn't?"

"He might have been under different circumstances." Tyme sniffed and looked in the mirror. "Oh, damn. My mascara's running."

"You can't leave me hanging now," begged Ivy. "Please finish the story."

"Sorry about that, kid." Tyme dabbed at the black streaks on her cheek and continued her story. "He was so sweet and good looking and I loved him dearly. He had this beautiful Stutz Bearcat we used to rip around in. God, we had fun."

"Did you break up with him?"

"No. Actually, we were engaged to be married." Tyme's hand shook and she stared into the distance. "Your father and grandfather were ecstatic. Everybody started planning the wedding."

"What happened?"

"Apparently, his father had laid down the law to him to be frugal. But frugal wasn't our style." Tyme noticed the ashes growing long and flicked them out. "Walter didn't tell me that his wild ways had just about ruined his father, even before the market crash. He gambled a lot, and played the stock market on margin. He just wasn't prepared for the consequences, since there was nowhere for him to land."

"You don't mean..."

Tyme nodded solemnly. "I'll never forget...it was a cold November day in 1929....his best friend found him...gunshot wound to the head...the official death certificate called it an accident, but I know better...he was so despondent...I know he took his own life."

"Oh, Tyme. I'm so sorry."

"That's not all of it." Tyme wiped away another tear. "Soon after Walter's funeral I discovered I was *in the family way*."

"No!"

"Yep. Well, you can just imagine the reaction." Tyme grimaced. "Daddy kinda wilted and Caleb went berserk."

"So he set you up with Chauncey?"

"You got it. He found someone in a remote area with the right financial ties that would be willing to take on a soiled bride. So I married him." Tyme shrugged. "What other choice did I have?"

"What about the baby?" asked Ivy. The air felt heavy and she thought she detected a slight vibration from the cosmetics scattered across the dresser. A tube of lipstick rolled across the surface of the dresser.

"Oh, it only took a few of Chauncey's beatings before that was all history." Tyme hung her head.

"You poor, poor thing. Thank goodness you didn't have any children with that monster." Ivy embraced her aunt and shivered. The room grew increasingly chilly.

162

"Humph. There wasn't much chance of that. I think that's why he was so mean. He couldn't be a man when it really counted."

The room temperature plummeted and Tyme's powder jar suddenly went flying across the room. It banged against a chair and scattered its contents on the Oriental rug. Both women jumped in fright, but Tyme recovered quickly. An expression of amusement spread across her face.

Horrified, Ivy searched the room, preparing to run. "Oh, my God! What was that? Was that Chauncey?"

Tyme laughed and slapped her knee. "He's having a tantrum because he doesn't like to hear the truth. You shouldn't have given him the idea."

"Tyme, I'm really scared now," said Ivy, her eyes wild with fright. "Maybe he *can* hurt us."

"No, kiddo, no. Don't let him get the best of you. That's what he wants us to think." Tyme patted Ivy on the shoulder. "He's probably used up so much energy with that stunt we won't hear from him again for a month."

"Are you sure?

"I'm sure." Tyme reached for her car keys and stood up. "Come on. Let's go. We can clean up later. I'm tired of this mausoleum."

Harry Fuller fidgeted with the stiff starched collar of his shirt and tried not to think about how much the new clothes had set him back. For the first time in his life he had money in his pocket that wasn't already earmarked for the care and feeding of some other family member. This new, carefree lifestyle would take some getting used to.

He followed his friend Clyde up the front steps of the building, reached up, and carefully removed his new straw hat. The crisp, clean brim felt strange to his calloused fingers. He smoothed the sleeves of his suit jacket and looked down to make sure the cuffs of his pants were straight. A tingling sense of excitement coursed through his body. What did he expect to find here tonight?

Clyde McKinney's eyes lit up at the sights and sounds of the dance. He practically bounced with enthusiasm. "Come on, Harry. Let's get in there before all the best dames'r taken."

Harry laughed and followed his buddy into the gymnasium. He stood and stared. He'd never been to a party like this. Tiny white lights strung from the rafters transformed the drafty old room into a warm, glowing fairyland and tables covered with white linen encircled the perimeter. A thick cloud of smoke hung in the air and red glowing embers from dozens of cigarettes lit up the room. People were everywhere, dancing and drinking and clapping for the band on the stage.

Three guys on trumpet and another on trombone set the place afire with their jazzy swing style, then stepped aside and waited while a little man with a huge smile twirled and strummed an upright base in a tempo so seductive, even Harry felt like dancing. The music's beat grabbed him, exhilarated him, and temporarily banished his anxieties.

"There's one over there." Harry pointed to a table in the farthest corner.

"Nah." Clyde shook his head and made for a table near the door. "Ya cain't see the dolls from way over there. Let's take this one."

Harry and Clyde staked their claim at the table and glanced around. The music changed to a slow, dreamy rhythm and couples crowded the dance floor, vying for a place beneath one of the spotlights. A thin man with a bow tie and slick-backed hair stepped up to the microphone and began crooning *I'm in the Mood for Love.*

"What'll ya have, fellas?" A pretty blonde waitress wearing a frilly apron over her uniform appeared. She put her hand on her hip, chewed her gum and held her pad and pencil while she waited for their order.

"We'll both have a beer," Clyde volunteered. "We're celebratin'."

"Oh, yeah?" She smiled, put her pencil behind her ear, and switched her hand to the other hip. "Whatcha celebratin?"

"My friend here just got hisself a big promotion," said Clyde.

"Issat right?" She smiled seductively at Harry through lowered lashes. "What line a work are ya in?"

"Um, CCC, ma'am."

"Yes'm, Harry just got promoted to full-fledged leader," Clyde announced proudly.

The waitress looked disappointed. "Well, congratulations. I'll bring your beers."

"See how easy it is?" Clyde ran his big, work-roughened hand through his curly mop of hair and then rolled a cigarette. "She likes you."

"She does not." Harry tugged at his collar, wishing he could get rid of the blasted tie that choked him. "As soon as she heard me say CCC she turned into an icicle."

"Well, you ain't got nothin' to be ashamed about. Me and my ma woulda starved if'n Mr. Roosevelt hadn'ta done something. Gets mighty old livin' in them Hoovervilles and bein' a hobo." Clyde bristled when he realized what Harry meant. "She's just a gold-digger out to find her some rich guy. We don't need some floozy like her who don't appreciate the Civilian Conservation Corp."

The waitress returned with two bottles of Schlitz. "It's on me." Harry laid down a quarter. "Keep the change." The waitress sniffed, scooped up the coin, and walked away, her hips swinging.

"Stuck up," Clyde commented as he watched her leave. "But ya gotta admit—she's got a cute little…"

"Welcome ladies and gentlemen," the bandleader boomed

into the microphone. "Is everything copacetic tonight?" The crowd cheered. "All right, everybody needs to dust off their ol' dancin' shoes, 'cause we've got a lollapalooza of a show comin' up. At twelve midnight we're gonna award this year's trophy and a twenty-five dollar prize to the couple with the meanest Lindy Hop." Another roar spread through the hall. "So let's all make whoopee! Please give it up for Jim—Jam—and the Jammers!"

Clyde scanned the room. "I gotta find the right gal." He took a swig of his beer with one hand and puffed his cigarette with the other. "I wanta win that prize."

"You're that good of a dancer?"

"Well, I'm kinda out of practice, but I know it'll all come back to me." Clyde's blue eyes lit up and he flashed a toothy grin. "My ma wuz a dancer on the Vaudeville stage. I grew up in show biz."

"Really?"

"Um hm." Clyde took another sip and then hung his head. "Never did know who my pa was. But Ma done real good fer a while. Taught me how to tap and everything. Made me a part of the act." He gazed sadly across the dance floor. "Then the shows just kinda dried up and she had to move over into burlesque. She had to dance the cootch just to put food in our mouths."

"Sorry, Clyde." Harry felt suddenly sad, thinking about his own parents who had both passed on. "Is she still alive?"

"Yeah. She just kinda snapped when the hard times got so bad. She's in a state-run nuthouse down in Texas. That's where all my government money goes, so she'll get a little bit better treatment."

Harry sighed, took a swig of beer, and looked up into the eyes of an angel. A gleaming, golden, heavenly vision—or at the very least, the most beautiful woman he had ever seen. Her eyes were green—emerald green—like he'd always imagined the Irish moors to be. Fresh and shining and brilliant. And her face—exquisitely perfect like the face of the china doll once owned by his long-lost little sister.

She stood next to another ravishing beauty—a tall, leggy blonde in black satin that could almost make a man weep from the pain of just looking. He could see by Clyde's expression that she affected him in just that way. None of the other girls in the room came even close to this pair's glamour, and Harry could only surmise they must have taken a wrong turn on their way to Hollywood.

The two breathtaking sirens sat down at a table not far from Harry and Clyde. He sipped his beer and tried to look away, wishing he couldn't see the copper fringe on her dress, or smell her perfume, or hear her tinkling laughter. What was the use? If a two-bit waitress wasn't interested, why would a goddess care about him?

A mad scramble of men suddenly lined up at the ladies' table. Clyde chugged the last of his beer, squared his shoulders, and rose. "I'm gonna dance with the blonde. Come on. You can dance with the other one."

Harry tugged on Clyde's jacket sleeve. "Ah, come on. They ain't gonna dance with the likes of us."

Clyde glanced around the room. "Last I seen, this was No-where's-ville, Arkansas. Don't see no Bing Crosbys or Fred Astaires or Clark Gables. There ain't nothin' here but hillbillies anyhow. If'n they wanted high class, I figure they'd go on up to St. Louie."

Harry grinned and waved his hand in dismissal. "Go on, then. I wish you luck."

He leaned back, sipped his beer and watched his friend join the throng of other men waiting to dance with the two women. He told himself he didn't care and he almost believed it.

Moments later Clyde bounded back to the table, success painted all over his face. "I'm number five." He was almost out of breath with excitement. " I told her I could do a real good jitterbug and she said okay."

"Swell," said Harry. He averted his eyes when he saw the golden angel glide by in the arms of another man.

"Aint'cha gonna dance at all?" asked Clyde.

"Nah. I'm not much of a dancer. I just enjoy listening to the music."

Clyde shrugged, then his eyes lit up when the band struck up *Flat Foot Floogey With the Floy Floy*. He saw a young lady sitting alone at a table, tapping her feet to the music and he jumped up and headed straight toward her. "I just *gotta* dance this one."

Harry leaned back and watched his friend lead the girl out onto the dance floor. Gee whiz, but he was good! He never would have guessed that Clyde, usually so awkward when it came to his work, could dance so skillfully. His movements were loose and fluid, evoking a sense of joy and abandon.

He sneaked a peek at the green-eyed angel. She sat alone at the table, but men periodically approached her. She always shook her head when the tempo was fast, he noticed. Her friend seemed to dance just about every number, but the angel only danced the slow songs.

Just like me, he thought. Jitterbugs and Lindy Hops were something he'd never learned to do. He wished he had the nerve to ask her to dance with him. What would it be like to slide his arm about her slender waist, feel the softness of her hands in his, smell the fragrance of her hair, and gaze into those lovely green eyes at close range?

Her beautiful blonde friend danced by and he noticed her watching Clyde with an approving smile. He leaned back and tried to relax, but he bumped his elbow on the cluttered table. He wished the waitress would bring some fresh beer and take away these dead soldiers.

When the song ended, Clyde plopped down into his chair. He grinned happily, breathing hard from the exertion. He saw the waitress walk by and motioned with his hand. "Hey, Jane! We need another round."

"You gonna sit this one out?" asked Harry. He tried to ignore the sight of his angel being led onto the dance floor by a half-drunken man with a paunch the size of Rhode Island.

"Yep. Gotta catch my breath. Next set's me'n the blonde. I'm hopin' she'll dance the contest with me." Clyde gave the waitress some money when she brought the beers. He pursed his lips suggestively and said, "Cash or check?"

"Sorry, mac. Bank's closed." She tossed her head and wiggled away.

"I'll be right back. Gotta go iron my shoelaces." Clyde jumped up and headed for the privy.

Harry picked up his beer bottle, but put it back down in surprise. The beautiful blonde siren stood staring at him. He nervously got up and glanced around to make sure her attention was on him and not someone else in the room. "H-hello."

"Hi, there." Her voice sounded sweet, like spun sugar. "Where's your friend?"

"Oh, uh. He'll be back in a minute." Harry pulled out a chair. "Would you like to sit down?"

"Thanks." She sat in the chair he offered and then signaled to Harry's angel, who was wandering around, seemingly lost. "Some Dumb Dora stole our table."

"W-Well, you're more than welcome to sit here," Harry stammered. He remained standing until the angel appeared. She smiled brilliantly when he helped her with her chair. Her nearness almost took his breath away.

"My name's Tyme and this is Ivy."

Her name is Ivy. Such a beautiful name. His mother always liked ivies. They were sweet and easy to care for and they'd grow tall, and clinging, and green, like her eyes. He imagined those beautiful arms of hers clinging to him.

Tyme looked questioningly at Harry and then pulled out a

cigarette. "You got a light?"

Embarrassed, Harry returned to earth and fumbled in his pockets. He usually kept a book of matches for just such an occasion, but he'd failed to put any into his new suit. "Sorry, I'm not a smoker."

Suddenly Clyde appeared, camel-decorated Zippo in hand. With a flick of the wrist he had the tiny flame burning. He held it out to Tyme like a knight in shining armor come to her rescue. "Here ya go, gorgeous."

"Ah, my hero." Tyme smiled and inhaled the cigarette.

"Uh, the ladies were just introducing themselves," said Harry. "Clyde, this is Tyme and Ivy. My name's Harry."

"Glad to make your acquaintance, Harry. Clyde and I have already met," said Tyme, and then turned to Clyde. "I saw you out there a while ago. You can really cut a rug."

"Well, doll. You ain't exactly no heeler yourself."

Tyme took a puff and smiled seductively at Clyde. "So, ya wanna be my gigolo for the contest?"

"Oh, baby. I thought you'd never ask." The band struck up another fast one. Clyde stood up and held out his hand to Tyme. "Come on. Let's go get warmed up."

Painful shyness overcame Harry when he found himself alone with Ivy. The starch in his collar seemed to tighten around his neck like a noose, but he forced himself to keep his hands away from it. He racked his brain for something to talk about and finally came up with something.

"Would you like something to drink? A beer maybe?"

"I'd like a 7-Up." Her voice sounded like honey.

Harry signaled the waitress. "Two 7-Up's, please."

The waitress stared disdainfully at Harry and Ivy, popped her gum, and headed for the kitchen.

"Will you just look at them?" Ivy pointed to Tyme and Clyde on the dance floor. "They look like they've been dancing together all their lives."

"Yeah, Clyde really loves to dance," said Harry. "He was hoping to win the contest tonight."

"Looks like they've got a good chance." Ivy took the 7-Up from the waitress and sipped it with a straw. "Thank you."

"Here you go." Harry handed the waitress two quarters this time. She grinned and winked, then sashayed off. He worked up his courage. "So, do you live around here?"

"Me? No, I'm from St. Louis," replied Ivy. "I'm just staying with my Aunt Tyme for the summer. And you?"

"Oh, I'm stationed out at the CCC camp. We're working on the new dam." Harry hoped his revelation didn't completely doom any chance he had with Ivy. He decided to embellish a little. "I just got promoted to work leader, but I'm studying to be a civil engineer."

"Really? That's fascinating." Ivy's green eyes shone like jewels beneath the dance lights. "Engineers have to be really, really smart."

Harry felt like a fraud and he tried to redeem himself. "Well, I'm not exactly in the engineering program yet. But I want to be. I'm planning on applying next week."

After the words were out of his mouth, he decided it was a good idea. He smiled and his confidence grew. He looked at her lips. They were full and ripe, like cherries. He wondered what it would be like to kiss them.

"Are you a good dancer like your friend?"

"Me? Oh, no. I've got two left feet." He made a face and kicked out a foot at an odd angle.

Ivy giggled. "Me too. I can do the slow ones, but I get completely lost with the Lindy Hop or the St. Louis Shag."

The half-drunken fat man Ivy had danced with earlier approached their table. He had now apparently had enough drinks since their last dance to qualify for totally drunk. "Say, baby. I've been lookin' for ya. They're about to start the dance contest." He grabbed Ivy by the wrist. "Come on."

"No," Ivy struggled and jerked her arm away. "I don't want to dance right now."

"Come *on*, baby." The man argued and staggered slightly. "Don'tcha wanta win the trophy?"

"Look, mister." Harry stepped between Ivy and the man. "The lady said no."

"Who da ya think you are, you little pipsqueak?" The big man bristled and raised his hands into fists. "You wanta fight me for her?"

Ivy looked as if she was going to cry. Harry glanced toward the dance floor. Clyde and Tyme danced furiously, oblivious to the drama that was taking place at the table. He looked again at the drunken man and made his decision.

"Come on, Ivy." He grabbed his hat, placed her wrap around her shoulders, and helped her to her feet. "Let's go outside and get some fresh air."

The man followed them, swaying and bumping into other people as he went. Ivy and Harry continued walking quickly. He put his arm around her protectively as they headed for the door. All he could think about was getting her safely out of there.

"Hey, buddy! Watch where yer goin'." A big, burly man dressed in overalls yelled angrily when his beer spilled down the front of his bib.

"Ah, shaddup," said the drunk, and then he yelled at Harry. "Get back in here with that broad."

Harry's anger got the better of him. He stopped, turned around, and stared at the man, then motioned for Ivy to go around behind him. Ivy appeared worried, but did as she was instructed. The party inside continued on, but a small group of people within sight of the altercation began gathering to watch the spectacle.

"Please go back inside and leave the lady alone." Harry spoke slowly, yet firmly. His hands formed angry fists and he felt his temperature rise. Ivy shrank back in terror. He fought to remain calm.

"Why, you liddle…" The man suddenly ran at Harry, his big beefy arms swinging wildly.

Harry ducked and caught him on the chin in an uppercut. Blood gushed from the man's mouth and he hit the ground, bellowing in pain and anger, like an injured bull. Harry winced at the pain in his knuckles, put his arm around Ivy, and stepped over the fallen giant. They walked through the door and welcomed the fresh night air.

"Oh, my God, Harry," Ivy shivered and Harry pulled her closer. "I was so scared."

"Me, too." Harry led Ivy to a bench near the front of the auditorium. The silvery light of the crescent moon helped to calm his jangled nerves and he breathed deeply of the smoke-free air.

"Gee, Harry. I've never had a fellow fight over me before."

"I've never fought over a girl before, either," Harry replied. He looked at Ivy and saw that her hat was askew. He reached up to straighten it and winced at the pain in his hand.

"Ohhh," Ivy pulled his hand toward her face and looked closer. She brought it to her lips and kissed it. "Your knuckles are beginning to swell."

"It'll be all better now," said Harry, just before he felt a sharp pain in his head. The last thing he remembered were the stars before his eyes and the sound of a woman's scream.

CHAPTER ELEVEN

Harry moaned, blinked, and attempted to focus his eyes. He licked his lips and tasted grit. Gravel scraped his cheeks and the dank odor of grass, dust, and alcohol irritated his nose. Face down on the ground, he tried to rise, but he was too weak and dazed.

Voices surrounded him, talking and shouting and sobbing. He saw dozens of legs and feet from a crowd of onlookers. Probing hands pressed down on him. Too close. He couldn't breathe. Mustering all his strength, he gasped for air, rolled over and sat up.

Intense pain set Harry's head to throbbing. He couldn't remember ever having such a terrible headache. He reached up and touched the back of his head. His hand came back wet and sticky. His nostrils twitched. Something—or someone nearby, reeked of whiskey.

"Son, are you all right?"

Harry gazed in bewilderment at the two identical men who knelt before him. His eyes fluttered, and his fuzzy vision focused. Now there was only one.

"Name's Doc Pruett. Can you tell me yours?" asked the gray-haired man.

Harry hesitated and then replied, "Harry Fuller."

"That's good, son. Okay if I take a look at your head? I'm a doctor."

Harry nodded and then winced in pain. Dr. Pruett placed his hand on Harry's head, carefully parted the saturated hair on the back of his head, and examined the wound. "Do you know what day this is?"

"Ouch!" Harry responded when the doctor touched a tender area. It stung like fire. "Uh, I think it's Saturday. No, wait. It might be Sunday by now."

The doctor's eyebrows rose and he bent down to look into Harry's eyes. "Can you tell me who's the President of the United States?"

Harry didn't hesitate. "Franklin Delano Roosevelt, sir." His head throbbed harder, but he tried not to let on. "He's a mighty fine man."

Laughter rippled throughout the crowd. Harry felt his face flush when he realized he was the center of attention.

"That's good, Harry. Can you stand up now?" Dr. Pruett stood first and held out his hand.

Harry accepted the assistance and rose. His knees wobbled, but the rush of cool night air filled his lungs and he grew stronger. He stood very still for a moment, making sure he had completely regained his balance.

"He'll be all right," the doctor announced and then patted Harry on the shoulder "It's just a bump and a little scalp wound. He won't need any stitches."

The momentary hush from the crowd ended. People began to talk and laugh and go about their business when they realized the crisis was over. Harry glanced around, wondering what had happened and why the smell of alcohol was still so strong.

"Harry, are you okay?"

His beautiful angel—Ivy—stood next to him. Her hairdo had come loose and half of her curls hung down to her shoulders. The front of her dress appeared to be soaked. She reached to embrace him and the stench of whiskey grew stronger.

Puzzled, Harry returned her embrace, as Clyde and Tyme approached. He glanced around and saw the big man who had bothered Ivy lying prone, being carried away on a stretcher and placed into the bed of a truck. Had he hit the guy that hard?

"What happened?" asked Harry.

"Oh, that big palooka got all soused," explained Clyde as he pointed beyond Harry. "And then you knocked him down, and he got real mad, so he came at you with a bottle of panther sweat. Then he hit you on your noggin."

Tyme held her nose and pointed to Ivy's dress and Harry's jacket. "You both smell like a distillery."

"But how?"

"Me and Tyme came out here when some people inside heard Ivy scream. They'd just awarded us the dance prize when everybody noticed all the commotion. We heard yellin' about a fight outside, and when we couldn't find the two of you we got worried." Clyde's eyes glittered as he related the story. "So we went outside and saw you layin' on the ground and poor Ivy, all soaked with whiskey and cryin' her eyes out. The big guy was standing there hollerin' and waving a broken booze bottle around. So I just politely returned the favor with this." Clyde held up the trophy, which was bent at an odd angle.

"You didn't kill him, did you?" asked Harry. He held onto Ivy and he didn't want to let her go.

"Nah. Doc said he just needs to sleep it off. He'll have a big headache in the morning, same as you." Clyde looked at the trophy, shook his head and said to Tyme. "Bet this woulda looked purty good on your mantle."

Tyme reached for the trophy. "It'll still look good. These dents just give it character." She smiled seductively up at Clyde. "It'll be a great reminder of how we first met."

A heavy-set man wearing a khaki uniform and a sheriff's deputy badge sauntered toward them. He scowled at Harry and Clyde and crossed his arms. "Heard you boys been stirrin' up some trouble here tonight."

Tyme's eyes flashed and her voice was filled with contempt. "You're more stupid than you look, Earl."

The deputy glanced disdainfully at Tyme and hitched up his britches. "Well, you're lookin' mighty dressed up fer a newly-widdered woman, Miz Renfro." He sniffed and spat a wad of tobacco onto the ground. "Ain't seen ya up at the church lately. Pore ol' Chauncey'd be rollin' in his grave if he knowed how you've been behavin'."

"Look, you wack," Tyme bristled. "I'm sick of guys like you who think just because I'm alone now I'm lookin' for some kinda lover-boy and you feel obligated to come sniffin' around. I suggest you keep your observations to yourself and stay out of my store, especially after closing time."

Earl glared at Tyme, shrugged, and turned to Harry and Clyde. "I think you two boys need to head on back to your camp now. Ya don't need ta be comin' into town, drinking and tearin' up stuff no more."

Protests rose up from the crowd. "They didn't start it."

Another person spoke up. "Yeah, it was that Dr. Ballew guy."

"I saw him take a swing at the young fella," A woman shouted.

"Me too, then he followed him and the girl outside and cracked him over the head with the whiskey bottle." Another man joined in.

Dr. Pruett raised his chin defiantly. "You'd better be careful about who you go accusing, Earl."

The deputy frowned and his shoulders twitched, forced to back down under the onslaught of protesting witnesses. "All right. I won't run either of ya in this time, but you'd both better skedaddle outta here right now." He spat on the ground again, swaggered off, climbed into a patrol car, and drove away.

"What a horrible man!" remarked Ivy. "Why did that deputy blame Harry and Clyde?"

Harry pulled Ivy closer, not caring about the pain in his head or the rude sheriff's deputy.

"Because the person my dear Clyde cold-cocked is one of those so-called *doctors* up the hill at that Baker Cancer Hospital." Tyme sniffed with disdain. "Baker's got all the law enforcement in this town right in his pocket, you know."

Ivy shuddered. "How could somebody like *him* be a doctor?"

"He probably bought his degree from a mail-order diploma mill," replied Dr. Pruett. "I shudder to think about what goes on up there."

"But my mother is up there right now being treated for cancer!"

"Don't worry, Ivy," Tyme soothed. "Your mother's all right. She doesn't really have anything wrong with her. It's like she's on vacation. She's having the time of her life."

"What?" Ivy stared at Tyme. "But she's always complaining about some sort of aches and pains. And I heard Dr. Baker himself say she had cancer, but that he was in the process of curing it."

"That's the way Baker works, miss." Dr. Pruett sighed. "He'll tell anybody they've got cancer, if that's what they want to hear. People like your mother, who aren't really sick at all, come here, spend a lot of money, and then go home *cured*. It's the ones who are really sick that make me sad, because they either miss out on real treatment or they spend their life savings on false promises."

Harry interrupted Dr. Pruett. "So why doesn't somebody do something about it? If what you say is true, why doesn't someone put a stop to it?"

"What I just told you is practically blasphemy in this town," replied Dr. Pruett. "If I tried too hard to rock the boat, they'd run me out of town and then there wouldn't be anybody to take care of the folks who really need doctorin'."

"Did ya'll hear the racket Baker was making last night?" asked Tyme. "He's always going up on the roof of his hospital and playing that thing he calls a *calliophone*. You can hear it shrieking all over town."

"Is that what that music was? I thought the circus was coming to town," said Ivy.

Clyde shook his head. "So what do we do now, Harry? Sarge isn't supposed to pick us up to take us back to camp 'til Monday night. We don't want the deputy harassing us all weekend."

"I tell ya what, boys. You stayin' at Miss Effie's boarding house?" Dr. Pruett asked and the two young men nodded. "I'll drop you off there tonight, then you can come out to my place and help me with some fishing tomorrow afternoon. I got a stock tank the size of a small lake that's just brimmin' with bass. Cain't catch 'em fast enough by myself. Then Monday evening we'll come back downtown for the big Fourth of July party." He turned to Ivy and Tyme. "You young ladies comin' to the social?"

Tyme looked at Ivy, smiled, and replied, "You couldn't keep us away if you tried."

Ivy practically floated up the stairs and into her bedroom. She'd never met anyone like Harry, never felt the way she did tonight. Her heart pounded when he looked at her. And the way her skin tingled at his touch was pure magic, unlike the emptiness in the pit of her stomach when she waved goodbye.

What was it about this man she knew practically nothing about? He wasn't movie star handsome like Jared. No, he was very different. His face was young and boyish, with unruly strands of brown hair that tumbled down across his forehead. His nose was just the slightest bit crooked, and he had a little scar on his left cheek. He was tall, thin, and tanned from years of hard physical labor in blistering heat. But his sky blue eyes reflected a gentleness and she knew that he was the one her soul had been searching for.

Ivy wondered if Harry felt the same way about her. She thought he did. There had been an undeniable connection between them. She'd noticed it right away. The feeling had been tentative at first, gradual. But the way he'd come to her rescue and defended her against that awful man had accelerated the process and cemented the bond. There was no doubt in her mind that Harry was the man of her dreams.

The grandfather clock in the hall bonged twice. Two in the morning. She needed to get to bed and get some sleep, but her mind was so worked up from everything that had happened, she knew it wouldn't be easy to settle down.

She ticked off in her mind everything she had to do for the next two days. Sleep late, and then attend evening mass with her mother at St. Elizabeth's. Monday was a holiday, so the store would be closed. Maybe she'd help Tyme by doing a little cleaning in the store. Anything to keep her busy and her mind occupied until she saw Harry again. How would she ever manage it?

Her thoughts swirled madly as she turned the knob on her bedroom door. Then she stopped. Was that music? The soft, tinny, tinkling of *Tea for Two* grew louder as she pushed the door open.

Ivy gasped when she saw her. Sitting on the edge of her bed, playing with her musical powder box, was a little girl. She appeared to be about seven or eight years old and she was wearing a long, old-fashioned dress with a white pinafore. The girl glanced up in shocked surprise and then disappeared.

"Tyme!" Ivy screamed and ran out into the hall. Her heart pounded and she sobbed in terror.

"What's the matter?" Tyme came running.

"I saw a ghost—in there!" Ivy shook as she pointed toward her bedroom.

"Was it Chauncey?"

"No, it was a little girl. She was playing with my music box."

"Really?" Tyme's eyes lit up and she smiled. "I've never

known them to venture upstairs before."

Ivy paced the floor. "Don't smile Tyme, it's not funny. I'm not sure I can deal with this. I don't think I'm cut out to coexist with ghosts." She shivered and glanced around the darkened hallway. The ticking clock seemed to intensify her fears.

"Honey, I wish I knew what to say to make you feel better, but I don't. Do you want to go home?" Tyme gently patted Ivy's back.

Ivy thought about her home. Papa was probably still in Joplin, so she'd be alone there. Even though she'd never seen or heard a ghost in her home in St. Louis, she didn't want to be by herself in that rambling old house. And Harry was here in Eureka Springs. If she left now, she might never see him again.

"No, I don't want to go home. I'll be okay." Her mind made up, she hugged Tyme. "I'm sorry I've been such a baby. We both need to get some sleep. Good night."

"Well, good night," replied Tyme. "Let me know if you need anything else."

Ivy returned to her room and began preparing for bed. She looked sadly at her beautiful evening gown, afraid no amount of cleaning would ever remove the whiskey smell. Tyme ought to send Dr. Ballew a bill to replace it, Ivy thought. After all, it was his fault for getting drunk, attacking Harry, and splattering her dress in the aftermath.

She sat on the edge of the bed and looked at the pewter music box. The delicate Limoges top displayed a miniature picture of a woman and a little girl dressed in Victorian costume. It really was a pretty little trinket. The picture must have reminded the ghost girl of something from her past.

When Ivy thought about the little spirit that way, she was no longer frightened. What could have happened to snatch her and her family away from life at such a young age? She felt sad at the thought and then ashamed at her previous fright. After all, the ghosts in this house had once been living people, with hopes and ambitions, feelings and pain. Even Chauncey—but she didn't want to think about him.

Maybe she should give the music box to the little spirit girl as a gift? The idea warmed her heart and she picked it up, preparing to take it downstairs. But hadn't Tyme said there were two children? She didn't want to leave the other one out.

She rummaged through her dresser drawer and found a little tin whistle she'd discovered in a box of Cracker Jacks the day before. That's good. She didn't know if the other child was a boy or a girl, but she figured either one would enjoy such a gift. She gathered up both items and headed down the stairs.

Ivy scanned the darkened store, no longer afraid of what she might encounter. Now where should she put them? She looked around and found a rocking chair in a back corner. Surely the children would find them there. She left the presents, returned to her room, and fell into a deep, peaceful sleep.

"Tyme, how long did it take after you met Walter before you knew you were in love?" Ivy pulled an apple pie out of the kitchen window where it had been cooling and set it on the table.

"Oh, I knew right away. It was love at first sight, as they say." Tyme smiled and looked at the pie. "That crust came out really nice."

Ivy grinned back at her aunt. "So, do you like Clyde?"

"Yes, I do. I like him a lot."

"Does he remind you of Walter?"

"Oh, heavens no," Tyme exclaimed and bent down to check the wood in the stove. "They're about as different as night and day."

Ivy looked puzzled. "I don't understand. How can you be in love with two people who are so different?"

"Now, let's not get ahead of ourselves. I never said anything about being in love with Clyde. I just said I like him. He makes me laugh and he's fun to be with—and boy can he dance!" Tyme closed her eyes and exhaled. "Don't get me wrong. I'm not ruling anything out at this point. It's quite possible I could learn to love him."

"I'm still confused. I thought you just told me you fell in love with Walter right away." Ivy wrinkled her brow and folded her arms. "Why is this different?"

"Oh, honey. Every relationship is different." Tyme put her hand on Ivy's shoulder and looked into her face. "Sometimes love just comes out of nowhere and hits you up the side of the head. Sometimes it tiptoes in softly, sneaks up on you from behind, and just makes itself at home until you finally notice it and realize it's there. There are as many ways to fall in love as there are hours in the day."

Ivy gazed thoughtfully out the window. "Well, I think I got walloped the first way you said." She giggled and rubbed the side of her head.

"I think you just might be right."

Ivy turned back to her pie. "Do you think Harry will try to bid on my box supper?"

"Of course he will. I just hope he brings lots of money. That's such a pretty box, he's gonna have to fight half the men in the county over it," replied Tyme. "Is your mother coming tonight?"

"Oh, I doubt it." Ivy picked up a knife and began slicing the pie. "She doesn't usually enjoy things like this—especially when it's outdoors. Why?"

"Just wondering. You haven't heard anything from Jared in a few days, have you?"

"No, thank goodness." Ivy shuddered. "I think he and Papa were meeting in Joplin this week. I wonder what he thought about my telegram?"

"I wonder what he would think about Harry."

"I know exactly, but I don't care. I already know Harry's

twice the man Jared is. So Jared had better just stay away."

"Let's just hope he does."

Ivy arranged the food on the Blue Willow china plate with care—fried chicken, potato salad, and corn bread. She put a generous helping of green beans into a small, lidded jar, and then included two large slices of homemade apple pie on a separate, covered dish. Carefully wrapping the food with wax paper, she then laid the plate, silverware, and other containers inside a red velvet covered hatbox. She picked up a yellow ribbon, tied it around the box, and made a neat bow.

"How does it look?"

"That's really pretty. The ribbon gives it a nice, finished look."

"Is that why you left it on my pillow this morning?"

"Left what?"

"The ribbon. It was lying on the bed when I woke up this morning." Ivy frowned and looked at the decorated box. "I thought you left it."

"No...I've never seen this ribbon before." Tyme looked pensive as she ran her fingers across the yellow satin. "It looks different from the ones I sell in the store. This one seems older." She bent down and sniffed. "It even smells old."

"You don't think?..."

"Think what?"

"Could the children have left it?" Ivy untied her apron and headed out of the room. "I've got to check on something."

Tyme followed Ivy down the stairs into the darkened store. Ivy went straight to the rocking chair in the corner. It was empty, but she thought she detected a slight movement and a faint creaking sound. Her imagination must be playing tricks on her. She scanned the room, looking for the music box and whistle.

"Did you move them?" asked Ivy.

"Move what?"

And then, as if from a great distance, Ivy heard a faint toot toot and some other sound she couldn't quite identify. She whirled around, trying to locate the source of the noise. An odd, tingling sensation coursed through her body, but she didn't feel frightened. "Did you hear a whistle?"

"Um hm," Tyme grinned at Ivy and then motioned for her to go back upstairs. "Come on. We've got to finish getting ready."

Ivy smiled as she followed her aunt up the stairs. A sensation of warmth and well-being surrounded her. She grew excited at the prospect of seeing Harry again and she absent-mindedly hummed along with the tune Tyme was singing.

Harry brushed imaginary lint off the sleeve of his jacket, straightened his tie, and scanned the crowd for Ivy. It had been almost two days since he'd seen her and he'd spent a lot of that time trying to clean the whiskey out of his only jacket. But he'd managed it and now he was so excited he feared he might burst. He hadn't been able to think of anything else, even while he reeled in the fish at Doc Pruett's place.

This celebration was completely different from the one he'd attended two nights ago. The Fourth of July festival was outside, in the center of town. Three fiddlers and a man on banjo entertained the crowd from a newly erected bandstand at the Basin Spring Park.

Earlier in the day there had been a parade and a picnic, with sack races and watermelon eating contests. But Harry knew Ivy wouldn't be here until later, so he'd stayed away until now. Brightly colored booths still lined the streets, selling everything imaginable, but they were beginning to shut down for the evening's entertainment. At eight o'clock, the party was just beginning. Now that the blistering July sun had finally begun its descent beneath the western ridge of the Ozarks, everyone could relax and enjoy themselves.

"Hey, Harry. Look over there." Clyde pointed across the

crowd of people seated at the long picnic tables that had been brought in for the occasion. "There they are."

Harry's whole body tingled with excitement as he and Clyde made their way toward the two women. His breath caught when he saw Ivy up close. She didn't look like a movie star anymore, but she seemed more beautiful than ever to him.

That pretty little blue dress she wore sure looked soft and frilly—but the best part was the way it showed off those perfect legs and slender ankles. Harry gave thanks to the fashion gods for letting the ladies wear their skirts a little shorter this year— almost to the knees.

He had to force himself not to stare at the satiny smooth skin of her bare arms and the little vee that formed right at the neckline of her frock, which hinted at the softly swelling bosom underneath. He liked her hair better this way too. Those bouncy little curls around her face made him want to reach out and run his fingers through them. His heart lurched when her green eyes flashed with recognition.

Clyde was the first to speak. "Hey, baby. Couldn't wait to see ya again." He walked over like he owned the place, straddled the bench, and sat next to Tyme.

"Me neither," purred Tyme, still playing the vamp even in normal street attire. She had abandoned the black mourning clothes, opting instead for a hot pink dress and matching beret. She bent forward and pecked Clyde on the cheek.

Harry stood awkwardly. He wondered what he should do, since an older lady sat next to Ivy. She was quite a stunning woman, with light brown hair piled atop her head in an old-fashioned, Gibson girl style. Her face was pale and drawn, and she appeared to be in shock as she stared at Tyme and Clyde.

Ivy broke the silence. "Mama, I'd like you to meet Harry Fuller. Harry, this is my mother, Mrs. Turner."

"How d'ya do, ma'am?" Harry removed his hat and bowed slightly.

"How do you do?" responded Winifred. Harry heard the suspicion in her tone.

"Scoot over, Clyde," said Tyme. She wiggled around until there was room on the bench for Harry. "There you go, Harry. Now you can sit down with us."

Harry felt about as welcome as an ant at a picnic when he saw the stare of mistrust on Winifred Turner's face. But when he looked into his angel's emerald eyes, all his discomfort melted away. She smiled at him and his heart sang with joy.

"Would ya just look at that." Tyme whispered as she leaned toward Ivy and Harry. She pointed to the front table where the mayor and other dignitaries were seated.

"Hm. I guess Doc Pruett was right. Dr. Baker's considered a VIP in this town." Ivy whispered back, wrinkling her nose.

So that's the infamous Dr. Baker. Harry gazed at the short little man in the dazzlingly white suit and purple shirt. He certainly acted like he owned the town, puffing on his big cigar, laughing, and slapping the mayor on the back. He thought about what Doc Pruett had said and frowned. He wondered how Ivy's mother could fall for such a charlatan.

The band struck up a fast hillbilly tune. A man dressed in overalls and a plaid shirt stepped up to the microphone and began calling the steps. Couples lined up, promenaded in front of the bandstand and the square dance began in earnest.

"Yee haw!" yelled Clyde. "It's a hoedown!"

"Oh, baby. Let's go." Tyme rose, and she and Clyde joined the dancers.

Winifred glared coldly at Tyme and Clyde as they sashayed and do-si-doed like experts. She sniffed and folded her arms. "Caleb would be furious if he could see his sister right now. It's only been a few months since she lost her husband, and just look at her. Her behavior is disgraceful!"

"Oh, Mama. Leave her alone," said Ivy. "She's young. She deserves to have a little fun."

Winifred turned and stared at her daughter. "Your aunt *had* her fun years ago. It's time for her to grow up and begin acting like a lady." She gazed out at the dancers, then turned back to Ivy, annoyance written on her face. "I'm not at all sure it's such a good idea for you to be staying with Tyme right now. I'm going to wire your father tomorrow and tell him he needs to take you home."

"Mama!" Ivy's eyes filled with tears, but she held them back.

"Don't argue with me, young lady." Winifred's tone was crisp and unyielding.

Harry's face grew red and his temperature rose as he listened to the argument between Ivy and her mother. He felt sorry for Ivy. Obviously she was totally embarrassed, but he didn't know how he could help her. His tie began choking him and he reached up to fidget with his collar, trying to remain invisible.

Ivy turned to Harry, ignoring her mother. "Harry, did you catch a lot of fish yesterday?"

Self-conscious beneath Winifred Turner's disapproving glare, Harry stammered. "Y-yes. C-Clyde and me both caught a big mess of bass and some perch. Doc fried it up for supper last night."

"Do you know how to square dance?"

Harry caught on to the fact that Ivy wanted an excuse to get away from her mother. "Um, not really. But I'm willing to give it a try."

He started to rise, but Ivy's mother suddenly turned toward him, her face a mask of anger. He sank back down. "I'd like to tell you something, Mr..."

"Fuller." Harry filled in the blank. His heart hammered beneath her scrutiny.

"Mr. Fuller...yes." Harry's name rolled off her tongue slowly, as if she was tasting a glass of buttermilk for the first time and not quite sure she liked it. "Were you aware that my daughter—Ivy—is engaged to be married?"

Harry's eyebrows rose and sweat beaded on his brow. "No, ma'am. I didn't know that."

"Harry, it's not true!" cried Ivy. "Mama…"

Winifred interrupted Ivy. "I'm afraid my daughter has developed a childish habit of indulging in flirtations with men and then playing hard to get." She gazed pointedly at Harry. "I thought it only fair to warn you. She will be marrying Mr. Jared Covington in the fall. I'm sure you've heard of him? He is the owner of Covington Lead and Steel of St. Louis, Missouri."

"Mama, I am appalled!" Ivy jumped to her feet and glared at her mother, her hands on her hips, her chest heaving. "I have told you and Papa over and over that Jared and I are through. How can I convince you of that?"

"Ivy, you are a mean, ungrateful child." Winifred's eyes flashed with anger. "Here I am, practically at death's door, and you treat me this way." She buried her face in a linen handkerchief.

"Oh, stop it, Mama!"

Winifred glanced up from her handkerchief, her eyes dry, and stared at Ivy. Ivy sat down again, folded her arms, turned her head, and gazed defiantly at the dancers. The tension between the two women was almost unbearable to Harry.

Winifred studied her daughter for several seconds before she turned her attention back to Harry. Harry felt like crawling off somewhere to hide. She stared at him, long and hard.

"And what is it you do, Mr. Fuller?" Her gaze impaled him.

He wiped the sweat off his brow with his handkerchief before he answered. "I'm a work leader on a CCC dam crew, Mrs. Turner."

Winifred thought for a moment. "I was under the impression the CCC only hired men with dependents. Do you have a family somewhere you're taking care of?"

Harry hung his head at the memory. "I used to send my pay

to my Ma and Pa and my little sister. But they've all passed on now. Little Denver died of diphtheria, and consumption got both my folks last spring. It's just me now."

Winifred didn't respond to Harry's revelations. She turned back toward Ivy and studied her face. When her daughter showed no sign of contrition, her face suddenly crumpled and she clutched her stomach. "Ohh! Dr. Baker told me to avoid too much stress. I never should have come here."

Ivy continued sitting with her arms folded. She stared angrily at Winifred. "Stop it, Mama. You always do this when you don't get your way. Everybody knows there's nothing really wrong with you."

"Ohhh," Winifred moaned again and fanned herself with the festival program. "This is just too much. I think I'm going to faint."

Harry looked frantically around, relieved when he saw Doc Pruett walking toward them. He motioned him over. "Doc, I think this lady needs your help."

Doc Pruett leaned down and spoke softly to Winifred. "May I be of some assistance, Ma'am? I'm a doctor."

"I feel weak and dizzy—too much stress." Winifred held her stomach, gazed pitifully at Dr. Pruett and then glanced at Ivy. "I'm a cancer patient of Dr. Baker's, but I hate to disturb him right now."

"There, there." Dr. Pruett patted her on the hand. "You probably just need to get away from the crowds and noise. My car's right over there. Why don't you let me take you back up the hill so you can get some rest?"

"Would you? That would be so nice." She turned to Ivy. "Will you come with me?"

"No, Mama." Ivy's voice was firm. "They're about to auction off the box suppers and I intend to stay."

Winifred sighed with resignation and moved lethargically. Her fighting spirit had deflated quickly. Doc Pruett helped her rise and winked conspiratorially at Ivy. "Come on Mrs. Turner. You'll feel much better in a little while—do you like to play bridge?"

"Oh, yes," replied Winifred, perking up. "I love bridge."

Ivy rolled her eyes when she saw Doc Pruett lead her mother away. She let out a sigh of relief. "What a life saver Dr. Pruett is. Harry, I'm so sorry you had to hear all that."

Before Harry could reply, the music stopped and the dancers found their way back to their tables. Several ladies began carrying the various box suppers for display to a table on the stage. A murmur of excitement raced through the crowd. The square dance caller stepped up to the microphone.

"Which one's yours?" Clyde asked Tyme.

"None of them, you big goof. This is just for the single gals."

"You're single." Clyde cocked his head to one side.

"I'm a widow," replied Tyme. "Big difference."

"Ladies and gentlemen," the announcer called for attention. "It's time for us to auction off these wonderful box suppers the single ladies have so graciously provided. Please be generous, the proceeds go to a good cause."

Ivy leaned toward Harry and pointed to the stage. "That red one with the yellow ribbon is mine." She giggled and placed her finger in front of her lips. "I wasn't supposed to tell."

"Okay, we'll start with this one." The auctioneer picked up a gaily-decorated box with sea shells glued to the sides and held it aloft. "What am I bid for box number one?"

"Two bits," someone yelled.

"Two bits. Do I hear four?"

"Four bits." A man in the back raised his hand.

"Six." The first bidder protested.

"I've got six bits," said the auctioneer. "Do I have a dollar?"

"One dollar." The man in the back boomed.

The first bidder frowned and closed his mouth.

"Going once. Going twice. Sold to the man in the back for

one dollar."

The winner of the box came forward to accept his prize. He handed over his dollar and was joined by a pretty young girl who smiled shyly and accompanied the winner back to his table.

The bidding and buying continued. Some boxes went for as low as twenty-five cents and one sold for as much as five dollars, with most averaging between one and two dollars. Part of the prize included sharing time with the young lady, as well as getting to eat the food she had packed. Theoretically, nobody was supposed to know which young lady had prepared what box, or what kind of food it contained. But cheating ran rampant, so most of the men knew ahead of time who—and what—they were spending their money on.

Harry reached in his pocket and counted his money. He was determined to win Ivy's box, one way or another. It sat toward the back of the table, so it was one of the last to be auctioned. He felt a thrill of anticipation when the caller picked up the red box and held it aloft.

"All right, the next box is this lovely red velvet—with a little yellow ribbon." He held it up and displayed it slowly to the crowd. "Do I hear a dollar for this lovely gem?"

"One dollar!" A middle-aged man in a brown suit bid.

"Two dollars," countered Harry.

"Three," came a voice near the back of the park.

"Four twenty-five," yelled somebody else.

Harry gulped nervously and cried. "Five dollars."

"I've got five dollars," cried the caller. "Do I hear six?"

"Twenty dollars."

A gasp rose up from the crowd. Harry was in shock. He craned his neck to see the bidder. It was Dr. Baker!

"Twenty dollars! Do I hear more? Going once, going twice..."

"Oh, Harry. You can't let him get it." Ivy looked like she

might cry.

Harry's heart fluttered. He was a child of the Great Depression. He'd grown up scrimping and saving and making do. There'd never been enough money to spend on anything frivolous. Every fiber in his being screamed at him not to do it. But he couldn't help himself.

"Thirty dollars."

The crowd gasped again. All eyes were on Harry.

"I've got thirty dollars," yelled the caller. "Do I hear thirty-five?"

Baker stared across the park at Harry and Ivy seated next to him. He shifted his cigar over to the other side of his mouth and made his bid.

"Forty dollars." He looked smug and puffed two smoke rings.

"I've got forty dollars. Going once..."

"Forty-five." Harry swallowed a lump. That was his entire months' pay and it was all he had.

"Forty-five. Do I hear fifty?" The atmosphere was charged with excitement.

Baker pulled out a wad of bills and thumbed through them. He shook his head and then shrugged and held out his hands. He whispered something to the mayor, who sent his assistant up to the dais. The crowd became restless. A private conversation with him and the auctioneer ensued.

"Sorry, no credit allowed." The auctioneer shook his head.

The mayor reached in his pocket and handed some money to Dr. Baker, who smirked at Harry and opened his mouth to bid again. The crowd went wild in protest.

"No fair!" Somebody yelled from the back. " Rules say you can't loan out money either. S'gotta be what ya have in your pocket."

The crowd was in an uproar. The mayor appeared worried, put his money back in his pocket, and shrugged. Dr. Baker scowled and sat down. His eyes raked across Harry and Ivy, but he didn't say anything more.

The caller nodded and continued.

"Forty-five dollars going once...going twice...sold!"

Harry exhaled with relief. Ivy giggled and clapped her hands, then together they walked up to redeem their supper. Harry could feel Dr. Baker's eyes boring a hole through his back, but he'd never felt so happy in his life. He might have to eat nothing but beans for the next month, but it would be worth it.

He'd just made the best investment of his life—and maybe the worst enemy.

CHAPTER TWELVE

Harry finished the last dollop of potato salad, gnawed one more time on a drumstick, and then wiped his mouth and fingers on his handkerchief before reaching for dessert. He took a bite of apple pie. Umm. Scrumptious. The flaky crust and sweet-yet-spicy flavor tickled his taste buds. Had he died and gone to heaven?

He felt guilty because he'd eaten most of the food himself, but Ivy didn't seem to mind his healthy appetite. A sweet, beautiful angel and she could cook, too. How lucky could a man be?

"Is the pie all right?"

"Mm hm." Harry nodded, his mouth too full to give a dignified answer.

"Oh, I'm sorry Harry." Ivy's pretty little brow wrinkled as she apologized. "I hate it when people ask me questions while I'm eating."

He swallowed and then replied. "That's okay. I shouldn't have wolfed it down so fast. Haven't had nothin' to eat this good in I don't know when."

Ivy's eyes sparkled. "I'm so glad you like it. I'm just sorry you had to pay so much." She shook her head. "That was a sinful amount of money."

"It was worth every penny. I just wish you'd eaten more."

"Harry, I appreciate you stopping Dr. Baker from buying my box supper. I just don't think I would have been able to stand it if I'd been forced to sit with him. I wouldn't have eaten *anything* if he'd been the winner." Ivy shuddered. "I'll try to pay you back somehow."

"Oh, no," Harry protested. "Don't even think that way. If I hadn't wanted to bid on your dinner box, I wouldn't have done it."

She rewarded him with a brilliant smile just before Clyde and Tyme came back to the table, panting from the exertion of the square dance. Clyde picked up a piece of crust with a little apple filling on it and popped it into his mouth.

"Hey, quit stealin'," protested Harry, slapping at his hand.

"Mm-mm-mm," said Clyde as he licked his fingers. "Got any more?"

"You got forty-five dollars?" Harry countered.

"Oh, baby, don't eat Harry's pie," Tyme purred, rubbing her hand along Clyde's back. "*I'll* bake you a pie of your own. Do you want cherry, apple, or lemon?"

"Whatever ya got in the pantry." Clyde gave Tyme a big, sloppy kiss. She giggled and kissed him back.

"Are you two gonna sit here all night?" asked Tyme when she came back up for air. "They're hitchin' a wagon for a hay ride up the mountain. We'll be able to see the fireworks better from there. Ya'll wanta go?"

Harry looked at Ivy and she nodded. "Sure, let's go."

Moments later they were all nestled in a mountain of fresh hay. The wagon was old and it had squeaky wheels, but it overflowed with young people eager for a ride in the moonlight. The wagon creaked and groaned as the last couple climbed aboard. The mules snorted and stamped their feet as they waited for the driver's signal to push off.

Harry's whole body tingled with excitement when the wagon jerked forward and Ivy fell against him. He smiled and put his arm around her and she snuggled close. He gave her a little squeeze, realizing that with her at his side, he was truly happy.

Darkness descended and the lights of town grew distant and faint. Guided only by the silvery light of the crescent moon and an occasional pulsing firefly, the mule team plodded up the steep mountain road. The atmosphere in the wagon was charged with excitement and a festive spirit as the people laughed and chattered happily. Somebody began singing *The Bear Went Over the Mountain* and several others joined in. Soon the raucous noise drowned out the shrill song of the bullfrogs and cicadas.

"Ride's not too rough, is it?" asked Harry. His teeth chattered from the bouncing of the wagon. He didn't mind it himself, but he didn't want Ivy to suffer any discomfort.

"Couldn't be better." Ivy reached for his free hand and laced her fingers through his.

He leaned back on the hay, held her close, and gazed up at the stars. Contentment. That's what he felt right now. If he had his way, this moment would last forever.

Harry glanced over at Clyde and Tyme. His eyes had adjusted to the darkness, but all he could see was the outline of their bodies, molded together in a passionate embrace. Ivy squeezed his hand. His pulse quickened and his temperature rose.

He turned toward her and lightly touched her hair with his lips. She trembled and turned toward him. Her eyes and alabaster skin gleamed in the moonlight. She looked innocent and trusting and he hesitated, not wanting to move too fast, yet his self-control slipped away.

He ran his fingers down her hairline and found her chin. He tilted it up and lowered his mouth until it found hers. She returned his kiss and a sweet, burning ache traveled throughout his body, turning his limbs into jelly and flipping his heart upside down.

When their lips parted, Ivy buried her face against his chest and he wrapped his arms around her. He never wanted to let her go. If he were to die right now, he'd go to meet his maker a happy man. He nestled against the hay, tightened his grip on Ivy, and stared at the stars.

"Ivy, look." Harry pointed toward the sky. "I just saw a shooting star."

"Quick! Make a wish." She turned around, and then pointed upward in excitement. "Look! There's another one!"

Harry sucked in his breath. The second star came from the opposite direction, and its trail of light crossed the first one's path. This must indeed be his lucky night. He closed his eyes and silently made his wish.

He cuddled her and asked, "What did you wish for?"

"I can't tell you, silly. If I do, it won't come true."

"Do you want to know my wish?"

"No, Harry." She giggled and buried her head in his chest again. "And don't you dare tell me."

Harry laughed and kissed the top of her head. He'd never felt this way about any woman before, never believed he could be so lucky. Up to this point, his life had been a mad scramble for survival; a constant challenge of keeping himself and his family fed from one day to the next. He thought of all the days and nights he'd spent riding the rails, traveling from one town to the next, hoping to find work of any kind. He remembered the months he'd spent hoping that the folks in the next place he came across in his wanderings would be kind enough to trade a little food for some chopped wood or slopped hogs, and maybe even let him spend the night in their barn.

Harry thought about the girls he'd known in his life. Although he was well past twenty-one, there hadn't been many. When he was sixteen his family had worked as sharecroppers in West Texas and he'd had a big crush on the landowner's daughter. But she'd been nothing but trouble—sassy and bold and wild. She'd turned out to be the kind of girl who could turn a man's heart inside out and then walk right over it and go find another guy before the first fella knew what hit him.

He'd been wary of romance after that. There'd been lots of opportunities while he'd lived the hobo life, but he just didn't feel right about casual matings. All the other fellas he knew jumped at every opportunity when they found a willing female, but he didn't want to deal with the consequences. Too many of the guys he knew came away with embarrassing itches or worse. Over the years he'd learned the benefits of a brisk walk or quick dips in a cold pond when he felt the need to stifle his urges.

The wagon jerked to a stop and people began to pile out. Harry helped Ivy down and brushed the hay from his clothes. Tyme jumped off the large bag she'd been sitting on, pulled out a blanket, and handed it to Harry.

"Here you go. I thought we could use a blanket or two." A flash of blue lit up the sky and Tyme motioned toward a secluded area. "Oh, good, the fireworks are starting. Clyde and I are gonna wander around a bit. That looks like a good spot over there for you two." Tyme winked at Ivy and then disappeared with Clyde into the darkness.

Harry led Ivy away from the others and spread the blanket on the ground. They sat down and Ivy leaned her head against Harry's chest. He put his arm around her and lowered his head until it rested against hers. He knew other people were around, but he and Ivy were the only two humans in the world, as far as Harry was concerned.

"Oohh! That's a good one." Harry pointed toward a bright orange sunburst in the sky, followed in rapid succession by a green one, a huge red burst, and then a shower of whistling white sparkles. The noise of the blasts echoed throughout the hills.

"Um hm. I love fireworks. Papa took me to see them every year at the Veiled Prophet parade in St. Louis." Ivy shivered and glanced down at her hands. "It was a year ago tonight I met Jared."

"Is that the guy your mother was talking about?" A sense of desolation washed over him at the thought of Ivy with another man.

"Yes, but what my mother said isn't true. I didn't flirt with him and lead him on." Ivy's tone was pleading. "I never wanted him. My parents insisted I be a debutante, and he saw me at the ball and decided he wanted me. I went around with him for quite a while, just to please my parents; but the more I got to know him, the less I liked him. He had the *nerve* to go to Papa and ask for my hand in marriage, without even consulting me. But I am not—I repeat *not*—going to marry him."

"That's okay." Harry patted her on the shoulder. "I believe you."

He kissed her again and it was just as sweet as the last time. He didn't want to stop, he wanted to keep kissing her forever. But the place where they sat was too public and his passion too heated, so he tore himself away when he heard the yells and claps from the other people as a volley of Roman candles whizzed and squealed and burst in the air.

They sat quietly for several moments holding each other, their bodies close, enjoying the splendor of the Independence Day celebration. Ivy was the first to break the silence.

"Harry, tell me about yourself. I want to know everything."

Harry had never been much for talking about himself. What was there to tell? "You want to know my life story?"

"Yes. Where do you come from? What was your family like? That sort of thing."

"Well, there's not much to tell." He looked up at the glowing fireworks. "Let's see. I was born and raised not too far from here. My Pa had a little farm over in Siloam Springs and he was a Primitive Baptist preacher."

"Oh, my. Did he have his own church?"

"No, he was more of a circuit preacher. He farmed for a living and every time there was a fifth Sunday in a month, he'd travel to other churches and preach. He never got paid, he did it out of love and because of his calling."

"He sounds like a wonderful man." Ivy sighed and gazed at the dancing lights in the sky. "My religious upbringing was very confusing."

"Oh?"

Ivy smiled. "Papa is a Presbyterian and Mama is Catholic. Need I say more?"

Harry laughed. "Well, that does make for differences in opinions."

"Tell me more, Harry. Tell me about your mother."

"Okay, if you insist. Wow! Look at that." Harry pointed to a giant fountain of sparkling white flames before resuming his tale. "Let's see. Okay. Ma worked hard to keep everything going, and you never saw her without a smile on her face or a song on her lips. No matter how hard the times got, she was always optimistic and happy."

"Sure sounds different from my mother."

"Well, I got the impression your ma has faced a lot of sorrow in her life and just doesn't know how to be happy. I think she's dealing with an awful lot of pain and nobody understands, because on the surface she's got everything so good. But deep down, she's wounded. Not everybody is born knowing how to deal with sorrow."

Ivy gasped and looked at Harry. "Do you think that's why she's always putting on that she's sick all the time? I never thought about it that way. I just thought she was self-centered and childish. It never occurred to me that she was sad. Don't they call that melancholia?"

Harry nodded. "You shouldn't be angry with her. Ma taught me to try to see the good in everybody. No matter how mean and ornery they are, you can always find a little spark of *something* to redeem them."

"Oh, Harry. Now I know why I like you so much. You

always make me smile." Ivy leaned over and kissed him and his heart skipped a beat.

He wanted to keep on kissing her, but she resumed the conversation. "Do you have any brothers or sisters? I'm an only child."

"I had a little sister named Denver." Harry's voice broke at the memory. "I was almost seventeen by the time she came along. I'll never forget the night she was born. We was livin' in Oklahoma and she came right smack in the middle of the worst dust storm I ever seen. Ma had already lost so many other babies, we all figured this would be just one more to bury. But Denver made it through and she was like a ray of sunshine in a dark, bitter world."

"You lived in Oklahoma?"

"Yeah. Pa lost his farm at Siloam Springs in 1933 when he couldn't pay the mortgage. We'd had a real good crop that year and made a nice profit. But Pa put all the money in the bank and then it failed. We lost every last cent we had, 'cept for Ma's butter and egg money."

Ivy's green eyes flashed in the moonlight and Harry heard the anger in her voice. "Did they sell your father's farm at auction?"

"Yeah, somebody from up north bought it. People who still had money snapped up all the farms real cheap."

Ivy hung her head. "I know someone who took advantage of people like your parents and I hate him for it—especially now that I've heard your story."

"Don't hate anybody, Ivy." Harry lightly touched his finger to her lips. "It just hardens your heart—that's what my Ma used to say."

"I wish I'd known her. Would you tell me what happened to your folks and Denver?"

Harry sighed. "Well, after my folks lost their place, we went to Texas and did share-cropping in the cotton fields. It was hard, dirty work, but we were lucky to get it. Then, we ran into some trouble with the owner and we had to pick up and leave. That's when we moved to Oklahoma."

"And that's when Denver came along?"

"Yep. But it was real hard to make a living there. No rain, nothing but sand and dust and tumbleweeds. The people who'd lived there before us had plowed the life out of the soil, and left nothin' for us. We couldn't get hardly anything to grow. And I think those constant dust storms just aggravated my Ma and Pa's lungs, 'cause a couple of months after we got there they both started coughing real bad."

"Did they have consumption?"

Harry nodded. "Later on they found out they had tuberculosis. They got so sick they could hardly work, so they decided to go to California, hoping for a better climate. The three of 'em piled everything we owned in an old Model T and they headed west. I went the other direction, looking for work. But there just wasn't any work to be had anywhere."

"How did you stay in touch?"

"It wasn't easy, but we managed. There's a whole network in the hobo world, so every time I was able to make a couple of dollars, I'd send it to 'em. They was livin' in these little shanty towns here and there, but it wasn't a healthy way for grown-ups to live, let alone a child." Tears threatened and he turned his head, but not before Ivy saw them.

"Oh, Harry. I'm sorry. If this is too hard on you, please stop."

"No, it needs telling." Harry took a deep breath and continued. "I completely lost touch with 'em for a while. I asked everybody I saw about 'em, but nobody seemed to know what happened. Then one day, a train conductor heard about my searching and he gave me a letter he'd been carrying around for several months. It turned out they'd all been moved to a TB sanitarium in Arizona. Even little Denver."

"Did you go see them?"

"No. The conductor gave me another letter from the TB hospital's office. They told me I'd have to join the CCC. I could go and work for the government, and if I wanted my family to stay in the hospital, I'd have to send all but five dollars a month to my family for their care. Well, that sounded like manna from heaven, I can tell you. A job, room and board, and the knowledge that my family was being cared for. I couldn't believe my good luck."

"Did you ever get to visit them?"

Harry hung his head. "No. I was too far away. They sent me to a camp up in South Dakota for a couple of years. I really liked the work and it sure took the pressure off, knowing where my folks were. We wrote lots of letters back and forth. I even saved up my money and sent Denver a little doll with a china head for Christmas one year. But I never got to see any of them again."

"So how did you get back to Arkansas?"

"When my first term was up, I decided to re-enlist and I requested Northwestern Arkansas. I decided to take a leave of absence and go down to Arizona. But when I got there, they were all gone. Denver had come down with diphtheria and Ma and Pa just gave up after she died. They were too sad to write and tell me about it. They were both sick, but I think her passing was just too much for 'em and they lost their will to live— now there ain't nobody but me." His voice cracked and he turned away again.

"Oh, Harry. Please don't be sad," Ivy pulled his face toward her and stared into his eyes. "You'll always have me."

Harry couldn't believe what she'd just said. "That's the sweetest thing anybody's ever said to me." He pulled her into his arms and held her, fighting back the tears. He wasn't usually so emotional. She returned his embrace and he thought he would die from the sheer joy of her touch. "I know we don't know each other very well. I know we just met a few days ago, but…" His tongue became dry and he couldn't get the words out.

"What is it?" She searched his face and his whole body quivered beneath her gaze.

"Would you…I mean, do you think…" The words refused to come. She would think he was crazy. They barely knew each other, yet he felt like he'd known her forever.

"Say it," she insisted. "I want to hear you say it."

Harry felt his pulse throb in his temples and he fought for the courage to say what was in his heart. He gazed into her eyes, took a deep breath, and took the plunge. "I'm in love with you Ivy—will you marry me?"

Dear God, he'd said it and he knew he'd die right then and there if she said no. His thoughts fragmented, suddenly worrying about how he could take care of a wife, with no money or home or car or…anything. "I mean, I know I don't have any money right now, but I promise I'll work hard—and I'll do anything to make you happy and…"

"Yes, Harry."

Harry looked confused. "What?"

"I said yes. Yes, yes, yes!" Ivy exclaimed and threw her arms around his neck. "I don't care about money. I don't care that we only met two days ago. It wouldn't make any difference to me if it were two years. I know how I feel about you and it's never going to change. I'm in love with you too. All I care about is you."

Harry stood up, whooped like an Indian on the warpath, and picked Ivy up from the blanket. He twirled her around and then kissed her long and deep. He'd made his wish on the falling star and it had just come true.

"Hm, looks like the two of you are getting along just fine," said Tyme. She stood beside Clyde, with her blanket under one arm and her other hand on her hip. Clyde ran his hands through his hair and then nuzzled the back of Tyme's neck.

"Harry and I are getting married!" Ivy squealed with delight and Harry grinned.

"My, my you shore do work fast," remarked Clyde, as he reached down and scooped up the other blanket. "Wagon's about to leave. Gotta go. Sarge's gonna be waitin' for us in town."

"Congratulations, you two," Tyme hugged them both, then turned to Ivy. "Your Papa's gonna blow a head-gasket."

"I know," giggled Ivy. "We need to keep it a secret for now."

"Mum's the word."

Harry's hand was gentle yet firm when he helped Ivy climb back into the wagon, protecting her as if she were made of fragile Dresden china. He couldn't believe he'd just become engaged to the sweetest, most beautiful, most wonderful, most—he couldn't think of words good enough to describe her—woman in the world. He tried not to think about Sarge, who would be waiting in town to take him and Clyde back to camp. Away from his betrothed. Hm. He'd never used that word before, but he liked the way it sounded.

Ivy's eyes glistened in the moonlight as Harry climbed in beside her and pulled her close. He glanced over his shoulder and saw that Clyde and Tyme had covered themselves with their blanket, even though the night was warm and balmy. Someone near the front of the wagon pulled out a harmonica and began to play the sweet sad melody of *Barbry Allen*. A girl beside the harp player sang the words, her voice low and quivery and poignant.

> *"Twas in the merry month of May;*
> *When green buds were a swellin';*
> *Sweet William on his death bed lay;*
> *For the love of Barbry Allen..."*

Harry leaned back and relaxed, cuddling Ivy while he

listened to the haunting verses of the ancient love song. The wagon trudged back down the twisting mountain road, the mules snorting and shaking their heads when a pair of deer stepped out of the woods and crossed in front of the wagon. A hoot owl swooped to the ground somewhere behind them, grabbed something in its mouth, and flew away.

"When he lay dead and in his grave;
She heard the death bells nellin';
And every stroke to her did say;
Hard-hearted Barbry Allen..."

The world still turned on its axis and life went on as usual. But there was nothing routine about this day as far as Harry was concerned. His life had changed forever. He was getting married!

Harry's spirits dropped when the wagon pulled into the parking area. He saw Sarge puffing on a cigarette and leaning against his old jalopy at the designated meeting place. It was time to say good-bye to Ivy. He took her in his arms and kissed her one last time, just as the girl was ending her song.

"They grew and grew in the old church yard;
Till they could grow no higher;
At the end they formed a true lovers' knot;
And the rose grew 'round the briar."

CHAPTER THIRTEEN

Ivy gazed at the view from the third-floor hospital balcony, wishing she was anywhere but here. She hated this place; hated her mother's disregard for her time; hated all the wasted hours as she waited for Winifred to appear.

Visiting her mother had become strained over the past three weeks. Ever since Winifred had met Harry, an icy wall of mistrust had sprung up between them. Even though Harry had urged her to be more understanding, she had found it impossible. She just wanted to say hello and leave.

"Mrrrr."

Ivy stared in amazement when a big gray tomcat jumped into her lap. He gazed at her with intelligent green eyes, circled once, and then made himself comfortable.

"Now where did you come from, pretty boy?" Charmed by the friendly animal, Ivy began to relax as she stroked the velvety softness of his fur. The cat rewarded her by stretching up to rub his head against her forehead and purring.

Such a beautiful, unusual cat. He had gray tabby stripes, and a spotted underbelly, somewhat like a lynx. The hair on his ears tapered into long pointed tips and his tail was bobbed. His feet were large, with extra toes on each foot.

"What *is* that creature in your lap?" Winifred's horrified voice startled both Ivy and the cat.

"Hello, Mama. I hope you're feeling better." Ivy stroked the cat to reassure him. "Isn't he beautiful? He must belong to someone here at the hospital—sweet kitty cat." She murmured softly, running her fingernails down his spine. The cat purred louder and lifted the angle of his backside.

"That is hardly a normal cat," remarked Winifred, her eyes narrowed and her expression grew wary. "It's much too big and wild looking. It looks like a bobcat to me. You should put it down before it hurts you."

"Oh, don't be so silly..."

Suddenly Ivy heard dogs barking and the thump of huge feet drawing near. The cat heard it too and instantly tensed, arched its back, and flattened its ears. His green eyes flashed, and his gray fur stood at attention, while his half tail frizzed into a ball. Two gigantic, slobbering brown heads poked themselves between the arms of Ivy's rocker and proceeded to bark insults at the cat.

The cat hissed and growled, displaying its fangs and claws as a warning to the dogs. Then like a flash, it leaped straight up from Ivy's lap, landed on the balcony railing, and was gone. The Saint Bernards went berserk, running around in circles, trying to figure out what had happened. They raced back inside the building, bumping into Winifred as they went.

"Goodness gracious." Winifred clutched her chest and sank into a rocking chair. "Such a shock. I think I might just faint!"

"Oh, for goodness sakes. You make such a drama out of everything."

Winifred ignored Ivy's comment. "What a terrible racket those animals make. And I thought they were going to trample me. It's quite disturbing to have creatures the size of ponies running free all the time. Dr. Baker really needs to do something about it."

Ivy rolled her eyes. "Here, Mama. Let me get you something to drink." She reached for a pitcher of lemonade on a nearby table and poured a glass.

"Thank you, dear." Winifred sipped, took several deep breaths and managed to compose herself. "I'm so looking forward to going home."

"You're going home? When?"

"On Monday. Dr. Baker has agreed to discharge me."

"Why, that's wonderful. So you're cured?"

"Dr. Baker says my tumor is almost gone. I'm doing much better now, but I'll need to continue taking my treatments at home for a while. He has graciously allowed me to purchase some of his wonderful medicine to take with me."

"Is Papa coming to get you?"

"Yes, and Ivy—your father wants you to come home with us."

"What?" Ivy froze. She wasn't ready to go home with her parents. In fact, she knew she never would be ready. All she wanted was to be with Harry. "I can't go home now. Tyme needs my help in the store."

"Tyme will get along very nicely without you. You need to have all your things packed and ready to go on Monday morning."

"But Mama—Papa said I could stay here all summer."

Winifred frowned. "That was before you started running around all over creation with that Harry person. And Tyme has been an utter disappointment to her brother—again…"

"Mama!"

"Don't deny it, young lady. This is a small town. People talk, you know." Winifred folded her arms and glared at Ivy. "I've heard it all—in sordid detail."

Ivy froze when she heard her mother's words. The past three weeks had been the happiest of her life. She and Tyme had worked out a system to meet with Harry and Clyde each weekend, and her time with Harry had been magical. The guys always stayed at Doc Pruett's farm and met with Ivy and Tyme in the evenings. Both couples had gone to the movies, gone dancing, and taken long walks in the moonlight. But never once had Harry crossed the line of propriety.

"I'm sorry, but I don't want to go back to St. Louis." She folded her arms and stared at her mother. "I don't know what kind of stories you've been hearing about Harry, but I can assure you nothing improper has occurred."

Winifred scowled at Ivy. "Your father and I think it will be better for you to be away from certain influences here. Everything will be much easier when we're back in St. Louis."

"I am not a child anymore," Ivy raged. "Is this the only reason you're going back? Because you don't trust me?"

"No, Ivy. That's not the only reason." Her expression changed to worry and she wrung her hands. She glanced over her shoulder to make sure nobody else was listening and lowered her voice. "Your father is going through some financial difficulties at the moment and he needs your cooperation. What happens next could make a difference in whether we can afford to continue the treatment I need."

"What are you talking about?"

"Jared has agreed to make certain investments in your father's businesses. These investments are vital if your father is to avoid bankruptcy." Winifred sighed and her voice took on a pitiful tone. "If your father loses all his money, I don't know what will happen to me—or any of us, for that matter."

Ivy felt the color drain from her face. "What do I have to do with it?"

"Jared was very hurt by the callous way you flung him aside. Your father and I are terrified that if he relinquishes his financial backing to your father's businesses we'll be ruined. We need you to come home and be nice to him. Please, just give it a try?" Winifred smiled hopefully at Ivy. "When everything gets back to normal, we can begin to plan your wedding."

Ivy stared at her mother. She obviously lived in a dream world. She never thought about anyone else's happiness except her own. Ivy knew it wouldn't do any good to argue with her mother about Jared. She'd tried to explain that she and Jared would never get married, but her mother refused to understand. Further discussion would be futile.

And there were apparently spies here twisting the truth about her and Harry. She knew she had to be careful until she had a chance to talk with Tyme and figure out what to do.

"Well, I guess I should go back to Tyme's and let her know I'll be leaving." Ivy stood, straightened her skirt, and put on her hat. "She'll need to hire another shop girl to take my place, and I've got a lot to do before Monday."

"All right dear." Winifred's smile lit up her face. "I'm so glad you understand."

"Have you seen my cat?"

Ivy looked up in surprise at a tiny, elderly woman standing on the balcony. "Was he gray with a stubby tail?"

"Yes, that's him. I've been searching for Bob everywhere." The old woman hobbled toward the two women and offered her hand. "How do you do? I'm Theodora Hardcastle. Are you patients of Dr. Baker?"

"Glad to meet you Mrs. Hardcastle. My name is Winifred Turner and this is my daughter Ivy," replied Winifred. "I'm a patient here, but I'll be leaving in a few days."

"Oh, that's so nice for you. I hope Dr. Baker has success with me as well." She glanced around the porch. "Did you see where he went?"

"I'm afraid Dr. Baker's dogs chased him off," said Ivy. "I think he might have gone up on the roof."

"Humph. Lucky for those dogs." Theodora craned her neck, trying to see up on the building's turrets. "He wasn't in the mood to fight today or he would have had them running for their lives."

"I thought it looked more like a wild animal than a domestic cat," said Winifred. "Do you think it's safe to keep it around a lot of sick people?"

"Oh, he would never hurt a person," replied Theodora. "He

just doesn't like dogs."

"He seemed very friendly to me," said Ivy. "What kind of a cat is he?"

"Well, his mama was a little gray tabby named Pixie. People don't believe me when I tell them this," said Theodora. Her eyes gleamed and her smile created even more wrinkles around her eyes. "Pixie got outside one day and I finally found her in the woods. Later on, she gave birth to a kitten. I believe that she mated with a bobcat, because how else would she produce a cat like Bob?"

Winifred sniffed and rose from her rocker. "I have never heard anything so ridiculous in my life. If you'll excuse me, I need to go lie down for a while now. Ivy, I'll see you on Monday."

"It was very nice meeting you," Theodora called to Winifred's retreating figure.

Ivy turned to Theodora and said, "I'm sorry for my mother's rudeness. I'd like to say she isn't usually like that, but I'd be lying."

"That's all right, dear. I hope to see you again real soon." Theodora smiled, patted Ivy on the shoulder, and went in search of Bob.

Ivy nodded, took one last look at the roof of the huge building and headed down the outside steps. Her mind whirled as she made her way through the hospital gardens and down the steep stone steps that descended into the town.

Ivy let herself into the dry goods store through the back door, surprised at how dark and cold it seemed. She glanced around, wondering why every window was shaded and the front door was locked. Then, to her surprise, she saw Tyme on her hands and knees in a corner of the back room. Goose bumps rose on her arms when she stepped into the frigid room. The electric lights flickered and buzzed.

"Tyme, what are you doing?"

But before Tyme could answer, Ivy stopped, frozen by the sight of a deathly pale, thin man standing in the opposite corner.

Ivy screamed. "Chauncey!"

Tyme looked up, startled by Ivy's outburst. Chauncey's head turned toward Ivy and her blood ran cold by the hatred in his gaze. He stared at her, and her knees buckled when she saw the pin in his lapel. She sank to the floor, overcome with terror.

Her eyes were riveted to the shining metal object on the jacket of his burial shroud. She'd seen that stickpin before. How could she ever forget the sight of the strange looking symbol—a dagger in front of a curved cross within a circle. Chauncey had worn it in his coffin. Now, seeing it again, she realized someone else she knew wore one too—Jared.

"Get out of here, you blasted monster!" Tyme shouted and hurled a pry bar at Chauncey's ghost.

His expression showed surprise and then he disappeared. The heavy metal tool hit a display case and broke it, sending hats and bags flying in all directions.

Tyme grinned, dusted off her hands, and stood up. "It's okay, honey. He's gone now. He's just like a cur dog. Throw somethin' at him and he'll turn tail and run."

Ivy kept her eyes squinched tight and covered them with her hands, afraid to look up. "Are you sure? Is he really gone?"

"I'm sure. Come on and get up. I've got something to show you."

Reluctantly, Ivy opened her eyes and gazed around the store, still shivering from the cold that hung in the air. When it seemed safe, she stood up and followed her aunt. In a far corner of the store's back room was a hole in the floor. "What happened to the floor?

"I pried up the boards," said Tyme. She put her hands on her hips and smiled. "I stubbed my toe while I was cleaning and that's when I noticed the loose nail. And then when I looked a little closer, I saw that the boards were uneven. So I got a lever and pulled 'em up to see what was down there."

"What's in there?" Ivy peered into the hole. She saw a bulging, burlap sack, covered with dust.

"I think it's Chauncey's treasure." Tyme rolled her eyes when the lights flickered again. "I *said* go away. You're dead, you moron. This isn't gonna do you any good any more."

"Is he going to start throwing things again?" Ivy's pulse quickened. "Maybe we ought to leave right now."

"Oh, no. That's just what he wants us to do. I knew he had to have some money stashed somewhere. I've been searching for it for months and I'm not gonna run away now. He's been prancin' around like a killdeer protectin' its nest every time I get too close, but I finally figured out his hiding place." Tyme reached into the hole and tugged on the sack. "Here, help me pull it out."

Ivy wrinkled her nose at the musty smell. The bag was heavy and awkward, but together they managed to lift it. A frisson of excitement coursed down her spine when she peered again into the hole. "Look! There're two more."

"That stingy bastard had even more money than I thought." Tyme wiped dust off her face and prepared to haul out the other ones.

"Money? Is that what's in these sacks?"

"I hope so." Tyme grinned, reached into her pocket for a knife and cut open one of the bags. Stacks of neatly bound currency held together by rubber bands fell onto the floor. "By God, we're rich!"

Tyme and Ivy laughed and giggled and hugged as they counted out the money, ignoring the growing coldness caused by Chauncey's anger. They could hardly believe their eyes when they opened the other two bags, which held jewelry, watches, and coins, as well as more cash. Together, the three bags held ninety-three bundles of bills and they estimated that each bundle contained at least five thousand dollars.

"Ivy, can you believe it? The cash alone is worth almost a half a million dollars!" exclaimed Tyme.

"But where did it all come from?"

"Remember I told you Chauncey ran several speakeasies? He also had partnerships in some moonshine stills scattered here and there. There was a lot of money to be made in corn liquor, especially before the repeal of Prohibition. God only knows what else he was involved in. Judging by the other loot, I would guess he had some kind of fencing operation for stolen goods. I know some of those big-time Chicago gangsters would come around now and then, but he always banished me from the room when they were here."

"But why did he hide it under the floorboards?"

"Well, he couldn't exactly put it in the bank, could he? How's a humble dry goods store owner gonna explain that kind of money to the Income Tax people?"

"Tyme, I've got a problem." In all the excitement, Ivy'd almost forgotten about her mother's ultimatum.

"What's the matter, kiddo?"

Ivy related the story to Tyme about her earlier encounter with her mother. "What am I going to do about Harry?"

"I thought you two were gonna get married?"

"But we don't have any money. Harry has to live at the camp and we don't have any place to go. Where would I live?"

"Consider this a wedding present." Tyme handed Ivy a bundle of currency.

"Oh, Tyme. Five thousand dollars? This is way too much."

"You're wrong," Tyme handed her two more stacks. "It's not nearly enough. Here's ten thousand more. That ought to get you and Harry a pretty good start."

"Tyme, I can't take this."

"Yes, you can." Tyme folded Ivy's hands around the money. "I'm not going to let that brother of mine ruin your life the way he did mine. Harry is the perfect man for you and I want to see you both happy together. I would say the timing is just about perfect."

"Are you going to stay here and keep putting up with Chauncey?"

"Actually, no. Now that I've found what I've been looking for, I think it's time to say goodbye to Eureka Springs." Tyme bent down and whispered. "Clyde and I have been talkin' about goin' out to Hollywood. We thought we might get work dancin' in the movies, so I guess it's about time we got hitched."

"Oh, Tyme. That's wonderful! I'm so happy for you."

"Thanks, kiddo. I'm happy too. I've really grown to love him. But I think we should all vamoose tonight, before anybody has a chance to stop us."

"What about the store? Won't it take some time to sell it?"

"Humph. I'm sure my brother will take care of that—you see, your dear Uncle Chauncey didn't see fit to leave the store or anything else to me. He left everything to Caleb."

"My father owns the store?"

"Yep. He's been letting his little sister live here for the past six months out of *Christian charity*, so he says. But I'm sure he'd be kicking me out real quick, now that he's having money problems *and* he's mad at me."

"Do you think he knows about the money?"

"Are you kidding? If he'd known about this, he'd have already been here with a wrecking crew." Tyme put her finger to her lips and then started scooping the treasure back into the bags. "He mustn't find out."

"Don't worry about me." Ivy giggled and helped her. "I'll never tell."

"We've only got a couple more hours before we meet the guys over at Doc's place. Why don't you go on upstairs and pack your things? I'll start loading up the car."

Ivy nodded and headed up the stairs, but halfway up, she

hesitated. "What about the children?"

"What children?"

"You know, the ghost children and their mother. We can't leave them here with Chauncey." Ivy glanced around the darkened store. "It just wouldn't be fair."

"You're right. I've been meaning to do this for a long time, but I kind of liked having them around." Tyme picked up the telephone and spoke to the town operator. "Hello, Mabel? Tyme...can you please connect me with Cordelia?...yes, I'm doin' fine. Thanks for asking...bye now...hello, Cordelia? Tyme...I've got an emergency. Could you come over and help me do a *cleansing*?...yeah, I'm in a big hurry...okay, I'll see you in a few minutes."

"Who was that?"

"That was Madame Cordelia. She does séances and spiritual cleansings." Tyme motioned up the stairs. "She'll help the spirits move on to the next level. Go on now, get packed."

Ivy went to her bedroom, pulled down her valise, and began packing her personal items. She pulled her dresses from their hangers, folded them, and stuffed them in her suitcase; everything she owned, reduced to two small bags.

She smiled when she thought about the adventure ahead. Harry would be so surprised when she handed him the fifteen thousand dollars. Why, that would be enough to buy a little farm some place, and get them started off right. She couldn't wait to see the look on his face.

Finished with her packing, Ivy walked downstairs with her luggage. A short, plump woman with long black hair sat with Tyme at a table in the back of the darkened store. She wore a red dress with a brightly colored shawl. She stood and smiled when she saw Ivy.

"Ivy, I'd like you to meet my friend, Cordelia."

Cordelia's gray eyes sparkled with warmth. "Hello, dear. Your aunt's told me so much about you. I'm glad we finally got to meet."

Ivy returned the greeting, sat in the vacant chair, and stared at the objects on the table—an abalone shell, a book of matches, and several gnarled, wooden sticks. Cordelia struck a match, lit one end of each stick, and placed them in the shell. Ivy wrinkled her nose at the odor of burning sage.

"Let us all hold hands," said Cordelia.

Ivy watched the ritual, fascinated with the medium's careful preparation. The three women formed a circle, their arms resting on the table, their fingers intertwined. She shivered when she noticed the lights in the other rooms flicker and heard the buzz of the electric lights.

Madame Cordelia closed her eyes and breathed deeply. The smoke from the burning sage lingered in the air. Ivy's pulse quickened when she felt the drop in room temperature. She tightened her grip on Tyme's hand.

"I sense four entities in this house," said Madame Cordelia. "Three are frightened and the other is angry—dangerously so."

"Can you see them?" asked Tyme.

"Yes, I see a young woman. Her face is covered in bruises and she's holding her arm as if it were hurt...there are two children with her, a boy and a girl...they're afraid of the other spirit."

"Chauncey." Tyme's lip curled when she spoke his name. The lights buzzed again and a light bulb exploded in the hall.

Ivy flinched, but Madame Cordelia and Tyme held her fast.

"Do not break the circle. He can't hurt you. The smoke from the smudge sticks will protect you."

Ivy nodded and gritted her teeth while Madame continued the ritual. They hadn't had any smoke or circles before. What had protected them then?

"The lady tells me she and the children ran away from her abusive husband and came to Eureka Springs in 1910...she'd heard that Carry Nation lived here and that she ran a shelter and refuge for women like herself."

Surprised, Ivy asked, "Carry Nation? The hatchet lady?"

Madame nodded. "She said Mother Nation took them in, doctored her wounds, and made them feel welcome. But her husband tracked her and the children down. He followed them to this very building and murdered them—and they haven't known what to do since it happened ...for the last twenty-eight years they've been waiting for someone to show them where to go."

"Oh, I feel so bad," said Tyme. "I wish we'd done this a long time ago."

"We can all help them now. Close your eyes and focus internally. Imagine a bubble of white light inside of you, deep in your body."

Ivy closed her eyes and tried to conjure up the imaginary bubble. But it wasn't easy to do with all the hissing and buzzing. By now the room was icy cold. She opened one eye just in time to see a bolt of cloth go flying off a high shelf. She closed her eyes again and prayed for it all to just go away.

"Imagine the bubble expanding in all directions, out past your body," Madame continued as chaos reigned. "Now imagine the white light pushing the negative energy until it fills the room and pushes it out through the windows and the doors."

Ivy felt the table start to shake and she heard the grandfather clock upstairs striking the hour over and over. She heard glass shattering and furniture rolling across the floor. The Victrola began to play a Rudee Valle song. Her instincts told her to get up and run, but instead she squeezed her eyes shut, clutched the other women's hands, and held on for dear life.

"It's working," exclaimed Madame, her eyes tightly closed. "They see the white light—they're running towards it—oh, no—the evil one is trying to stop them—he's chasing them—he's got the little girl's pinafore in his hand—tugging on it..."

Ivy tensed with fear and then she heard it; the shrill, piercing blast of a whistle. She heard a thump on the table. Afraid to look, she kept her eyes tightly shut.

"He let her go to cover his ears—they made it—the white light is gone—the evil one is now alone."

Silence descended on the room and the temperature instantly warmed. Ivy opened her eyes and glanced around the room. If a tornado had blown through, she doubted the destruction would have been greater. The three women relaxed and let go of each other's hands.

"Will you look at that?" Tyme pointed to the middle of the table.

Sitting in the abalone shell, nestled between the burning smudge sticks, was the little Cracker Jack whistle she had given to the children weeks before.

Ivy exhaled and rubbed her arms. She still had goose bumps from the long exposure to the frigid air and the horrifying experience. "Are they really gone?"

Cordelia nodded. "Yes, thank goodness. The family has gone on to the next level. But Chauncey is still here. He refused to go."

"I guess he's not ready to burn in hell yet," remarked Tyme. "Cordelia, thank you for everything you've done." She stood, put her hands on her hips and gazed around the room. "He certainly did make a mess, didn't he?"

"Yes, he did. I've never seen so much rage. He's used up a lot of energy, but you should go as quickly as possible before he starts back up again." She reached into a pocket in her skirt and pulled out a jar of white crystals. She poured some into her hand, and tossed it around the room. "The salt will keep you safe for a while, but you shouldn't wait too long. Goodbye and good luck," said Cordelia.

Tyme embraced Cordelia, then pressed a hundred dollar bill in her palm. "Please don't tell anybody about this."

Cordelia nodded and thanked Tyme profusely. She hugged

Ivy, gathered up her paraphernalia, and left.

"Well, are you about ready to go, kiddo?"

"I think so." Ivy glanced around. "I can't wait to get out of here."

"Me neither. But we probably ought to go upstairs and take one more look around. I don't want to forget something important and then have to come back. There's not much room in the car, so we've gotta travel light. I'm afraid the guys are gonna have to sit on our luggage in the backseat. Chauncey's loot completely filled up the rear steamer trunk. "

The two women cautiously climbed the stairs, carefully stepping over the debris from Chauncey's rampage. Ivy's nose twitched when she noticed a scorched smell, but she dismissed it, assuming it to be residual odor from the smudge sticks.

"Do you hear that?" asked Tyme. "It sounds like music."

Ivy stopped and listened. The hairs on her neck stood on end when she too heard the faint, tinkling melody. She opened the bedroom door and gasped when she saw the music box lying on the bed. Tears ran down her cheeks as she picked it up. She deposited the whistle inside the powder box, carried it down the stairs, and followed Tyme to the car.

The children wouldn't need their gifts any more.

"So long, Chauncey." Tyme saluted and the two women left the house together. They put their suitcases inside the car, and then backed out of the garage.

Ivy turned in her seat and glanced back at the building. The darkened windows were like black, staring eyes. She shuddered, wondering if Chauncey watched them as they made their get-away. Her heart jolted when she saw a bright orange light at the upstairs window. Could the place be on fire? Then she noticed the setting sun reflecting on the windowpanes of surrounding buildings and concern for the store they were abandoning left her mind as the car made its way out of town.

She turned around, relaxed in her seat, and prepared to live happily ever after.

"Hallelujah, we're on our way." Tyme pulled out a cigarette, lit it, and exhaled. "What a relief."

"I know. I'm still in shock over what just happened."

"Um hm." Tyme tapped her cigarette out the window. "Happy days are here again."

Ivy stared wistfully at the passing scenery. "I know Harry and I are going to have a wonderful life. But I feel kind of sorry for Mama and Papa now."

"Why do you feel sorry for them?"

"Because they're both so miserable. I can't ever remember a time when they were happy together."

"I do." Tyme finished her smoke and threw the butt out the window. "They were really happy right up until Danny died."

"Who?"

"Danny. Your baby brother." Tyme glanced nervously at Ivy. "You don't know about him?"

"I had a baby brother?"

"Don't tell me they never told you?"

Ivy stared at Tyme. She felt her temperature rise. "No they didn't. This is news to me."

"Oh, dear. I guess the cat's out of the bag now." Tyme sighed and related the story. "You weren't much more than a year old when he was born, just barely walking. But you always wanted to hold him. You used to call him your dolly."

"I have no recollection of him." Ivy shook her head. "What happened to him?"

"Well, of course you were way too young to remember. He seemed so big and healthy. Everybody just loved him. Then, when he was about four months old, he just died in his sleep. Nobody knows why. The doctors called it crib death."

"So that's what happened to Mama." Ivy wiped a tear from her face. "Harry said she'd been wounded somehow and that's why she acts the way she does. Now I know."

"Yes, Ivy. But most people go through a grieving stage and then continue on with life. They pick up the pieces and love the ones who are left. But your Mama didn't do that. She just withdrew into herself."

"What did Papa do?"

"Well, he wanted to try again. Everyone said they should have more children to help fill the void left by Danny. But your mother wouldn't have it. She moved out of Caleb's bedroom and took up a career as an invalid."

"Poor Papa."

"Humph. Don't feel sorry for him. He just went out and got himself a mistress. He did just fine."

"Did Mama know about that?"

"Sure, she knew. She acted like she was hurt, but in truth I think she was relieved. It just gave her an excuse to continue down her own path of destruction."

Ivy's mind reeled. What a day of discovery this had turned out to be. She braced herself for the turn as Tyme drove the car down Doc Pruett's bumpy old driveway.

"What time is it?"

Tyme glanced at her watch. "We're a little early. They'll be along soon." She pulled up to Doc's house and parked. "Boy, are they gonna be surprised."

"Tyme, are you going to tell my father where you've gone?"

"Look, honey. That's something I've got to talk to you about." Tyme turned in her seat and gazed at Ivy. "I've got to disappear for a while. When everything blows over, I'll write to you. But until then…"

"What are you talking about?"

"Do you remember Earl, the sheriff's deputy? Well, he's been sniffin' around ever since that little brouhaha at the dance. He's threatening me with an inquest."

"For what?"

"For Chauncey, of course. He's beginning to question the

way he died."

"I thought he died of natural causes."

"Well, that's what Doc Pruett put on the death certificate. Bleeding ulcers is what it says. But there was a little more to it than that—it was actually something he ate."

"What are you trying to tell me?" Ivy shivered.

"Let's back up a little before you go jumping to conclusions, okay?" Tyme's hand shook as she lit another cigarette. "I want to tell you what happened."

Ivy nodded and flexed her shoulders.

"We had a visitation that day from some G-men out of Washington DC. They were snooping all over the place like they owned it and Chauncey was nervous. I was tidying up in the store, minding my own business, when one of them came up to me and started asking questions."

"Do you think they knew about all that money he had hidden?"

"I don't know. That's not the type of thing he was asking me. I remember he had a face like a bulldog's and he acted real tough. Said his name was J something Hoover. Anyway, he told me he wanted to buy his sister a red satin corset, and he needed it in a rather large size. So I took him back to the ladies' intimate apparel section."

"He was buying a corset for his sister?" Ivy laughed and covered her mouth.

Tyme rolled her eyes. "That's what I thought. But he kept holding it up to himself and looking in the mirror. I swear, his sister must have been really fat, because it would have fit him!"

"Did he buy it?"

"Um hm. And then Chauncey saw us and I knew I was in trouble."

"Oh, gosh."

"After they left, Chauncey pulled me upstairs and read me the riot act about flirting with other men. I tried to tell him I wasn't that guy's type, but he just smacked me across the jaw. He loosened this tooth right here." Tyme pointed to her mouth. "Then he pulled out a knife and ran the tip across my right breast, going just deep enough to slice the skin. He promised me that the next time he caught me talking to any man he'd cut it off." She opened her blouse and showed Ivy the scar.

"Oh, Tyme. What did you do?"

"Well, I knew he meant business and I'd had enough. So after I got my breast to stop bleeding, I walked into the kitchen and began preparing supper."

"How did you manage to cook after what he'd done to you?"

"Oh, I really enjoyed it. I made him all his favorites. Chicken fried steak, green beans, mashed potatoes, and cream gravy. Only I added a little extra ingredient to the gravy. He gobbled it down like it was his last meal—hm, I guess it was."

"What did you do?"

"I simply used my own, secret recipe." Tyme grinned and lowered her voice. "A pinch of salt, a dash of black pepper— and a cup of rat poison."

CHAPTER FOURTEEN

"You killed Chauncey?" Ivy shrank back, suddenly repulsed by the aunt she had grown to love so much.

Was Tyme a cold-blooded killer? She couldn't believe it. Even though Chauncey had been an evil, domineering sadist, she still couldn't condone murder. There must be more to the story than what appeared on the surface.

"Yes, Ivy. I did. And that's why I have to run away." The expression on Tyme's face pleaded for understanding. "But I assure you, it was in self defense."

Ivy reached for Tyme's hand, ashamed at her flicker of doubt. She had faith that what her aunt was about to tell her would explain everything. "I'm sure it was. But why don't you just go to the authorities and tell them what happened? There's no need for you to be a fugitive."

Tyme shrugged and lit another cigarette. "It's not that simple."

"Oh, yes. I guess you'd have to give up the money."

"No, it's not the money, although I guess in a way it's all intertwined. I can't go to the authorities. I already tried that once."

"After he died, or before?"

"Before." Her hand shook and tears welled in her eyes. "When things got so bad I feared for my life, I went to the sheriff and told him I thought Chauncey was trying to kill me. But he just laughed. You see, my husband was a charter member of the *Good Ole Boys Club* in this town. The sheriff must have told

Chauncey what I said, because things just got worse after that. My complaints are probably the reason Earl got so suspicious of me afterwards."

"But surely they'd understand, after the way he treated you?"

Tyme sniffed. "They didn't care. But I knew for a while he was planning something. He'd been giving me little hints for several weeks that my days were numbered. Making remarks about what he'd do when I was dead and how glad he'd be when he was rid of me."

"He actually said that?"

"Um hm. Twice in that final week he came up behind me while I was washing dishes and held my head underwater until I thought I was going to drown—and another time he shoved me down the stairs while I was carrying laundry. Stuff like that really amused him."

"Such an evil man." Ivy shook her head.

Tyme reached under her car seat and pulled out a large brown envelope. "I found this in another of Chauncey's secret stashes the morning he—ahem—died. I walked in on him while he was hiding it inside a panel in the wall of our bedroom. He didn't know I saw him and when he left the house I pulled it out. When I realized what it was, I knew for certain he was planning to kill me."

Ivy opened the envelope and stared. Inside was a book entitled *The Coming Race*. A narrow piece of paper protruded from the top of the book and she pulled it out. It was a one-way passage ticket for a ship bound for Bremerhaven, Germany. The date of embarkation was February 12, 1938—one week after Chauncey's death.

"What does this mean? Was he going to Germany?"

"Apparently so. And as you can see, there was only one ticket, and he wasn't planning to return." Tyme tapped her ashes out the window. "There's no way he would have left me alone—and alive."

Tyme reached for the ticket and turned it over. On the back, someone had handwritten the words *Thule Society* and beside it was a crudely drawn picture of a dagger atop a broken cross within a circle. Ivy gasped when she recognized the emblem.

"That's the same symbol on the stickpins Chauncey and Jared wore. It also reminds me of that horrible necklace my father gave me to wear to the debutante ball."

"Oh, my. Is Jared mixed up with them too?"

"Mixed up with whom?"

"The Thules. Chauncey called it a fraternal organization, but it's really a secret society. I'm not surprised Jared's a member after what you've told me."

"Papa is a Mason. Isn't that the same thing?"

"Not at all." Tyme stubbed out her cigarette. "I've heard that the Masons participate in secret rituals and handshakes and such. But these other groups—they're deeply involved in the occult, maybe even satanic worship. I think there's something very evil about the Thules."

Ivy shivered, grateful she hadn't given in and married Jared like her parents wanted. "Do they practice witchcraft?"

"I don't really know what they do. But I did snoop around and hear some very disturbing things."

"Like what?"

"Well, I think Chauncey was involved with another sect within the Thules called the *Vrils*. I heard him talking to one of his *brothers* about some kind of flying saucer machine the Nazis had been building in caverns in Bavaria—I think Hitler himself is a member."

"Oh, my gosh. Do you think that's why Chauncey was planning to go there?"

Tyme shrugged. "Your guess is as good as mine. But I do know that I want to distance myself from this place and you should too. If that money was earmarked for the Nazis, it could prove dangerous for me and Clyde."

Ivy shivered when she remembered what her friend Margot had said about Jared selling lead to the Nazis. Her father had laughed at her, but now she knew it must be true. Her instincts had been correct.

The sound of a car coming up the driveway interrupted the somber moment. But despite the day's disturbing events and revelations, Ivy smiled when she saw Harry in the back of Doc's old truck. She climbed out of Tyme's car and ran to meet him, not even waiting for him to get out before she kissed him.

"Are you girls all right?" asked Doc.

"We've been worried sick about ya," said Clyde.

"We're fine," replied Tyme. "Why've you been worried?"

Doc leaned against his truck, folded his arms, and replied, "'Cause right about now, your store's burnin' to the ground."

Harry cuddled Ivy and stared out the back window of the car. She sighed softly and rested her head against his chest. A sense of wonder and excitement filled him to the bursting point. He ran his hand up and down her arm just to make sure she was really there and that he wasn't dreaming.

He couldn't believe what had just happened. The workweek had dragged by; he'd been so anxious to see Ivy again. He'd expected to spend the evening with her watching James Cagney's latest movie, but instead, here they were riding in the back seat of a car on their way to Fort Smith to get married.

"How're we gonna get a license this late in the day?" Harry leaned forward and looked at Tyme. "It's after five. Courthouse is closed."

"Doc has all that taken care of."

When they arrived in town, they followed Doc Pruett's truck onto a quiet, tree-lined street and parked in front of a big Victorian house.

"Whose place is this?" asked Ivy. She climbed out of the

back seat and followed the others up the front steps.

"My friend, Tom's. He's one of my fishin' buddies," explained Doc as he rang the doorbell. "He's also the county clerk."

Tom welcomed them all inside, they went into the dining room, and sat at the massive oak table. He was already prepared for them, with the necessary paperwork spread out and ready to sign.

"Sure was glad Doc managed to get hold of me b'fore I left the courthouse." Tom smiled warmly. "Always like to help nice young people who wanta get hitched."

Their next stop was a used car lot owned by another of Doc's friends. Tyme and Clyde wandered around and gazed at the inventory. They made their selection, handed the salesman some cash, and then transferred the steamer trunk, along with Tyme's and Clyde's possessions into the new car.

"Here ya go, Harry." Clyde tossed him the keys to Tyme's Model A.

Harry made the catch and looked at Clyde with a question in his eyes. "What's this for?"

"It's yours." Tyme replied. "We've got no use for two cars now."

"But…"

"No arguments," Tyme scolded. "Just shut up and follow us."

He couldn't believe her generosity. Ivy'd told him her aunt had given them some money to get them started—and now she was giving them a car too! Ever since the box-supper auction, he'd been broke and forced to bum money off Clyde, but he'd kept a close tally. He'd sworn to repay every cent when he got paid.

Now he felt guilty about leaving the CCC so abruptly, but he knew it was necessary. After the girls had explained what had happened, he'd written a hasty note to Sarge, letting him know that he and Clyde wouldn't be coming back. He'd sealed the envelope, stuffed it into Doc's mailbox, and raised the flag.

Ivy giggled and climbed into the front seat beside Harry. He started the engine and followed the two lead cars down the street, caravan style. They drove to the edge of town and then turned into a driveway beside a small country church. Harry parked, helped Ivy out, and followed the others into the parsonage.

The pastor greeted them at the door and motioned for them to come into the parlor. A plump, elderly woman walked in, wiping her hands on her apron.

"My wife, Martha, will play for the ceremony," said the minister. She smiled, went over to an upright piano, and began to play the wedding march.

"Licenses all in order?" The pastor scanned the documents, his bifocals riding low on the tip of his nose. When he was satisfied, he nodded to his wife at the piano and she stopped playing. "If everyone's ready, I'll ask you to please stand here and join hands. Martha, we'll need you and Doc to act as witnesses. Do you have any rings?"

Harry and Clyde looked at each other and shrugged.

"Doesn't matter. You can always get 'em later," said the pastor and then proceeded with the ceremony.

Moments later, both couples repeated their vows. Overwhelmed with joy, Harry had to fight to keep the gravel out of his voice. He promised to love Ivy forever, for better or for worse, in sickness and in health, until death do they part—and he meant every word of it.

"I love you, Harry," Ivy whispered.

Choked with emotion, Harry just smiled and obeyed the pastor's invitation to kiss the bride. He couldn't believe it. She wasn't Ivy Turner anymore. She was now Ivy Fuller. And he was the happiest man in the world.

Doc Pruett beamed at both sets of newlyweds. "Well, I guess it's about time for me to head on back to my place." He stuffed the completed marriage licenses in his jacket pocket. "I'll make sure these get filed first thing Monday morning. Write me when you get settled and I'll send you your copies. Sure am gonna miss you all."

"Thank you so much for everything," Tyme said. She and Ivy hugged him and the men shook his hand. "We'd never have been able to pull this off without your help."

"All right, now. Ya'll go on and git."

The four newlyweds waved at Doc as he pulled his old truck onto the road and drove away. Harry put his arm around his bride and turned to Clyde and Tyme. "So now what?"

"So now we all go start our new lives," replied Tyme. She reached over and embraced both Ivy and Harry. "We'll try to contact you when everything settles down, okay? Goodbye. Love you both."

Harry and Ivy stood and waved until the car disappeared into the gloom.

Darkness descended on the newlyweds as they drove south on the winding forest road. They'd left the Ozarks far behind, but now the elevation rose again as they made their way through the Ouachita Mountains. Intermittent rain made driving difficult and reduced visibility. Ivy's body tensed as the car's headlights sliced a path through the thickening fog. Not wanting to distract Harry, she remained silent.

"Honey, are you all right?"

Ivy nodded, but then gasped when she saw a movement at the edge of the road. But Harry's reflexes were good. He saw the buck in time and successfully applied the brakes before the animal stepped into the road. Her heart pounded as she watched the deer stare at the car before shaking his head with its massive rack and ambling to the other side.

Harry exhaled. "Maybe we need to stop somewhere for the night."

"I think that's an excellent idea," Ivy agreed. "Aren't we coming up on a town pretty soon?"

"I think so. We passed Pine Ridge a while back, so we can't be too far from Mena. Do we have enough money for a tourist court? Or do you want to see if we can stay with Lum 'n Abner?"

"We most certainly do." Ivy laughed and squeezed his hand. "I don't intend to spend my wedding night in either this car or at some silly radio comedian's place."

When they reached the outskirts of town Ivy pointed to a neon light in the distance. "Look, Harry. I think that's a motel right there."

Harry pulled the car into the driveway and parked in front of the office. Ivy gazed at the dingy little buildings. It was a far cry from the Ritz Carlton where Jared had said he'd wanted to take her when he married her, but she wouldn't have traded places. She'd rather live under a bridge with Harry than in a palace with Jared.

When Ivy pressed a bill into Harry's hand he gazed at it in disbelief. "A hundred dollars?" He picked it up and stared at Benjamin Franklin's face. "I don't think I've ever seen one of these before. I never dreamed Tyme would give us this much."

Ivy smiled at his innocent wonder. She hadn't told him about the rest of the money yet because she wanted to surprise him when they got to their room. She thought about the little farm they would buy in Texas—and the home they would make together—and the family they would raise.

"Why don't you wait here and I'll go get us a room?" Harry climbed out of the car, but Ivy opened the passenger door and followed him.

"I want to go with you."

She took his arm and followed him into the motel's office. The bell above the door jingled, and an obese man glanced up from his newspaper, hitched up his pants, and waddled to the front desk.

"C'n I help you?"

"Uh, yes sir," Harry replied. "I'd like a room for me and my wife."

"Yer wife, huh?" The man cocked an eyebrow at Ivy's bare ring finger and sniffed. "That'll be two bucks, in advance."

Harry handed the man the hundred-dollar bill.

"What're you, some kinda wise guy or somethin'?" The man picked up the bill and held it up to the light. "I ain't got that kinda change. And besides, how do I know it ain't counterfeit?"

Harry turned red and fumbled in his pockets. He counted out three quarters, a dime and four pennies. Ivy reached over, snatched the bill out of the desk clerk's hand, and emptied the contents of her purse onto the desk. When he was satisfied with the correct amount, the clerk handed Harry a room key.

"Check-out's ten a.m." He turned, glanced over his shoulder, and then waddled back to his chair.

"Sorry, Ivy." Harry opened the car door and then hurried around to the drivers' side, preparing to park the car near their assigned unit. "Ain't never stayed at a motel before."

When Harry found the room, he unlocked the door, flipped on the light switch, and deposited their bags on the floor. Ivy started to walk in, but he put his hand on her shoulder and stopped her. She turned and stared at him, wondering what he was doing.

"Wait a minute, honey." He swept her into his arms and carried her into the room, kicking the door shut behind him.

Ivy wrapped her arms around his neck and kissed him. He carried her into the room and laid her on the bed, without their lips breaking contact. There was a tingling in the pit of her stomach, a raw, aching need unlike anything she'd ever known before.

She felt his hands moving up and down her body, propelling her senses beyond anything she'd ever experienced. He tore his lips from hers and began kissing her neck and caressing her limbs, sending fire through every nerve in her body. She felt his male hardness pressing against her thigh and she trembled in his arms.

He pulled away and stared at her. "I'm sorry, Ivy." His eyes were filled with worry. "I didn't hurt you, did I?"

"Oh, Harry. I love you so much."

They didn't have to wait any longer, now that they were married. No more kissing and feeling the passion, but being forced to withdraw. She wanted to know for herself what it was her body yearned for, to quell the burning fire in her loins. She reached for him and their kiss deepened. Her senses throbbed with the strength and scent and feel of him.

He fumbled with the buttons of her dress and she reached up to help him, anxious to be rid of it. She wanted to feel her bare skin against his. He raised himself off the bed to remove his own clothing.

"Would you turn off the lights, please?"

Harry walked over to the light switch and flipped it off. Ivy pulled her dress over her head and then removed her chemise. She felt her temperature rise in anticipation when she heard the thud of his belt as he dropped his clothing onto the floor, and felt the bounce of the mattress as he joined her on the bed.

His hands set her body on fire as they traveled across her naked flesh. Her nails massaged his back and she trembled at the feel of his hard, aching need rubbing against her belly. Primitive desire consumed her and she gave herself over to him with sweet abandon. A hard knot of desire twisted in her stomach when she felt him enter her, thrusting slowly at first, and then harder as his passion increased.

She gasped at the sudden pain, and felt the warm blood flowing down her thighs. But seconds later, the pain was forgotten as she reveled in the incredible power of his surging body. Instinctively, her hips lifted in a sensuous invitation and the moment of ecstasy exploded around her. She felt him jerk inside her and was consumed by a dizzying, uncontrollable burst of joy.

Afterward, they lay in silence, just holding each other. Ivy sighed happily. She hadn't known it would be like this, never dreamed the act of love could be so wonderful, so totally fulfilling.

She turned toward Harry and kissed him. And then it all started over again.

Harry's stomach growled when he awoke the next morning. He thought about the little café across the street. It had been closed last night, but he figured they'd be serving breakfast now. He and Ivy had both been more concerned with satisfying a different kind of hunger last night to worry about the dinner they had missed.

He turned on his pillow and saw his angel there beside him. His heart swelled with love for her and he reached over and ran his finger down the curve of her breast. Her nipple hardened and she squirmed beneath his touch, then opened her eyes and smiled. She was even more beautiful this morning, with her hair spread out on the pillow, and the glow of their lovemaking still fresh on her face.

He leaned over and kissed her deeply and a fire in his loins soon replaced the growl in his belly. They made love again, and this time was no less sweet than the others. When they were finished he held her tightly, and she curled into his arms. He didn't want to let her go, but his empty stomach betrayed him.

"Sounds like you're as hungry as I am." Ivy sat up and stretched.

"There's a diner across the street. You wanta go get something?"

"Would you mind bringing the food back here?" Ivy pulled the sheet up to cover her breasts. "I'd like to freshen up before we leave."

"Don't hide 'em from me." Harry playfully jerked the sheet back down and buried his face in her chest.

"Would you stop it and get out of here?" She swatted at his head and giggled. "We've gotta get out of bed sometime."

"I don't wanna get out of bed." Harry nuzzled her neck.

"Go on, now. Put your clothes on and get out of here." Ivy laughed and gently shoved him. "If we stay too much longer, that big goon'll be demanding another two dollars and we're just about out of small change." She emptied out her purse and he put the coins and the hundred-dollar bill in his pocket.

"What would you like to have?"

"Scrambled eggs, toast, and coffee. Cream and two sugars, please."

"Okay. Be right back." Harry kissed her goodbye, walked across the road, and entered the diner.

He went to the lunch counter, sat on a stool and placed his order, making sure to let the waitress know he needed it to go. He glanced around the room, noting the people scattered throughout the café, sipping coffee and eating breakfast. It seemed to be a popular place for the locals, as well as travelers.

The waitress brought out Harry's order and he'd just reached in his pocket to pay when he noticed a hush fall over the diner. He glanced over his shoulder when he saw the expression of alarm on the waitress's face. Three men in uniform with shiny badges walked in and went straight to Harry.

"You Harry Fuller?"

"Y-Yes sir," Harry stammered. "Is something the matter?"

The officer chewed his tobacco and hitched his fingers in his belt loops. "Got a warrant fer yer arrest outa Carroll County."

"For what?" Harry stared at the officer and then glanced around the room. Everyone was looking at him like he was some kind of criminal. He had no idea what this could be about.

"We'll get to that later, boy. Just turn around now and let me put the cuffs on ya."

Harry put his hands behind his back and turned around. But the sound of a woman's screams from outside caused him to jerk around. Something was wrong with Ivy!

He shoved the officer as hard as he could, knocking him off balance, and ran for the door. He heard Ivy scream again and when he looked toward the motel he saw her. Two men had wrapped her in a blanket and were forcing her into a car, kicking and screaming.

Panic rose up in his throat and he ran toward the car, trying desperately to reach her. He made it to the car and banged on the window just as it began to pull away. He saw her face through the window and heard her terror-filled cries, but he was powerless to stop it. He didn't know what else to do, so he ran.

Until the report of a gun reverberated in his ears—and the pain in his left leg rose up and burned him like white-hot fire—and the beat of his heart as he lay on the ground drowned out the haunting echo of his wife's frantic screams.

Harry's leg hurt. Bad.

He groaned and blinked his eyes, then tried to sit up. Cold steel chains at both wrists held him fast.

"Hello? Is anybody there?"

He glanced around the darkened room, noting the rows of metal cots lining the walls and the bars that covered the windows. Where the hell was he? His nose wrinkled at the stench of disinfectant, mingled with human waste, and he heard a moan from the other side of the room. He tried to twist his body around to see, but the pain stopped him cold and he lay back, gasping for breath.

His left leg throbbed painfully, his hair was drenched in sweat, and he felt like he hadn't peed in a week. He didn't know where he was or how long he'd been there, but relieving the pressure on his bladder was his top priority at the moment.

"I see you're awake now." A heavy-set woman in a nurse's

uniform peeked through the door. "Need a bottle?"

"Excuse me?" Her *don't-bother-me-now* expression startled him. He licked his dry, chapped lips and tasted the sourness of his own breath.

The nurse took an empty milk bottle out of a cabinet near Harry's bed, pulled back the sheet and held it in place. Humiliated, Harry turned his head so he wouldn't have to look at her. He couldn't decide which was worse—the pain in his bandaged leg or the embarrassment.

Thank goodness she wasn't the talkative sort. Her task complete, she marched out of the room and left Harry alone. He pulled again on the restraints. The chains clinked against the metal bed frame. He tried to move his left leg, but agony overcame him. Chains or not, he wouldn't be able to get very far on that leg.

"Well, well, well." Harry started when he saw Earl, the sheriff's deputy come into the room. "Guess you're gonna live after all, huh Fuller?"

"Why'm I here?" Harry squirmed from his supine position, wishing he could at least sit up.

"'Cause Sheriff Miller over in Polk County was forced to shoot you after you attacked one of his deputies and then tried to run off." Earl grinned and crossed his arms. "Too bad he just got ya in the leg. If'n he'd aimed a little higher it shore woulda saved the taxpayers some money. You been wallerin' in this bed fer nigh on three days now."

Memories came rushing back and he panicked. "Where's my wife?"

"Wife?" Earl cocked his head to one side. "Din't know you was married."

"Ivy's my wife. Where is she?" He clutched the bed sheets, frustrated by his captivity.

"You talkin' 'bout the little gal they dragged outta that cheap touristy court?"

"Where is she, damn you?" Harry jerked at the restraints, causing the bed to shake. "What have you done with my wife?"

"If you're talkin' 'bout Miss Turner..." Earl smiled, walked over to a trashcan and spat. "Her daddy done took her back to St. Louie."

"Her name's Ivy Fuller." Harry felt his temperature rise. "We got married on Friday. Me and Ivy, and Clyde and Tyme. Just ask Doc Pruett. He was gonna file the marriage licenses for us."

Earl shook his head and folded his arms. "Now that's just too bad."

"What?" Hairs on the back of Harry's neck prickled.

"Pore ol' Doc." Earl walked slowly around the room before he continued. "Found him in his truck a couple days ago near Thompson's crick. Looks like he just skidded right off the road and hit the bottom of the bridge...truck caught on fire. If he had any marriage licenses on him, they're toast now...same as Doc Pruett."

Harry lay back in the bed and closed his eyes. He should have known it was all too good to be true. Ivy—the money—all of it. Now she was gone and Doc was dead. Nothing good ever happened to him. Everything always ended in tragedy.

"They're gettin' up a grand jury tomorrow," said Earl. "They put it off for a couple of days when it looked like you might not make it, with your fever and all."

"A grand jury? For what?"

"Well, let me see if I can 'member all the charges they're plannin'." Earl grinned, poked out his fingers, and counted. "There's arson, grand theft auto, bank robbery, kidnapping..."

"Arson? Bank robbery?" Harry spluttered. "I didn't do none of those things."

"Let me spell it out, Fuller," Earl's eyes glittered. "We got reason to believe you and your partner McKinney set fire to the Renfro Dry Goods store last Friday."

"No, we didn't," Harry argued. "We worked all day Friday at the camp and then when we came through town we heard about the fire, but we didn't go near it."

"Hm. Well, we'll see. There's also the car you stole."

"I didn't steal any car. Clyde and Tyme bought a new one, so they gave her old one to me and Ivy."

Earl sniffed. "Wasn't hers to give. Belonged to Caleb Turner. He inherited it from Chauncey Renfro after he died."

"What about the money? I didn't have nothin' but a hundred dollars that Tyme gave us for a wedding gift."

"Yeah, that's what tipped us off to the whole thing." Earl smirked and leaned on Harry's bed. "Man at the motel called the local sheriff Friday night. Said you'd been tryin' to pay for a two-dollar room with a counterfeit C-note. So they checked it out and discovered the car you was drivin' was stolen too. Our men do fast work. S'why you got caught so quick."

"It wasn't stolen." Harry clenched his fists and tried to ignore the throbbing pain. "And you think I robbed a bank just because I had a hundred dollars?"

"Hoo boy!" Earl chortled. "I ain't no accountant, but best I can figure, you had 'bout fifteen thousand dollars in your suitcase."

"What?" Harry gasped.

"Um hm. That was a nice little chunk of change, my boy. Where'd ya get it?"

"I have no idea what you're talking about." Harry lay back on the pillow and closed his eyes.

"People's been speculatin' 'bout that money. Couple men robbed a bank over in Bentonville back last January." Earl scratched his head, sending dander flakes flying. "We think maybe it was you and McKinney done it."

"I wasn't even here then. I was still working for the CCC up in South Dakota. I didn't come to Arkansas until April."

"You got any proof of your whereabouts?"

"Well, yeah. I could get proof. All I gotta do is write to my old unit."

"We'll let your lawyer take care of that. Meanwhile, you're still in a messa trouble. But you're damn lucky they caught ya when they did." Earl hovered over Harry, staring him in the face. "Just a little bit farther and youd've crossed the state line with the little gal. Then we'd have to turn ya over to the Feds for interstate kidnapping."

"Yeah, lucky me."

"What about McKinney? You know where he went with Miz Renfro?"

"No. They didn't say where they were going."

"You sure you don't know where they went?" Earl poked at Harry's injured leg with his finger. "'Cause you might as well tell us. We'll find 'em one way or the other."

Harry stifled a scream and broke out in a cold sweat. A thousand burning needles gnawed at the edges of his frayed nerves, but he remained silent.

Earl pulled back the sheet and stared at Harry's leg. He ripped the bandage off and Harry almost passed out. The gaping wound where the doctor had removed the bullet was still raw and puffy, but appeared to be healing. Earl stood and studied the wound for several seconds, then roughly tied the bandage back in place. Harry bit his lip, refusing to cry out.

"Yeah, that's what I thought." Earl sneered as he headed for the door. "Ain't that bad no more. I'll tell the doctor you're ready to leave the infirmary and go back to your jail cell."

CHAPTER FIFTEEN

"Are you sure she'll be ready by then?" Jared's dark eyes glittered and his mouth tightened. "It's been more than three months since she's spoken with me. It's almost October, you know. I have to make the reservations for our ship or we'll never make it to Paris by New Year's Eve."

"Yes, yes, of course she'll be ready." Caleb smiled, lit a cigar, and held out his lighter to Jared. "She's been through a trauma, remember? Just takes a little time. But the doctor says she'll be just fine. I see no problem in having the wedding on December third."

"Well, what's the matter with her now? Why won't she see me tonight?" Jared puffed on his cigar and scowled.

"She's got a touch of the flu," said Winifred. "Her eyes are all puffy and her nose is red. She's in no condition to entertain anyone right now. Did you bring the sketches?"

"Oh, yes. Here they are." Jared pulled some drawings out of his briefcase and spread them on the drawing room table.

"These are lovely. I think that one will do quite nicely." Winifred studied the pictures of wedding gowns, pointed to the third one in the set, and handed Jared an envelope. "Here are her measurements for the seamstress."

"Don't you think we ought to consult Ivy before we make the final decision?" asked Caleb.

"Very well. If you will excuse me, Jared, I'll take these upstairs and show them to her."

"Winnie, Jared and I are going to the club for a drink. I

shouldn't be too late, but don't bother waiting up. All right?"

"Of course, dear. It was nice to see you again, Jared. I'll show these sketches to Ivy."

Winifred turned and walked slowly up the stairs. They were all fooling themselves if they thought Ivy would be ready to marry Jared by December. It had already been more than two months since they'd forced her to come home, yet she was still crying over Harry.

She stopped on the stair landing and held her aching head. The tension from all the unhappiness in the house was getting to her. Dr. Baker had advised her to avoid stress, yet she found herself bombarded with it daily. As soon as she finished with Ivy she would go take a dose of her medicine and lie down. She just hoped the tumor wasn't growing again.

She could still hear Jared and Caleb's voices from where she stood upstairs. She paused to listen.

"Will you be certain she wears the necklace? She was wearing it the night we met, you know. It's very important she wear it at our wedding, too."

"Of course, Jared. The necklace is safely locked away. Nobody's going to touch it until then."

The slamming of the front door echoed throughout the house.

Winifred sighed when she thought about the unusual diamond and sapphire pendant cross. Caleb had taken it, along with a matching ring and pair of earrings, off a dead German officer when he was away fighting in the Great War. He'd sold the ring and earrings before they married, but she'd worn the necklace at their wedding. She reached up and touched the scar on her neck, still faintly visible after all these years.

She'd never liked the necklace. From the moment she first saw it, she'd sensed something cold and unfriendly about it. But Caleb had insisted she wear it and she'd kept her anxiety to herself; afraid he would think her insane if she told him about the way it seemed to cut off her breath—or how the sharp edge had dug into her neck, leaving tiny droplets of red on her wedding veil.   And then the scratch hadn't healed properly, leaving a scar to remind her of her irrational fear.

Caleb had locked it in the safe after their wedding and she hadn't looked at it in years. But then two years ago, when times grew hard, Winifred suggested he sell the necklace. Together they'd taken it to a local jeweler with a reputation for honesty. The jeweler's appraisal had been astonishing.

Winifred shivered, remembering the excitement on Mr. Schmidt's face when he looked at the necklace. The jeweler's wife had then entered the shop, picked up the necklace, and tried it on. She was wearing the earrings and ring Caleb had sold years before, and the proximity of the stones together flashed like fire beneath the overhead lights. Mr. Schmidt had grown angry and barked something in a language Winifred didn't understand, which sent his wife scurrying in tears from the room after removing the necklace.

He recovered quickly from his outburst, rummaged around on a bookshelf behind the counter, produced an old, leather-bound book, and flipped through the pages. An artist's rendering of the necklace, earrings, and ring appeared on page fifty-seven.

Caleb laughed when the jeweler read the story beside the picture, but Winifred took it seriously. According to legend, an eighteenth-century Romanian jewelry-maker had been commissioned by a member of European royalty to manufacture the set for her daughter. The precious gems were delivered to their destination, but the necklace was never paid for. Unable to collect the debt, the jeweler put a curse on whoever wore the necklace.

Mr. Schmidt then proceeded to tell them that the necklace was a priceless antique, that it belonged in a museum, and that it would be impossible for him to pay Caleb a fraction of its true value. This explanation had seemed to satisfy Caleb, however, for he had taken it home and locked it up. The next time Winifred saw it was on the night Ivy was crowned Queen of the Veiled Prophet Ball—the night she met Jared.

Ivy hadn't liked the necklace either. She'd complained about feeling choked when she wore it at her début last year. Yolanda, the maid, had called it unlucky.

Winifred steeled herself and knocked. Silence. She put the key in the lock and opened the door. The room was cold, yet airless and stuffy. Winifred's heart skipped a beat when she looked around and couldn't find her daughter. Then she heard the retching and she hurried inside, dropping the portfolio onto Ivy's bed.

"Sweetheart, are you all right?"

Ivy knelt on the floor, hovering over the chamber pot. Her face was a tortured mask, her complexion ashen, and her eyes sunken and hollow. She wiped her mouth with the back of her hand and slowly rose to her feet.

Winifred's stomach heaved at the sickly smell, but she covered her nose with her hand and hurried to help Ivy. "Darling, are you sick again?" Winifred put her arm around Ivy and walked her back to the bed.

Ivy groaned and lay down. She turned her face to the wall and curled herself into a ball.

"Ivy, I'm getting very worried about you. I think it's time to call the doctor again." Winifred sat on the edge of the bed and ran her fingers across Ivy's forehead. She didn't have a fever, but her chestnut hair had lost its shine and her complexion seemed pale and sallow.

"You won't like what he tells you. You know very well what's wrong with me, but you don't want to admit it."

Winifred stared back at her daughter and shook her head. "Oh, Ivy. You've got all the symptoms I had months ago. Do you think you might have cancer?"

Ivy closed her eyes and her lips curled in a grimace. "You

are such an actress. You know very well that I'm with child. I'm going to have Harry's baby."

Winifred recoiled. "How can you say such a thing? You're not even married!"

"I was married. Until you and Papa had me declared incompetent and got my marriage annulled." The dark circles under Ivy's sunken eyes grew more pronounced as they filled with tears. "I will never forgive you and Papa for what you did to me."

"That so-called *husband* of yours is nothing but a common criminal. He's sitting in jail right now and I hope they never let him out." Winifred's heart began to palpitate and she held her hand to her chest, gulping in shallow breaths.

"Well, that makes two of us," Ivy spat. "I might as well be in jail too. I haven't been out of this room in over two months."

"Your father and I had to work very hard to convince the judge to let you come home at all. You were acting like such a lunatic, he wanted to have you committed to an institution. I thought I would die from shame when they brought you home wearing a straight jacket."

Ivy sniffed. "I wish you had sent me to the hospital. At least then I might have been able to go outside occasionally."

"Is that what you want? To go outside?"

Ivy sat up and took Winifred's hand, her eyes pleading. "Mama, if I don't get out of here soon, I'm going to lose my mind. I'm sick of this room—sick of this house. Won't you please let me see some of my friends?"

Winifred hesitated. "Jared will be back in a little while. Would you like to see him?"

"No! You know how much I hate him." Tears rolled down her cheeks and her eyes darted around the room. "I want to see Margot. I heard her at the door yesterday asking for me. Please let me talk to her? Please?"

"Oh, sweetheart. You know how your father feels about

her." Winifred embraced Ivy and the sketches fell out of the portfolio onto the bed.

Ivy picked up a drawing and stared at it. "What is this?"

"They're sketches of wedding gowns from Jared's designer. He wants you to pick one out so she can begin sewing."

Ivy screamed, picked up the drawings, and began ripping them apart.

Winifred gasped and jerked them away. She stood up and stared at her daughter. "What is the matter with you?" She backed out of the room, clutching the portfolio.

Ivy collapsed onto the mattress, sobbing uncontrollably. Winifred's heart lurched when her daughter's mournful wailing seemed to increase with the click of the lock. She retreated to the safety of her bedroom.

She stood with her back to the wall, trying to catch her breath, her lungs ready to explode. How much more could she endure? Her head pounded and she was reminded of another time, when the pain in her head and the crying of her child had been too much to endure.

Almost blinded from the pain, she felt her way to her bathroom. She reached into the medicine cabinet with shaking hands and rummaged through the bottles. Nothing in here would be strong enough to help her now.

She stumbled back into the bedroom and opened the closet, kicking aside mounds of hatboxes and shoes until she found what she was looking for. The little wooden chest hadn't been opened in years, but she knew that what she needed was inside. She groped through the tiny blankets and shirts and booties until her fingers touched the cool glass bottle.

Mrs. Winslow's Soothing Syrup.

She carried it into the bathroom, poured some into a tumbler, and drank. She closed her eyes and waited for the precious serum to work its magic. Within seconds her mind cleared and the pounding in her head abated. She breathed deeply and smiled. Her stress had vanished.

Winifred stared at the label on the bottle. A picture of a pretty Victorian lady dangling a toy above a plump baby adorned the bottle. The words *for children teething* were prominently displayed across the front. A Pure Food and Drug Act tax stamp dangled loosely from its stopper. Such a wonderful product. It used to be available everywhere, but now you couldn't even get it any more.

She carried the bottle down the hall, placed the key in the lock, and entered her daughter's bedroom. Her mother's heart ached at the sight of her child, crumpled on the bed. Ivy was crying again, her sobs pitiful and hopeless. She sat on the bed and rubbed Ivy's back, her words low and soothing.

"There, there, my darling. Mama's here now. Please don't cry. Mama has something to make you feel better." Winifred reached for a spoon on the bedside table, opened the bottle and poured some liquid into the spoon.

Ivy turned over and looked at her mother, her nose twitching from the pungent odor. "What is that?"

"Some nice medicine to make you feel better," replied Winifred. Her hand shook as she held the spoon toward Ivy. "Baby Danny liked it when he was cutting teeth. It always made him sleep so well."

Ivy gasped and knocked the spoon out of Winifred's hand, spilling its contents on the bed. She grabbed the bottle out of her mother's other hand and stared at the label. "Mama, this has morphine in it."

"Now look what you've done!" Winifred snatched back the bottle and hugged it to her body. "How will I ever get the baby to stop crying?"

"Mama, is that what happened to Danny? Did you give him that syrup?"

Winifred stared at Ivy, confused. How did she know about Danny? She and Caleb had kept his existence a closely guarded secret from Ivy all these years. But now somehow she knew and the pain she'd kept bottled up inside suddenly came pouring out, threatening her composure, as well as her sanity.

"He wouldn't stop crying." Winifred stared at Ivy. She had to make her understand. "He cried and he cried and he cried. There was nobody here to help me. Caleb told me he was taking Ivy and the maid to church and he left me alone with Danny. But I know he was really with that trollop." Her face turned red with anger and then crumpled in pain. "My head hurt so much, and the louder Danny cried the more it hurt."

"Mama, you're scaring me." Ivy reached for Winifred's hand, but she batted it away.

She paced and wrung her hands. "Don't you see? I tried everything. I changed him. I fed him. I rocked him. But nothing worked. He just kept screaming. So I gave him some syrup. But he kept on crying. So I gave him some more." Winifred stopped and stared out the window. "And then he stopped crying."

Winifred stared at Ivy's horrified expression. Her mind jolted and she realized what she had done. The horror she had suppressed so many years ago stared her in the face, raw and bleeding.

"I'm sorry...sorry..." Winifred stumbled backward, clutching the bottle. She fled, locking the door behind her.

Knowing what she had to do, she walked into Caleb's upstairs study and removed a painting from the wall. She reached for the combination lock and moved the dial, backwards and forwards, and then back again until she heard it click. The safe opened and she took out the sapphire necklace, making sure to close the door and re-hang the painting.

Like a zombie, she walked into her bedroom and stared at the crackling fireplace. Caleb didn't like to have a fire this time of year, but Winifred seemed always to be cold. No matter what she did, she could never get warm enough. She stoked the fire until it blazed with a fierce heat.

She spread her fingers toward the hearth, still holding the necklace in her right hand until the cold metal and stones began to heat up. Her fingertips grew hotter and hotter, until the pain from the heat became unbearable, and she dropped the necklace into the flames.

Winifred watched in fascination as the jewels burned and the gold chain melted. They cracked and popped until nothing was left but black, charred remains. What was left of the necklace gave one last, agonizing hiss before she added three more logs and the flames leaped up again, reborn. She then sat down at her desk, composed a short letter, sealed the envelope, and placed it on her bedside table before walking out into the hallway.

She stopped on the stair landing and listened, but Jared and Caleb had not yet returned. The silence reassured her as she made her way back to Ivy's room and unlocked the door. Her daughter's rhythmic breathing told her she slept. Tears welled in her eyes as she gazed at Ivy before closing and locking the door one last time.

Then she walked back to her bedroom, lay down on the bed, and drank the rest of the bottle of Mrs. Winslow's Soothing Syrup.

Margot glanced over her shoulder as she knocked on the back door of the Turner house. She tapped her foot and waited, praying that the note Ivy'd slipped into her hand at Winifred's funeral had been correct and that her father would indeed be gone. After everything that had happened, the last person she wished to confront was Caleb Turner.

The door opened and Yolanda motioned for her to come inside. Margot followed the maid through the deathly quiet house, noting the dozens of flower arrangements scattered here and there. The scent of dying roses filled the house. She shivered and climbed the stairs.

Yolanda glanced over her shoulder before knocking on the bedroom door. "Miss Ivy? Are you awake?"

"What is it Yolanda?" Ivy's shaky voice came from the other side of the door.

"Miss Margot's come to see you." The young black woman glanced at Margot, nodded, and then retreated down the stairs.

"Oh, Margot. Thank goodness you've come," said Ivy, her voice trembling. "Everything's been so horrible."

"Kid, are you all right? I can't believe your father won't trust Yolanda with the key to your room." Margot sank to the floor and leaned against the door, speaking into the keyhole. "I'm sorry it's taken me so long to get here. I've been out of town all summer and I'd assumed you were gone, too. I came over the minute I heard you were in town, but they wouldn't let me in."

"So much has happened. Did you know about Harry and me?"

"Yolanda told me. I still can't believe it. It's all so incredible."

"I thought my parents loved me." Ivy's voice quivered. "I never would have believed they would do this to me."

Margot choked back a sob and wiped her face with her hand. "Your father's not starving you to death, is he? When I hugged you at the funeral yesterday you felt like a skeleton."

Ivy's voice seemed to recapture a tiny spark of her old self. "No. I'm getting plenty to eat. I've just been having a hard time keeping it down, although I'm trying to do better. I've heard it's normal to lose weight for the first few months."

"Oh, my God." Margot sat upright and stared at the keyhole. "Are you trying to tell me…"

"Yes. Isn't it wonderful? Now I have something to live for."

"Does your father know? Why is he keeping you locked up

like this?"

"I'm not sure if he knows, or not. If he does, he's not saying anything to me. In fact, he's barely spoken to me at all since the night he found Mama. I think he blames me for what happened." Ivy sighed.

"How could he blame you? What he's doing to you is criminal."

"I told Mama I was pregnant the night she died, but I don't think she said anything to Papa. She just went into her bedroom and drank that bottle of poison."

Margot sucked in her breath. "I wondered what happened. Ivy, I'm so sorry for your loss."

"Don't be. I lost my mother a long time ago—and apparently my father, too. I just hope Mama's finally at peace."

"So what happens now? Have you heard anything from Harry?"

"No. All I know is he's in jail. Papa won't tell me what he was charged with or if he's gone to trial, or anything. But whatever it is, I know he's innocent."

"Ivy, this is absolutely insane," said Margot, jumping to her feet and glancing around the hallway. "I'm going to go find something to break this door down and bust you out of here right now."

"No, don't do that." Ivy's voice was filled with panic. "It'll only make things worse for Harry."

"Then what can we do? I can't stand to let your father do this to you."

"Isn't your fiancé, Sydney, a lawyer? Maybe he could help Harry?"

"Of course, he can. I'll ask him tonight."

"Oh, Margot. That would make me feel so much better. Papa took all that money Tyme gave us away from me, so I know Harry doesn't have any money to pay a decent defense lawyer."

"Don't you worry about money, kid." Margot squared her shoulders. "If anybody can get him off, it's Sydney. I'll have him working on the case first thing in the morning."

"Thank you for everything, Margot." Ivy 's voice trembled. "You'd better go now, before Papa comes back. I've got this terrible feeling he's about to do something else—something I won't like."

"Like what?"

"I don't know. But I don't think he's given up on his plans to force me to marry Jared. In fact, I think he's more determined than ever. I'm beginning to think he's going to keep me imprisoned forever unless I give in."

Margot wiped away a tear and spoke softly into the keyhole. "Keep the faith, kid. You've got somebody else to think about now. Goodbye—for now."

Margot stifled a sob as she walked down the darkened steps. She went into the kitchen and saw Yolanda standing at the stove, stirring a pot of soup.

"I'm going now, Yolanda. Thank you for letting me talk to Ivy."

Yolanda nodded and smiled. She laid the spoon on a tureen, led the way to the back door, and opened it. Margot stepped outside and then turned back to Yolanda.

"Did Mrs. Turner leave a note?"

Yolanda nodded and glanced over her shoulder before she whispered. "It said *Ivy must be saved. The cancer is spreading.*"

PART THREE

JOURNEY'S END

CHAPTER SIXTEEN

Emma woke up, shivering and gasping for breath.

She was cold—oh, so terribly, horribly cold. She could barely breathe and her body wouldn't stop shaking.

Something covered her face. She reached up to pull it away and then tried to sit up, but she banged her head. Terror began to build as she lay there and wondered where she was. She'd never experienced such bone-chilling cold—or such absolute darkness—or such total silence.

Panic-stricken, Emma's hands groped her surroundings. Her fingers touched cold, wet ice. It was all around her. Freezing her. Devouring her.

She whimpered and strained to see through the blackness. Terror threatened to overcome her, but she fought it back. Somehow, she had to remain calm. Breathing deeply, she counted to ten and worked to compose herself. The gelid air tortured her nose and lungs, but she continued on until her thoughts became more rational.

Wherever she was, the enclosure was small. She reached upward, testing her surroundings. The frigid ceiling was only inches from her face. The cold, hard surface beneath her intensified her discomfort. Her left arm brushed against the icy wall and she shuddered.

She explored to the right. Her fingers touched something solid and dry, covered with cloth. She yanked at the covering and pulled it forward.

Whatever lay beside her was cold and rock-solid. Wondering

what it could be, her fingers grazed its surface. Course, grainy sandpaper chafed her fingertips. Traveling upward, its texture became smooth. Then she touched something soft. It felt like hair.

Cautiously, her fingers traveled back down across the rough surface until they found a gap. Her heart lurched when her fingers brushed against an uneven row of smooth, stone-like objects and she realized what she'd touched.

Teeth.

Emma screamed, over and over. Terror consumed her. She beat on the walls of her prison. She kicked the ceiling. When the violence of her struggle caused the corpse lying beside her to roll nearer, she wrenched up the volume.

And then suddenly, light and warmth came pouring in.

"Help me—please," begged Emma. Loud, wracking sobs tore from her throat when she saw a man wearing a billed cap peering down at her. She'd never been so glad to see another human being in her life.

Strong, calloused hands grasped her shoulders and pulled her backward. She gasped when she saw the body of an old man whom she had touched moments ago. His sunken, dead eyes stared gruesomely from a skeletal face; his cancerous lips were peeled back, as if snarling in eternal agony. She turned her head and tried to banish the vision and the smell of death from her mind.

The man who had rescued her picked her up as if she was a feather and set her down lightly onto the floor. He wrapped her in a blanket and then guided her to a small folding chair. She sighed with relief, and then looked into the face of her savior.

He was a big, lumbering, giant of a man with innocent eyes like a child's. His mouth opened in disbelief, displaying a set of yellowed, crooked teeth. He wore a dark blue uniform, with the words HOSPITAL SECURITY – ANDY FARMER printed on a name tag.

"Miss Anna, are you all right? We thought you was dead."

Emma's teeth chattered and she pulled the blanket tighter. Frigid air penetrated the room, but a pungent chemical smell burned her eyes and nose. The odor reminded her of the biology lab in college. She glanced toward the source and saw the open door from which she had been pulled. The cadaver's head was barely visible, but she could still remember its macabre face, staring sightlessly. She was relieved when the security guard went to the freezer door, slammed it shut, and latched it.

What had he called her? Miss Anna? Confused, she stared at her surroundings. This room looked familiar, but she couldn't quite place it. When had she seen that long, steel table attached to the sink? Or the wooden door of the built-in freezer? Or the room over there with the shelves lining the walls?

She remembered going back to the hotel after Allen and Phoebe's wedding reception. Her head had ached, but she hadn't wanted to spoil Zan's fun. And then...no, it wasn't possible. She must have dreamed all that other stuff.

But how did she end up in the freezer? And why did this strange man call her Anna? A sudden, twisting pain in her abdomen almost felled her, and she doubled over, gasping for breath. She clutched her stomach and noticed her hands.

They were the hands of a stranger.

She gasped and spread her fingers. They were long and thin, with short, rounded nails. And freckles? They were all up and down her arm. Where did those come from? What had happened to her tan and her white-tipped French manicure?

Emma jumped up from the chair and ran to the mirror above the sink, fighting back the intense pain in her stomach. She looked at her reflection, stunned by the face that stared back at her.

She gazed into the mirror, confused, as she ran her stranger's fingers across the hollowed planes of an alien face. This woman, whoever she was, looked emaciated and ill, with sunken eyes and dull, brittle red hair. Her skin was ashen and her boney frame wasted, but her abdomen was hard and swollen, straining grotesquely against the thin cotton gown she wore. The stench of illness enveloped her. Another sharp pain tore through her gut and Emma clutched her distended stomach.

"Miss Anna, you'd better come back and sit down." The guard put his arm around her and helped her back to her seat.

"Who are you?" Emma stared at the man, trying to recall where she'd seen him before.

He looked surprised. "You don't remember me? I'm Andy. We wuz good friends until…"

"Until what?"

"Well…until you died, of course." He cocked his head to one side and stared at her. "I sure am glad they wuz wrong about that."

"Where are we?" Emma gestured around the dimly lit room.

"I'm afeared this be the morgue, Miss." He lowered his voice and glanced over his shoulder. "Hospital patients ain't s'posed to see whut's down here—least not the live ones."

So she was back in the basement of the hotel. But everything seemed very different and bizarre. She thought about her recent experiences—being trapped inside the wall, the hospital emergency room, and seeing her dead family in Heaven. And then she remembered the corpse on the gurney that first night and she knew that it and the face in the mirror were one and the same. She must still be dreaming, but it certainly seemed real. This was the longest, most vivid dream yet.

"Andy, what's in there?" Emma stood up and walked toward the room with the shelves, shocked by what she saw. Dozens of jars lined the walls, filled with strange objects. She shuddered when she saw a human hand suspended in formaldehyde, a brain, and other body parts she couldn't identify.

"Miss Anna, you oughtn't be lookin' in that room." Andy hustled her aside and slammed the door shut. "Come on, let's get you outta here."

He wrapped the blanket around her skeletal frame and guided her down the hall. Her bare feet were cold as they touched the stone floor. They passed the hotel's laundry room, but it looked very different now, with old-fashioned wringer washers and big steel tubs. The place where the New Moon Spa had once been was now a bowling alley.

They walked toward an elevator and climbed inside. It was quite different from the one Emma remembered. Andy showed her to a little seat in the corner where, presumably, the operator would normally sit. She huddled on the chair while he closed the door, and then the folding cage. Then he pulled backward on a controller and the car began to rise. It stopped after going up only one flight, but Andy had to juggle the controller several times before he managed to make the elevator car align with the floor.

"Sorry, Miss Anna." Andy apologized for his awkwardness. "I'm not too good at runnin' this thing."

They walked out of the elevator, past the lobby, and down another hallway. Emma craned her neck and gawked at the purple paint on the walls, the brightly painted beamed ceiling, and the Art Deco posters. The red velvet Victorian chairs and pipe organ were gone. A cubist art painting hung in the spot where Morris the Cat's photo had been.

Andy led her down a hallway, past a door marked *Dr. Baker's Office* and into a room bearing the sign *Nurse's Station*. She felt suddenly weak in the knees and Andy helped her to a chair when she stumbled.

"You'd better sit down, Miss Anna," Andy said. "I'm gonna go see if I can find somebody on duty. Okay?"

Emma nodded and sank into the chair. A savory smell caused her empty stomach to growl and hunger pangs momentarily outweighed the intermittent, stabbing pains. She saw a bowl of soup with steam still rising and a plate of crackers sitting on a desk. The tantalizing smell was sheer torture.

She stood and walked over to the food. She glanced over her shoulder to make sure she was alone. Surely one little sip wouldn't hurt, and maybe a cracker or two. Her hand trembled as she reached for the spoon and popped it into her mouth. It was delicious, and before she knew it, she'd ravenously drained the entire bowl and devoured all the crackers. She felt a lot better and some of her strength returned.

When the food was gone, guilt overwhelmed her. She wondered if she'd get into trouble for her thievery. And then she noticed the desk calendar, turned to the page marked Sunday, October 23. But it was the year that caused her to gasp and to make her eyes widen.

1938.

Emma glanced up, startled when she heard voices approaching. Andy and a pretty young woman in a nurse's uniform walked into the room. Caught in the act. She'd eaten this poor woman's meal.

"I'm sorry," Emma apologized, hanging her head in shame. "I was just so very, very hungry."

"Oh, you poor little dear." The nurse put her arm around Emma and helped her back to the chair. She wrapped the blanket around her and tucked it under her feet. "Of course you were hungry. You were in a coma for almost three weeks. You must be starving by now."

"Hadn't we oughta find Miss Amiss and tell her what happened, Jennie?" Andy frowned and glanced from Emma to the nurse. "She's cold and barefoot. She needs to get back to her room and go to bed."

Jennie looked pensive. "Her room's already been reassigned to somebody else. The hospital's pretty full right now." She put her hands on her hips. "Where's Dr. Ballew? I thought he was on call tonight."

"Ahh, he's off drunk again. I ain't su'prised he made a

misstep, declarin' her dead an' all. I doubt it's the first time."
Andy wrinkled his nose and waved his hand in dismissal. "He's
prob'ly in his office, sleepin'. Where's Miss Amiss at?"

"She took the rest of the night off," said Jennie. She patted
Emma on the shoulder. "That big facial mole is bothering her,
so her mood's even worse than usual. I hate to wake her up for
this. She'll be furious, and I don't want her to take it out on poor
Mrs. Schmidt."

Emma sat and listened to the exchange between Andy and
Jennie. Apparently they thought she was somebody named
Anna Schmidt, who had been in a coma and been declared dead
by a drunk doctor. Judging by the looks on their faces and the
tones of their voices, this Miss Amiss was not a pleasant person.
How much more detailed was this dream going to get?

"What're we gonna do? It's almost four in the mornin',"
asked Andy.

"I know a room that's empty on the second floor. It's really
just a storage room, but there's a bed in it." Jennie's face
appeared excited, then changed to an expression of uncertainty.
"Do you think it would be all right to put her in with Michael?"

Confused, Emma glanced from Jennie to Andy. Had she
heard it wrong? First she'd said the room was empty, and
then she'd indicated the room already housed someone named
Michael. At this point, she was so cold and exhausted she didn't
care who she roomed with as long as she could just climb into a
nice, warm bed—anything but a morgue freezer.

"Come on, sweetie. You wanta give it a try?" Jennie looked
at Emma expectantly. "You're not afraid of him, are you?"

"Afraid of who?"

"Ain'tcha never heard of Michael?" Jennie's lips turned up
in a smile. "He's the mischievous spirit on the second floor.
Been here since before this ol' building was complete. That
one's always on the make when it comes to the ladies. He knows
I'm Irish too and he always manages a little goose or hikes up

my skirt whenever he's feelin' devilish." She apparently noticed Emma's alarm and added. "But he's harmless. He just likes to pull pranks now and then."

"A spirit? As in ghost?" Emma'd just escaped from a morgue. She wasn't sure she wanted to bunk with a randy poltergeist.

"Ah, Jennie. I don't think that's such a good idea," said Andy. "Poor Miss Anna won't get no rest with that scamp lurkin' about."

"Wait! I have it," Jennie's eyes danced excitedly and she clapped her hands. "We'll take her up to Mrs. Hardcastle. She's got that double room with the extra bed and it's right next door to Mrs. Schmidt's old room. I'm sure she wouldn't mind."

"That's a great idea, Jennie," said Andy. He turned toward Emma. "You remember Mrs. Hardcastle, don'tcha?"

Emma shook her head, confused. She'd only been to this place once before and that was—what? More than seventy years in the future? She could hardly explain that to them. Even though she knew this was all just a dream, she still felt compelled to play along. "Sorry. I must have lost my memory while I was asleep."

"Don't you worry, Mrs. Schmidt." Jennie helped her stand and walk toward the elevator. "We're gonna take good care of you now."

They rode the elevator to the fourth floor and turned left to a long hallway. A hint of recognition washed over Emma. Everything was the same, yet different. The walls were no longer pink and the formerly green carpet was now red. *Dr. Baker's Lounge* no longer existed. But she recognized the door when they turned right at the end of the hall—the same room she and Zan had shared a lifetime ago, according to this dream.

Emma held her breath as Andy knocked on the door. She heard the creak of bedsprings and the shuffle of feet across the floor. The rasp of the deadbolt echoed in the cavernous hallway and the door creaked open.

A tiny, elderly woman peeked out through the open door, a worried expression on her wrinkled face. "Is something wrong?" She pulled her robe closed with one hand, glanced at the three people standing in the hallway, and then gasped. "Anna! Oh, my God. Where have you been? They told me you were dead!"

Emma's breath caught when she recognized her. This was the woman in her dream who had saved her from the evil nurse in the portal. But then, she was still dreaming, wasn't she? Which dream was she having now? She was getting confused, with all the different dreams converging.

A sudden, stabbing pain sent her reeling and clutching her stomach. The others hustled her inside and laid her on the spare bed. She bit her lip and writhed in agony. What was the matter with her and why couldn't she wake up? And then she realized that in all her previous nightmares, she'd never before experienced pain or cold or hunger. The only tangible sensation she'd felt before was fear.

And then it hit her. This wasn't a dream! It was really happening. It was like she'd traveled back in time. But why was she inhabiting a stranger's body? Was she losing her mind?

Unbearable anguish jerked her thoughts back to the present. It gnawed at her innards and she almost fainted. She writhed in agony, her misery complete. She clutched her stomach and stared at the three worried faces that hovered above her. She felt herself drifting away.

"She's going into shock!" Jennie shouted. "The pain's gonna kill her. She needs morphine."

"Here, give her some of mine." The old woman reached into a bedside cabinet and pulled out a hypodermic needle and a vial of liquid. She handed them to Jennie and jerked up Emma's sleeve. "She needs a constant supply to keep her as comfortable as possible."

Jennie expertly filled the syringe and injected it into Emma's arm. Within seconds the pain began to subside and Emma relaxed. Her mind soared briefly and then returned to earth. She felt one hundred percent better. But the word *morphine* worried her. She knew how easily a person could become addicted to such a powerful drug.

"Anna? It's Theodora. Do you remember me?"

Emma blinked. Theodora? Wasn't she the ghost who broke the champagne glasses? She sat up in the bed and looked around the room. The slanting attic walls looked familiar, but they were now plastered white. No turquoise paint or gold stars. A small iron cot replaced the velvet swooning couch. There was no sign of a television, microwave, refrigerator, *or* coffee maker.

She peered into the other bedroom and her heart skipped a beat when she saw it—the little door in the wall. How did she go from being trapped inside the wall to being trapped in time?

"I'm sorry, I don't remember anything," said Emma.

"Mrs. Hardcastle, would it be all right if Mrs. Schmidt stayed in here with you until we can make other arrangements?" asked Jennie. She explained how Anna had been mistakenly declared dead, taken to the morgue, and subsequently rescued. "I'm sorry for the inconvenience..."

"Of course she can stay," interrupted Theodora. "I'm just happy Andy was so alert. He's quite the hero."

Andy blushed and shuffled his feet. "I'd do just about anythin' for Miss Anna."

The entire group looked up when the bathroom door creaked open. A beautiful young woman wearing a pink flannel nightgown peeked out. She cautiously entered the room, holding a huge gray cat in her arms. It jumped down and ran toward Theodora, purring and rubbing against her legs.

"Ivy, dear. Did we wake you up? I know it's awfully early." Theodora patted the cat on the head before turning back to Emma. "Anna, this is Ivy Turner. They gave her your old room a few days ago. She shares a connecting bath with us. And my cat, Bob, of course."

"Ivy Fuller," she corrected. "It's nice to meet you, Anna. I heard the voices in here and I was just wondering if everything was all right."

"Sorry, dear. Of course. Ivy Fuller."

Emma's eyes widened. Ivy Fuller. This was Zan's grandmother! But where was Grandpa Harry? She remembered the story at the wedding rehearsal dinner about Jonathan's parents having met in Eureka Springs in 1938.

She searched her memory, trying to recall Moonbeam's predictions when she'd read her palm. Hadn't there been something about taking a trip that would change her life? Then she remembered the final prediction—the one about Emma dying and coming back. Could that be what had happened? But if it were true, what was she doing so far back in the past? Would she be able to get back to Zan, or would she be trapped here forever?

Theodora turned back to Jennie. "Where has Anna been all this time? Nurse Roberta told me she'd passed away almost three weeks ago."

"She's been down in the Annex. Miss Amiss calls it the Intensive Care Unit," Jennie answered. "But she doesn't let the newer nurses like me go in there."

Andy snorted. "It's more like an asylum, if ya ask me. I seen what goes on in there—and it ain't pretty."

"Anna, do you remember what happened to you down there?" asked Theodora.

"I don't remember anything at all." Emma shook her head. "Everything's a blank."

"Sounds like you've got amnesia," Theodora replied, then turned back to Andy. "What were you talking about just then, Andy. What goes on in the Annex?"

Andy lowered his voice and glanced around the room. "Turrible stuff goes on in there, Miz Hardcastle. I heard 'em say that when somebody couldn't pay no more but didn't have no place else to go, they just took 'em in there and let 'em waste away 'till they died. That's prob'ly whut happened to Miss Anna."

"How could that happen?" asked Theodora. "Don't you think somebody would hear them screaming?"

Andy bent low and whispered. "They got th' walls all padded up and sound-proofed. Only reason they let me in there that one time was 'cause they needed me to help 'em with a man whut wuz too big fer em ta handle by theirselves." He glanced toward the door and nodded. "They think I'm too stupid to know better. But I ain't. I know what they're doin'. Told ma Pa 'bout it once. I wuz hopin' we could help put a stop to it all, but he told me to shutup, not ta go gettin' myself fired. Said we needed the money too bad ta go causin' trouble. "

Everyone froze when someone rapped against the hallway door. The cat's eyes blazed and his ears folded back. His hair instantly fluffed and he growled low before slinking toward the door in the wall. He nudged it open with his nose and disappeared inside.

A hush settled over the room and Emma's heart quickened in dreadful anticipation. Ivy scurried back through the bathroom and closed her bedroom door. Andy and Theodora stood like statues, waiting. Jennie turned pale and wrung her hands as the door swung open.

Emma's nightmare had returned.

CHAPTER SEVENTEEN

"*What* is going on in here?"

A tall woman dressed in a gray robe and tattered house shoes stood at the door. Her eyes blazed with fury as her stare raked across the group. Emma shuddered when she recognized the glaring face—the same one that haunted her dreams.

Even without the nurse's cap and uniform, there was no mistake. But now, instead of a scar, an angry red lesion extended across her left cheek. Emma tried to tear her eyes away from the festering wound, but she was too late.

The woman automatically raised her hand toward her face when she noticed Emma's stare. "What're you lookin' at?" Then surprise replaced fury. She gasped and pointed, then backed away. "This can't be! You're dead…"

Theodora chuckled. "Oh, lighten up, Roberta. You act like you've just seen a ghost."

Roberta bristled, then turned her attention to Jennie. "I demand an explanation. Right now."

Jennie cowered, her face ashen. "Well, ya see, Miss Amiss…"

"I found Miss Anna locked away in th' cooler," interrupted Andy. "She warn't really dead. Dr. Ballew made a mistake."

"But that's impossible. I checked her vitals myself." Roberta appeared uncertain, and then she stared at Emma with suspicion in her eyes.

Emma opened her mouth to reply, but nothing came out. She felt her new body break out into a cold sweat. Anxiety overwhelmed her. After the horrible dreams she'd been having, coming face-to-face with the nurse terrified her.

"Leave her alone, Roberta. Don't you think you and your cronies have put her through enough already?" asked Theodora. "You gave her room away, so she's going to stay here with me."

"Who made this decision?" Roberta's eyes narrowed. She glared at Jennie and Andy. "She doesn't have any more assets to pay for further treatment. She can't stay here."

"*I* decided," replied Theodora. "Dr. Baker's been well paid for his services. What happened to her sapphire earrings?"

"I don't know what you're talking about." Roberta looked surprised at Theodora's remark and then shifted her eyes away.

"As I recall, one of Dr. Baker's policies is that he will never turn away someone who needs help if they have no money. Isn't that true?"

Roberta ignored Theodora's question and said, "But we thought Mrs. Schmidt was dead."

"Well, then. There's nothing more to discuss, is there?" Theodora put her hand on Roberta's arm and steered her out the door. "Everyone makes mistakes. Anna will stay here with me and you will continue her treatments."

Theodora closed the door and the group expelled a collective sigh of relief when they heard the bad tempered nurse stomping up the north penthouse stairs. Jennie sniffed and wiped a tear from her face. Moments later, Ivy paused in the connecting bathroom doorway.

"Is it safe to come in?" she asked.

"With her, you never know," said Theodora. "We should keep our voices down."

Jennie turned to Andy. "We oughta get back down to our posts or there'll be hell to pay from her. Will you be okay now, Mrs. Schmidt?"

Emma nodded, suddenly feeling very tired. Now that Nurse Amiss was gone, the effects of the morphine were making her relax. All she wanted to do was sleep.

"I'll see to her," said Theodora. "You and Andy should get back to your duties. Ivy, go back to bed dear. It'll be morning soon enough."

When the others left, Emma settled back against the pillow. Her eyelids fluttered and drowsiness swept over her. She'd worry about what was going to happen tomorrow. Theodora gently stroked her hair and then pulled the covers up around her chin. The fragrance of lavender hung in the air and the warm memory of a similar moment flitted across her mind before sweet oblivion overtook her.

Emma awakened to excruciating pain. A thousand burning knives stabbed and twisted in her gut and she writhed in agony. She groaned and clutched her stomach. What could be causing her so much pain?

"She's awake."

Emma stared up through a fog of misery when she heard the voices. She moved her hand, but pulled it back when the knives stabbed again. Someone picked up her hand and poked her in the arm with something sharp. And then the pain drifted away and her mind cleared. She blinked and focused her eyes.

"Anna? Can you hear me?"

Confusion overtook her. She stared at the elderly woman and the young girl who hovered nearby. Then she remembered. Theodora and Ivy. The nightmare was reality.

She sat up and gazed around the room, her heart pounding. Sunlight flooded through the windows in Theodora's room, which connected with hers. "What time is it?"

"It's almost noon, dear. We didn't want to disturb you," replied Theodora. She held a glass of orange juice. "Would you like something to drink?"

"Yes, please," replied Emma. She licked her dry, cracked lips in anticipation. Her hands shook, so Theodora guided the cup to her lips. She drank it all and then collapsed back onto the pillow.

Ivy brought a tray with two hard-boiled eggs and crackers and set it on the bedside table. Emma watched as she picked up a knife, buttered the crackers, and then sliced the eggs. She placed them on the crackers and offered them to Emma, one at a time.

"Thank you," said Emma after finishing the food. She remembered that Zan had once told her his grandmother had worked as a nurse's aide at a veteran's hospital during World War II. "You'd make a good nurse."

"I think I'd like to do that someday," Ivy replied and then gave Emma more juice to drink.

"What's today?" asked Emma.

"Monday."

Emma glanced at Theodora before plunging ahead. No matter how strange it would sound, she had to know the answer to the next question. "What's the day, month, and year?"

Ivy looked surprised, but Theodora answered. "It's Monday, October 24th, 1938."

"That's what I thought." Emma turned her head and stared at the wall. For a moment, she'd hoped Theodora would say 2011.

"Well, I'd better get back to my room before Miss Amiss catches me in here." Ivy smiled and disappeared back through the bathroom. The big gray cat jumped down from the windowsill and trotted after her.

Emma glanced at her arm, saw the needle mark, and panicked. "Theodora, should you be giving me these injections? I don't want to become a drug addict."

Theodora sighed, took Emma's hand, and patted it gently. "You really don't remember anything, do you?"

"Not a thing." Emma looked down at her hands. The sickly, yellowish skin was freckled and bony, with short broken nails.

They were the hands of a stranger's, yet they responded to her mind as if they belonged to her. She shuddered at the memory of the gaunt face with the hollow eyes she'd seen in the mirror. Even her voice sounded strange. She still found her predicament hard to believe. And then a terrifying thought struck her. She almost choked on her words. "Am I dying?"

"Yes, dear. We both are," Theodora replied. "It's too late for you and me. Our cancers are well advanced, so the morphine is the only thing that makes our existence bearable. We knew that before we came here, but we both wanted to believe what Dr. Baker told us. He was our last hope."

"And Ivy? What about her?"

Theodora waved her hand. "Ivy's completely healthy. The only thing that's wrong with her is she's pregnant. And in my opinion, I don't consider that an ailment."

"Ivy's pregnant?" Emma gasped. "Then what's she doing here?"

Theodora slumped down in a chair. "Her horrible father sent her here. She told me all about it." With frequent pauses for breath, she related the story of Ivy's marriage to Harry, her subsequent annulment, and her imprisonment by her father. "She's been here about three weeks, but she's refusing treatment for her *cancer*."

"Why does her father think she has cancer?"

"Ivy doesn't think he really believes it. But before her mother committed suicide, she left a note indicating Ivy had cancer. And of course, Dr. Baker diagnosed her with it, like he does with everybody." Theodora sniffed. "I met her mother when she was a patient here and supposedly Dr. Baker cured her of cancer, but Ivy says it was all in her head. She thinks her father is using it as an excuse to send her here in hopes she'll have a miscarriage."

Emma's heart lurched when she did the math. It was October 1938 and Ivy was pregnant. She would have the baby

in the spring of 1939—and she remembered Jonathan Fuller—
who would one day become her father-in-law. His birthday was
April 15, 1939. If she lost this baby, it would mean Zan would
never be born either. She would never meet him, marry him, or
love him. Her mind reeled at the possibility.

"We've got to do everything we can to see that nothing
happens to either Ivy or her baby." Emma sat up and reached for
Theodora's hand. "We can't let those monsters hurt her. We've
got to figure out a way to help her husband, too."

Theodora smiled and squeezed Emma's hand. "Anna, you
are just the sweetest thing. You don't even know her, yet you're
ready to fight her battle. What do you propose we do?"

Emma sank back onto the pillow, lost in thought. What could
she do? She was caught in some kind of time warp, trapped in a
body that was quickly being eaten away by a malignant tumor.
What she wouldn't give for a computer and the World Wide
Web right now. With those tools, you could find the answer to
just about anything.

The sound of knocking and people shouting in another
room arrested Emma's attention. She sat up and strained to
hear. "What's going on?"

Theodora gazed in the direction of the noise and replied,
"Sounds like Roberta's trying to get Ivy to take her medicine
again." She chuckled and walked toward the bathroom so she
could hear better. "That girl's got a lot of spunk."

"What are they trying to give her?"

"Some sort of herbal concoction Dr. Baker's dreamed up."

"Do you know what kind of herbs he uses?" Emma realized
that the knowledge she'd gained of herbal remedies while
designing the computer database for Zan's pharmacy might
come in handy now.

"I don't know. He keeps his formulas a secret, but he claims
they're just natural herbs."

"Well, she's right about refusing the treatments. She

shouldn't let him give her anything she's not sure of." Emma tried to rise, but she didn't have the strength. "The right combination of certain herbs can cause uterine contractions and she could lose the baby."

"Now how did you know that? Was your granny one of those hillbilly medicine women?"

"Something like that." Emma smiled, remembering the times she and Zan had discussed the various herbs and their effect on humans. She flinched when she heard the rap on the door to their room. "Oh, no. Not that awful nurse again."

Theodora hobbled toward the door and pulled it open. Emma sat up in bed and gasped when she recognized the short little man in the white suit, lavender shirt, and purple tie standing next to a glowering Nurse Roberta. She'd seen his face before in pictures at the Crescent Hotel.

He shifted the cigar from one side of his mouth to the other, walked straight toward her, and reached for her hand. She shrank back, but not before he'd grabbed her with a firm grip. "Welcome back, Mrs. Schmidt. Don't you remember me? Dr. Norman Baker, at your service."

Emma trembled beneath his penetrating gaze. She remembered the stories on the ghost tour about how he charmed innocent victims into believing he could cure their health problems and then swindled them out of their money and property. Is that what had happened to Anna Schmidt?

"Afternoon, Dr. Baker."

"Afternoon to you, Miz Hardcastle. How's the treatments goin'?" Baker fixed his stare on Theodora.

"Oh, I get by as long as I have my pain medication." Theodora nodded and shuffled back to her bedroom. She sat down in a rocking chair, picked up a skein of yarn and began knitting.

Baker turned his attention back to Emma. "Well, I guess we're gonna have to rename you *Lazarus*, ain't we?" He winked at Emma and then at Roberta, who attempted to smile. But with the suppurating sore on her face, it seemed more like a grimace. "Yessiree, this is one for the record books! Comin' back from a coma after what? Two-three weeks?"

Emma shrugged. "I don't know. I've lost my memory."

"Well, what *do* you remember?"

Emma felt like she was being interrogated. Her instincts told her to hold back as much as possible. "The first thing I remember was waking up in the freezer. Then the guard got me out and brought me upstairs and they put me to bed in here. That's about it."

"Hmm." Baker chewed on his cigar. "I wanta conduct a couple of tests, if I may? Can you sit up and dangle your legs for me?"

Emma nodded, but she was so weak, Nurse Roberta had to help her. Her skin crawled when the odious woman touched her. She looked with dismay at the thin, bony legs, covered in soft golden peach fuzz and dotted with bruises.

Nurse Roberta handed Dr. Baker a small metal reflex hammer and he tapped her knee several times before he found the right spot. When her leg finally jerked, he seemed satisfied. He pulled back her thin, lank hair and peered into her ears. Then he put an odd looking stethoscope, with red rubber hoses and a flared metal bell, to her chest. He moved it back and forth until he located her heart, listened for a moment, and then smiled. "Everthin' seems normal there. I'm gonna ask ya a few questions now. Can ya tell me what today is?"

That was easy. Theodora had just told her that one. "Monday, October 24th." She didn't tell him the year.

"Good." He nodded. "Who's the president of the United States?"

"Barack Obama—," she responded, then realized her mistake.

"Do what?" Dr. Baker's eyebrows shot up.

What a goof. She scanned her memory, but her mind went blank. "Uh, Truman?" No, that wasn't right. "Herbert Hoover."

Nurse Roberta gazed at Dr. Baker and rolled her eyes. He pulled his cigar out of his mouth, squinted, and peered closely at Emma's face.

"Wait! I've got it! Franklin Delano Roosevelt." Emma grinned, knowing FDR was correct.

"Okay, I think that about does it," said Dr. Baker. He rose and helped her lie back down. "We'll continue back on the same treatment plan as before."

Theodora looked up from her knitting, raised her voice, and said. "She's gonna need morphine."

"All right. Roberta, see to it." He nodded and exited the room.

Roberta approached Emma, her damaged face twisted in a sneer. She jerked the covers back, rolled her over on her side, and proceeded to administer an injection in her hip. Emma gasped at the rough handling, but set her mind to endure it. She had to keep this poor, frail body alive long enough to figure out a way to help Ivy and her unborn baby Jonathan—and ultimately, Zan.

By the time Nurse Amiss left, Emma was exhausted. She lay back and closed her eyes, wondering what she should do in the short time she had left. Who was Anna Schmidt and what had become of her? She had so many questions, but she didn't know how to ask them.

Using all her strength, Emma rose and went into Theodora's room. The short walk exhausted her, and she sank into the nearest chair. "Theodora, can you tell me something about Anna—I mean, about me? It's terrible not being able to remember anything."

Theodora smiled, reached into a drawer on her bedside table, pulled out an old red velvet pouch with a yellow drawstring tassel, and handed it to Emma. "Here, I think this may answer most of your questions."

Inside the pouch was a small composition notebook. She pulled out the book and gasped when a ring fell into her lap.

Her engagement ring. The ring Zan would give her almost seventy years into the future.

Emma picked up the ring and asked, "Where did you get this?"

"Bob, my cat, dragged it out of his hiding spot a few days ago." She pointed to the door in the wall. "He was batting it all over the room, playing with the tassel. It's yours. Does it jog your memory?"

"Sort of…" She couldn't explain the truth to Theodora. She would never understand how one day this ring and Zan, the man who would give it to her, would mean more than life itself.

"Well, for all the details, just read the notebook. After all, you wrote it." Theodora put down her knitting and rose. "I'm going to take a walk. These old legs are growing stiff."

Emma's hands trembled when she opened the notebook. She didn't recognize the handwriting on the lined pages, but she was eager to read it, hoping whatever Anna had to say would give her a clue to her purpose in this bizarre adventure. She settled herself in the chair and began to read.

My name is Anna Bernstein Schmidt. I am thirty-three years old, childless, and a widow. Today is Sunday, October 2nd, 1938 and I am a prisoner of Dr. Norman Baker. I know that I am somewhere in the hospital, but I do not know where. By the time you read this, I will most likely be dead. It is with hope in my heart that I remain coherent to tell my tale so whoever reads my story will understand my plight, and perhaps take action to halt the evil that is perpetrated in this place.

The room in which I find myself is small and dark. The only furnishings are a small metal cot, a wooden stool, and a chamber pot. There are no windows and the walls are covered with some sort of spongy material. A single fixture on the ceiling is my only source of light, and the shadows make writing difficult. I apologize if this is hard to read, or if I ramble.

I found this pencil in a crack in the floorboards. The point is dull and I must guard against breaking it, as I have no means to sharpen it. When they brought me here, they left my valise, which contained a few of my personal possessions. They took away my *Torah*, calling it *Pagan*. But I am grateful they did not remove this small writing tablet, as it gives me something to do and serves as an outlet to assuage my fear.

They took my sapphire earrings, but I managed to hide the matching ring and bring it with me. The ring is very old and beautiful. It is made of pure gold and is set with a large diamond, surrounded by sapphires. My beloved Manny gave it to me, along with the earrings, so it is very precious to me. That is what they really want, but I will die before I let them have it.

The pain in my belly grows stronger every day and I know that I am dying. I had so much hope when I came here two months ago, but now I see that it has all been an exercise in futility. My doctor back in St. Louis told me that the cancer in my ovaries had spread too far, but one never wants to give up hope.

Monday, October 3rd. A long, miserable night has passed and I find myself weaker and in more pain. I intend to write something every day for as long as I am able. I fear that writing in this journal will be the only thing to prevent me from going mad. I jump at every noise I hear, afraid one of them will walk in on me and catch me writing. If they knew what I was doing, they would take this notebook away and then I would be left with nothing. I hide it inside a loose plank in the floor beneath my bed and I pray they will not find it.

Nurse Amiss came to tend me this morning, if you can call it tending. She brought some thin gruel and water. And she emptied the chamber pot. She brought out a syringe I know was filled with morphine and held it out where I could see it. I felt so relieved, thinking that my pain would at last go away. But then she asked about the ring and I refused to tell her, so she took the needle and left. I am in agony.

Tuesday, October 4th. I lacked the strength to get out of bed when Miss Amiss came into my room. This time she brought eggs, bacon, and coffee. It smelled good, but I was too weak to rise. And then, remarkably, she gave me the morphine injection, and I felt much better. I drank the coffee and ate the eggs like a starving dog, but my faith would not allow me to eat the pork. She sneered at me and called me *finicky*, but she promised me she would return later that evening. There was nothing in the chamber pot to empty because I was so weak, but she did change my nightgown and bed sheets without scolding me for making a mess.

I am suspicious of her kindness. It is most likely a ploy to confuse me and make me give up the ring. But I have it hidden away, where I keep this notebook, and I am determined not to tell. The days and nights are growing more and more difficult to distinguish, locked away as I am. I will continue my daily prayers for as long as I am able, especially through this holy season after *Rosh Hashanah*. I was greatly comforted after the morning *shaharith* and the afternoon *minhah*. The evening *maarib* will help me through the night.

My only reference of time is the smell that slips

through the cracks in the door: the smell of coffee tells me it is morning and the odor of disinfectants means the maids are at work in the afternoon. When one is devoid of all stimuli, one notices small things.

Today I smelled beans and it reminded me of the *cholent* I used to make, which was Manny's favorite. He always insisted on remaining Kosher. How I miss him and the life we shared in our home above the jewelry shop in St. Louis.

Sometimes I wonder if the antique sapphire earrings and matching ring he purchased several years ago were not the beginning of our troubles. The man who sold them had been down on his luck and was happy that Manny had been so fair. But with this great Depression that has dragged on for years, Manny was never able to sell them, so they became mine.

But it wasn't until two years ago when the same man and his well-dressed wife returned, that our bad luck began in earnest. This time he wanted to sell a necklace, which matched the earrings and ring.

I was in the shop and, admiring the necklace, I picked it up and put it on. Manny got angry and made me take it off. I was humiliated and left the room. I did not hear what else transpired. All I know is that Manny did not buy the necklace because, he said, it was cursed. Six months later I discovered I had cancer.

I am sure you think this is all just the crazy rambling of a dying woman, but my instincts tell me to stand firm. I feel there is something sinister happening and that if I give up the ring something terrible will be perpetuated.

I fear every day for the plight of my relatives in Europe, being persecuted by the madman named Hitler. I have no faith that the *Munich Pact* signed last week between the European nations will ensure the peace they hope for. Something tells me that if I let the ring go, it will somehow end up in the hands of the Nazis.

The last time I spoke with Manny on the hospital telephone he told me some men had come to the shop asking about the necklace and that he had felt threatened. He said he recognized the younger one from the newspaper social pages as a rich businessman named Covington. The other one was tall and paunchy, with bad teeth and foul breath. The young one kept waving an old, out-dated pawn ticket, insisting it was for a sapphire and diamond necklace he wanted to redeem.

Manny tried to explain that he didn't have it and that the ticket had been for something else, but this had only enraged the rich man. He'd walked around the shop, smashing the glass of the display cases with his silver-tipped cane, while the big man stood with his arms folded, as if daring Manny to react. That was when he'd noticed the stickpin on Covington's lapel—shaped very much like the necklace he was seeking. It was then that Manny knew something terrible was about to happen.

The very next day, Manny was dead, killed in a fire that destroyed the jewelry shop, our home, and everything we owned.

That same day, Dr. Baker informed me that since my husband was dead, he would need my jewelry to fund my treatment, room, and board. When I refused to give the jewels to him, they took the earrings from my ears and locked me away in this padded cell when I refused to tell them where I'd hidden the ring. Now you know how I came to be here.

Wednesday, October 5th. I spent a tolerably good night last night. Miss Amiss came in the evening with a delicious meal of soup and bread. Today is *Yom Kippur*, the Day of Atonement, and normally I would fast today. But since I am so ill and under the circumstances, I am sure God will forgive me. Miss Amiss gave me morphine and even brought me an extra blanket. She is now coming to feed me twice a day. But I noticed her staring under the bed. Something is up.

Since my strength has returned and the pain has been mitigated, I now find myself restless. After my prayers on this Holy day, I spent the afternoon testing the walls, trying to find a breach of some sort. In the far corner behind the bed, I found a loose nail near the baseboards. I chipped at it with my soup-spoon until it came loose and discovered a small opening in the wall, just big enough to use as a hideaway for my treasures.

Thursday, October 6th. More of the same. She is still feeding me twice a day and relieving my pain. But the monotony is wearing. There has been no more mention of the ring. My pencil is almost out of lead. I must cut this entry short.

Friday, October 7th. Today I heard something gnawing inside the walls. I peeked into my hiding place and came face to face with a big brown rat. He'd been chewing on the corner of my tablet and I worried he would carry off the ring. I found an old velvet reticule in my valise and I will keep my tablet and ring inside it from now on. I hope the rat will leave it alone.

Saturday, October 8th. I am losing ground. I am no longer sure what day it is. Solitary confinement is a terrifying experience. It takes all my strength now to bear down hard enough to make this pencil write. I keep hearing the rats inside the walls. They are all around me.

Sunday, October 9th. I have been in this place for a week now. I know that it is Sunday, because nobody has been here all day to feed me or give me my injection. For some strange reason, Dr. Baker refuses to provide medical treatment to any of his patients on Sunday. But at least in the past we were fed. I am so hungry and the pain is unbearable. Writing this has completely exhausted me.

Monday, October 10th. Miss Amiss has shown her hand. Today when she brought me breakfast, after going all day yesterday without anything to eat or drink, she asked me about the ring. I lied and told her I had lost it down the toilet. I could tell she didn't believe me, but she let me eat.

When I glanced at her face, I noticed for the first time that the mole on her face, the blemish she once called her *beauty mark*, seems to be changing. Facing my own demise, I fear she may have melanoma and the awareness must have shown in my face. She grew furious and stomped away, without giving me any morphine. How I wish I had never looked at her.

Tuesday, October 11th. I am back to gruel and water—once a day and no pain medication. My strength is all but gone. On her last visit, she didn't even bother to change my soiled nightgown or bedclothes. What a sorry, wretched state I am in. I must conserve my strength to make certain I can hide this tablet away.

Wednesday, October 12th. All I do now is lie in bed. I can't believe I am still alive. My goal today is to get this notebook back into the wall before I am discovered.

It is getting harder and harder to put the boards back in place. I am afraid if they clean this stinking cell, they will discover it.

Thursday, October 13th. Today I heard a great flurry of squeaks from the rats in the wall, followed by a feisty feline growling. Then I heard a familiar "meow" and saw a furry gray paw poking through the hole in the wall.

I forced myself to my hiding place and found Bob, Theodora's cat, inside the wall! He was licking his paws after feasting on the rat he'd caught, and I felt like I was greeting an old, dear friend. He noticed the tassel on my reticule and began to play with it, which gave me an idea.

This will be my last entry, because I am counting on the cat to carry away my reticule, with the tablet and ring inside. I know Bob roams throughout the walls of this building, so I hope he will carry it off someplace where Dr. Baker or Miss Amiss can never find the ring. Perhaps someday someone will find this journal and know that I was here. I look forward now to joining my beloved Manny in Heaven.

Emma finished reading the journal, stunned. Such a sad, brave story. She picked up the ring and stared at it. The last time she'd seen it, the ghost had thrown it into the space behind the wall of her Crescent Hotel room. And now here it was again, many years into the past.

But what was she going to do with it? After everything poor Anna had been through, she couldn't allow Dr. Baker or Nurse Amiss to get their hands on it. She searched her memory to the night of the wedding rehearsal dinner. Jonathan had said one of his mother's friends had given it to her, so she knew that she was supposed to give it to Ivy. But how should she approach her? They had just barely met, so Ivy wouldn't understand if she just handed her the ring without explanation. She decided to guard it for the time being and wait for the proper moment.

Emma looked up, startled when she heard the hallway door creak open. Theodora entered with her arm around a pale and frightened Ivy.

"What's the matter?" She gathered her strength to help Theodora lead Ivy to a nearby chair. Ivy buried her face in her hands and wept. Emma's heart lurched, worried about the baby.

"There, there, dear." Theodora patted Ivy and then turned to Emma. "Ivy tried to leave the hospital, but that despicable ex-sheriff's deputy Dr. Baker has hired stopped her and brought her back."

"Earl," said Ivy, her pretty face contorted in anger. "I hate him."

"Where were you trying to go?" asked Emma.

"I was going to see Madame Cordelia. She's a medium." Ivy sniffed and wiped her face with Theodora's handkerchief. "Mama's trying to contact me. She came to me while I was taking a nap, but I can't understand what she's trying to tell me."

Emma was confused. "I thought your mother was dead."

Ivy sighed and nodded. "She is."

Theodora stared at Ivy, her eyes wide. "What did your mother say?"

"She said '*Death has opened my eyes*'."

CHAPTER EIGHTEEN

Caleb Turner grabbed the crystal highball glass and hurled it at the wall. He buried his face in his hands, desperately trying to banish the specter of his dead wife. He was going mad! She'd haunted him for weeks—staring—accusing. Why wouldn't she leave him alone?

He lifted his head and gazed at the mess in the parlor through a drunken haze. The whiskey dripped down the wallpaper and puddled on the polished wooden floor. Shards of glass lay scattered across the Aubusson rug, mingling with an accumulation of empty liquor bottles, dirty glasses, and other debris that cluttered his once pristine home.

The ghost was gone now, but he didn't feel any better. His week-old chin stubble disgusted him and the rancid taste of whiskey-sodden breath increased his self-loathing. He was alone. October would soon be gone, along with everybody in his life. He'd fired the housekeeper, Winifred was dead, and Ivy had been at the Baker Cancer Hospital for almost a month. The stillness was so complete that every little noise startled him.

God, how he wished he could take it all back! The guilt he felt for his actions was enough to kill any man. He had nothing left but unbearable memories. Maybe he deserved to be haunted.

The first time Winnie's ghost had appeared, her accusing eyes had tortured him with unspoken guilt and recriminations. He'd never forget the terror of that first visitation. She'd awakened him two nights after her funeral and he hadn't had a moment of peace since. He remembered how he'd felt her icy touch when she jerked the covers off his bed, appearing misty and incorporeal. But her identity was unmistakable.

Winifred had returned.

She stood next to his bed, stared sadly, and then faded away. After that, he'd been unable to sleep at all unless he was good and drunk.

Caleb groaned as he thought about that terrible night, three nights later—the night of October 1st— the night he had made the biggest mistake of his life. He'd just begun to think he'd imagined her visit when she came to him again. This time he'd been in the parlor, drinking and brooding over the mess he'd made of his life. He'd tried to ignore her, but she'd been insistent and agitated as she slammed books and flicked the lights on and off. When the ashtray, with a smoldering cigar resting on its edge, went sliding to the floor he knew she meant business.

He'd given in and followed her as she floated up the stairs toward her bedroom. More than a little drunk, he'd staggered slightly as he climbed. He continued on, however, bolstered by his Dutch courage as curiosity replaced fear. What the hell did she want from him?

He hadn't been inside her bedroom since the night he'd found her dead. After they'd taken her body away, he'd locked the door himself and forbidden anyone to enter. To his amazement, however, Winnie's ghost had simply extended her arm and the door creaked open.

He'd followed her toward the fireplace, where she turned, looked back with anguish in her eyes, pointed toward the hearth, and disappeared. Bewildered, he flipped on the light, grabbed a poker, and probed the ashes. He touched something solid and pulled it out.

Caleb had studied the twisted hunk of metal speared by the fireplace poker, wondering what it could be. Several seconds passed before he realized it was the diamond and sapphire necklace. It was barely recognizable. Its gold chain was hopelessly warped and the stones were cracked and charred.

Then someone had rapped at the door downstairs and Caleb glanced up, startled. Who would be calling at this hour? He stood still and waited, then realized that Yolanda was gone for the evening. He wrapped the charred necklace in his handkerchief, placed it in his pocket, and went downstairs.

"Is everything all right in here?" Jared and a heavy-set man stood on the darkened porch.

Caleb stared at the men, sobered by the cool night air. "I'm fine. Why'd ya ask?"

"May we come in?"

"Oh, sure, sure." Caleb opened the door and motioned them into the parlor. "Sorry 'bout the mess. Dropped my ashtray a little bit ago."

Jared removed his topcoat and hat, and then settled onto a big leather chair. Caleb sat in his own chair, but the other man remained standing. The man looked familiar, but he couldn't place where he'd seen him. "Have a seat, Mr..."

"This is Earl Twitchell. He's my new bodyguard," said Jared. The big man stood behind Jared and nodded, his hands clasped behind his back.

"Body guard? What'cha need that for?"

"In this dangerous world, you can never be too careful." Jared smiled and relaxed in his seat. He reached toward the whiskey decanter and poured himself a drink. "May I?"

Caleb grunted. "What'd ya mean a while ago? Why wouldn't everything be all right?"

Jared ignored his question again. "Is Ivy here?"

"Of course she's here," replied Caleb. "She's upstairs asleep. Where else would she be?"

Jared swirled the amber liquid in his glass before he took a drink, ignoring Caleb's question for the third time. "Were you aware that my fiancée has been in contact with Margot Hollander?"

Caleb's eyebrows rose. "That's impossible. She's been under my nose or her mother's since late July. The only time she's been out of this house was when she went to the funeral—and I can assure you she was with me the whole time."

"Well, I don't know how she did it, but that lawyer boyfriend of Miss Hollander's is stirring up trouble over Harry Fuller's case."

"What? That can't be. Fuller's already been convicted and sent to prison."

"Um hm." Jared nodded. "But apparently Sydney Lowenstein entered his appearance as counsel for Fuller and has filed an appeal."

"On what grounds?"

"I don't know, I haven't seen his brief. But I'm sure we don't have anything to worry about. I've contributed to the campaigns of most of the judges on up the circuit. I just wanted to make sure you were aware the case had been reopened, in case you get a subpoena—although I doubt it will get that far."

Caleb's hand shook as he poured himself another drink. "Well technically, he *did* steal that car. It didn't actually belong to my sister and she had no right to give it to him. I heard they almost acquitted him on the stolen money charge, citing reasonable doubt or some sort of foolishness."

Jared chuckled. "People serving on juries need money just like everybody else. It wasn't hard to bribe one of them into standing firm until the others just wanted to get it over with and go home."

"Sure wish they coulda pinned the arson on him," Caleb brooded. "Damned brother-in-law of mine let the fire insurance lapse on the store," he said, looking up when the bodyguard cleared his throat. He felt a chill at the sardonic grin on the man's face.

"Which brings us around to the reason for my visit," said Jared.

"Been wonderin' when you'd get to that."

"Time is running out. It's already the first of October. Do you believe that Ivy will be willing to marry me in December? Or is it time to give up and cut our losses?"

Caleb hung his head. "Jared, I just don't know. She's been through so much lately. The loss of her mother—and all the previous events…"

"Well, then." Jared straightened in his seat. "How much would you take for the necklace?"

"Huh?" Caleb stared at Jared, startled. One moment he wanted to marry Ivy and the next he implied that he wanted to break the engagement and buy that cursed necklace. Was that what he really wanted all along? Suspicion, replaced by a premonition of dread shocked him into full sobriety. Perspiration dotted his forehead when he thought about the contents of his pocket. "Why do you want the necklace?"

"I have my reasons." Jared's dark eyes glittered and his lips thinned in derision.

"I don't have it anymore."

Jared's eyes flashed. "Where *is* it, then?"

Caleb shrank from Jared's anger. Something warned him not to be truthful. "I pawned it."

"You *pawned* it?" Jared's face became a glowering mask of rage. "For God's sake, why?"

Caleb shrugged and continued his lie. "You know how hard up I've been, Jared. My wife just died, ya know. I had the choice of either payin' the undertaker or makin' payroll at the sawmill. What was I s'posed to do?"

Jared closed his eyes and composed himself. "Do you have the pawn ticket? I'll get it out of hock in the morning." His voice held a contemptuous note.

"Sure, Jared. I think it's somewhere in here." He rummaged through a cabinet drawer and found an old ticket that read *Schmidt's Jewelry Store*. Caleb couldn't remember what this particular receipt was for, but at least it might pacify Jared until he could collect his thoughts. "Does this mean the engagement is over?"

"That depends on your daughter," Jared replied. He stood up and put on his outerwear. "I leave for Europe in early December, so I haven't got time for much more of her foolishness."

"I'll have a talk with her in the morning."

"Very well. I'll let you know when I retrieve the necklace."

Caleb poured himself another shot of whiskey when the door banged shut behind the two men. He searched his memory. Earl Twitchell? Wasn't he the Arkansas deputy who'd testified in Fuller's trial? What was he doing working for Jared?

Several drinks later his courage returned and he set his mind to solving the problem of what to do about Ivy. He feared his plans to marry her to Jared were now history, but he had to do something. His dead wife would never let him rest until he figured out what she wanted him to do.

Winnie's suicide note had been very cryptic, saying something about Ivy having cancer. But Caleb knew that was a lot of claptrap. Anybody with eyes in his head could see the truth. He filled a whiskey glass and drank; then another; and another. He closed his eyes and let the alcohol carry him away—and then he had a thought.

In a drunken epiphany, he had seized upon the note as if it were from the Gospels and early the next day he'd whisked Ivy away to the Baker Cancer Hospital. Dr. Baker had been very obliging, agreeing with Winnie's cancer diagnosis from beyond the grave. Ivy was immediately admitted for treatment and, Caleb hoped, Dr. Baker's ministrations would soon rid her of the bastard growing in her belly.

Now here he was almost a month later, back in St. Louis, scared and confused. He'd wandered around in Arkansas and southern Missouri for awhile after he'd left her, dreading his return to a lonely, empty house. He'd spent practically his last dime making sure Ivy would be well cared for at the hospital and he'd felt good about his choice—until he got back in town and learned about the mysterious fire at Schmidt's Jewelry Store.

Miserable, he looked up from his musings and groaned when he saw Winnie again. What the hell did she want now? She didn't speak. Perhaps she couldn't. But whatever it was, she was relentless.

He slung back another drink and watched the spectral woman glide toward the window. She glanced back over her shoulder, wrote with her finger in the condensation on the glass, and disappeared.

Caleb stood and walked toward the window. He read the words with astonishment. Now everything was clear. He knew what he had to do.

HELP HARRY.

His purpose now clear, he pulled out the telephone directory and turned to the L's. He ran his finger down the page until he found the residential number for Sydney Lowenstein, Esquire. With trembling hands he dialed the number and waited.

"Hello, Sydney Lowenstein here."

"Mr. Lowenstein? This is Caleb Turner. Sorry to bother you at home so late at night, but I have some information for you that can't wait…"

Emma paced and intermittently stared out the window, chilled by the bleak landscape below and the realization of her own impotence. Days of constant rain soaked the gardens and a blustering north wind howled outside, but armed guards continued to patrol the hospital grounds despite the miserable conditions. What was she going to do? She was beginning to despair.

Almost a week had gone by since she'd awakened in a stranger's body in the distant past, yet in her own time, it had been more like a month. She supposed time and space must be vastly different when a person is hovering between life and death. How long had she been out there floating in la-la land?

Ivy and Theodora huddled around an iron steam register for warmth. They both had their knitting or embroidery to occupy their minds, but Emma had never learned to do either. Having grown up in a different era, she wasn't sure she possessed the patience for such an activity. How did people fill their time without going stir crazy before the invention of television, the Internet, or DVD players?

Of course, there was a radio. Theodora's was lovely. Made of wood, it had a curving, cathedral-style top and ornamental speaker openings. She'd proudly tell anyone that it was a Philco Model 60B—the latest technology available when she'd bought it in 1935.

And, Emma must admit, in the past week she'd found the radio shows to be quite entertaining. Who would have thought she could become as interested in Charlie McCarthy, Jack Benny, or Radio Orphan Annie as in her weekly television favorites—*Desperate Housewives* and *Glee*?

"Are they still parading around out there in the rain?" asked Theodora.

"Like little wooden soldiers," replied Emma. "Very wet and miserable soldiers."

"I'll bet Earl's not out there," Ivy remarked. Her lip curled disdainfully and she stabbed at the cloth with her needle. "I wonder what happened to his job with the sheriff?"

"I haven't noticed him for a few days," remarked Theodora. "But Jennie told me the sheriff fired him. Something about him being accused of causing the death of a local doctor and setting fire to a local dry goods store last summer."

Ivy stopped her needlework and stared in horror. "Do you mean Doc Pruitt?"

Theodora shrugged. "I'm not familiar with the locals. Jennie just said there'd been an inquest. Apparently there hadn't been enough evidence to charge him, but he was dismissed from his duties anyhow. She said the sheriff and the mayor had a falling out with Dr. Baker after he hired Earl. Looks like the town officials are finally waking up to the fact that Baker's no good."

"So what does that say about us? Why are we still here?" Emma put her hands on her hips and felt a sudden stab in her belly. She staggered to the bed and lay down, holding her side.

"I think you just answered your own question, dear." Theodora slowly rose and followed a quicker, more nimble Ivy to Emma's bed. "Do you need another shot?"

Emma gazed at her friends as they ministered to her needs. Such a pathetic trio. She knew Anna's body was giving out and Theodora's breathing seemed to have grown more labored during the past few days. An ominous rattle emanated from the old woman's chest every time she coughed, which seemed to be growing more and more frequent. How much longer would they be able to protect Ivy?

Together they'd formed a conspiracy to thwart Dr. Baker and Miss Amiss from their attempts to feed the herbal concoction to Ivy. With sly and cunning, they'd managed to trade their meals with Ivy, just in case Miss Amiss tried to lace her food with the medicine. So far it seemed to have worked, but who knew how long it would be before they would catch on?

A sudden rap at the door startled them and they all glanced up, frozen with dread. At five forty-five in the afternoon, supper had already been served. Today was Sunday, so nobody was going to get any medical care today. Theodora rose and slowly walked to the door, stopping every few steps to catch her breath.

She hesitated. "Who is it?" More raps answered her. "All right, all right. Hold on." Theodora undid the lock and pulled the door open. A short, plump woman wearing a shawl over her black hair stood at the door, her eyes darting furtively back and forth. "Yes, may I help you?"

"Yes, ma'am. My name's Cordelia. I'm looking for Ivy."

"Cordelia! How wonderful that you came." Ivy grabbed the woman by the hand and pulled her inside. "How did you know I needed you? I tried to come see you days ago, but Earl stopped me—Theodora, Anna, this is Madame Cordelia, the psychic I tried to visit on Monday."

"I'm a medium, dear. I'm not gifted with precognition." Cordelia embraced Ivy and shook hands with Theodora and Emma. "I'm simply a messenger—a conduit between different plains of existence."

"But what made you come here?" asked Theodora.

"Ivy's mother has been bombarding me with messages all week, but today is the first time I've been able to slip through the guards." Cordelia pulled off her wet shawl and draped it across the register to dry. "Did you know they're stopping everyone who tries to come up here? And they're carrying machine guns!"

"Machine guns? Oh, my goodness. You're so brave," said Ivy.

"How did you get in?" asked Theodora.

"Jennie distracted the guard on duty by flirting with him and giving him hot coffee long enough for me to slip in. But if they find out I'm here, she'll get in trouble."

"Then we must be quiet," said Ivy. She smiled and her face lit up.

Emma's heart lurched. When Ivy smiled, her mouth and eyes looked just like Zan's.

"We haven't much time. Let's all put our chairs in a circle, shall we?" Cordelia pulled Theodora's card table into the middle of the room and they arranged their chairs. She pulled a small, cone-shaped object from her bag and laid it on the table, along with a short, fat candle. A glossy wooden board with scrolled letters and numerals, along with a small planchette came next. She then brought out some incense sticks, laid them on a metal tray, struck a match, and lit the incense and the candle. The spicy aroma wafted around the room.

"Is that a Ouija board?" Theodora's eyes were wide as saucers. "Those things scare me to death."

"We don't have to use it if it makes you uncomfortable." Cordelia moved the talking board and planchette to a dresser in the corner.

"Shall I close the drapes?" asked Ivy.

"Yes, thank you," replied Cordelia. "Oh, I almost forgot. Do you have something that used to belong to your mother? Any kind of small object will do. It'll help make the channel more clear."

Ivy thought for a moment and then headed toward her room. "I think I know just the thing." She returned a moment later with a musical powder box. "How's this?"

"Perfect." Cordelia ran her fingertips across the box and then positioned it on the table next to the voice trumpet. "If a spirit decides to speak, we'll be ready."

Emma froze when she saw the powder box. She recognized the round pewter base and the dainty porcelain top—a picture of a woman and a little girl wearing hoopskirts. It looked just like the one she'd owned as a child. Ivy opened the lid. Inside was a toy whistle. The music box began to play *Tea for Two*. Amazing. She hadn't seen hers in years. She wondered what had become of it.

"Ahem." Madame Cordelia cleared her throat and reached around the table. "Are we ready to begin?"

The four women sat around the table in the darkened room and held hands. The wind blew mournfully around the building turrets, contributing to the eeriness of the moment. Madame Cordelia closed her eyes, took a deep breath, and began to hum. Goose bumps rose on Emma's arms. She'd never been to a séance before, but she was fascinated. Remembering the accuracy of Moonbeam's palm reading session and everything else that had happened recently, she wouldn't dare be skeptical.

The room grew quiet as they all concentrated. The only sound now was the moaning of the wind as Cordelia fell deeper and deeper into a trance. Emma tightened her grip on Ivy's hand, wanting to cry from the poignancy of the contact. She'd never felt closer to Zan, yet so far away.

Cordelia's eyes closed and her head swayed gently as she spoke. "I'm walking through a forest. The air is fresh and birds are singing overhead. I feel the warmth of the sun on my shoulders as it peeks in and out through the trees. I hear the sound of water, like a babbling brook and smell the fragrance of the cedars. My path makes a turn and I see a stream; its busy waters rush over and around smooth stones, producing tiny rapids."

She paused and inhaled deeply before continuing. "Up ahead I see him, standing tall and proud, like a sentinel. Such a regal bearing, his face so wise, his feathered headdress so colorful. I approach and he greets me warmly, as always. He is my spirit guide—Nantan."

Cordelia's head began to sway faster and her breath became labored. "I'm following him through the forest. The path is now descending, becoming steeper and steeper. Large boulders lie across the path. I'm afraid I'll twist my ankle. It's difficult to keep up with him. Nantan—slow down—please." She moaned, her head snapped limply to the side, and then her neck became rigid.

Suddenly, the scent of roses overpowered the incense and its curling smoke changed direction. The candlelight flickered, sending shadows dancing across the slanted attic walls. The temperature in the room plummeted and the hairs on Emma's arms and neck stood erect.

Cordelia's head slumped forward and then she twitched. She opened her eyes, stared around the darkened room, and Emma was instantly aware of the difference. There was a noticeable change in the personality of the hand she held. The face was the same, the body was the same, but Cordelia was gone.

"II....veeeeeee..." A strange, sad voice spoke from Cordelia's mouth.

"Mama! Is that you?" Ivy tensed and stared at Cordelia. Tears welled in her eyes.

"II......veeeeeeeee...I'm sorry...so sorry..."

Emma shuddered at the plaintive voice of the indwelt spirit, but she didn't break the circle. She glanced at Theodora across the table; her wrinkled face and sunken eyes made her appear even older in the flickering candlelight. Emma's heart went out to Ivy, as well as to the poor, tortured soul who spoke to them from beyond the grave.

"It's okay, Mama. I forgive you," said Ivy, between sobs. Tears flowed freely down her face. "I understand now. You didn't know what you were doing. I love you."

"Love...you...too..." the spirit of Winifred paused and then continued. "Dan-nee...I'm here with Dan-nee...and your Papa..."

Cordelia's face twisted into a half-smile and then her head lolled to one side like a rag doll. Her body suddenly went limp and her eyes closed, but her hands didn't lose their grip on the circle. The music box began to vibrate, rattling back and forth on its legs before scooting across the table and landing against Cordelia's bosom.

"What was that?" Ivy stiffened and stared at Cordelia as the music box spun like a top in slow motion. "What did she mean about Papa?"

Emma felt another change in the grip of the hand that held hers. It was strong, powerful, and no longer feminine. The odor of cigar smoke replaced the rose smell. An icy chill ran down her spine when Cordelia's body twitched convulsively, and then slowly raised her head. She opened her eyes and gazed around the room. Cordelia was gone—Winifred was gone—some other spirit had pushed out Winifred and replaced her.

The plump woman seemed to grow taller and her face changed. "Har-ry..." An agonized male voice boomed loudly from Cordelia's mouth and then faded away.

"Papa! Is that you?" Ivy's eyes were wild with fear. "What about Harry? Is he all right?"

"Please help me..." a feeble female voice sounded from the trumpet, then faded away as a different male voice interrupted. "I'm dying...Please let me ou...." Different voices came and went, as if someone were twisting the dial of a radio.

Cordelia's head bobbed back and forth before her mouth opened again. The voice seemed to labor, struggling against the commotion from the trumpet. "Har-ry...I told ...the truth... about Har-ry...he's free ...he's ...coming ...for...you."

"When, Papa? When?"

The trumpet was now a cacophony of lamentations, as if vast multitudes were struggling for a microphone. Emma cringed at the chaotic sound. What did they all want? It was impossible to understand what any of them were saying—but then one of the messages caught her attention.

"Emma...it's Tommy..."

"What about Harry, Papa?" Ivy's voice shrieked above the uproar.

Emma sat forward and strained to hear the voice through the tumultuous noise. Had it been her brother Tommy? And then she heard it again. Tommy's voice. "Emma...tell Zan...lockbox... tea for two...four one nine..." The voice was interrupted again, and then it returned. "They want ... your... heart."

"Papa," screamed Ivy. "*When* is Harry coming?"

Cordelia's face twisted grotesquely in the candlelight. Her body moved spasmodically, as if she were battling for control. The rotation of the music box increased. When Caleb's voice came again, it was barely audible and then drifted off into static.

"Tonight...he's coming...tonight...in...the...mor..."

Ivy screamed and wrenched her hands loose, breaking the

circle. The music box spun wildly across the room, hit the wall, and came apart. Cordelia's body collapsed forward. Emma grabbed her shoulders to prevent her from falling into the candle's flame. The babble of voices ceased.

Cordelia stirred and gazed around the room. "What happened?" She shook her head and stared at the sobbing girl. "I'm completely exhausted."

"I—heard—my father's—voice," replied Ivy, between sniffs. "He must be—dead." She broke down and sobbed even harder. "Harry must be dead too."

"Oh, honey. Why do you think Harry's dead?" Theodora pulled Ivy close in her feeble grasp and patted her shoulders. "Please don't cry."

"Because—Papa—said he was coming—in the—morgue."

"I don't think that's what he was saying, Ivy. I think he meant *in the morning.*"

Ivy pulled away from Theodora and stared at her. "But he said tonight. He said 'Harry is coming tonight.' Why would he then say in the morning?"

Cordelia held her hand to her chest and tried to catch her breath. "What the spirits say doesn't always make sense to us."

Emma interjected. "Harry can't be dead. There were only two spirits speaking through you. Right, Cordelia?" She knew Harry was going to live a long, productive life. Didn't she? Her confidence wavered when she thought about her own strange adventure. Everything she'd believed in had been turned upside down in the past week.

"Of course he can't be dead," agreed Cordelia.

Theodora's head shot up and she pointed toward the window. "Oh, my God. Ivy, is that your father?"

Emma turned in the direction Theodora pointed. She gasped and grabbed the sides of the table, afraid she might faint. She was terrified, but she couldn't tear her eyes away. The hazy figure of a man had materialized in the corner. He appeared young, had long wavy hair, and wore overalls. Could it be Harry? She felt sick at the thought.

"Nooo. I don't know him." Ivy wailed, buried her face in her hands, and curled up in a ball.

"Then who is it?" asked Emma, her heart pounding. It obviously wasn't Harry, or Ivy would have acknowledged him. Things were growing weirder by the minute.

Cordelia raised a finger to her lips and cocked her head to one side. "Wait...he's speaking to me...he says his name is Michael."

Emma tensed, remembering Jennie and Andy's conversation about a ghost named Michael on the second floor, as well as the story about the Irish stonemason on the Crescent Hotel ghost tour. Could this be the same Michael?

"What's he doing here?" asked Theodora. She put her arm around Ivy and pulled her close.

Cordelia stared at the specter in the corner and strained to listen to a voice nobody else could hear. "He says he normally stays on the second floor, but he felt the energy from our séance and came up here to see what was happening," she replied, acting as an interpreter. "What was that?...yes, I know...the people who run this place now are very bad...yes, I agree... thank you, Michael. I'm sure we all appreciate your help."

The specter disappeared in a windy exit, extinguishing the candle in its wake. The temperature warmed immediately, but the room remained dark even after Emma pulled back the drapes. She flipped on the overhead light.

"It's all right. He's gone now," said Theodora. Ivy clung to the frail old woman.

Ivy wiped her cheeks with the back of her hand and turned to face Cordelia. "What did you mean about Harry in the morgue?"

Cordelia appeared blank. "I don't know, dear. This was my first experience with transfiguration." She shuddered. "Usually, the spirits simply talk to me and I relay their messages. But this time, Nantan couldn't hold them back—there were so many of them."

"So many what?" asked Emma. "Spirits?"

Cordelia nodded, her brow knitted as she glanced around the room. "I've never seen anything like it. This place is full of earthbound spirits, begging for help...so much sorrow and despair...they're overwhelming." She shuddered, leaned back in the chair and closed her eyes.

Theodora rose and assisted Ivy from her chair. "Ivy needs to lie down for a while. She mustn't be subjected to any more stress. Come on, dear." Ivy went with Theodora through the connecting bathroom door, leaning against the old woman's stooped shoulder.

Emma noticed the broken music box in the far corner. She bent over to pick up the pieces and a miniature photograph of an early twentieth century family fell out from a thin compartment between the base and the lid. She stared at the young man, woman, and two babies. She turned it over and read the inscription on the back—*Caleb, Winifred, Ivy & Danny – Christmas 1921.*

So this was the Turner family during happier times. Emma had never seen any pictures of Caleb or Winifred before and she had only heard about the baby boy. When things settled down, she would ask Ivy about it, but now was not the time. She placed the picture back where she found it, screwed the lid back in place, and set the powder box on the card table.

Cordelia gathered the objects on the table into her bag and then helped Emma move the card table and chairs back. She picked up her shawl and draped it across her head and shoulders. "This was an extraordinary experience, but I must be going now."

"Thank you for coming, Cordelia," said Emma, more confused now than ever. She couldn't stop thinking about her brother's message, or the one from Ivy's father. What did they mean?

Cordelia stopped suddenly before she reached the door and tapped the side of her head. "I am so forgetful. Can you please tell Ivy something for me? It's very important."

"Of course."

"Tell her I got a letter from her Aunt Tyme. She and her husband are doing fine. She says Clyde has been very lucky at the race track and she sent a rather large sum of money to Ivy and Harry, in care of me." Cordelia gazed at Emma expectantly. "Since we know Harry's coming back soon, what do you think I ought to do with it? Should I open a bank account in their name?"

Emma drew in her breath at a sudden thought. The words *race track* jumped out in her mind. She'd been listening to the radio this morning and the announcers had been talking about the upcoming horse race on Tuesday at Pimlico, Maryland. Jennie had said Dr. Baker and Dr. Ballew were excited about the money they hoped to win betting on War Admiral.

"Today is Sunday, isn't it?"

"Uh, yes…Sunday, October 30th. Why?"

Emma bubbled over with excitement when she thought about the DVD she'd forgotten to return to Blockbuster before she and Zan had left on their trip. The late fees were probably piling up by now, but that was okay. She and Zan had enjoyed the movie so much; they'd watched it twice and she remembered the date of the story's climax—which would be the day after tomorrow.

"Cordelia, do you know anybody here who can place bets for you?"

"Um hm. Frank at the feed store is the town bookie."

Emma placed her hands on Cordelia's shoulders and stared into her eyes. "You must trust me on this—take Ivy's money to Frank and put every penny on Seabiscuit."

CHAPTER NINETEEN

Harry stared out the car window at the retreating scenery, grateful for his liberty. He'd been imprisoned for over three months, so freedom was a true and precious blessing. The cold, wet landscape and the growing gloom looked like heaven to him. He'd despaired of ever seeing Ivy again, but now the miracle had happened. He was on his way back to Eureka Springs to get her. He bowed his head in a silent prayer of thanks.

"You okay, Harry?"

"Hm? Oh, yessir." Harry opened his eyes and smiled when he felt a touch on his shoulder. "Just givin' thanks to the Lord."

Sydney grinned and steered the car around a crooked mountain turn. "Good men like you don't belong in jail."

"Sure do appreciate all your help, Sydney," said Harry. "My Pa was a preacher, an' he'dve been real upset if he'd thought I was on the wrong side of the law."

Sidney laughed. "Mine's a Rabbi, and he's not happy I went into law."

"Well, I'd sure be up a creek if you hadn't."

"We're still not out of the woods, you know," Sydney warned. "I had to do a lot of fancy footwork to get Judge Trimble to grant a Writ of Habeas Corpus to hear your appeal. You wouldn't have been released without Caleb Turner's testimony, so we've got to make sure we do everything by the book. If we don't show up in Federal Court in Little Rock on Wednesday, he'll send you back. Are you sure you don't want to wait until after the hearing to get Ivy?"

311

"Oh, no, Sydney!" Harry's heart skipped a beat at the thought of waiting. "You heard what Margot said. She's worried Dr. Baker might cause Ivy to lose our baby." He choked back a sob. "I just gotta get her before it's too late."

"That's okay, Harry. I understand." Sydney frowned and grew silent.

"What's wrong? D'ya think the judge is gonna deny me?"

"Oh, no. Your case is rock solid. I was just trying to think of the best way to tell you something—something that's going to upset you."

"What?" Harry's heart fell as he waited for more bad news.

"Caleb Turner is dead." Sydney maneuvered the car into a parking space in front of the county jail. "His house burned last night. The firemen found him lying in bed with a cigar in his hand, but the police don't think it was an accident."

Harry gasped. "How come?"

"Because his whole house *and* his body had been soaked in gasoline. Thank goodness he swore out his statement in time."

"Poor Mr. Turner…such a horrible thing to happen…poor Ivy."

"Mm hm. Same thing happened to that doctor here in Eureka last summer."

"You mean Doc Pruett? Who would've done something like that?"

"If I had to guess, I'd say one of Jared Covington's goons." Sydney set the parking brake and opened the door. "You stay out here and wait while I talk to the sheriff. Okay?" He bowed his head against the wind and walked away, splashing through the puddles on the sidewalk.

Harry waited in the car while Sydney went inside the jailhouse. He had no desire to ever go back in there. He would spend his time, warm and dry, dreaming about Ivy.

Twenty minutes later Sydney returned. His expression appeared bleak when he climbed behind the wheel of the car.

"Looks like we're on our own."

"What do you mean?"

"Sheriff was real sympathetic, especially when I showed him a Federal court order," replied Sydney. He frowned and stared into space. "But we're not gonna get any help from him. Apparently, Norman Baker's gone off the deep end when it comes to defending his hospital. He's got a whole bunch of hired guards with an arsenal of automatic weapons. The sheriff has been warned to stay away and he won't send his deputies anywhere near that hospital unless he's got the National Guard behind him. He says the only people they're letting through in the evenings are the undertakers, because there're so many people dying up there—and Sheriff's not anxious to give the ghouls any more business. I think we'd better wait until morning and hope we can bluff our way through."

"I can't take the chance, Sydney. I'm gonna get her one way or another. Tonight." Harry opened the car door, intent on marching up the hill alone, if necessary.

"Not so fast." Sydney jerked Harry by the shirt-sleeve. "Don't be a fool. You're not gonna do her any good if you're dead."

Harry's eyes widened at the sudden idea that popped into his head. "That's it! We'll go see an undertaker."

"What?" Sydney stared at him as if he were mad—but by the time Harry finished explaining his plan, Sydney was smiling.

Theodora staggered and held her handkerchief to her mouth when she reentered the bedroom. Emma gasped and ran to her aid when she saw her pale face and the red-soaked cloth. "Oh, my goodness! What happened?"

The old woman collapsed onto the bed. Her voice came out as a gurgle before she managed to clear the blood from her throat. "My tumor's …burst …hemorrhaging …won't be long…now."

Bob jumped down from the dresser and stared at Theodora, his back arched and his short tail standing at attention. He mewed softly and hopped onto the bed. He rubbed his head against Theodora's forehead several times, curled into a ball, and then lay beside her with his head resting on her chest.

Panic swept over Emma at the thought of losing her friend. "Theodora, you mustn't speak that way. I'll go call for help."

"No." The ancient, claw-like hand gripped Emma's with obviously waning strength. "Don't tell…about me…'til after… Harry comes."

Emma nodded, feeling sick. "All right, but what do I tell Ivy?"

Theodora pointed to her closet. "Luggage…bring my Bible…please."

Emma pulled out the heavy suitcase, wincing from her own pain, but trying not to let it show. She found the worn black book and carried it to the dying woman. "Here it is. Do you want me to read to you?"

Theodora shook her head and reached for the Bible. Bob meowed when she moved and she stroked his fur to reassure him. She gasped for breath as she opened the Bible to a marked page. Inside was an envelope. "My Will…already written…need a…witness…" Her breathing was labored. "Will…you sign?"

"Of course." Emma handed her an ink pen from the bedside table.

Theodora signed the document with a shaky hand and then collapsed backward onto the bed. Emma signed beneath, making sure to write the name *Anna Schmidt*.

"I feel…at peace…now," said Theodora. "So grateful…you came back…when you did…will you…make sure…Ivy gets… this?" She handed the Will to Emma. "I never…married…my family…all gone…don't want…Baker…to get it."

"I understand. Of course I'll give it to her," replied Emma, choking back tears.

"There isn't...much...just a small ranch...in Texas... between Dallas and...Fort Worth...About fifty acres...and a... farm house." She had another coughing fit, which left her even weaker and the towel Emma had given her even redder, but she seemed to want to talk. "Several...years ago...fella leased...my land...for horses. Had a...racetrack nearby...called Arlington Downs...but had to close...last year...betting outlawed...in Texas." She coughed again and struggled for breath. "Maybe it'll be...worth something...someday."

Emma listened in amazement. Now she knew how Zan's family had come to the area where they'd settled. She wondered if the pharmacy, which sat at such a bustling intersection in Arlington, had once been a part of Theodora's ranch?

"Anna?" Theodora's breathing rattled and her eyes appeared weary. "You aren't...really Anna...are you?"

Emma shook her head and wiped away her tears. What was the point in lying any more? "No. My name is Emma Fuller— and I come from the future." By the time she'd finished telling her story, her handkerchief was soaked. "And I don't know if I'll ever see Zan again. I know this all sounds incredible. Do you believe me?"

Theodora smiled and nodded. "I believe you...I knew... when I saw you...eating Ivy's ham sandwich...and just now... when you signed the Will...with your...left hand...something was...different..." Theodora relaxed on the pillow and closed her eyes. "Please take care...of...Ivy...I'll see you...again... soon..." She gasped once, exhaled, and became still.

Emma closed her eyes, her heart aching with sadness. When she opened them again they filled with tears. She wiped her face with the sodden handkerchief and stared one last time at her friend, taking comfort in the knowledge that death had washed away her pain. Desolation swept over her when she realized that her own time drew nearer, yet she still had much to accomplish.

Pulling the blanket up to Theodora's chin, she smoothed out the wrinkles and tucked her in. If she hadn't known better, she would have thought her merely sleeping. Bob howled mournfully and began licking the old woman's still face. When she didn't move, he let out a sigh, curled up on her chest and lay down.

With one last look, Emma slipped the Will into the pouch with Anna's diary and her ring, and went into the bathroom. She knocked on Ivy's door, but there was no answer. The doorknob turned and she went inside. "Ivy, are you awake?"

A chill black silence surrounded her. The room was empty.

Ivy awakened to a blinding headache and a sickly, sweet smell that hung in the air. She gasped at her surroundings; she was lying on a canopy bed in a room with darkened windows that curved into a semi-circle, draped with lavender and purple satin.

"Hello, little darlin'. I see you're awake now."

Ivy flinched when Dr. Baker's head popped up from below as he climbed the stairs into the loft bedroom. She shrank back, clutching the purple counterpane to her chin. Where in God's name was she and how did she get there?

"Sorry we had to take such extreme measures to get you outta your room," said Baker. He picked up a wet handkerchief from the floor and deposited it onto a table on the other side of the room. "But you wuz so hysterical when I tried to talk to you, I had to do somethin' to calm you down." He gestured around the room and grinned. "Welcome to my private penthouse."

Ivy ignored his bid for admiration and sniffed the air. Her stomach heaved at the odor. It reminded her of the operating room when she'd had a tonsillectomy as a child. What was Dr. Baker referring to? She didn't recall being hysterical. The last thing she remembered was waking from a sound sleep and seeing Earl's ugly grin just before something covered her face.

Outraged, she spoke with loathing. "What do you want

from me?"

Baker sighed and sat in a rocking chair. "I have some very sad news, my dear." He reached over and took her hand. She tried to wrench it away, but he held it firmly. "Sorry to tell you this—but your father has passed away."

Tears formed in her eyes and she looked away. "I already knew."

"You did?" His eyebrows shot up above his wire-rimmed glasses. "How'd you know? It happened last night, but the St. Louis Fire Marshal called me just a bit ago when he found out you wuz here." His eyes narrowed suspiciously. "Somebody been up here 'n tole ya?"

Ivy ignored his question and asked, "There was a fire? I didn't know how it happened."

Baker scratched his head and nodded. "Yep, I'm afraid your home was totally destroyed. Your daddy was in bed at the time."

"Poor Papa." She buried her face in her hands and sobbed. "What a horrible way to die."

"There, there, dear." Baker patted her on the back and tried to embrace her, but she pulled away.

"Please don't touch me!"

Baker scowled and his lips thinned with displeasure. "There's more." He reached into his pocket, pulled out a cigar, and lit it. He wrapped his left thumb around a lavender suspender and leaned back in the chair. "They suspect arson."

"Arson! But who?"

"Well…" Baker drew on his cigar, blew out a puff of black smoke, and stared at the ceiling. "Coppers arrested your fiancée, Mr. Covington. Apparently, somebody saw him leavin' your house just 'fore it burned."

"Jared?" Ivy's skin prickled. She'd always known he was bad. But murder? She would never have considered such a thing. "Jared's in jail?"

"Not any more, I'm afraid." Baker puffed thoughtfully.

"They found him hangin' in his cell this mornin'."

Ivy collapsed onto the pillow and digested this new information. Jared was dead, but she felt no emotion, other than surprise. There had to be more to it than what she'd been told. Jared cared only for Jared. He would never have committed suicide.

She closed her eyes, put her fingers to her head, and massaged her temples. Pain stabbed above the bridge of her nose just before she felt a slight shiver in her womb, like the flutter of a butterfly's wings. Her eyes grew wide and her hand flew to her belly, her headache forgotten.

Baker must have noticed her movement. He leaped up from the chair and sat on the side of the bed. Before she could react, he wrapped his arms around her and kissed her. She gagged at his fetid breath.

"It's all right, my little darlin'." He caressed her even as she struggled against him. "I know your secret and it's okay with me. Never been a daddy b'fore, but I wouldn't mind helpin' ya raise this one." He placed his nicotine-stained hand on her abdomen.

"Get your hands *off* me. You're old enough to be my grandfather," shrieked Ivy. She struggled, but Baker chuckled and tightened his grip.

"Maybe what you need is somebody old enough to tame ya. Had my eye on you ever since the night I lost out on yer box supper. But I always win in the end. How 'bout we get hitched tomorrow—on Halloween! My favorite holiday."

Ivy spluttered and wiped at her mouth with the back of her hand. "I'm not going to marry *you*. Besides, I'm already married—to Harry."

Baker's mouth twisted. "Last I heard, that little creep wuz doin' hard time in the state pen. If that's his kid ya got there, it'll be all growed up long b'fore *he* ever sees the light of day. You don't want your baby's daddy to be a jail bird, do ya?"

Ivy placed her hands on Baker's shoulders and pushed as hard as she could, but he held her fast. "Please. Let me go!"

Baker laughed and pulled her closer. "My, my, but you've got a lotta spirit. And purty too! You'll be perfect for the new Madame Tangley. You'd like that, wouldn't ya?"

"I don't know what you're talking about." Ivy shuddered in his grasp.

"No, I s'pose you wouldn't know 'bout that." Baker's eyes gleamed. "Back b'fore everybody got all googaw over the movin' picture shows, they used to get their entertainment from live Vaudeville acts. I produced the greatest show of 'em all— Madame Pearl Tangley, The Mental Marvel. We traveled the entire country puttin' on mind reading shows that astounded and entertained."

"What's that got to do with me?" Ivy stared at Dr. Baker with growing horror.

"Oh, I just had a little yen to reinstate the show on a part time basis. Who knows? Maybe we could even make a movie."

"What is *she* doing in here?"

Ivy looked up in surprise. Nurse Amiss stood at the top of the stairs, her hands on her hips and her chest heaving. Her damaged face was a glowering mask of rage. Sparkling blue earrings at her ears were shockingly juxtaposed against her crisp white uniform and no-nonsense nurse's cap.

"Thought I told you to move yourself and your stuff back downstairs, Roberta." Baker scowled and his face turned red. "I didn't say you could have them earrings. Take 'em off right now." He released Ivy and stood.

"Norman, don't do this to me." Roberta's face paled, and she put her hands to her ears, her lesion becoming even more pronounced. "Ten years I've devoted to you—loved you. You can't just throw all that away now. Not for this little—whore!"

"You'll mind your tongue, woman! Give 'em to me."

"I thought *I* was gonna be the new Madame Tangley,"

whined Roberta. Her voice was a shrieking assault to the senses, like the creaking of an unoiled hinge. "You promised me."

"Have you looked in the mirror lately? Nobody—including me—wants to look at you anymore." Baker sneered and reached for a cigar. He lit it and blew the smoke straight at Miss Amiss. "Madame Tangley must be beautiful."

Roberta's eyes flashed and her face contorted. "I *used* to be beautiful. At least that's what you told me." She put her hand to her cancer-eaten face. "Why isn't your precious cure working for me? Maybe you *are* a quack like everybody says. A short little quack!"

"Get *out*!"

Miss Amiss stared with loathing at Dr. Baker, walked to the dresser, picked up the radio, and jerked the cord out of its socket. Ivy shrank back, terrified she was going to hit her with it. But then the rampaging woman turned, slammed the radio against the wall, and threw its remains down the stairwell.

"You'll pay for that," Baker hissed. His eyes flashed and his hands balled into fists.

Roberta's twisted smile changed from triumph to fear when she read the fury in his expression. She backed away, the sapphires still flashing at her ears, and then turned and stomped down the stairs. Ivy cringed when from somewhere downstairs she heard more shouting, crashing noises, and then the sound of heavy footsteps ascending. She smelled Earl Twitchell long before she saw his repulsive face peek into the bedroom.

"Everythin' okay up here, boss?" He flashed a gap-toothed grin at Ivy and patted his front shirt pocket which held the sapphires. "Got the jools back. Hoo boy! Was that bitch ever mad."

Harry lay in the pine box, willing himself to remain calm as he fought against the claustrophobia that threatened to engulf him. Pitch black surrounded him. He could barely breathe. But he'd experienced worse than this in jail, so he knew he could handle it. He mentally relaxed, put his finger to his neck, and counted off the rhythm of his pulse until it slowed.

The hearse made a sharp turn and Harry braced himself against the narrow sides of the casket. The sway of the ride made him queasy and he practiced deep breathing until the sensation passed. He couldn't afford to be sick now. He was on his way to get his wife.

The anticipation of seeing Ivy again cheered him and he tried not to think about the dangers ahead. He smiled when he remembered the look on Sydney's face when he heard his outrageous idea. Most folks would have laughed in his face and called him insane, but not Sydney. He'd seen the inherent possibility of success and agreed to help.

They'd chosen an undertaker who lived above one of several funeral homes in town. He'd been surly at first, called away from his favorite radio show on a blustery Sunday evening for an *emergency* pickup at the Baker Hospital, but the promise of cash in advance had softened his attitude. No, it couldn't wait until morning, Sydney had assured him. It must be tonight or not at all.

The mortician had been furious when Sydney chose the cheapest, flimsiest casket in his inventory. But the offer of an extra hundred dollars for his after-hours service held great influence and the bargain had been struck. Now Harry's biggest concern was finding Ivy once he was inside the hospital.

Harry's heart thudded when he felt the vehicle stop, then reverse, then stop again. The banging of the driver's door told him they had arrived. He counted to thirty before he reached forward and slowly pushed the coffin lid up. It wasn't hinged, so it slid easily to the side and he crawled out.

He scrambled to the front of the hearse and climbed out through the driver's door just in time. Darkness and a tall hedge that bordered the building provided adequate hiding. Its leaves were wet and the cold and damp soaked through his cotton shirt and onto his bare head. He held his breath and watched the men argue.

"I just told ya! You're s'posed to have a corpsie ready fer me ta pick up. Fella said it was some kinda 'mergency."

"Don't know nothin' 'bout no bodies tonight." The security guard scratched his head. "Been real quiet-like. We wuz just about to listen to ole Charlie McCarthy."

"Humph. Guess I'll miss half of it 'cause of this wild goose chase." The undertaker grumbled and spat on the ground "That feller better not ask fer a refund." He climbed in the hearse and drove away without noticing the disturbed coffin.

"Andy! I'm goin' on break. Take over, will ya?" Harry watched the guard light a cigarette and heard his footsteps as he walked away.

Once the guard was gone, Harry crept out of the bushes and gawked at the huge building. He was at the rear of the hospital near the lower level service entrance, but even from there it was an awe-inspiring sight. From a distance, it had always seemed surreal, like a medieval fortress floating in the clouds. Up close it appeared even bigger, like a hungry giant waiting for him to come closer so it could snatch him up.

Near the back door Harry noticed a large brick incinerator with smoke rising from a tall, round chimney. Even from a distance he could feel the heat that emanated from the closed metal door, yet a chill ran down his spine. *A goose just walked over my grave*, he thought—at least that's what Ma always said.

He shook his head to banish such fanciful notions, glanced over his shoulder, and sidled through the open door. Harry jumped when the outer door swung to with a bang behind him. He squinted in the darkness and followed a distant light, holding his breath as he crept carefully through a narrow hallway.

Shadows played with his imagination when he stepped into a dimly lit room. He stared in horror at the stainless steel tables and shining surgical instruments neatly spread out, ready for use. His foot stepped in something wet and sticky. He gagged at the smell of the thick red liquid oozing slowly down the drain in the floor.

He glanced to the right and saw the specimen jars, full of unspeakable things, lined up on the shelves. He put his hand to his mouth, gagged by the smell of chemicals and death—and then he froze when he felt something cold and metallic poke him in the ribs.

"Okay, mister. Hold it right there."

CHAPTER TWENTY

"Get your hands up and turn around. Now!"

Harry froze and raised his hands. The distorted shadow of a man loomed large in the murky dungeon and the unmistakable click of a gun's hammer being cocked sent his heart racing. He'd barely gotten inside the hospital. Had he come this far, only to fail?

With his hands in the air, Harry turned to face his captor. After being ordered around in jail over the past several months, he automatically obeyed. Despair settled over him, his pulses slowed, and his stomach felt hollow. His feet and hands grew cold with fear.

"Who are ya and what're ya doin' here?"

A sudden vision of his beautiful wife skittered across Harry's mind and adrenalin coursed through his veins. He'd come here to save her and he couldn't fail. He must be brave—for Ivy's sake.

Harry sized up the security guard. His nametag read HOSPITAL SECURITY – ANDY FARMER. At six feet one, Harry considered himself taller than average, but this guy was practically a giant, towering several inches over him. He looked too big and strong to easily overpower, and besides, having the drop on Harry with a .38 revolver definitely gave him the advantage.

Hoping to put a little space between him and the firearm, Harry took a step back. His shoe slid in a puddle on the floor and his foot made a sucking sound. "What kinda place is this?"

"It's a hospital morgue," Andy replied without changing expression. "Come on. What's your name? Ain't got all day."

The big man waved the gun and Harry stepped back even farther, studying his face. He didn't have the cocky attitude or sense of superiority of the jailers who'd spent their time making his life a living hell over the past few months. A glimmer of hope began to grow.

"I'm looking for somebody who's a patient here—a girl."

The guard lowered his gun a notch. "What's her name?"

Harry hesitated. If he blurted out whom he was searching for, he might lose any chance of saving Ivy. On the other hand, he had no idea where to look for her in this gigantic building. He needed help. He cautiously reached in his pocket and pulled out the wad of cash Sydney had given him. Bribery might work when all else failed.

"Her name's Ivy. I can pay you." He held the money toward the guard. "Will you help me?"

Andy lowered the gun the rest of the way, stared at Harry and grinned, but he didn't reach for the money. "Ivy? Are you looking for Ivy Fuller? You must be Harry."

Harry nodded, amazed.

"I seen your picture one time on her bureau an' she tole me 'bout ya. She's Anna's friend." A tender smile transformed the big man's face. He pulled an extra security cap and jacket off a peg and tossed them to Harry. "Here. Put these on. I'll take ya to her."

Emma returned to her room, frantic with worry and fearing for Ivy's safety. She'd heard the screaming and cursing about a broken radio from the penthouse above. She was certain Ivy was in Dr. Baker's clutches. But what could she do? Sick with fear and fighting back the agonizing pain that gnawed at her belly, she paced the room.

Zan had always told her she needed to be more spontaneous,

to relax and go with the flow. But that kind of thinking made her panic, fueling her terror of the unknown and loss of control. She only felt comfortable when she was on a precise schedule. She missed her BlackBerry almost as much as she missed Zan.

Here she was, alone in a strange time and place, with her and Zan's entire destiny hinging on her ability to *fly by the seat of her pants*. Could she do it without her organizational tools? She had no other choice.

A movement from the corner of the bedroom caught Emma's attention. She glanced at Theodora, lying on the bed, with her cat still guarding her body. Her skin prickled with goosebumps when she felt a draft. The misty outline of a long-haired man appeared, lifted something from the dresser, and then faded away.

Michael was back.

Emma's heart beat faster as she watched the Ouija board float across the room and settle on her bed. Apparently, Michael wanted her to communicate with someone. Did Theodora have something else to tell her?

She sat on the edge of the bed and placed her fingers lightly on the planchette, hoping she was doing it correctly. The last time she'd used a Ouija board had been at a slumber party when she was thirteen. She remembered it needed at least two people to operate, but apparently not this time. The small triangle-shaped object began to vibrate and glide across the board.

Emma's fingers tingled from the energy of the planchette. It seemed to move with a purpose and she watched in awe as whoever—or whatever—communicated with her.

are you michael spelled out across the board.

Emma pushed the planchette: *no*

what is your name came the reply.

She spelled out: *emma fuller*

are you a spirit

Emma's eyebrows rose and she moved the planchette: *no*

who and where are you

The planchette moved again: *ryan pittman crescent hotel*

Emma gasped and replied: *im at crescent hotel too* then added: *baker hospital 1938*

are you dr bakers patient

yes then, before it could reply, she spelled out: *what day is it for you*

October 30 2011

im from 2011 too but trapped in time

how

do not know was in room 419 hit head

are you woman on news

Emma's heart jumped and she eagerly moved the planchette: *do not know must get message to zan fuller can you help*

She held her breath as she waited. Excitement filled her at the thought of communicating with someone across time.

will try what is message

Emma scanned her memory for her brother's message at the séance, hoping she had heard him correctly. She had no idea what it meant: *tell zan lockbox tea for two 419*

will try

find ring inside wall room 419 please

will try

thanks

is that all

She thought for a moment before adding: *tell zan I love him he lives in texas address is…*

The planchette suddenly jerked out of her control, as some unseen force spelled out *husband at hospital rogers ar*

A premonition of dread coursed down her spine as she asked the question: *why am i on news*

in coma they want your heart

Emma jumped when someone rapped on the door and the Ouija board's energy suddenly ceased. She'd lost the connection into the future. Who could have interrupted at such a crucial moment? And what was all this business about her heart? She rose, took a deep breath, and opened the door.

"Andy...and Harry?" She gasped and motioned them both inside. Except for his sandy brown hair, Harry looked exactly like Zan's brother, Allen. "Come in, come in..."

When the two men stepped into the room, it took all of Emma's self-control not to throw her arms around Harry's neck. He greeted her politely as he gazed at his surroundings.

"Miss Anna, Harry's lookin' for Miss Ivy, but she don't answer her door. D'you know where she is?" Andy glanced toward the bedroom and saw Theodora. "Is Miz Hardcastle feelin' porely?"

Emma looked at Theodora, not quite ready to tell Andy the truth. She put her finger to her lips. "She's napping right now. We probably shouldn't disturb her. I'll make sure Harry finds Ivy. Okay, Andy?"

"Sure thing, Miss Anna." Andy's face lit up. "I'd best get back downstairs or else they'll get mad. I won't say anything about Harry visiting."

Andy closed the door behind him and Emma turned her attention to Harry. She put her hand on his arm and glanced at the ceiling. "Thank God you've come. Ivy's in Baker's penthouse. We need to hurry."

Harry's voice was tinged with panic. "How're we gonna get Ivy away from Baker without him knowing?"

"I have a plan. It's risky, but it ought to work." Emma had a plan, all right. A half-baked one, but she couldn't let Harry know that.

She led the way to the door in the wall next to Theodora's bed. Bob's green eyes glowed and his half-tail twitched, but he didn't budge from his mistress's side. Fear began to coil inside her when she peeked into the dark hole, recalling the terror she'd faced when she'd been thrown in there before. How could she send Harry there after what had happened to her? Her heart sank when she saw how dark it was. "I know there's a ladder that goes up to the penthouse. But it's so dark…"

Harry fumbled in the borrowed jacket and pulled out a flashlight. "We're in luck." He flicked on the light and the tunnel lit up. "I see it." He moved the light in different directions. "There seems to be a whole network of passages."

Emma's heart pounded. So the legends had been true. If their luck held out, Baker's secret tunnels would be Ivy and Harry's means of escape. If only she could figure out some way to distract Baker.

"Baker's got armed guards patrolling the hospital grounds, so you've got to be careful. I was told a tunnel runs somewhere near the elevator and out into the woods. If you can find your way, you stand a good chance of getting out safely," cautioned Emma. "Do you have anyone outside the hospital that can help you once you're free?"

Harry nodded. "Um hm. My lawyer, Sydney, is waitin' for us in town."

Emma had a sudden premonition. "Harry, you must be very careful. If Baker and his goons find out what you've done, they'll follow you. Ivy told me what happened to Doc Pruett. I think Earl Twitchell is the pyromaniac who's been setting all the fires, so watch out for him."

Harry grinned and Emma's heart flipped when she saw the Fuller smile. "Oh, I'll steer clear of Earl, all right! Sydney's fiancé, Margot, is waitin' for us out by the lake. Her daddy bought her a new Stinson Reliant and she's gonna fly us to Little Rock. I ain't never been in an airplane before."

Emma and Harry looked up in surprise when the radio suddenly came on and the announcer's voice boomed into the room, "The Columbia Broadcasting System and its affiliated stations present Orson Welles and *The Mercury Theatre on the Air* in *The War of the Worlds* by H. G. Wells…"

"How'd that happen?" Harry scratched his head and stared at the radio.

Orson Welles' satiny voice caressed the airwaves. "We know now that in the early years of the twentieth century this world ..."

Emma tensed. The radio had come on by itself, so she assumed *somebody* was trying to get her attention. With all the ghosts in this place, nothing surprised her anymore. But she couldn't help being awed by what she was hearing. She'd read about this famous radio broadcast in history books and she knew how the realism of the presentation had panicked the entire nation. Could they use it as a diversion long enough to let Harry and Ivy get away?

"That's *it!*" cried Emma. "I'll tell Baker Earth is being attacked by Martians."

Harry stared at her like she was crazy. "But it ain't nothin' but a radio play. It ain't real."

"You know that, and *I* know that." Emma smiled. "But they don't. It's worth a try, isn't it?"

Harry shrugged. "I guess so. We gotta do something."

Emma searched the room for Ivy's music box, but she couldn't find it. She grabbed Anna's reticule. She pulled out the diamond and sapphire ring and Theodora's Will. "Now listen to me, Harry. When you find Ivy, give her this ring. Tell her I want her to have it. When your oldest son takes a wife, it'll go to her, and then later on to his son's wife. Remember. This is very important."

Harry sucked in his breath. "Are those real diamonds? It's beautiful. Ivy'll love it. Thank you."

"That's not all." Emma nodded toward Theodora. "Mrs. Hardcastle wanted you and Ivy to inherit her farm in Texas. This is her Will, so don't lose it."

"She's dead, ain't she?" Harry put the ring and the paper in his shirt pocket and laid the reticule on the floor inside the wall.

"Nobody coulda kept on sleeping when that radio came on."

Emma nodded. "Yes, she's passed on, but she was very ill and now she's at peace. But don't worry about that now. You need to get up that ladder and rescue your wife. I'll go upstairs and raise a fuss about the Martian invasion. I'll do my best to get Dr. Baker and Earl out of the room."

"Earl?" Harry recoiled. "What's he doing here?"

"He works for Dr. Baker now." Emma rolled her eyes. "He seems to get around a lot. Now listen, I think the ladder comes out in a closet, so when you get up there, just listen and I'll try to signal you somehow."

Emma walked into the hall and banged on the door that led to the penthouse. After several minutes, she heard a deadbolt disengage and the door creaked open. Earl peered out with irritation on his face.

"Whadda ya want?"

Emma took a deep breath for courage before she gave a performance worthy of an Academy Award. "Have you been listening to the radio tonight?"

"What's goin' on?" Dr. Baker asked as he stomped down the stairs.

"We ain't been listenin'," sneered Earl. "What happened? Did Charlie McCarthy give ol' Edgar Bergen a splinter?"

"You need to turn on the radio. Martians are attacking the Earth. They've already destroyed someplace called Grovers Mill," replied Emma.

"Martians?" Earl slapped his knee. "Hoo boy! I told ya that broad was a nut, boss."

"Shut up, Earl." Dr. Baker gave him a warning look. "You say it's on the radio right now?"

Emma nodded. "It's very scary and you need to be aware of what's happening, Dr. Baker. After all, you're responsible for the lives and safety of every person in this hospital." She turned and motioned for him to follow. "Please, come listen."

"We got a radio here. Come on." Baker turned and started back up the stairs.

Emma reluctantly followed, her stomach twisting in agony as she climbed. Now what would she do? She thought Baker's radio had been broken earlier. If she couldn't control the station, would he catch on that it was all a hoax? She needed to lure him downstairs and out of the penthouse so Harry could save Ivy.

"Humph, that's strange." Dr. Baker stared at the radio. "I don't remember turnin' it on."

Emma heard the radio playing before Baker and Earl reached the living room. Gasping for breath from her climb up the stairs, Emma found a chair and settled down to listen. She forced herself not to smile as Orson Welles described snake-like tentacles wriggling out of the shadows.

Emma watched Dr. Baker and Earl stare at each other with worried expressions as the radio show continued. She had to place her hand over her mouth to hide her smirk.

Emma turned when she heard a hiss and a low growl behind her. Bob stood at the top of the stairs, his back arched and his hair fluffed. When Baker's St. Bernards noticed him, they jumped to attention. Barking and howling, they charged down the stairs in pursuit of the cat. As they rushed through the room, their massive bodies bumped against the table and the radio crashed to the floor.

"Damn those dogs!" yelled Baker when silence filled the room. "Come on, there's a radio downstairs in my office." Both men stomped down the stairs.

Emma couldn't believe her luck. She rushed over to the closet in the corner, noting the machine guns hanging on the wall. Jerking open the door, she tapped on the wall and heard an answering rap. A loose panel slid to the side and Harry climbed out.

"They're gone, but I don't know for how long," said Emma, pointing to another set of stairs. "She must be up there."

Harry loped up the stairs and Emma did her best to follow. She gasped when she saw Ivy bound and gagged on the bed. Tears formed in Emma's eyes as Harry freed Ivy's arms and legs and then gathered her in a staggering embrace.

"Oh, Harry. I can't believe it's you," sobbed Ivy when their kiss finally ended.

"Come on, you two. There's not much time," interrupted Emma. "You can kiss each other later all you want." Fighting for breath, she led the way down to the living room. "Go on. Get out of here."

"Anna, we can never thank you enough." Ivy's eyes brimmed with tears and Harry's grin lit up the room. Ivy embraced Emma. "We'll never forget you."

"I won't forget you either. Now go on." Emma pushed them toward the closet. "Be careful. And be happy with each other." She watched them disappear into the dark hole, closed the closet door, and turned to leave.

"Whadda ya think you're doin'?"

Emma was on the floor before she realized she'd been hit. When she looked up, she saw Earl step over her and head toward the closet. Dazed by the rough blow to her back, she watched in horror as Earl opened the closet door, slid back the secret panel, and drew his weapon.

Her mind reacted automatically. Somehow she found the strength to pull herself up, walk over to the guns hanging on the wall, pull one down, and carry it to the closet. She watched as Earl climbed inside and mounted the ladder. She raised the heavy weapon.

Emma had no idea how to use a machine gun, but she knew how to swing a baseball bat. She pulled the gun back and then swung it forward. She heard the crack of splintering bones as it hit him full in the face, heard the scream of pain, saw the gush of red, and felt the vibration of his fall.

CHAPTER TWENTY-ONE

"Dude," exclaimed Ryan Pittman when he sensed the sudden disruption of psychic energy.

He stared with dismay at the Parker Brothers Ouija Board. Only moments before, his Toys-R-Us purchase had been animated beyond his wildest dreams, but now the planchette sat like a lump of molded plastic. Flicking it with his fingertip, he tried to resurrect the connection. It refused to budge.

His hands shook as he retrieved his video camera from its tripod and played back the footage. He sucked in his breath. Even though he'd just experienced it, watching the plastic triangle glide back and forth across the Ouija board and hearing his own voice narrate the proceedings thrilled him.

Finally. The proof he'd been waiting for.

Ryan smiled like a cat licking cream. He'd been coming to the Crescent Hotel for over three years trying to capture the ghost of Michael, the Irish stonemason, on camera. He always requested Room 218, and Michael usually teased him with a little headboard knocking or electric light manipulation. But never anything big. Never anything he could prove. Until now—and this hadn't even been Michael!

He carefully packed his camera in its case, linked the strap around his shoulder, left the room, and headed for the lobby. He was on a mission.

"Jimmy," said Ryan when he got to the front desk. "Hey, man. Glad you're here."

"What's up, Ryan?" Jimmy smiled at the tall, skinny,

335

twenty-something and leaned his elbows on the counter.

"Dude, you're not gonna believe what just happened." Ryan briefly explained about his Ouija board experience and then pulled out his video camera. "Just watch."

Jimmy frowned as he watched the amazing video. "Do you think it's the same Emma Fuller who got hurt here?"

Ryan shrugged. "I assume so. Apparently, she's trapped in some kind of time warp or something. She wants me to get a message to her husband and find her ring. Can we go look for it?"

"I don't know Ryan," replied Jimmy. "Management's closed Room 419 until we've had a chance to make sure it's safe for guests."

"Good. Then there's nobody staying in it tonight."

Jimmy looked uncertain, then pulled out a walkie-talkie. "Larry, this is Jimmy, come in…"

The instrument squawked. "Larry, here. Whassup? Over."

"I need you to meet me at the north end of four ASAP. Over."

"Ten four."

"I'll be on four if you need me," said Jimmy to the desk clerk. He turned to Ryan and motioned. "Come on."

A few minutes later Larry joined Jimmy and Ryan in front of Room 419, his tool belt jingling. "Oh, man. Don't tell me we're goin' in there again."

"Sorry, Larry. Something's come up."

Jimmy unlocked the door and flipped on the light switch. Ryan followed the others inside, staring at the month-old chaos. He felt a chill run down his spine when he saw the yellow police tape that stretched from the door in the wall to the bathroom.

"…so, Ryan here wants to see if he can find her ring." Jimmy pointed to the door after explaining about the Ouija board to Larry.

Larry shook his head. "If that ain't the dangedest thing I ever heard tell. Poor little thing. I heard on the ten o'clock news that ole judge done ordered the hospital to pull the plug on her by noon tomorrow."

"No way," gasped Ryan. "They're gonna appeal, aren't they?"

"From what I heard, the Fifth Circuit's already turned 'em down and they don't expect much from the Supreme Court either. Somethin' 'bout a precedent in a Florida case." Larry sighed and pulled the yellow tape away.

Jimmy tugged on the door and it creaked open. A cloud of dust blew in their faces. "Nobody's been in here since the night they pulled her out. What a mess." He shivered. "Man, there's a helluva draft in here."

Larry turned on his torchlight and poked it inside. "If I see them blue eyes again, I'm leavin'." He waved the light back and forth and then stopped. "Wait! I see somethin' shiny."

"Is it the ring?" asked Ryan.

"I don't know," replied Larry. "It's back in that corner, but I'm too big to get in to reach it."

"Here, let me try." Ryan reached for the flashlight.

"No, Larry." Jimmy placed his hand in front of Ryan. "If the boss finds out we let a guest go in there, we're dead."

"Please, let me try," begged Ryan. "I've just gotta help Mrs. Fuller."

Jimmy paused, lowered his hand, and backed away. Ryan grinned, ducked his head, and climbed through the door. He scooted into the crevice left by the cave-in and shone the light in the direction Larry indicated. Sure enough, caught in the flashlight's beam, diamonds and sapphires winked back.

"Found it!"

He reached for the sparkling ring and plucked it out from beneath a rotted board. Ryan admired the ring for a second before placing it in his jeans pocket for safekeeping. His hand touched something soft and he tugged at it. It was a rotting velvet bag.

He threw the bag out through the door and then shivered when his arm made contact with a blustery updraft. He pointed the flashlight up above the collapsed walls. The flash of two blue objects suspended in midair caught his eye.

"Whoa, dude. What is that?"

"What's it look like?" asked Jimmy

"Two blue shiny things hanging down."

"Oh, Jeez," said Larry. "It's the blue-eyed monster again. Time to go."

"Wait a minute," said Ryan. "I think I can just about reach 'em." He strained his arms and legs until the objects came into reach. He snatched them loose from the rotted cloth that barely contained them. Sapphire earrings. Might even match Mrs. Fuller's ring, for all Ryan knew.

He shone the light higher toward the source of the earrings. And then he saw it. The partially mummified remains of a man hanging upside down in the shaft.

Ryan moved the light up and down. The skeleton's foot seemed to be caught on something in the wall, while the rest of its body dangled in midair. Whatever had happened, he'd been in there a long time. The extreme updraft through the shaft must have carried any smell up and out through the roof. Ryan noted a nametag pinned to the man's rotting shirt. It was upside down, but he transposed the letters.

HOSPITAL SECURITY - EARL TWITCHELL.

Senator Grayson Talmedge stared at the television in his daughter's hospital room in Memphis. His stomach churned as the TV report showed the helicopters circling like vultures over the crowd of protesters outside the Arkansas hospital. He sighed, feeling saddened and ashamed to be at the center of such a gruesome media circus.

A pretty blond in a bright red suit spoke into a microphone. "This is Lora Lapinski reporting live from Rogers, Arkansas where an emotional crowd stands vigil, awaiting news of the latest ruling by Judge Jerry Covington in Zan Fuller's last-ditch effort to save the life of his comatose wife."

The wind blew a lock of golden hair across the reporter's face. "Emma Fuller has been unconscious and on life-support for more than a month, after an accident at a Eureka Springs hotel left her with a brain hemorrhage. Her injuries are allegedly similar to the recent accidents that claimed the lives of actors Natasha Richardson and Gary Coleman. Doctors at the trauma unit have advised the parties that Mrs. Fuller's condition is not likely to improve and tests suggest she may already be brain dead.

"Just prior to the accident, Mrs. Fuller had scheduled routine medical tests and had subsequently executed a legal document known as an Advance Healthcare Directive or Living Will, which included an organ donor addendum. Although Mr. Fuller acknowledges that he himself witnessed his wife sign the document, he refutes the fact that she would wish her life support be terminated at this point and has sued to have the Living Will declared null and void.

"At the center of the controversy is U.S. Senator Grayson Talmedge whose twenty-one year old daughter, Monica, is currently on the waiting list for a heart transplant. If Mr. Fuller loses on appeal, his wife's life support will be terminated and Miss Talmedge is scheduled to receive her heart. Senator Talmedge, who we understand has aspirations for the White House, has been under fire for the past month by critics who claim he used his political clout to bully his daughter's way to the top of the list. We have the hospital administrator, Ms. Rachel Hughes, here now. Ms. Hughes. Would you care to comment?" The reporter thrust the microphone toward Rachel.

"Thank you, Lora," said Rachel, smiling for the camera and holding an umbrella. Her short black hairdo maintained its perfect helmet shape despite the howling wind. "This has been a long and difficult ordeal for everyone involved. But I can assure you Monica Talmedge has not received preferential treatment over anyone else as a heart donor recipient. There are many factors to be considered when deciding which patient receives a donated organ and in this case, it was a matter of an almost perfect tissue and blood type match, in conjunction with Monica's place in line. We seldom see such an ideal match in these situations, especially when we're dealing with extremely rare blood types."

"Why weren't the identities of the donor and recipient kept confidential?" interrupted Lora.

"Normally, they are," Rachel shrugged. "But unfortunately, Mr. Fuller decided to pursue litigation and to sensationalize this business before the media."

"Thank you for braving the rain and cold to speak with us this morning, Ms. Hughes."

An angry-looking man carrying a wet, curling sign that read SAVE EMMA pushed his way forward. Lora held the microphone toward him. He glared at the camera and shook his fist. "If they pull the plug on her, it'll be murder. God will punish the sinners."

A woman carrying a sign that read OBEY THE LAW – RESPECT EMMA'S WISHES elbowed her way toward the camera. "By signing that Living Will, Emma Fuller declared she wouldn't want to live like a vegetable. I know I certainly wouldn't." She rolled her eyes and gestured toward the crowd. "If we allow these right-wing Zealots to have their way, decades of progress on human rights issues and personal choice will be lost."

A handsome man in an Armani suit joined the reporter. His mouth curled in a smile, but his eyes showed no warmth. "Thank you, ma'am. You've exactly summed up what's at stake..."

A wild-eyed woman pushed her way up front. "If everybody has a choice, then how come they lock you up if you attempt suicide?"

A roar of both agreement and dissention raced through the crowd. A police officer pushed her back behind the barricades.

Lora took back control. "We're speaking with Paul Murphy, attorney for the defense." She returned the microphone to the man in the expensive suit.

"Thanks, Lora." He faced the camera. "Emotions are high right now. Everyone's sympathetic to Mrs. Fuller's situation and her husband's grief, but this is a landmark case that will go down in history as a testament to the sanctity of a person's right to choose their quality of life. I have confidence that justice will prevail, especially considering the precedent in a similar case a few years back in Florida. We believe our case is even stronger, since we have a valid, legal document and we're not relying on a family member's testimony."

"What about Mr. Fuller's argument that these Living Wills are being pushed as routine paperwork on people who haven't thought out their implications?" asked Lora. "Mr. Fuller argues that if someone buys a vacuum cleaner and has buyer's remorse, they'd have three days to cancel the contract. Why would that not apply in this situation?"

Attorney Murphy shrugged. "That argument is ludicrous and has been struck down repeatedly. Living Wills can be revoked at any time, as long as a person is competent. Emma Fuller's been on life support for over a month and she hasn't waved a white flag to say she wants out of the contract. You have to draw the line somewhere."

"Daddy?"

Senator Talmedge turned off the television when he heard his daughter's voice. He went to his wife and daughter and kissed them on the cheek. His heart lurched at the sight of Monica's pale complexion, the dark circles beneath her eyes, and her slight form in the wheelchair. "Did you enjoy your outing?"

Monica nodded. "I've decided to have the transplant from

the other donor."

"Are you sure? Remember what the doctors said. Your chance of rejection would be much greater." he stared at his wife, Tess. "Did you know about this?"

"Yes, Tally. We've been discussing it for the last hour." Tess Talmedge helped Monica climb back into bed. "She's old enough to make her own decisions and I've told her I'll stand behind her, whatever she decides."

"I want to do this, Daddy." Tears glistened on Monica's pallid cheeks. "The tissue match isn't as good as with Emma Fuller's, but there's no question about the prognosis of the donor. The heart's already arrived and they're prepping the operating room now."

"You're having the operation today?"

He felt conflicted. On one hand, he wanted Monica to receive a strong, healthy organ to replace her own virus-damaged heart. But on the other, he was miserable from all the controversy and the moral dilemma. If he'd had any idea what would happen, he would never have sent out those e-mails to the hospitals. He'd taken a lot of heat about those messages, even though he'd meant them only as a reminder to those in charge of the donor lists to keep her in mind, not an attempt to circumvent the system. He'd sent them as a concerned father, but his motives had been misunderstood and the fallout had helped him reach a decision not to run for President after all.

"Daddy, would you do something for me? Please?"

"Of course, sweetheart." The senator choked back a tear. "Anything."

"Call a press conference." The light behind Monica's bed framed her head like a halo. "Tell them I don't want Emma Fuller's heart. Tell them they have to let her live."

Zan looked up when the door opened and his brother Allen came into the room. His eyes were tired and he absent-mindedly fingered his beard that had grown, long and untrimmed, for more than a month. He felt like hell and he knew he probably looked it, but he couldn't make himself leave Emma's side long enough to shave. Like his darling Emma, the rhythmic whoosh of the ventilator and the steady beep of the heart monitor were the only things that kept him functioning.

"Senator Talmedge just gave a press conference," said Allen. "His daughter's in surgery right now. They found a different heart donor and he's made a plea to Judge Covington to grant our injunction."

"Oh, thank God," said Zan. He dropped his head in silent prayer. Then he looked up and grinned. "So it's all over?"

"Not yet, but it's a good sign. We've still got to wait for the judge's ruling." Allen glanced down at his vibrating cell phone. "Maybe this is it. You want to come downstairs with me while I make my call? Phoebe and Moonbeam'll stay with Emma while we're gone."

Zan felt as if a huge weight had been lifted from his shoulders. He smiled and carefully patted Emma's arm. "I'll be back, sweetheart," he whispered in her ear. "And when this is all over and you're well, we'll fill the house with babies." He grinned at the girls and followed Allen to the elevator.

When they got to the exterior waiting area, Allen pulled out his cell phone and called his legal assistant. The news wasn't good.

Allen ended the call and turned to Zan. "Our injunction was denied. We've only got a few hours before they turn off the machines."

"How can that be? Surely he ruled before the senator's announcement."

"I'm afraid not," replied Allen, staring into the distance. "He ruled that Monica Talmedge's decision to receive a different transplant was irrelevant."

Zan groaned and sank to his knees. Anger boiled inside

and he fought for control. A suffocating sensation tightened his throat and his vision clouded over. He barely noticed the tall, thin man who approached.

"Excuse me. Are you Zan Fuller?"

"I'm Allen Fuller. Can I help you?" Allen put his hand on his brother's shoulder.

"Yes, sir. My name's Ryan Pittman. I have a message for Zan—from Emma."

Zan recoiled.

"Is this some sort of cruel joke?" cried Allen.

"Please, I know this sounds crazy. But I swear, I've been in communication with Mrs. Fuller." Ryan reached in his pocket, pulled out a diamond and sapphire ring and matching earrings, and handed them to Zan.

"Where did you get these?" Zan gasped.

"Emma told me where to find them at the Crescent Hotel," he replied. "Look, can we go somewhere and sit down? I've got a lot to tell you."

"Okay, Barbara. Tell Dad to look in the guestroom closet. Maybe it's in there someplace."

Zan tapped his foot and glanced at the *low battery* light on his cell phone. He'd never been more nervous than now, while he waited for his father to find Emma's mother's lockbox at his home in Texas. He wished Allen was with him, but he'd gone back to the courthouse to file a new appeal.

"He found it," cried Barbara.

"Good. Let's assume Emma's message is the combination. We never knew what it was before, so we've never tried to open it."

"Okay, son. Now what?" asked Jonathan. "It's got both letters and numbers on the lock."

"Try T-4-2-4-1-9." Zan held his breath and waited.

"It worked! There's a music box inside with a porcelain top.

It's a picture of a woman and a little girl in Victorian costume."

Zan heard a tinkling, musical sound. "I can hear the music. Is there anything inside it?"

"No. Nothing."

Zan's heart sank. He'd expected to find something important, something that would help Emma.

"No, wait. Zan, you won't believe what we found!" Zan had never heard his father so excited. "Barbara unscrewed the top of the music box and found some old black and white photographs inside."

"Old Photographs? Of what?"

"Well, there's a family picture of my grandparents taken with your Grandma Ivy when she was a baby, of all things. And there are some photos of a young couple, but I don't know who they are. They look like some of those instant photo strips you get in a booth at a mall."

Zan shook his head, confused. "How strange. I wonder who they are?"

"I don't know, but wait. There's writing on the back," replied Jonathan. "It says *Tess and Tally July 4, 1983*. That's weird. The man looks like a younger Senator Talmedge. Say, isn't his wife named Tess?"

"Yes, it is. I still don't know what the connection is, but I think Emma's trying to tell us something important. I need you to scan those pictures into a computer and send them to Allen's BlackBerry."

"Send it to Allen's what? Barbara, what does Zan want us to do?"

Barbara took the phone and Zan repeated his request. "I understand. Leave everything to me."

"Bless you, Mom." Zan smiled when he heard what Barbara said just before the battery died.

"Jonathan, did you hear what Zan called me? He called me Mom!"

§

Allen paced before the bench, nodded to the court reporter and smiled at the TV camera. "Your honor. If it may please the court, I hereby file a motion for his honor to recuse himself from this case on the grounds of conflict of interest."

The judge scowled. "This had better be good. Proceed."

"Thank you, your honor. I'd like to offer into evidence what I've marked as Exhibits A and B."

Judge Covington frowned. "What've you got, Fuller? A voodoo doll? If you *dare* introduce any more video *evidence* of Ouija boards or ghosts or time travel to 1938, I'll hold you in contempt." He leaned forward and smirked. "Today's Halloween. I'm surprised you're not in costume."

Nobody laughed.

Allen ignored the remarks and continued. "Exhibit A is a photo strip of Senator Grayson Talmedge and his wife Tess, dated July 4, 1983. Exhibit B is a recording of Mrs. Talmedge's sworn statement to me over the telephone less than an hour ago regarding these photos."

"Objection," cried Paul Murphy. "I haven't received notice of this evidence."

"Sustained. My patience is wearing thin, Mr. Fuller."

"Sorry, your honor. But this evidence just came to light very recently. And this is an emergency hearing, since time is running out for my client." Allen pulled out two transcripts and handed one to the defense attorney. "May I approach? I've taken the liberty to provide these transcripts for your convenience."

Judge Covington grunted and took the transcript. He stared at the photos, then waved at Allen to continue. Allen pressed a button on a tape recorder.

"My name is Teresa Schmidt Talmedge. I'm sorry I can't be there in person. However, my youngest daughter, Monica, is undergoing a heart transplant operation here in Memphis and my presence in court is impossible. I refer to Monica as my youngest daughter, because I am convinced that Emma Fuller is also my daughter and her father is Senator Talmedge. The reason their tissue match is so close is because they are sisters. "

Gasps echoed throughout the courtroom.

"Please allow me to explain...I met Tally when I was a freshman in college and he was a senior. That was in 1983. We fell in love and I got pregnant. I never told him. I was afraid it would destroy his political career, so I kept silent."

"I lied to my parents and told them I was going to Paris for a semester as an exchange student. But instead, I went to a private maternity home in Arkansas. While I was there, an old woman named Cordelia visited the home and gave me an antique music box. I'd never seen her before, but she said it belonged with my baby."

"After my baby girl was born, I had a change of heart and I wanted to keep her. But an elderly nurse with a horribly disfigured face took her away....I'm sorry, but the memory's just so horrible...I chased the nurse all over the building, all the way to the top floor, and she dangled my baby over the stairwell... she threatened to drop her if I didn't sign over parental rights... so I did."

"She took me into the office and made me sign the paperwork. I begged the young attorney who handled the adoption to allow the music box to go with the child to her new home and he agreed. When he wasn't looking, I slipped the pictures of Tally and me inside the secret compartment, hoping she would find them someday."

"A few years later, Tally and I got married. I was ashamed of what I'd done and, until now, I've never told anybody... not even my husband..." A long pause ensued. "But I never forgot about my daughter and several years ago I hired a private investigator to try to find her. He discovered that the maternity home had been shut down years earlier and those involved had been charged with illegal baby brokering. Papers had not been properly filed and most information has been permanently lost. But I did discover the name of the attorney who handled the paperwork...his name was J. R. Covington."

Allen snapped off the tape recorder. The courtroom grew silent.

Judge Covington's face turned red and his fingers gripped the edge of the bench. "Would you kindly explain what is being implied?"

"Yes, your honor. We are alleging that you were the young attorney who handled the illegal, coerced adoption of Tess Talmedge's baby. That you would have been disbarred and sent to jail had your influential family not paid to have the charges dropped and your record expunged, and that until this matter is properly investigated, you should not have the power to decide the fate of Emma Fuller."

Judge Covington's eyes narrowed. "Do you have any physical proof of these outrageous allegations?"

"Not yet, your honor. My investigator is working on it, but it will take some time. Therefore, my client hereby moves the court to issue an Order of Recusal in this case, and asks that our Motion for Injunction be reopened and transferred to a different judge for consideration on the merits of the case."

Judge Covington's eyes burned with rage before he spoke. "Counsel, your motion is hereby *denied*." He bent forward in his chair and his lip curled in a sneer. "Although we are all highly entertained by Mrs. Talmedge's *true confession*, it does not change the facts of the case. The assertion that I was the attorney who handled Mrs. Fuller's adoption some twenty-eight years ago and that I was *ever* charged with any sort of crime is preposterous. Until you can come up with hard evidence to support your assertions, this matter will not be considered. The motion to recuse is dismissed in its entirety." His eyes flashed as he pounded his gavel.

"But your honor!"

"Mr. Fuller, I've had just about enough of this case and your shenanigans." He looked at his watch. "In approximately forty-five minutes there will be an end to this spectacle. And unless you can find some other judge in a higher court who's willing to buy into this nonsense about Ouija boards and ghosts, the taxpayers of this state will finally receive some relief. I hereby order the execution," he paused for effect. "...of the order to terminate Emma Fuller's life support at twelve noon today. Good day. Court is adjourned."

"Oh, my goodness," cried Moonbeam. "It's Jonathan and Barbara."

Zan looked up from his haze of misery, too numb to speak. Emma's hospital room was crowded, with the entire family, a permanently posted nurse, and an armed guard outside the door.

"How did you get here so fast?" asked Phoebe.

"We've got friends in Bentonville who own a private jet," replied Barbara.

"Alexander, are you all right?" Jonathan asked. Zan noticed the love and concern in his voice. "You look terrible."

"Allen just called. He's exhausted all the appeals. There's nothing more he can do."

"I'm sorry, son. I'm sure Allen did his best."

"It's all my fault, Dad," replied Zan. He put his head in his hands and rambled. "I should have fought harder...shouldn't have let her sign those papers...it's like the world's gone crazy...all we wanted was a family of our own..." He groaned and stared at his father. "She's the same age Mom was when we lost her...the same kind of headaches..."

"Zan, you can't blame yourself. I tortured myself for years the way you're doing now," said Jonathan. "Your mother had an aneurism. You can't compare her with what happened to Emma. I just wish we'd had the diagnostic tools we have now. Things might have turned out differently."

"I'm not impressed with this hospital's diagnostics," sniffed Moonbeam. Chief Whitefeather stood behind her with his hands on her shoulders as she stared at a black oval object in her lap. "If they're so smart, why can't they tell Emma's pregnant?"

"What's that?" asked Zan.

"It's right here, plain as day, in my scrying mirror."

"Oh, I see it," exclaimed Phoebe. "There I am with Emma, and we're both holding babies!"

Everyone huddled around Moonbeam and stared at her mirror. Zan didn't see anything except black glass. "How could she be pregnant? Dr. Ballew told us they'd already tested her." He turned to the poker-faced nurse who stood at Emma's bedside. "Did she have a pregnancy test?"

The nurse frowned and flipped through the chart. "Yes. She's been tested three times. Each time came back negative."

Moonbeam pulled an EPT test kit out of her purse. "Why don't we see for ourselves?" She headed toward Emma's catheter bag.

"I can't let you do that." The nurse planted herself between Moonbeam and Emma's bed. "Guard!"

The security guard ran into the room, his hand poised over his gun. "I need everybody to step away from the patient."

Chief Whitefeather reached inside his shirt, but Moonbeam stayed his hand and shook her head.

"She's my wife," gasped Zan. "We need to run a test."

"I got orders. Nobody touches the patient, including the family."

Zan's heart hammered, his breathing grew ragged, and his thoughts raced. He had to leave. Had to get out of this room before he started breaking things—or killing people. He touched the hard lump in his jacket pocket. Could he really do it? His mind went numb at the thought. So instead, he fled, running faster and faster, ignoring the stares of the onlookers.

He ran until he saw a door marked *Exit*. Pushing on the door, he found himself in a stairwell. It wound around and down, but he blundered on. Maybe he'd end up in hell. It couldn't be any worse.

When the stairs ended in the basement, he collapsed on the floor and let himself go. Weeks of stress, poor nutrition, and sleep deprivation caught up with him and he cried like a baby. He was losing her and there was nothing more he could do. If he couldn't have Emma, he didn't want to live.

He reached in his pocket and pulled out the Glock. It felt cold and alien in his hand. He and Allen had gone to the gun range from time to time for target practice and he'd enjoyed the sport. But could he use it now in defense of Emma? What other choice did he have? He'd played by the rules and lost. In less than twenty minutes they would unplug Emma's ventilator and she would die. He couldn't allow that to happen.

"Hey, big guy. Don't take it so hard."

Zan felt a hand on his shoulder and he gazed up through a haze of tears. He had to think for a moment before he recognized the man. "Dr. Wilson! Where've you been?"

"Oh, I've been around."

Zan hauled himself up, his voice cracking. "We've lost the case. They say they're gonna kill Emma, but they'll have to kill me first." He pulled back the firearm's slide. His resolve strengthened when he heard the click of the chambered round.

"Do you have any idea how many laws you've already broken just by bringing that thing into a hospital?"

Zan bristled. "What good are laws to Emma? An inmate on death row has more rights than she does. If I don't do something soon, it'll be too late."

"You're absolutely correct, but why don't you let me play the bad guy?"

"I have to do this myself." Zan straightened his spine. "She's my wife and I have to be there for her."

"Exactly my point. You won't be there for her if you're sitting in jail. I don't have anything to lose and I've got a score to settle with Rachel Hughes—always wanted to do something like Denzel Washington in *John Q.* Loved that movie." Dr. Wilson smiled sardonically, took the Glock from Zan's hand and stuffed it into his waistband. "Come on, let's go clean up this mess."

Zan followed Dr. Richard Wilson through the hospital corridors as chaos reigned. He flinched when the fire alarms clanged and flashed and the overhead sprinklers popped out. The cold water drenched him, but Dr. Wilson didn't seem to even notice. Was the building on fire? Zan's pulse raced, thinking about his family—and Emma.

They turned the corner and headed for Emma's room. People were running everywhere, shouting and screaming. The security guard outside Emma's door looked confused. Dr. Wilson grinned and pulled the gun from his pants.

"Stick 'em up."

The guard gasped and held up his hands.

"Okay, you can go." Dr. Wilson fluttered his hand. "I'm takin' over security."

The guard turned and ran. When Dr. Wilson and Zan entered the room, the alarms ceased and the sprinkler heads popped back into place. Emma's bed was soaked, but her life support machines labored on.

"Zan! Is the building on fire?" Jonathan wiped the water that dripped down his face. "What'll we do about Emma? We can't move her without disconnecting her respirator."

"It's okay, Dad. There's no fire," replied Zan. He grabbed a towel from the bathroom and tried to pat Emma dry. "Dr. Wilson and I are taking control of the situation."

"Dr. Wilson?" The nurse froze. Her voice became a frightened squeak and her eyes went wide with shock. Dr.

Ballew stood beside her, his face almost as white as his lab coat.

"In the...yeah, it's me," he replied. "Nice to see you, too, Mildred—Frank."

"Wh-what are you doing here?" asked Dr. Ballew. He sweated profusely and the front of his slacks appeared wet.

"Good grief, Frank. Mildred, I believe we've got us a *Code Yellow* here." Dr. Wilson grimaced and held his hand over his nose and mouth. "Uh oh. Now I think it's a *Code Brown*."

Dr. Wilson waved the Glock toward the telephone. "I've come to take care of unfinished business. Mildred, Call Rachel and tell her I want to talk to her—and call downstairs and tell that cute little reporter to come up here with her camera crew. Go on. Stat!"

Several minutes passed before Zan heard more commotion in the hallway. He peeked out and saw the reporter and cameraman approach. An army of policemen moved to let them pass. Frightened-looking people milled about and gawked, but nobody else came near Emma's room.

Zan stepped back as Lora and her crew entered the crowded room. Lora wrinkled her nose at the smell. Dr. Wilson leaned nonchalantly against the wall and twirled the handgun. The camera panned across the comatose woman in the bed and paused on the wall clock, which read *eleven fifty-five*. She held the microphone and faced the camera.

"This is Lora Lapinski, reporting live from inside Emma Fuller's room at Northwest Regional Hospital in Rogers, Arkansas. With only five minutes to go before the scheduled time for removal of Mrs. Fuller's breathing apparatus, we seem to be in the midst of a hostage situation. Mr. Fuller, can you tell us what's going on?"

Zan froze when the camera turned toward him. He had no idea what to say. Public speaking had always been one of his greatest fears. He glanced toward Dr. Wilson, who smiled and nodded. He took a deep breath and the words began to flow.

"Uh, yes," he gestured toward the gunman. "This is Dr. Richard Wilson. He was Emma's original treating physician. I'm sorry things had to come to this. I'm not usually violent. I'm a law-abiding person, but this just isn't right..."

"Hey," Dr. Wilson interrupted. "*I'm* the one with the gun. The violence part is all my idea."

Zan smiled and continued. "All I'm asking for is a little more time for Emma. Give her a chance to come back. Ever since this all started, there's been a mad rush to unhook her life support. She's been caught in the middle of a tug-of-war between legal and moral issues. But everybody seems to have lost sight of what's really at stake—humanity."

A murmur of agreement buzzed through the room and Zan's confidence grew.

"I'm not condemning the concept of Living Wills or organ donation. On the contrary, they're two of society's most important tools. Why, I believe that the fact that science allows us to share our organs with each other is nothing short of a miracle. And Living Wills are an ingenius instrument for notifying everyone that we want to share the gift of life—but only when the time is right. If everyone, all over the world, would take the time to use these two incredible tools, properly and thoughtfully, organ shortages would disappear. But Emma's situation exemplifies the potential for abuse if such tools are taken completely at face value without regard to circumstance."

Lora spoke into the microphone. "Mr. Fuller, do you think the evidence you used in your motions hurt your cause? You've got to admit that legal testimony relying on Ouija boards and ghosts is a little unorthodox."

"Yes, I know it seems strange," Zan replied. "A month ago I wouldn't have believed in anything supernatural either. But just because we don't understand something, doesn't mean it's not true. Science makes new discoveries every day. Who are we to say ghosts and spirits don't exist?"

Lora turned toward the clock above Emma's bed. "It's now twelve noon. Emma Fuller is still alive and we seem to be at a stalemate. Zan, can you tell us what your demands are?"

"Well, we're basically just asking for time. My brother's investigator is still gathering information regarding Judge Covington. We're hoping to get Emma's case transferred to another judge who will give us a chance to make certain whether she's going to get well or not. That's all."

"What about the revelation that Emma might be Senator Talmedge's daughter? Do you think the fact that Monica Talmedge has already received a heart transplant from a different donor will make a difference to her case?"

Zan shrugged. "It didn't make a difference before. I'm not asking Congress to run out and enact a new law. All I want is for her to get a fair hearing and not be rushed out of life." He gazed at his wife. "Before you got here, we wanted to do a simple pregnancy test on Emma, but the hospital wouldn't allow it."

"A pregnancy test?" asked Lora.

"Let me explain," interjected Dr. Wilson. "It is my professional opinion that, given more time, Emma Fuller will not only make a complete recovery from her injuries, but she'll also reveal a wonderful surprise. I'd like to conduct a little demonstration here on live TV." He turned toward the group. "Has anybody got a pocket knife?"

The Chief nodded and pulled out his hunting blade. As if reading his mind, Moonbeam unwrapped a pregnancy test kit and with a quick slice of plastic tubing, she collected the sample and then dropped the end of the tube into a wastebasket. Everyone stared at the test strips and waited.

"Well, while we're waiting on that, I think I'll just take a look at the chart." Dr. Wilson flipped through the records and frowned. "Hm. Just as I suspected. It's missing."

The cameraman zeroed in on Dr. Wilson and Lora spoke into the microphone. "What's missing?"

"About six days after they brought Mrs. Fuller in, I asked her nurse, Bridget, to do a blood test for pregnancy..." Wilson turned and stared at Dr. Ballew. "Yes, Frank. I know. You were officially her doctor by then, but you know me. Can't keep my nose out of stuff." He turned back to the camera. "By then, my employment was officially terminated, and I was barred from entering the hospital. Bridget got the test for me anyway and brought me a copy of the results. Mrs. Fuller's blood had much higher than normal hCG levels, which indicated a positive pregnancy. That's when I confronted Rachel." He turned and stared at the cowering nurse. "By the way, where is Bridget?"

"Sh-she doesn't work here anymore."

"Why am I not surprised?" Dr. Wilson shrugged and gazed at Dr. Ballew, who was clawing at his tie. "Maybe you'd better check him out, nurse. He looks like he's about to have a coronary." He shook his head. "I told him over and over he needed to lower his cholesterol."

Phoebe pointed at the test strips in the urine cup and squealed.

Zan shouted when he saw the lines appear. "Look! It's positive!" The camera zoomed in on Zan's grinning face. "I'm gonna be a father!"

Dr. Wilson smiled like the Cheshire cat as he slapped Zan on the shoulder. "Congratulations, big guy. Rachel, are you watching out there in TV land? Guess you didn't want to meet me face-to-face, huh?" He moved closer to the camera. "How about you, Judge Creep-o? Bet you're sorry now. Guess you'll have to rescind your order to kill an innocent woman, won't you? And then right after you do that, why don't you let the janitor out of jail? He's not the one who murdered me. If you want the *real* guilty party, you'd better arrest Rachel Hughes."

Lora gasped and grabbed the microphone. "What are you talking about?" She shouted as the camera panned the room.

Dr. Ballew's face was a tortured mask of terror as he pointed at Dr. Wilson and started backing away. The cameraman kept filming. "You're not real...I went to your funeral two weeks ago...you're dead!"

The overhead lights suddenly went out. The sound of the ventilator and heart monitor ceased.

A deathly hush settled over the room.

CHAPTER TWENTY-TWO

The screech of unstable wheels and a wobbling, swaying movement plucked Emma from the depths of unconsciousness. She felt as if she were being tortured. The stabbing pain in her gut assaulted her and she moaned in agony.

"Won't you ever die?" Nurse Amiss muttered. She stopped the gurney and jerked the sheet away from Emma's face. Her eyes were filled with loathing as she punched the elevator button.

Emma gazed up at the nurse, too weak and helpless to move. Her strength was almost gone. All she had left was her misery.

Her eyelids fluttered and then she saw them, clustered at the end of the hallway. Dozens of people stood there, transparent and hazy, silently staring. Emma could see right through them, as if they existed somewhere outside the mortal realm. A pretty girl in a long white dress stood among the group and Emma vaguely recognized her as the ghost who'd jumped from the balcony a lifetime ago.

She felt a rough jerk as the elevator dropped. Through a haze of misery she endured the ride until, with a harsh bounce, the elevator stopped. The doors opened and Miss Amiss pushed the gurney, twisting and turning to its final destination. Emma recognized the narrow stone walls and the dank, gloomy darkness of the basement. She felt the sepulchral coldness and smelled the nauseating odor of formaldehyde.

Emma wasn't dead, yet somehow she knew where Nurse Amiss was taking her. The morgue.

"No…please," Emma begged when she saw the freezer and the stainless steel autopsy tables. Her consciousness faded and she fought to stay awake.

"You've been nothing but trouble," Nurse Amiss parked the gurney and glared at Emma. "What were you doing up in Dr. Baker's room?"

Emma groaned and her mind languished. A sharp slap brought her back.

"I asked you a question." The nurse's eyes glowed with madness. "What happened to Ivy? Did she run off with Earl?"

"Don't…know…what…you're…talking…about."

"Dr. Baker was *not* happy when he discovered you tricked him with that stupid radio play. Where did they go, damn you?" Miss Amiss slapped Emma again and she tasted blood.

"Stop that!" someone shouted and Emma watched as Andy stepped forward.

Roberta whirled around, her eyes flashing. "Mind your own business, idiot!"

Andy's face turned red and his big hands formed fists. "I saw what you did to Miz Hardcastle." He reached out, grabbed Roberta's arm and jerked her away from Emma. "You're *not* gonna put Miss Anna in the 'cinerator."

Roberta screamed with rage, lunged at Andy, and then grabbed his gun from its holster. She cackled triumphantly as she raised the weapon, pointed it at his heart, and pulled the trigger. The gun's report echoed against the stone walls. Andy screamed, and his lifeblood spurted. Like a felled tree, the giant man toppled forward and Emma watched helplessly as his body grew still and his blood seeped slowly down the drain in the floor.

Emma's mind grew numb. Her hearing and vision began to fade, as she heard Roberta's maniacal laughter and saw the cushion descend over her face.

§

The next thing she knew, she was back in the vortex, hurtling upward. This time, however, there was no life review. No Ferris wheel ride. No lovely panorama of the Earth or the solar system. There was nothing but a headlong rush through a dark, frightening tunnel, toward the white light.

A slight movement in Emma's peripheral vision distracted her and she saw a glowing bulge in the tunnel. It reminded her of the portal she'd slid through before and she wondered if the tunnel and the portal were actually the same conduit between life and death. She felt a tightening sensation from behind, as if she were attached to a bungee cord that had grown taut and was about to snap.

Her silver cord.

If it broke, she could never return to earth. Never return to Zan. Never have his children.

She felt confused. What had been the purpose of this bizarre journey? Yes, she'd helped Ivy and Harry get away together. And she'd even managed to overcome her rigid anxieties and learned to view possibilities she'd never before considered.

But why like this? Her parents had told her it wasn't her time to die; yet here she was again, heading back to Heaven. What about the children she was supposed to have? And what about Zan? Would she never see him again? A sense of abject failure washed over her.

Panic-stricken, she blindly reached toward the bubble. A hand came out of the bulge, seized hers, and dragged her inside. The tension immediately eased on her lifeline.

She felt encompassed by warmth and love as Theodora's spirit embraced and comforted her.

And then she woke up.

Emma gagged and tore at the respirator. Panic filled her as she fought the tube lodged in her throat.

"She's awake!" yelled Zan. He cradled her in his arms. "Calm down, honey. We'll get you loose in a minute." He motioned for the nurse.

"Take a deep breath and blow it out," urged the nurse. "That's it...good."

Emma coughed and her throat felt raw. She blinked and focused her eyes. Zan's bearded face was the first thing she saw and she wept with relief and happiness as he cradled her in his arms.

He held her like a drowning man who'd just found air; like a starving man who'd just found food. Her heart soared as he held her to his heart and rocked her back and forth.

"Oh, God. Emma. I thought I'd lost you forever."

"Love you...." Emma's voice came out in a harsh rasp, but the soreness of her throat was nothing compared to the joy she felt at having returned to him and her own time.

"Don't try to speak." Someone handed Zan a cup filled with ice chips and he spooned them into Emma's mouth. "I have so much to tell you. I didn't want to live without you, but now everything is perfect. We're going to have a baby!"

Emma tried to talk, but she was too weak and her vocal chords were too raw. She pointed at her belly and then croaked, "Me?"

Zan nodded and his eyes sparkled. "Moonbeam did a test on you. Isn't it wonderful?"

Emma batted at the wires that still connected her to the IV and heart monitor. "Pregnant...now?"

Zan nodded and happiness bubbled up until Emma thought she would burst with joy. She tore her gaze away from her husband and saw the others. People she loved—Jonathan, Barbara, Phoebe, Moonbeam, and the Chief suddenly surrounded her. They were laughing and shouting and crying all at once. Allen came rushing in and in the far corner she saw a man with a television camera and a woman with a microphone.

The overhead lights suddenly came on and the machines at her bedside came to life, buzzing and whirring and beeping.

"Where's the gunman?" The reporter snapped to attention and turned to the cameraman. "Are we back up? Just keep it rolling….ladies and gentlemen, I think we've just witnessed a miracle. Emma Fuller has awakened!" She approached the bed where Zan held Emma in a tight embrace. She thrust the microphone toward Allen. "Did you see Dr. Wilson leave?"

Allen shook his head. "The police wouldn't let anybody come upstairs, so I was down in the lobby watching TV. Then when the power went off, there was so much confusion, I slipped past 'em and ran up the stairs. But I didn't see anybody else leave."

"What was all that stuff about Dr. Wilson being dead?" asked Phoebe.

"Oh, honey. You should have seen it on TV." Allen grabbed Phoebe and hugged her. "Everybody thought it was some kind of trick photography. You could see right through him, like he was smoke."

The reporter's cell phone rang. "Yes? Um hm…um hm…I see…okay, thanks." She straightened and spoke. "We've just received breaking news. Moments ago, police arrested hospital administrator Rachel Hughes in connection with the recent murder of Dr. Richard Wilson. She was apparently caught in the act of tampering with the hospital's electrical system and was allegedly the cause of the power outage a little while ago. She is now considered a suspect in the shooting death of Dr. Wilson. Meanwhile, earlier footage of the man purported to be Dr. Wilson remains a mystery. This is Lora Lapinski, reporting live from Northwest Regional Hospital in Rogers, Arkansas."

She motioned to cut and the cameraman halted filming. She grinned and said to Emma, "Congratulations on your recovery and—everything else. Welcome back."

EPILOGUE

One year later

Emma exhaled, opened her eyes and smiled when Moonbeam walked into her office. She uncurled her legs, wiggled her toes, and stretched before rising from the cushioned Yoga mat. Phoebe jumped up as well, ran to her friend, and hugged her.

"How're the cousins?" Moonbeam headed for the cradle where both babies napped, side-by-side.

Phoebe's face lit up. "Ivy Ann just started crawling."

"And what about Harry Theodore?" asked Moonbeam, her voice crisp. Emma noted the absence of the tongue piercing. She'd let her hair grow out, cut back on the makeup, and her face glowed with an inner radiance.

"Teddy won't be far behind," replied Emma, smiling at her sleeping son. "He's already trying to sit up and I think he's cutting a tooth. What's up with you?"

"The Chief and I are getting married!"

Phoebe grabbed Moonbeam and pulled her around to face her. "You're holding out on us. Tell us the rest."

"Okay, okay, you've got me," Moonbeam giggled. "It's a boy! See?"

She pulled out her scrying mirror and, to Emma's amazement, she could clearly see the image of a fat baby boy in the black glass. So much for sonograms.

"Moonbeam, that's wonderful," replied Emma. Nothing shocked her anymore. The three women embraced and chattered happily.

"Have you decided on a name yet?" asked Phoebe.

"Um hm. He'll be a Junior, after his daddy."

Emma paused. "Well, now I'm curious. I've always wondered. What *is* the Chief's first name?"

Moonbeam smiled and replied. "Chief."

Emma laughed. She'd always thought it was a title. "When's the wedding?"

"This weekend. There was a cancellation at Thorncrown Chapel, so we grabbed it."

"We're going back to Eureka Springs?" Phoebe squealed and jumped with excitement. "I've got to call Allen." Her face suddenly fell. "I forgot. Didn't you promise our new client we'd finish his web page this weekend so he can launch his IPO next week?"

Emma shrugged. "Some things are more important than business. Where're we going to stay?"

"Where else?" Moonbeam grinned. "I've already made reservations at the Crescent for everybody. I also invited your parents and Monica."

Emma picked up the phone and called Zan to tell him the news. "Yes, honey…me too…I can't wait either…" She winked at her friends. "I agree. It's time to start working on a baby sister for Teddy…okay, see you later…love you too."

"I'm glad we're finally going back," said Moonbeam. "Theodora and Great-Granny Cordelia want to see the kids—and Emma."

"They want to see me? How do you know?"

"My scrying mirror. I see them all the time through it and they talk to me," said Moonbeam. "Great-Granny has permanently moved into the Crescent with Theodora. They're helping the earthbound spirits who are still there find their way to the other side."

"What about the bad spirits—like Dr. Baker, Roberta, and Earl?"

"I'm not sure, but I think they've either crossed over or their ghosts are somehow contained. They don't seem to have the power to cause trouble to the hotel guests anymore, thanks to you."

"Thanks to me?"

Moonbeam nodded. "Great-Granny and Theodora told me that if it hadn't been for you, evil would have completely taken over the hotel. The spirits who remain are simply lost souls who are working their way toward the next level. Except for Michael. He'll never leave."

Emma looked around at the evidence of her happy life. She had her son, a husband she adored, a wonderful family, and her friends. She was so lucky. What more could she ask for?

She paused to remember what she would always think of as her Dark Night of the Soul—the painful process in which consciousness became clouded by uncertainty—where only her love and courage sustained her through an ocean of fear—where awareness of her true place in the universe was ultimately revealed—her Night Journey.

ABOUT THE AUTHOR

Goldie (Beth) Browning's twisted imagination and fascination with the paranormal began in early childhood with her grandmother's ghost stories and her brother's retelling of classic fairy tales, such as Snow White and the Seven Little Frankensteins and Cinderacula. Almost every vacation she takes includes a stay at a haunted hotel or castle, as well as visits to famous cemeteries or catacombs. She loves anything by Edgar Allen Poe, Stephen King, or Nathaniel Hawthorne.

Her first and favorite job was as a secretary at a military mortuary in West Germany, followed by more mundane employment which included being a newspaper reporter, a real estate agent, a substitute school teacher, and a legal secretary. She finally settled down to a long career as a courtroom deputy clerk for two federal judges before retiring and getting to do what she wants to do when she grows up—be a writer.

Not long after finishing Night Journey she was stricken with cardiomyopathy. She received an implanted cardio-defibrillator and was evaluated for a heart transplant, which ironically paralleled the plot of Night Journey. Luckily, time and medication worked their miracle and she made a full recovery. Her experience, as well as someone near and dear to her in need of an organ transplant, has transformed Goldie into an advocate for Organ Donation and Living Wills.

The best thing she ever did was marry her high school sweetheart Alan a long, long time ago. She's living happily ever after with husband and family, which includes a menagerie of fur people, on a wooded hill in rural North Texas.

Visit Goldie at www.GoldieBrowning.com